# The Book of Chaos

## The Dragons' War–Book 3

By Ray Strong

## if
**Impulse Fiction**

# The Book of Chaos
## The Dragons' War – Book 3

By Ray Strong

Cover art: S. C. L. Benini

ISBN 979-8-9990605-0-1

Library of Congress Control Number: 2025914862
LCCN Imprint Name: Impulse Fiction, Pleasanton, CA

*Dedicated to:*
*Marina, Yuri, Veronica, and Elizabeth*

**My brightest stars are you.**

# Other Books by Ray Strong

| *The Dragons' War* | *Available On* |
|---|---|
| 1 Zephyr's Flight | Amazon Now |
| 2 The Wounded Sky | Amazon Now |
| 3 The Book of Chaos | August 11, 2025 |
| 4 Aeterna's Wings | November 3, 2025 |
| 5 Angel of Death | December 2025 |
| 6 The Storm Queen | February 2026 |
| 7 The Empress's Winter | May  2026 |

| *Hope's War* | *Available* |
|---|---|
| 1 Home: Interstellar | Amazon Now |
| 2 Pandora's Razor | Amazon Now |

# Contents

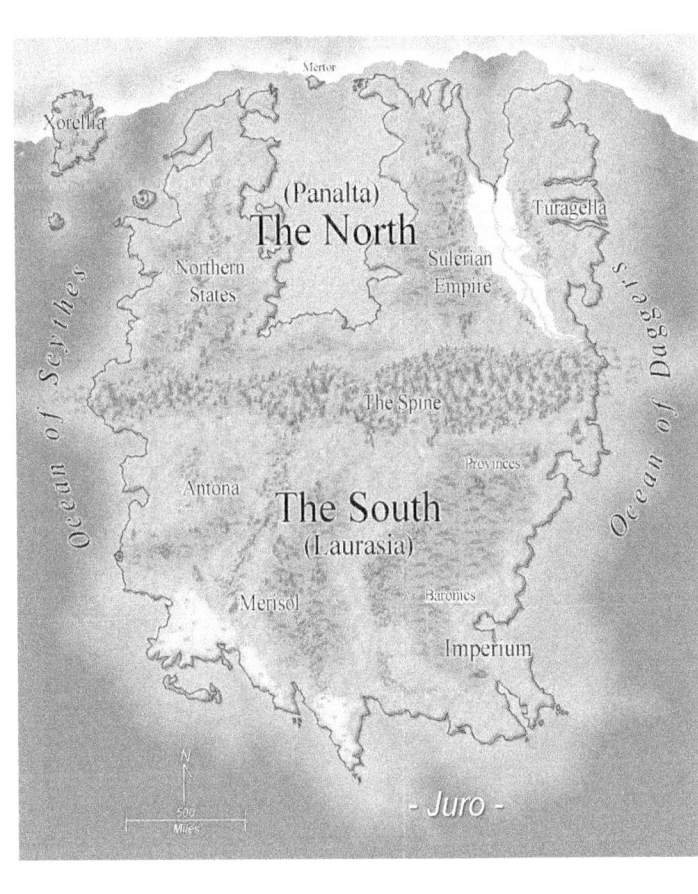

# Part 1 The North

### *From "The Singer's Oath"*

*There was History before history,*
*A time before men tilled the soil*
*And wrote the Book of the One God;*
*A time before the Wandering when people roamed the*
*land;*
*And even earlier, before the Chaos,*
*When men lived like animals in perpetual winter.*

*There was History before history,*
*When Juro wore our civilization like a crown,*
*And women flew like birds.*
*A time when we knew the ages of the stars,*
*Before we forgot who we were . . .*

*Now, we know nothing of this History but myths and*
*fairy tales.*
*But our ignorance of it does not mean we can escape*
*it.*

*The Singer's Oath, v.2/s.4*

# Chapter 1
## Arrow in the Heart

Like an arrow, trouble seemed to follow Diana, and this time it was about to catch her.

In the early evening before the moons rose, 14-year-old Diana Stewart sat up in bed and listened. A tree branch brushed the roof and masked the noises of the barnyard, and she closed her eyes.

In a break in the wind, she heard the cowbell and a soft moo. Moments later, a lamb bleated in the shed.

Barefoot and in pajamas, Diana crept outside, worried for her dogs, but heard nothing.

*Everything is fine.*

One of her dogs barked, but then whined and was silent.

*Wolves?* she thought and backed up toward the house as another dog whined and became silent.

"Dee!" her mother shouted from behind her. "To me!"

With one hand on a rapier, her mother reached out with the other to grab Diana's hand and they raced home and slammed the door. Just as it closed, a battleaxe split the door in two, and men charged through with torches. Tearing loose from her mother's hand, Diana ran to her bed to retrieve her new bow and quiver and the dirk that lay alongside it.

Diana slapped the dirk into her mother's left hand as the stockman she had argued with earlier that day raised his sword to slash her. She cowered, but her mother parried the sword with her rapier and thrust the dirk into his neck. His eyes fixed on Diana's, and with his bloody hands covering the wound, he stumbled backward and fell over a chair.

"Run!" her mother shouted as another attacker swung his blade. "To the tower!"

Diana scurried through her parents' bedroom, scooping up the dragon-tooth box from the dresser. Outside the back door, she peeked through the crack to see her mother with rapier and dirk fending off two attackers.

Silver glinted from the bootheels of their soft leather boots as they slashed at Katheryn. Afraid for her, Diana turned around and covered her ears to block the sounds of steel and death.

After a moment of quiet, Katheryn found Diana's hand and together they ran into the rising fog and acrid smoke. On the way to the tower, Diana found one of her dogs lying on the ground and pulled free of her mother's hand. Her dog was dead, with a crossbow bolt through his neck.

"I'm sorry," Diana said. She stroked his head and looked up as big gray wolves attacked her bleating sheep.

"Come, Dee," her mother whispered, took her hand, and pulled her away. But when they reached the moat, they found the tower engulfed in flames, and they ducked behind a bush. The farm manager, Ted, found them there.

"Lady Katheryn," he said as he gave them blankets. "The defense of the tower is a diversion. We can't hold. You must ride with us to Richard."

"Aemgarde is closer."

"Bandits roam there. The militia is our only refuge."

Through the forest, they followed Ted to waiting horses where four surviving guards joined them. Together, they raced east to Richard's camp.

Only the blanket kept the chill wind at bay on the back of her mother's horse. The thick fog and billow of her mother's robe hid the rising moons, so little was visible except for the occasional reflection of Ted's torch on a buckle or button.

In the dead of night, the horsemen found the clearing and ranch house and pulled to a stop. Katheryn jumped from one horse and ran to the door and banged her fist on it. Diana slid off and followed as the guards ran to the four corners of the house. Lights flashed from inside and a man came to the door.

"Katie, what in heaven brings—"

"No time, Will. Our home is in flames. I fear they are close behind."

"Eddie!" William yelled to a ranch hand. "Fresh horses!" He turned to Katheryn and stepped aside.

But before they entered, a crossbow bolt felled Eddie, and another struck the doorframe. Inside, her uncle bolted the door closed as her mother found a bow and quiver and hid between windows.

Diana hid under a table as arrows and crossbow bolts flew around her. At the window, her mother, Uncle William, and his farm crew defended his farmhouse from killers who fired from the foggy night outside. With her new bow and quiver of no use, Diana scuttled out of her hiding place and collected arrows to lay by her mother's side.

"Stay hidden!" her mother hissed.

Smashing through the rear door of the great room, an assassin ran and cut down a farmhand with a sword. Katheryn's arrows found the killer, and he fell in front of Diana, his dead eyes fixed on hers. Red twinkled from the silver inlay of his bootheels, and she glanced up as sparks fell from the thatch roof blazing high above her.

"The roof won't last, Katie," William shouted as smoke filled the room. "They aim to trap us inside while the house collapses upon us." He pointed to the kitchen. "In the pantry floor, there's a hatch. When you close the hatch, it'll hide itself. That will give you a head start."

"You can't stay here, Will," Katheryn said.

He scowled. "We'll make for the horses and take those nearest to glory."

"It's suicide. Come with us."

William shook his head. "Not enough time. We'll defend your escape, or there'll be none." He grabbed Katheryn and hugged her. "This is not your place to die or hers."

Without another word, Katheryn kissed him.

"Raise shields and form up!" William shouted, and the farm crew formed in two columns behind him with shields in front and above. "Draw swords, charge!"

As William and his crew ran out the door into the yard, Katheryn grabbed Diana's hand and led her to the pantry. Down the hatch they climbed, and in the musty tunnel, Katheryn lit a torch from the sconce with a sparker. There she stopped, kneeled, and took Diana's shoulders.

"Dee, when we surface, we must be silent," Katheryn said, signaling with her hands. *Do you remember the hand signs?*

Diana nodded.

*Never surrender,* Katheryn signed. *Promise me.*

Diana nodded again and crossed her heart as Katheryn pulled the cord to close the hatch and seal it with debris.

Insects and roots slithered through Diana's toes and fingers as she followed her mother through the muddy tunnel on her hands and knees. Three hundred feet later, Katheryn stopped at the ladder and doused the torch. When she cracked open the hatch to peek out, the light of two full moons crept into the tunnel. The path clear, Katheryn and Diana crawled out.

Outside on her belly in the damp grass, Diana peered back through the mist to the yard where shadows of men fought in the light of the blazing house and barn. At a shout behind them, Katheryn stood, grabbed Diana's hand, and raced for the safety of the forest. But after a whoosh and a wet thunk, her mother fell on her face, hard.

*What is it?* Diana asked in sign and helped her mother to her feet.

*Hurry! Hurry!* Katheryn signed back.

On foot and with Katheryn leaning on Diana's shoulders, they could not outrun the attackers. Stumbling through the tangled brush in the dark, Diana found the hollow trunk of a burned-out tree in a thicket at the bottom of a dry gulley far off the trail. There, she hid her mother and left to gather brush to scrub their tracks.

In the moonlight, Diana could not tell branch from bramble until a thorn or thistle cut her hands. Unable to cry out, she licked her palms until the sting eased. But when the bright moon, Elein, rose full, it exposed Diana, who hurried back to her mother. After sweeping the branches across their tracks, Diana wriggled inside the hollow trunk and hid the entrance behind brush. There, she sat on her mother's lap and hid her bleeding hands under her armpits.

"Tear a strip of cloth from the hem of your nightshirt," Katheryn whispered. "Now tie it around my arm near the shoulder." She gave Diana a sturdy stick. "Tie this into the knot and twist it tight."

Diana turned to face her mother and twisted the tourniquet. Katheryn cringed as she bit down on another stick which pulled on the scar that crossed her cheek to her ear. When Diana finished tightening the tourniquet, Katheryn spit out the stick.

"Mama, why don't you cover your scar?" Diana said quietly as she tucked the end of the stick under the cloth to secure it.

Katheryn ran her fingers along the scar. "This old thing?" she whispered.

Diana nodded.

"Because when I growl, I'm fearsome." Katheryn scowled with her teeth exposed and Diana widened her eyes and leaned away. Then her mother grinned. "And when I smile, no one seems to care."

Diana didn't care either, smiled in return, and settled into her mother's lap.

"Why'd they come for us?" Diana whispered.

The light of all three moons shined through the top of the shattered tree trunk to highlight the pain lines in her mother's face.

Katheryn winced. "Your father frightens the Sulerians because he defeated them."

"How did they find us? Papa's soldiers are between us and the Sul."

Katheryn nodded and wrapped her cape around them. "Good question. Some in the capital are not our friends." Diana wiggled and Katheryn winced again. "The Sulerian Emperor has a magic book they call the Book of Chaos, with which he can tell the future."

"What's a book?"

"It's like a scroll cut up into sheets and bound along one edge. Tell your father there's a copy in Branwyn."

"Can't the Dragon Riders help us again?"

Katheryn smiled. "They're too far away, Dee. Did Papa tell you of a Rider named Astria?"

"Tell me again, Mama."

"Well, when you were a sprout, the barbarian Hordes swept into Derryh and defeated the Army of the North. Their goal was the South, across the high mountains of the Spine, and in their way were the peaceful valleys of the Dragon Riders. When your father took command of the defense of Derryh, a beautiful young Rider came to him on a dragon. Her name was Astria Sannfjaer."

Diana snuggled into Katheryn's lap. "And her dragon?"

"Zephyr was small for a dragon, but brave and fierce, twenty feet from nose to tail and wings that spanned a clearing." Katheryn showed her teeth. "His features were gruesome, with fangs the length of your arm, claws on each of his four paws, and eyes like an eagle."

Diana smiled and closed her eyes. "Dragons aren't pretty."

"But they're very charming, and the moment I looked into his eyes, I knew he was a friend. I went right up to him and scratched between his eyes, and they sparkled. Well, that same year, Astria fell in love with a young lieutenant. And in gratitude for introducing them, she gave me the dragon-tooth box."

From her pocket, Diana took the box which twinkled in the moonlight as if it captured the stars. She could not see the details, but her fingers knew it by heart: a carved burlwood box inlaid with pearlescence in intricate patterns, smooth and warm to the touch as if it lived. Her mother once told her the inlay came from the teeth of dragons. When her father wove fantastic stories of the heroes who rode the monsters of myth, she held the box tight and wished they were all true. And as it sparkled in the moonlight, anything within it was blessed with magic.

"She and her friend Yana were couriers between her Clan Council and your father. Two years later, Astria led her people and the Dragon Riders to victory over the barbarian Hordes." With her hands, Katheryn mimed a dragon diving on soldiers. "She was brave and beautiful and . . ." Katheryn tensed and inhaled sharply. "And she was my friend."

"What happened to her?" Diana asked.

"It is said that the vicious leader of the Hordes cursed her and Zephyr, and they vanished in the mist. But her friend Yana thinks Astria and her dragon went to the Source."

"Where the dragons are born and go to die."

"That's right. And I've missed them ever since."

As Diana listened to the familiar fairy tales, she shivered in her mother's lap and gripped her bow and quiver. Mimicking her father's archers, she stuck the arrows point down in the dirt next to her.

*This is my fault, all because I made the stockmen angry. And I put Mama and our guards in danger.*

"I'll find the book, Mama, and bring it to you. I promise. And we'll never be so afraid again."

Torches flickered through the brush outside the tree trunk.

"Mama," Diana whispered, but Katheryn did not stir.

A tickle caused Diana to reach behind her, and her fingers returned with a sticky wetness and the scent of iron. *Blood!* Diana bit her fist to avoid crying out.

"Mama," she whispered and shook her. "Mama, please."

At the crunch of footsteps in the nearby thicket, she raised her little bow and nocked an arrow, heedless of her sore hands for the rush of fear. Her little bow was no good at ten yards and no good at even two. But she might have one shot, one chance at a target a few feet away.

The footfalls stopped in front of their tree, and through a gap in the cover, she saw the boots—boots of soft leather with silver inlay in the heels that glinted in the moonlight—boots like the dead assassin's in her uncle's farmhouse. Struggling to pull the bowstring back, she aimed at the entrance of the hollow trunk. One move of the brush that hid them and she'd let fly. Her fingers hurt and arms trembled, but she held her position.

A whiff of acrid smoke drifted into their hiding place, and Diana wiggled her nose to quell a sneeze. And still she held her position.

A whistle echoed from a distance, and the hunter outside whistled back. On the damp leaves outside, a spark fell, hissed, and disappeared under the boot. Footsteps sounded again, but trailed off, and with her weary hand and shoulder burning, Diana relaxed the bow.

*Mama might die without help, but they might capture or kill us if I leave cover.*

Bound by fear and her promise, Diana could do nothing but shiver in the cold mist and weep until she fell asleep.


A dim red glow peeked through the top of the tree trunk and woke Diana. Shivering in the morning fog, she brushed her hand over her mother's cheek and the scar that crossed it.

"Mama," she whispered, "wake up."

Katheryn did not move.

The sun crept into the stump and shone on her mother's ashen complexion.

"Mama, Mama, please, please!" She shook her gently, but still her mother did not wake.

Fear for her mother outweighed fear of capture, and Diana could wait no longer. She peeked out of the hollow trunk through the brush and crawled out to scout over the edge of the wash. With no one in sight, she went back to their hiding place.

She laid her bow and quiver on her mother's lap, as if it might protect her by its presence.

"Mama, I'm going for help," she said and restored the scrub to hide the entrance.

Under a crimson sky, Diana walked in widening circles through the morning fog to find a trail. Instead, she found the smoldering ruin of her uncle's house and barn and his body in the courtyard. The dim glow of sunrise behind her pointed to the road east and the militia. And there she ran, intent on running the entire way if needed.

A quarter mile down the road came the rumble of galloping hooves. Fearing her attackers, she scanned the nearby tall grass for shelter but hesitated.

*Assassins or not doesn't matter anymore: Mother will die unless I bring help.*

Without knowing who or what raced toward her, Diana stood in the road, stained with blood and caked in mud, and waved her arms.

# Chapter 2
# Ashes and Roses

Under a blood-red dawn galloped a cavalry troop of the elite Company A, led by Diana's father, Field Marshal Richard Stewart.

"Papa, come! Mama's hurt!"

Richard jumped from his horse and ran to her. "Aye, lass, where is she?"

"There." She pointed at the forest. "Hurry, hurry!"

But her father would not let her go. "Are you injured?"

"No. Hurry, please!"

He raised Diana's sleeve, soaked red with blood, her mother's blood. Diana stopped struggling and stared at the stains with open mouth and eyes wide.

"No!" she cried, pushing him away, and ran into the trees. She led him to Katheryn, unconscious in the hollow tree, a hunting arrow having torn through the artery of her upper left arm.

With Diana riding by his side, Richard carried her mother in his arms on the ride to the Le Pegre militia camp and laid her on his bed.

There, Diana and Richard, both soaked in blood, held Katheryn's hand as the medics ripped open her sleeves and examined her. One sewed the wound in her inner arm where the arrow severed the artery. But when he finished, he frowned and shook his head.

Together, they sat beside Katheryn as her life slipped away, with Diana holding her mother's hand to her cheek, unwilling to let go when Richard tried to pull her away.

When Katheryn sighed her last breath, Diana gasped and put her hand to her heart, as if the arrow that killed her mother struck her as well. With a kiss, Diana laid her mother's hand by her side.

After brushing his hand along the scar on Katheryn's cheek, Richard kissed her forehead. He picked Diana up and carried her away so she would not see the attendants who came with shrouds to prepare Katheryn for her funeral.

Diana did not cry that day as Maggie, Richard's portly housekeeper, helped her clean up. Nor did she cry when she sat with her father on a couch within the labyrinth of drab tapestries and canvas that defined his quarters. Only her father mattered to her now, and she hugged his arm tight. She hid her injured hands, but he grimaced at the stain of her blood on his sleeve. Without a word, he kissed her palms and field dressed them before calling for a healer.

Through the afternoon, the cool sea breeze from the Wye River Delta fluttered the tapestries. Late that evening, Diana fell asleep on the couch beside her father, holding his palm to her cheek.

Outside, the soldiers prepared for a major redeployment, and Richard's adjutant entered the tent.

"General Shirmet requests orders, sir."

"Malveaux leads the contingent to defend the Pelsuk," Richard said. "Beyond that, General Henlow is in command and Shirmet will follow him."

"Sir, the officers ask that you lead."

"They will follow Malveaux."

"But sir—"

Richard shook his head. "In time, Sam. Not to-night," he said, brushing aside a lock of hair from his sleeping daughter's cheek. Almost in a whisper, he repeated, "Not tonight."

"Yes, sir." His adjutant saluted and left.

Later that night, Richard woke to find Diana staring up at him, her brows furrowed. She sat up, and he put his arm around her. "What is it, lass?"

"Will they come again?"

He held her tight. "Don't worry. You're safe here with me."

Diana bit her lip and turned away. After a long pause, she shook her head and faced him. "I mean will they come for you?"

"Not here," he said, but his grim expression did not comfort her.

\*\*\*

At sunrise the next morning, soldiers formed up with unit banners along the banks of the Wye River for Katheryn's funeral. The cloudy sky washed the color from the pennants, and the light breeze stole the life from the flags.

Held in the old way, they laid Katheryn in a boat filled with runes and honors to announce her status as she entered heaven. The Le Pegre bugle corps played a lament and salute while priests in linen capes burned incense and prayed.

Diana pulled her hand from her father's grip and went to Katheryn, her face still gray around the edges of the makeup meant to make her pretty for the gods.

Wiping the tears from her eyes, Diana ran her tear-damp finger along the scar that crossed her cheek.

"When you smiled, we never cared," she said. *But I'll never see that smile again.*

She kissed her on the forehead and blessed her with the sign of the arrow on her chest. Richard and the soldiers from Company A joined her, and they pushed Katheryn's funeral boat into the river.

"May Lon and Juro welcome your daughter Katheryn's spirit home to heaven," the priestess said, marking each blessing with the sign of an arrow. "And join the spirits who await us at the End of Times when all things are blessed with eternal life and the brotherhood of the gods. May Demetris forever fill your senses with rose and forest green. May Artemia carry you to heaven on a white elk . . ."

At twenty yards out, when the boat caught the current, a single flaming arrow found the boat and set it ablaze. As the burning ship drifted out to the Inland Sea, Diana held the single thing left from the ashes of their home, her mother's small dragon-tooth box. With tears tracing her cheeks, Diana set her jaw.

*What better vengeance than to find Mama's book of magic and wield against the Sulerians? Never again will I be defenseless, unable to protect those I love.*

At her side, her father stood stonelike and impenetrable. When Diana reached up to hold his hand, he gripped hers, and she understood he vowed something as well.


After a brief appearance at the feast, Richard took Diana back to their tent with a plate of snacks. Alone at last, little Diana spoke.

"Papa, Mama said there's another book."

"What book?"

"The Sulerian Emperor's book of magic. Mama called it the Book of Chaos."

Richard stopped pacing and drank from a tankard. "Your mother brought that myth with her from Nordes. I'm not partial to ascribing an enemy's victories to magic, lass. It gives us an excuse for our lack of foresight or skill."

"I want to go get it, Papa."

"If the Sul Emperor has it, then it's in their capital of Mokdar. That's too dangerous for any of us, lassie. We're too valuable as hostages."

"Mama said there's another copy in Branwyn. Where's that?"

"I hear it's a fine town in the South."

"Can we go there and get it?"

He shook his head and opened the tent door to the parade ground. "It's a long and treacherous journey across the Spine. And word is the Imperator embroils himself there in civil war."

Tears filled Diana's eyes, and she pursed her lips tight.

*This is all my fault!*

"I miss her too," Richard said, sat by Diana's side, and put his arm around her.

She looked up at her father. "No, Papa. This was my fault. I angered the stockmen who killed everyone. Mama and Uncle William and Ted . . ."

"No," Richard said with narrowed eyes. "The stockmen weren't there to buy sheep. They were killers who deceived us."

"But I could've saved Mama if I'd called out. They were only a few feet away, and she was hurt. Mama needed help, and I . . . I let her die. I was afraid."

"No, no," he said and hugged her tight. "This isn't your fault, lass. You can't blame yourself for the evil that others do. What was the last thing your mother told you?"

"Never surrender."

He nodded. "Your mother believed death would be preferable to capture. You're blameless, lass. She knew what would happen and chose freedom for you. You did what she asked, which was the right thing to do."

Diana pushed him away and stood, knocking over a plate of fruit. "You would choose my freedom over her life?"

Richard winced, and his face softened. "I respect the choice your mother made."

As she stared at her father, his adjutant pushed a tapestry aside.

"Emissary Higell to see you," the guard said.

"Not now, Sam."

"Says it's urgent, sir."

Richard gazed at Diana, but nodded to Sam. A moment later, a man with narrow eyes in colorful silk robes entered and whispered into her father's ear.

Richard stepped away from him. "Negotiate? Never! You knew, emissary. Your people knew and said nothing!"

Maggie entered at the shouts and took Diana's hand.

"She stays," Richard said. "This is about her as much as anyone."

The emissary handed Richard a parchment note. "The Emperor offers attractive terms," he said with the look of a cat eyeing a cornered barn mouse.

Richard glared at him and showed his teeth. "You hope to pick on our bones while we mourn? We'll see who offers terms." He crumpled the note and threw it in the emissary's face as Sam led him out.

Diana ran to Richard and put her arms around him, and they returned to the couch. The clouds that gathered all that day thundered, and rain beat on the tent as General Jon Henlow entered with a bottle of whiskey and glasses.

"Higell insults us with terms for surrender," Richard said as he put his arm around Diana.

Jon poured two glasses and offered one to Richard. "I heard."

"They couldn't have broken the picket along the Wye Delta," Richard said. "I inspected it myself."

"That was months ago," Jon said. "The militias have come south to defend Derryh, which leaves the inner coasts poorly defended." He shook his head. "The Quarajii Hordes did this, Richard. And they fight for the Sul."

Richard nodded again. "If the target wasn't Cherbourne and the entire North, I'd as soon let them rot in Derryh."

Jon scratched his chin. "Perhaps despair was the purpose."

"Wait," Richard said, rising. With a furrowed brow, he paced with his hands behind his back. A few moments later, he stopped and turned to Jon with a feral smirk. "That arrogant bastard. Higell studied our rituals and would know we would still be here in mourning for Katie for weeks. If her death or capture, or Diana's, was meant to trigger a war, their cavalry could be on our necks by then. Our scouts could alert us only a day or two in advance."

He clapped Jon on the shoulder. "Our emissary, in his greed, was too quick. If we leave now, we can be right behind Higell's courier and meet the Sul on our terms, not theirs."

"You need to lead," Jon said. "We can't hold the army back any longer, and they'll throw themselves at the Sul without you. They need your temperance."

Richard emptied his glass and kissed Diana on the forehead. "I'm not feeling temperate, Jon. We leave to support Malveaux."

***

Diana's father, Richard Stewart of Cherbourne, was the man who united the Northern States to keep the Sulerians and their barbarian mercenaries out of Cherbourne and neighboring Derryh. His was an army of tribal leaders and militia commanders of the sovereign states who followed a militia colonel in their first common command. It was *his* army that stopped the Hordes from conquering the mountain clans and drove the Quarajii Hordes back to the Pelsuk River. It was *his* army that named him Field Marshal, Commander of the Army of the North. And *his* army was enraged by the treachery of Katheryn's murder. Before the traditional fortnight of mourning passed, Richard prepared to leave for war.

In a misty rain, Diana stood at Richard's side and held his hand. When the red war moon peeked through the clouds, they gazed at the troops assembling on the parade ground.

*He would stay here with me if Mama hadn't been murdered.* She made a fist and glared into the distance. Bitterness like lemon peel curled her lip and tightened her fist until her arm shook. *It's the Sulerians and the Quarajii. As long as I live—*

Richard kneeled by her side. "This is hard, lass, but don't let the hatred numb your grief. The things you cling to define you, and—"

"Like honor and virtue?" she asked.

He hugged her close. "Those are big words. I mean to cherish the things you love, the way your mother loved you. She never shied from what needed to be done to care for and protect you, even to give her life, and she never let the hatred overwhelm her."

He took her clenched fist, bloodless from the strength of her grip, and opened her fingers.

"This is your mother's favorite flower," he said, and on her palm placed a swamp rose her fist might crush. "And she said it reminded her of you."

Diana held the flower without the angry grip, and as the tears gathered in her eyes, Richard closed her fingers gently around it. She hugged him, and he stayed with her until Jon walked up, leading their horses.

"Come inside, child, or you'll catch your death," Maggie said as she came out and held an umbrella over Diana.

But Diana stood in the rain and watched Richard mount his horse. What she wanted most was to be with her father, surrounded by an army of soldiers. Instead, Richard rode straight into danger at the tip of the spear aimed at their enemy. With Jon at his side and most of Company A in the fore, Richard rode away with the bulk of the army.

And Diana was alone again.

# Chapter 3
# The Book

At dawn the week next, Diana jerked upright in bed after another nightmare of her mother's death. She rose from bed, threw on a linen shirt and jumper, and ran through the maze of tapestries out to the fence. With her elbows on the fence rail and chin on her hands, she waited for the courier.

In the bivouac below, the camp was just waking up. Through the morning fog, smoke from cookfires that had burned for hours carried with it the aroma of fresh bread and bacon.

At home, her dogs were her companions when no one had time for a child, and her comfort when she was sad or mad. But now they were gone, and she was alone. She closed her eyes and blessed her dogs with the sign of the arrow across her chest, praying they were at her mother's side in heaven to comfort and protect her.

The scent of breakfast overwhelmed her patience, and she snuck behind the mess. There she grabbed a bacon and egg sandwich and cup of strong tea and wandered into her father's command complex.

A tent of many tents, the complex was partitioned into functional areas by canvas walls and tapestries. A firepit, cold now, cut the audience chamber into halves. On one side stood chairs she guessed were for

Richard's staff. In the middle stood an immense chair made from stag antlers and white furs, and she climbed onto it, her elbows barely reaching the arm-rests. Across the firepit lay cushions on a dais which would raise the seated person's eyes almost to the same level as Richard's, but not quite.

*So what's my plan?* she thought as she finished her breakfast. *I promised Mama I'd get the book, but I only know the name, not how to get it. Papa won't go unless he believes it's real and can help us. And I can't defend myself if I search alone.*

"Milady, that chair was a gift to Richard from your mother's people in Nordes," a sergeant said in a reverential tone. "Your mother once wore that polar bear fur."

*Milady.* No one addressed her so formally. She was Dee, or Diana, or lass, or most often just brat. But this was her father's adjutant, Sergeant Sam Rickets, an archer from her father's guard, Company A of Cherbourne, handpicked by General Jon Henlow and fiercely loyal.

"Morning, Sam," Diana said and ran her hands along the fur. "Why the gift?"

"For ridding them of Sulerian slavers."

"And the fur?"

"The white fur implies elk," he said. "But no one in Nordes would act so profane. My guess, it's likely polar bear."

Diana hopped down from the chair. "Do you know where Branwyn is?"

"I'll bet the cartographer has a map somewhere. Come, lassie," he said and waved her to follow.

Sam led her to a tent with a large table and barrels filled with scores of rolled up maps. Leaning against them were tripods with instruments at the peak. A long table with drawing tools and small survey scrolls dominated the middle of the tent.

Climbing the chair to the table, and with her knees on the seat, she leaned over a scroll with a grid which called out the parade ground. And from it, she deduced the layout of the camp and the accommodations for the Sulerian delegation.

"Morning, sergeant," said a voice behind her. "How can I help you?"

"Alcore," Sam said, "This is Richard's daughter, Diana."

Diana straightened up in the chair and turned to the cartographer.

"Well, I'm pleased to meet you, lassie," Alcore said. "And how may I be of service?"

"We're looking for a map that shows Branwyn in the South," Diana said.

"Now that's a request I don't get every day," he said and rummaged through a barrel. "Ahh, this might do."

On the table, he unrolled a map showing an outline of the continent of Juro, with their home in the northwest, Suleria to the northeast, the Imperium to the southeast, and Antona to the southwest.

"Here," he said and pointed to a dot near the eastern edge of Antona. "It's almost straight south of Cherbourne, but between 'em are the lofty peaks and glaciers of the Spine."

"How do people cross the Spine?" Sam asked.

Alcore laughed. "They don't." With the dividers, he scaled the distance to her goal. "Even if you cross, it's another five-hundred miles. The easiest way is the long way: west to Royax and take a ship south."

*That looks impossible.* "How about Mokdar?" Diana asked, and Alcore pulled out a map of Suleria and Derryh. And within it, the boundaries of the major provinces, but without other details.

"Suleria is insular, so its geography is a mystery." He pointed to the mountains that bordered the Great Rift separating Suleria from Turagella where the Quarajii and Turajii dwell. "It's here in the western edge of the Pamir Kush Mountains. It's said to be a religious sanctuary, but I hear it's a fortified palace."

"How do I . . . How does one get there?"

"By crossing a thousand miles through Sulerian lands, either from the north or south."

"Not by the Inland Sea?"

He shook his head. "The sea is treacherous with shifting bars and too shallow unless you keep to the coast and the currents of the Wye and Pelsuk."

Diana smiled. "Thank you," she said and jumped from the chair as Sam and Alcore traded smiles.

*Branwyn it is, then.*

Across the parade ground came the sound of galloping hooves, and Diana ran back to the fence. At the sight of her, the courier pulled up short, reached into his pouch, and handed her an envelope.

"What was it yesterday?" he asked.

"A purple thistle," she said. "Papa has crossed the Wye?"

"I can't say, lass," he said and waited for her to open the envelope. Inside was a pink petal from a swamp rose.

Diana squinted and pursed her lips to curb a tear. "Thank you," she said and returned to her quarters with Sam close behind.

In her room, Diana took her mother's dragon-tooth box and added the rose petal. Beside it in the box were other flower petals, a blue ladybug, and brief notes with fond wishes. His gifts told her little of his location but reminded her that part of every day, despite the stress and danger, he thought only of her.

She closed the box and held it to her heart and stewed.

Her father had arranged for her safety in Le Pegre, surrounded by a personal guard and a thousand militiamen. But safety did not mean happiness, and it was her burden to manage the loneliness and grief, her father gone to war, and her mother gone forever. Adrift without the anchor of her father, her bitterness grew.

From the next room, Maggie called. "Diana, you're behind in your needlepoint."

"Mama would let me tend my sheep by now."

"Your sheep aren't here, and I'm following your father's orders."

Diana tiptoed from earshot through a gap in the tapestries and escaped to a sunny day. At the low fence separating her tent from the Sulerian compound, she stopped, and her jaw fell open.

Twenty yards on the other side of the barrier were two people close to her age. One, a bare-chested teen boy dressed in loose-fitting silks sparred with an adult half-again the teen's size with wooden weapons that clacked and banged. At the door to his tent kneeled the other, a girl in a plain dress who watched them.

She smiled that she might find friends in a camp of soldiers and smoothed her jumper. *What would I say? Do they understand my language?*

"That's War-Chief Garfann Sineura," Sam said as he approached her. "High Lord of Sinefora, heir to the throne of Takut, Speaker for the Fallen, and more such nonsense. He's the son of Makashti, the Governor of Sinefora next door to Derryh. The white and silver ribbon declares he attends the emissaries of the Sulerian Emperor."

The corner of her lip rolled up. "Sulerian." *His people sent the killers who murdered my mother. But he might know of the book.*

"And the girl? A servant?" she asked.

"A slave, most likely."

Garfann turned to her with his feet apart and fists on his hips as if all this land were his and the fence meant to constrain a ferocious animal rather than protect a boy.

"He's not grown into his titles or his conceit," she said, and Sam blurted out a laugh.

*If I'm to find the Book of Chaos, I'll need to be a warrior too.*

"There you are," Maggie said, as she approached with a fist on her hip. "Your lessons await." Taking Diana's hand, she led her back to their quarters, leaving Sam with a smile.

After an endless hour, Diana finished her lesson and needlepoint, rushed to her modest closet, and tore through her clothing.

"Maggie!" she shouted, "I have nothing for the hunt."

"Just what might you be hunting here?" Maggie asked through the tapestry from the sitting room.

"Can you find me something less . . . frilly?"

"Sorry, milady," Maggie said. "We only have clothing suitable for a proper young lady."

Diana tapped her foot and crossed her arms. After changing from her dress to dark tights, she readied to tear the sleeves from a blouse, but stopped and pouted.

"Maggie, these clothes are mine, right? To do with what I want?"

"Well, ahh, of course, dear."

Without delay, Diana ripped the sleeves off the blouse to resemble a jerkin.

"What was that?" Maggie asked, as Diana raced out the door with her bow and quiver. And behind their tent, Diana, went to practice out of Garfann's sight.

She was terrible, even at three yards, the bow too stiff and string too fine, her shoulders too weak, and her palms still healing.

"I'm dreadful," she said when Sam approached.

"May I?" he asked, and she nodded. He walked to her target, removed it, and returned to her. "Don't worry about the target, just work on your form. Now, pull the bowstring to the same spot on your chin and align the string to the arrow," he said, and she shot a flight.

"Don't hold your breath, lass. And elbow even with your shoulder."

Her wrist hurt and arm ached from the pull, but somehow the arrow found the bale.

Sam took an arrow and flexed it. "You need shafts to match your bow," he said. A few minutes later, he returned with new broadhead archers' arrows to replace her target arrows, a bracer, and a sheath to thicken the bowstring. After an hour of practice, Diana could hit the same region of the bale at five yards.

She did not complain but reached back to massage her aching arm. Sam took her hands and flipped them to find cracked and bleeding scabs on her palms and red fingertips.

"Time to quit," he said.

"The bow is too stiff for me."

"Your body must grow into it."

*Waiting is not an option.* "I want to use it now."

"Grow faster," he said.

Diana's shoulders fell.

Sam kneeled and put a hand on her shoulder. "Meet me here tomorrow."

She raised her head and smiled at him, then ran to her tent. Out of Maggie's sight, she cut up an old pair of leather riding gloves to copy the shooting gloves archers used to protect their fingers. As she worked, Sam dropped off two jars to Maggie: salve to heal Diana's hands, and liniment to ease her aching arm and shoulder. But neither were enough to help her sleep through the night.

\*\*\*

Every morning for a week, Sam moved the bale farther away. When Diana could not hide her practice behind the tent, he moved the bale to the wide clearing next to the fence. Every day, in sight of Garfann, Diana practiced until her fingers and arm hurt. At the end of each day's practice, Sam put up a target to coach her aim and gauge her improvement. Within a week, she could hit small stationary targets at fifteen yards.

But today, across the fence, Garfann and his servant set up a target as well and practiced archery. His bow was half again the size of hers, and his targets, each another ten yards distant, so Sam moved their practice ground out of his range.

"Sam, who is familiar with Sulerian culture?" she asked.

"Well, Lieutenant Denys, your father's translator, but he's with your father."

"Anyone here in camp?"

He shook his head. "But those who might are across that fence."

She nodded. "Garfann?"

"Aye. And his mother, Makashti."

*But why would they tell me anything?*

At dinner, Diana sat with Maggie at a table outside their tent.

"Maggie, how can I get someone to tell me something they don't want to tell me?" she asked and dipped her spoon into a dish of sliced peaches.

Maggie smiled. "And might this be meaning a boy?"

Diana blushed. "Yes."

Maggie coached Diana on how to attract a young man's attention and how to manage relationships until Diana interrupted.

"And what about finding out things?" Diana asked, distracted by a little four-winged wheezit buzzing around the torch. She smiled, imagining a little dragon ridden by a fairy.

"Well, lass, one way is to pretend you already know all about it without being specific," Maggie said and cleared the dishes. "They'll confirm it by their actions and may volunteer even more if you're a good actress."

"What would they say?"

"Not what they say, but what they do," Maggie said with a hand on her hip. "If they enquire into it, that could mean they're unaware and want to find out too. But if they deny the existence of the information, act to cover it up in speech or action, that could be confirmation of what you seek. And if you make them angry, they might just blurt it all out." She leaned over and smiled. "Can you tell me what this information is you want or who it is you want it from?"

"No. Not yet."

"Well, be careful. If this boy discovers your game, he may get mad or distrustful. If you have plans for him, that may push him away, and you won't get him back. Boys don't like it when they find out how clever we ladies are. You hear me?"

Diana nodded as a flitterbie swooped by to snatch the wheezit from the air and gobble it up.

Rain prevented practice the next day, and Maggie came to her.

"Child, you can't wear those rags anymore," she said, handing her a small package. Pleased with herself, Maggie smiled as Diana untied the string. "The men hunted for days to find something ..."

Within the package, Diana found a smaller version of the leather and linen hunting garb typical of the North.

"Thank you," Diana said but pursed her lips.

"What's the matter, milady?"

"Ah . . . they're new," Diana said and kissed her.

Maggie put her hands on her hips. "Well, of course they're new."

A moment later Diana smiled. "These are mine to do with what I want?"

Maggie crossed her arms and frowned. "I won't let you tear them up like your blouse."

"I promise I won't. They're mine then, right?"

"Well—"

"Thank you, Maggie!" Diana said and rushed outside into the rain with her new clothing.

Finding a suitable mud puddle, she ground the clothes into it with a stick until she had to dig to find them. Then she tied the muddy bundle behind a horse to drag around and work out the newness.

"That's better," Diana said and smiled after unballing the well-worn outfit. Soaked and covered in mud, she reported to Maggie.

"You're mad, child," Maggie mumbled, crossing her arms, and tapping her foot. And when Diana handed her the mud-soaked clothes, Maggie shook her head, but smiled. "No. Go change, and when you come back, I'll teach you to wash them yourself."

On the next sunny day after the leather was dry, Diana snuck out to her archery range in hunting attire that appeared as if worn in the bush for years. The clothes had shrunk, and with her budding womanhood, less modest than Maggie would allow. But Maggie wasn't there.

Garfann and his servant stood near his tent as she began her practice. But when she checked a minute later, Garfann was gone.

Her next arrow hit the target, and from behind her, another arrow whizzed past her and hit her target. Startled, she turned with wide eyes as Garfann approached the fence with his bow in his hand.

# Chapter 4
# Hard Targets

"You're improving," Garfann said from across the fence.

Sam ran to the fence to stand between him and Diana, and Garfann's guard did likewise which put the two soldiers nose to nose.

"Let him pass, Sam," she said.

Sam shook his head. "Not with a weapon."

Garfann and his guard turned, and Diana followed their gaze to the top of the rise where a beautiful woman with sharp features stood in robes that shimmered in the sun. The woman nodded.

"That's Governor Makashti," Sam said. "Emissary of the Emperor and Garfann's mother."

Garfann handed the bow to Sam, but the guard stopped the young man from crossing the fence and spoke to him in Sulerian. When finished, Garfann waved him away and vaulted over the fence.

*Don't show fear.* She turned back to her target and nocked another arrow. *I have a deadly weapon too.* "What did your guard say?"

"He warned me that within the fence is considered Sulerian territory where I am granted immunity from your laws and protected by diplomatic protocol. But on your side, I am not."

She nodded. "You speak our language well."

"I'm expected to communicate with my . . . adversaries," he said.

She turned back to the target and drew her bow. "So I'm your adversary?"

"No. That bedevils our parents and need not concern us."

She loosed her arrow. "Was that your mother?"

He nodded and smiled a charming smile as he walked toward her, and with each step, he became larger. From a distance, when compared to a Sulerian warrior, he was a boy. But standing in front of her, a head taller with chest bared, he was a man, and she blushed.

"I noticed your arm tiring and elbow falling during practice," he said.

She pursed her lips and raised an eyebrow.

"Use your shoulder to pull the string, instead of your arm. Let me show you." Garfann moved closer, and Sam took a step toward them. "Now, prepare to shoot but leave the string relaxed." When she nocked an arrow and raised the bow, he tapped the back of her shoulder where the muscle arced around the joint. "Pull from here where you are stronger."

She glanced at Sam, who smiled and nodded. As she pulled back, Garfann repeatedly tapped her shoulder at the same spot.

"Feel it?" he said.

"Yes." She fired and hit her target.

"Your shoulder will get stronger and your arm less tired," he said but remained close.

Her body reacted to his closeness, and the blood rushed to her face.

"Excuse me," she said and took a step back.

He smiled. "How about a contest?"

Diana turned to Sam. "Please?"

Sam nodded and handed Garfann his bow and quiver. "Stay within four feet of him," he said to Diana.

They took turns with the bale at thirty yards. At that distance, she matched him.

"Farther," he said and moved the bale another ten yards out. But from this extra distance she could not hit the bale without elevating the arc of her arrow and he won every round.

"My bow doesn't have the distance of yours," she said.

"Try mine," he said with a smile but narrowed eyes.

Diana took the bow and strained to pull it, but she could not pull to her chin, and the arrow went wide.

*That's to intimidate me with his strength.* "Where did you learn?" She asked as she returned his bow.

"In Mokdar," he said, admiring the bow. "This is the same bow as the Elites use in battle, the most skilled soldiers in the world." He said it with pride and thrust his chest out as if their glory accrued to him.

Diana smiled. "My father would disagree. If they're the best warriors in the world, why did they lose in Invernell?"

"Bah, those were Quarajii," he said with a scowl. "And no match for the fearsome Sulerian Elites."

She took a chance. "Quarajii with silver inlay in their bootheels," she said and flexed her bow.

He nodded as if this were common knowledge but gave her a side eye.

*So it was them!* "Men with such boots attacked my home and killed my mother."

He spun to face her with a furrowed brow. "Quarajii," he said and looked away.

*He didn't know who! Back off or he'll see through my questions!* "Perhaps the Elites are brave because the Emperor has a magic book to guarantee victory."

He glared at her.

"I didn't mean to anger you," she said with an inno-cent smile.

From across the fence, the guard shouted, and Gar-fann replied testily in Sulerian.

"Good day," he said, jumping the fence and return-ing to his tent.

Diana turned to Sam. "Do I need a new bow to get more distance? Garfann's bow is much bigger."

"Leave it to the master bower," he said and took the bow.


The next morning, Sam returned her bow with curved bone tips and new arrows.

She took the bow and pulled the string to her chin. "It's not that much harder."

Sam nodded. "That's the idea."

When she went to the range, she began at the usual thirty yards. She stepped back yard by yard and shot until she could confidently hit the bale at fifty yards.

Garfann appeared near the barrier, clothed in the style of a Sulerian huntsman with a hawk on his pad-ded shoulder. When Garfann spotted her, he stood feet apart with hands on his hips but did not glance at her.

She smirked. "Another costume," she murmured and tried not to stare.

Garfann's servant let loose a small rabbit that sprinted toward the nearby trees on her side of the fence. Garfann removed the hawk's hood and let the bird fly. The bird caught up to the rabbit after it ran under the fence and brought it back bloody, still twitching to free itself. He laughed as the bird tore pieces of flesh from the little thing.

*The bird is the weapon, but he's the killer. And he wants to show me he has more range than me.*

"Moving targets, then?" she mumbled with a hand on her hip.

From the supply tent, Diana scrounged materials and crafted a device with pulley, wood, and rock. With it, she practiced hitting moving targets: as the rock fell, it pulled a yarn ball across her field of fire. Garfann saw her and joined her with his bow.

"Are you still angry with me?" she asked.

"Don't be silly," he said. "Arguing with a woman is beneath a Sulerian warrior."

*Uh-huh.*

"May I?" he asked.

She went to set up her target device, while Garfann faced her, an arrow nocked in his bow, and Sam a few yards away.

*I won't show fear of him or weakness in his presence.*

They took turns with the moving targets, five shots at a time. But for all his training, he was only slightly more accurate, which earned her his scowl.

When finished, they sat in the grass, and Garfann signaled his servant. Soon after, the girl brought a blanket to sit on and a basket with pastries and a carafe of juice. The servant walked with an odd gait caused by a chain between her ankles and a lack of both big toes. Silver glinted in the sun from a ring on her pinky toe. After pouring drinks, the girl sat on her haunches by Garfann's side with her hands folded.

Diana smiled at her. "What's your name?" she asked, but the girl remained silent. "Is she mute?"

"She has whatever name I give her," Garfann said.

Diana glared at him. "Then what is it?"

Garfann leaned back and sipped his glass. "Today, her name is Tina," he said, as the girl stared at the hands in her lap.

Diana picked up a pastry but stopped before biting into it. "Can she eat with us?"

"No," he said. "She eats with the other . . . servants."

"Other slaves?"

"If you wish."

"We don't hold slaves in the North," Diana said and raised her eyebrows as she bit into the honeyed pastry.

"Our holy book, the Chiniferra, grants us the service of slaves if we maintain our vows to virtue and service."

"What do the slaves worship?"

"The same, and they are content."

"When did you last ask them?" Diana asked over the rim of her cup.

Garfann scowled, and Tina pursed her lips but smiled with her eyes.

From the hill, Garfann's guard called, and they turned to find Makashti again.

"Excuse me. My mother calls," Garfann said and walked to the fence.

"Makashti," Diana mumbled. She imagined her beautiful face with a snake's crescent eyes and forked tongue, the evil made flesh that killed her mother.

When Garfann crossed the fence, Diana turned to Tina. "Are you really content?"

"Don't be stupid," Tina said and lowered the shoulder of her tunic to expose the brand of a slave. "This hurt, a lot, but I'm alive, which is more than my father."

"What happened?"

"My family are merchants from Venaro caught by a Sulerian corsair."

"I'm sorry."

"It could be worse. Slaves do everything of value in Suleria: builders, farmers, infantry. Everything except rule. My brother works in the shit and piss of the sewers all day long, and my mother is a whore. Garfann is at least clean."

"Did you lose your toes when they captured you?"

"No. I ran away," Tina said. She glanced over her shoulder and whispered, "That's the prescribed punishment in their holy book."

"Did it discourage you?"

Tina narrowed her eyes. "I still have eight more."

Diana withheld her questions, thinking the answers might shame her. But Tina pulled her smock to cover the bruises on her legs and glared at her.

"I see that look in your eyes," Tina said. "Don't pity me. Get me the Hel out of here."

Diana inspected the simple locks on the hobble cuffs, but Garfann interrupted with a call from the fence.

"My mother asks when your father will return," he said.

Diana smiled. "After he defeats your army, is my guess," she said, and Tina smirked.

Garfann waved his mother away.

"Can I buy Tina from you?" Diana asked, and Tina gasped.

After a side-eye to Tina, Garfann said, "No. She pleases me."

*Would he hurt her? Change the subject, just in case.*

"Why did you and your mother come here?" Diana asked.

"My mother came to make friends with your father and have our peoples trade together."

She glared at him. "And murder is how you negotiate? My father said the Quarajii fight for you."

Out of his sight, Tina frowned and shook her head.

Garfann clenched his jaw for a moment, but his expression softened. "I'm sorry for your mother's death.

Makashti determined that the Emperor's emissary, Higell, hired the Quarajii. She has evened the score for the attack on you."

Diana scowled. "Nothing can even that score, with me or my father."

"Then take it as comfort if you can. Kidnapping and murder are unworthy of warriors."

"Higell asked for our surrender," she said.

"And Mokdar would have been grateful if his ploy had worked. But the treachery was not of my mother's doing. Higell betrayed her as well as you."

*I named the Quarajii to Garfann. Did they kill Higell because of me? Am I now responsible for his death? But I didn't kill him.*

She softened at his apology for things he did not cause, and regretting her harsh words, she took his apology to heart.

With a gentler tone, she asked, "You mentioned you spent time there in Mokdar."

He nodded. "For many years at the Empress's invitation. They taught me . . . many things there. Some I desired, like skill in battle and respect at court." He sighed and turned away. "But each brought their burdens."

"I've heard Mokdar is glorious," she said and her heart beat in her chest as she fished.

"It is. With white marble cathedrals and palaces climbing the mountains as if levitated by the prayers of the Envoy. Within the holy city are all the diversions allowed by law." He smiled wistfully. "And many that are not. Has your father taken you to Wikkert?"

"No. I've spent my life on our farm. I have something of a reputation as a shepherd," she said, restraining the pride in her voice.

He scoffed. "A peasant's job."

She pursed her lips. *A peasant's job! Is that all he sees in me?* And distracted by anger, Diana fished too deep.

"Did you see the magic book in Mokdar?" she asked. "The Book of Chaos?"

He hesitated and glanced at her. "You know of the book?"

"Of course. And it's used to advantage in war."

Garfann scowled. "The book does not guarantee victory."

*It's real! Courage!*

"Did you see it?" she asked.

"No. Only the Emperor has survived the sight of it."

"Is Mokdar where the Emperor keeps it?"

Within moments, Garfann's expression changed from confusion to disappointment. His eyes narrowed, and he scanned the field behind him.

"There are too many ears close by," he said. "Meet me tonight at my tent after your maid sleeps, and I will answer more of your questions."

As Garfann walked away, Tina packed up the lunch kit. And with deep creases in her brow, mouthed to Diana, "No!"

When Maggie's snoring reached a crescendo, Diana rose and changed from her nightshirt into her hunting clothes.

*He's different from the boys at home: poised, confident, skilled with the bow, charming, if arrogant. And he's alone here too and must want a friend.*

*If I go, I may learn more of what I seek. But can I trust Garfann? He's been friendly and hasn't shown me a reason not to. He's bigger and stronger than me.*

*But I'm quick and surrounded by soldiers. He'd never risk harming me.*

*My mission is worth it. Isn't it?*

*And what do I bring to this meeting? What does he expect of me? Information on troop maneuvers? Dispositions? They've told me nothing, so I can't betray my people. What other interest would he have in me?*

*Then if all I have is my charm and wit, I will bring that.*

As she passed her dressing table on the way out, Diana grabbed a hairpin that could be bent into a lockpick. To evade her guards and those of Garfann, she slipped under the edge of the tent into the rain gully and waited for the sentry to pass. In the pale red of the war moon, Fures, she ran to the woods at the edge of her compound and over the fence.

The trees shielded her until she was within a short walk to Garfann's compound. As she approached, the guard stood in front of the entrance with his spear blocking her path and spoke to her in Sulerian.

She dismissed him with a wave of her hand. "I'm invited."

He eyed her, smirked, and inspected her for weapons. But as she was unable to hide things in her tight-fitting hunting gear, he escorted her inside

The growing wind billowed the canvas and fluttered the silks that hung from ropes as she entered. Warmed by a central firepit, it was not decorated as a warrior's like she'd supposed, but more like a palace bedroom: inviting, colorful, and comfortable.

On the table stood carafes of red and white liquids which a sniff proved to be wines. And bowls held exotic foods she did not recognize. In the corner of the room, with bruises on her legs and welts on her arms, kneeled Tina picking up pieces of broken pottery.

"Hello, Tina," Diana said.

Tina jumped to her feet and turned. "Run!" she whispered. "Get out! Quick."

As she slipped a small package into Diana's pocket, Tina found the hairpin and tucked it under her waistband. And within the package, Diana found a silver bracelet.

"Ah, Tina," Garfann said from behind her.

Diana stuffed the bracelet and wrapper into different pockets and turned to his voice.

"Let's not upset our guest," he said, grabbed Tina by the arm, and hustled her out while Tina mouthed "Run!" At the entrance to the tent, he gave Tina to the guard.

"I thought the refreshments might amuse you," he said.

"What happened to Tina?" Diana asked, tense.

"The clumsy girl fell and broke some pottery."

His dress tonight was white silk with a green sash belt and shirt open at the chest. And something in his movements was restless, like a tiger itching to jump from his skin with dark eyes wide and alert.

"These foods aren't familiar to me," she said.

"Ah, yes. The farm girl." He took two shriveled dark things the size of her thumb from a bowl, bit into one, and gave the other to her. "Try this."

"They don't grow these in Derryh," she said and bit into it. "It tastes like raisin."

"It's a date from an island in the far south, liberated by corsairs off a merchant ship bound for Venaro."

"And so, all the more interesting," she said with a tense smile before eating the rest.

"Sit, please," he said and pointed to the couch. As she sat, he poured red wine into glasses and gave her one.

*Danger!* "I'd prefer water."

"If you wish." After pouring her a glass from a pitcher, he gave her half of a yellow fruit with a purple inside. "And these are figs . . ."

"Conjured by a gypsy queen from the rarest of oases?"

"Just so," he said with a pleasant smile. "Peel the skin off and eat the inside," he said and demonstrated.

She followed his lead and tasted it. "It's like raspberries and honey."

"I promised to tell you more about Mokdar." He smirked. "If you plan to go there without me, say to them, *'Il ente formic emperian. Confinus Et.'*"

"What does that mean?"

"It's a special phrase to tell the priests to speed your way to the palace in Mokdar. Repeat after me now. *'Il ente formic emperian. Confinus Et.'*"

When satisfied with her pronunciation, he slipped closer, his arm on the back of the couch, his hand near her shoulder. "I'd hoped we might have a different conversation."

"And the subject?" she asked as the breeze stopped, and a light rain tapped on the tent.

When he put his arm around her shoulders, she jumped to her feet.

Garfann dropped his charming smile. "You deceived me."

*Uh-oh.* "Why would I do that?" she said as the blush rose to betray her.

"The Book of Chaos is not the Emperor's but belongs to the Empress, and only she possesses the gift to use it."

*Nuts*! "Please excuse my slip of the tongue. It makes no difference to me which of your rulers uses it when the purpose is the same: advantage in war against us." She stood and went to the table. "And what are these?"

"Mangos." He stood. "You played me. Flirting with me to—"

She raised her eyebrows in surprise. "Flirting? No, I—"

"To pry information from me."

She scoffed. "Come now, I knew about the book and that your rulers owned it. You didn't tell me that. You didn't think they could keep something so valuable a secret, did you?" she said and smiled. "Really?"

Garfann scowled and stepped toward her, and she backed up against a tent pole. She stepped to the side, but he blocked her escape, like his hawk adjusting to the rabbit's zigzag.

The peril of her situation struck her.

*Would he dare? And why not? His people already dared to kill the wife of the Commander of the Army and risk tens of thousands in war. What's one soldier's daughter?*

He stuck his hand into her pocket, retrieved Tina's bracelet, and held it to Diana's face.

"A bribe to enlist your help in her escape?" he said.

"Nothing of the kind. It was a gift. She merely—"

"Why would a slave with no other valuable possessions decide to give it to a stranger?"

He grabbed her, held both her arms, and pressed her against the pole. "While you're on this side of the fence, your laws do not bind me or protect you."

He put his mouth on hers. But she bit his lip, and when he pulled back, she cracked his nose with a head butt.

He licked his sore lip and scowled. "So now the gentle shepherdess bares her teeth." He took another step toward her.

"Your people killed my mother and threatened my father and me, why should I be gentle with you?"

From a tent pole hung leather armor with a bronze helmet and beside it, a spear with a bronze tip. But when she glanced at it, he stepped closer to the weapon.

From the tent flap, the guard said something in Sulerian, but when Garfann replied, he returned to his post. During that moment of distraction, Diana lunged for the spear and pointed it at him.

"You'd be dangerous if you could use the weapons at your fingertips."

She thrust the spear out, but he side-stepped. As the spear tip passed him, he gripped it and pulled, dragging her toward him. He reached for her arm again, but she grabbed the bronze helmet and hit him in the temple until he stumbled backward and fell to his knees. Then she ran from the tent past the guard and into the trees.

Outside, Garfann stopped halfway to her and paced parallel to the tree line, but the night and the shadows hid her.

When he returned to his tent, she stood with her back to the tree and slowed her breathing to calm her beating heart, as the rain cooled the battle fever.

*Stupid! How naïve and trusting I am. Never again. What will this cost me if they tell Maggie or Sam?* She bit her lip. *Or my father.*

As she crept to the back of her tent, a voice came from behind her,

"Out for a late walk, lassie?" Sam said with his fists on his hips.

Diana stood in the rain soaking wet and turned to him with an innocent smile. "I couldn't sleep."

"Well, I hear there's been some commotion over by our young War-Chief's compound, so you'd best not be wandering about over there."

By his stern expression, he knew where she'd been.

"Don't worry," she said, "I'll never go there." *Again.*

Inside her bedroom, Diana checked herself in the lamplight, wincing at the tender purple bruises on her arms.

*Just like Tina's. But with a hobble chain and missing toes, Tina couldn't escape the way I just did.*

At the thought of the slave, Diana remembered Tina's crumpled note and reached into her pocket. After smoothing it, she read:

My name is Eavlyn Moretti. If you can, please
see that my family in Venaro gets this note and
tell them I am alive and love them all. EM

Diana put the note in her dragon-tooth box, sat on her bed, and gazed at her reflection in the mirror.

*Tonight, Garfann was not the boy I first met. Maybe he did want a friend. He said I was flirting! Am I suddenly so attractive? Or is this a different man tonight? I used him. I pushed too hard, too fast. What he might have told me voluntarily, I pried out of him. Why wouldn't he be different? Who will he be if we meet again?*

*And how close was I to something no one could ever fix?*

She lay back on her bed and doused the embers of the battle fever with tears.

\*\*\*

Maggie's voice sliced through her gloom the next morning.

"Sergeant Rickets is here to see you, dearie."

In the foyer, Sam fidgeted with a cloth bag under his arm.

"Mornin,' milady," he said and bowed.

She curtsied. "Morning, Sam."

"The boys and I thought you might want some company." He reached into the bag and took out a little round ball of fluff streaked white and gray with two tiny black buttons . . . and the buttons blinked.

"Old Sadie threw some pups last month," Sam said. "And this little one is lonely."

Diana took the puppy whose little pink tongue licked her nose. "What's his name?"

"Up to you, milady."

"I'll call him Bo," she said with moist eyes, hugging his little body as she would her sheep dogs.

"Here's some mush and milk so he doesn't get . . ." he said, but Bo stole her attention, and Sam backed away to the door.

From the corner of her eye, Diana caught him turning to leave. "Oh Sam, thank you," she said and ran to hug him. "Thank you and thank the men for me please."

Sam, a soldier and unfamiliar with the blessings of children, blushed.

And for the rest of the morning, Diana stayed in her tent playing with the puppy and making a home for him in her discarded clothing.

Her bitterness disappeared, and in its place grew a calm resolve.


The next morning, Diana dressed in her hunting gear but streaked wet ash on her cheeks and forehead like war paint, the fierce image broken only by the head of her puppy poking out from the game pouch at her side. She put the bag down and set up her targets in the clearing between the compounds and started her routine. And across the fence stood Garfann, unsmiling with his hawk on its perch. Eavlyn was nowhere in sight.

*Where is she?*

"Sam, did you hear anything about Garfann's slave, Tina?"

"No, lass," Sam said.

Still confused about the prior night, she questioned her judgment.

*Was that the real Garfann or someone else? Will he apologize? If he does, maybe we can still be friends, and I'll have someone to talk to.*

At first, he watched her with his nose in the air and eyes narrowed, but as she trained, he glowered.

With each bull's eye, Diana's confidence grew, and Garfann's power to intimidate her waned. It showed her skill with a weapon she could use to defend or attack, to project her will in any direction she chose. She was the master of her fate, and this arrogant young man could not control her.

To Garfann, her attitude was intolerable.

Bo shattered the tension when he jumped out of the pouch and yipped near the fence in an invitation to play. Garfann glared at her and removed the hood from the hawk. Returning the glare, Diana tapped the point of her arrow to return the threat. He snarled at her and shook his fist.

"Curse your mother that she didn't die before you were born!" he shouted.

The short wick of her patience burned out. She nocked an arrow and let it fly to hit the hawk's wooden perch, which stood less than a foot from Garfann. The bird hopped off and fluttered about, still constrained by its tether. Diana nocked another arrow and glared at Garfann.

From her side, Sam put his hand on the head of her arrow and pointed it at the ground.

Garfann's expression turned stony, and he backed away.

"Garfann!" his guards called. They ran to surround him and hustled him out of range.

Sam came to her and grinned. "I think that's enough demonstration for today, lass."

Sam came to visit her as she watched the stars after dinner with Bo on her lap and Maggie in a chair by her side. With a nod to Maggie, he approached Diana.

"You beat him, milady," he said with a broad smile.

"Garfann?" she asked, and he nodded. "I didn't harm him or his stupid pet."

"You harmed his reputation, and for a Sulerian that's worse than a wound. You humiliated him. His guardians protested." Sam laughed. "They protested that their war-chief was in danger from a little girl . . . ah, no offense milady."

"None taken," she said and smiled.

"His guards will never have such easy duty again—if they live." He took out a small leather bag secured by drawstrings and handed it to her. "The lads asked me to give you this."

Diana opened the package to find a silver arrowhead, too soft for game or target, strung with a black cord through the tang to wear around her neck. But it was the letters C/A engraved into it that mattered most to her, and she jumped to hug the soldier.

The archers made the arrowhead from the scant jewelry of the men of Company A of Cherbourne. This was her father's unit, his first command and loyal to a man, composed of his most trusted soldiers, personal guards, and couriers. The same C/A was on the pennants that led the army. This was their way to tell her she impressed them with her courage.

"The bowyer wants to meet you, lass," Sam said.

She hugged him. "Thank you, Sam. And please tell the soldiers how pleased I am for their kindness."

He smiled and left, and she caught Maggie's gentle smile as she too turned to leave.

The gift moved her, but she could not smile, for the courier had not come today with the package from her father. Her hatred grew, for the war-chief's people were responsible for the absence of those she loved most, and neither her puppy nor the silver arrowhead could quench it.

She sat again and stewed, staring up at the constellation of the Warrior poised with his sword running through his enemy's chest.

# Chapter 5
## A Throne

The night of the silver arrowhead was the last time Diana smiled.

All week the couriers had not come. Every morning she waited for them at the fence rail with the dragon-tooth box in her hand. Every day the courier did not appear, she dressed and took her puppy to practice archery until her shoulders ached and her bitterness ebbed. And while everyone else in camp worried for the fate of the army and their country, Diana worried only for her father.

Waiting at the fence again this morning, the courier shouted as he galloped passed. "The militias return!"

"And Richard?" she shouted, but the courier rode out of earshot.

*Who will return as leader? Papa or another? In victory or defeat?*

Rough men she did not recognize followed, dirty and grim. The riders who bore Richard's C/A standard stopped at the command complex where a squad ran for the Sulerian tents.

Not seeing her father with the passing soldiers, she slipped past the guards and peeked through an overlap between the tapestries. And from under them came the pungent scent of weeks on the march, exhaustion, and contempt.

*Is this the air of conquest? Whose?*

She could go no farther, because two armed soldiers stood on the other side. Shouts in Sulerian filled the room, and she followed their glares to her father's chair. She gasped and put her hands to her mouth to stop from crying out.

In Richard's enormous chair sat a man she did not recognize, unshaven in leather armor, cold and fierce. Around him stood generals holding banners decorated with Quarajii runes. Diana recognized Jon standing proudly next to the chair.

*Jon would die rather than betray my father and would never leave him. But who sits in the chair?* She studied the unshaven man more closely. A blink of a blue eye, an impatient tap of his finger.

"Papa," she whispered.

Opposite Jon, across the cold fire pit, sat Garfann's mother, Makashti. Expressionless in silk robes, she placed her embroidered slipper on a large rolled-up carpet. At her side, Garfann shouted curses at Richard and Jon and slandered their lineage until Makashti commanded her son be gagged and restrained.

Jon ignored the delegates and spoke to Makashti. "This is not a negotiation."

Makashti remained silent while the emissaries shouted.

"Take that up with your emperor," Jon said to them. "He violated the truce."

The translator protested, attempting to disown the mercenary Horde.

Jon raised his hand to interrupt. "If the Horde does not fight for the Emperor, they will be judged as common criminals and hung before sundown."

The room fell silent, and the priest gasped. "They would never enter heaven!"

"And the Hordes would slaughter us in vengeance for causing it," said a delegate.

"That will be on you," Jon said. "We cede nothing and now control Derryh. All of it. Your rearguard lies dead. You have nothing between here and Sinefora. Return home or request sanctuary. Everything remaining on Northern soil in two weeks belongs to the North, including you. Your only response is compliance. This audience is over. There's nothing further to discuss."

Richard rose to leave, but the priest spoke.

"Please, sire," he said. "With all the unrest in the country and your armed men in control, we're afraid some may take revenge on us. We fear for our lives and request you escort us safely to Suleria."

"I will grant you safe passage to the border," Richard replied, "but that will not help you in Suleria."

"Your pardon, sire, but the risk from your soldiers will end at the border."

Richard shook his head. "You should be more afraid of your emperor than my soldiers. He betrayed you as well as us, and you're now of no value to him or to me. You might reconsider a request for sanctuary."

Makashti's entourage fell silent at the realization of the threat from their own emperor. With a wave of her hand, Makashti's escort removed Garfann from the room, still gagged and struggling. She followed, leaving the carpet behind. The contingent from the Northern Militias retired as well, leaving only Jon, Richard, and Denys, the translator.

Moments later, Makashti reentered alone and walked up to Richard. Jon went to protect him, but Richard raised his hand. Makashti approached, handed him a note with a small package, nodded, and left.

"Unroll the carpet," Richard said to his guards.

Dark reddish-brown stains appeared as they unrolled it. Inside was the body of a thin man in elegant robes: emissary Higell, his throat slit, and by the smell of advanced decay, had died weeks ago. In the middle of his chest were four bloodstained feathers.

Diana put her hand over her mouth. *Did they kill him because I named the Quarajii to Garfann?*

Jon reached down and picked up the feathers: two white, half of a red and brown striped of a hawk, and one white and brown striped of an of an owl. "This is from the Sylvan Horde of the Quarajii. An ambush in two days with two squads of men. He knew."

Richard nodded. "And Makashti wanted us to see this." He turned to Sam and pointed to the dead emissary. "Burn this with the carpet and scatter the ashes. Leave no trace they ever existed."

Richard turned to Jon. "Come. You too, Denys," he said to the translator and led them to an anteroom.

Diana snuck behind the throne and peeked between the tapestries separating the rooms. In the dim light and hard shadows of a brazier, Richard read the handwritten note with deep furrows between his eyes.

"What does it say?" Jon asked.

Richard shook his head and threw the note into the brazier. After it was burned, he used the poker to stir the ashes to dust.

She frowned. *Why would he not read the note aloud?*

From within the unmarked package Richard removed a carved wolf with a feather on its back and held it up to the light.

"What is this?"

Denys raised his eyebrows and whistled. "I've heard of these but never seen one. It's called a charm or token, a symbol of obligation. Only the blood descendants of the old prophet-kings may use them. The wolf is the symbol of the Sineura family. The object tied to it shows the type of promise: a cord represents gold, an arrow troops."

"Those are both expendables, commodities," Jon said.

"And if a feather is attached?" Richard asked.

"That's the big one, sir," Denys said. "A personal obligation."

"For what?" Jon asked.

Denys shrugged. "Anything."

"What do you mean, 'anything'?"

"Anything within the person's power to provide," Denys said.

Richard raised his eyebrows. "Can one renege on such an obligation?"

Denys shook his head. "Not without humiliation and the risk of assassination."

"Does that mean the holder is at risk?" Jon asked. "To renege on the promise?"

"No, sir. The obligation can be passed on to heirs and can't be discharged by death," Denys said.

Richard rubbed his thumb across the charm and showed it to Denys. "What of the inscription?"

"Sorry, sir. I recognize the Sulerian script, but I can't read it." Denys smiled. "But I recognize this symbol of a grizzly bear here. That's how they refer to you." He took the object and ran his thumb over the message, but frowned and gave the charm back to Richard.

"Thank you, Denys. Dismissed." When the translator left, Richard turned to Jon and raised his eyebrows. "This is unexpected."

"Makashti indebts herself to you," Jon said. "In your hand you hold the key to the East."

"We can't be allies with a Sulerian governor."

"But you may need a favor," Jon said. "Congratulations, sir, you now have a powerful friend in Suleria."

"I'm not so sure, Jon. This has the smell of foreign intrigues," he said and put the charm in his pocket.

"Enough business of state. I have a long overdue meeting to attend."

When Denys tried to pass her, Diana stood and stopped him. "Denys, what does *'Il ente formic emperian. Confinus Et' mean?*'"

Denys put his hands on his hips and laughed. "And where did you learn that?"

"From a soldier."

"Well, never say it to a Sulerian. It means 'I aim to kill the Emperor. Arrest me.'"

As Denys walked away, Diana frowned and sat on Richard's antler throne with her cheek on her fist.

*Garfann lied. Even before we fought, he betrayed me. And Makashti, whose people killed my mother, wants to influence my father. What other information is tainted? The Book?*

Richard found her there on the throne. "It suits you."

Diana leaned forward with wide eyes and open mouth. But Richard dropped his dour expression, kneeled in front of her, and smiled through his beard.

"Hello, darlin'."

Diana jumped into his open arms, closed her eyes, and nuzzled into his neck. He hugged her tight and carried her to their tent, where he sat and gazed at his daughter's smiling face.

"You're a princess now," he said and puffed out his chest like a self-important official. "'By declaration of the Assembly of Parliaments in Wikkert, Lady Diana Stewart of Cherbourne, Princess at the Court of Richard Stewart, King of the North, and heir to the throne.' That's how the entire Sulerian Empire will address you now."

Diana's smile turned to wide eyes and open mouth. "No!"

"Don't you want to be a princess?"

She shook her head. "No, Papa. I don't want to live in the capital or wear those frilly dresses and shoes. Do we have to go?"

"Not if you don't want to."

Diana smiled, happy again, but soon after gripped his arm and frowned. "Papa, don't leave me! Don't go without me!"

"Never again. We're going home."

Her eyes widened. "Together?"

"Together," Richard said and nodded. "I only need to convince others it's the right thing to do."

***

Diana woke the next morning to familiar voices arguing nearby. Grabbing a muffin from a table, she kneeled by the tapestry to listen with Bo in her lap.

"You know her, Richard, she's not fragile," a voice said followed by grunts of assent in the room. *That's General Malveaux.* "She can adapt to the winds of change in the capital."

"Of course she would adapt," her father replied. "But she's only fourteen summers, and like a tree on a clifftop, such a steady wind will bend her in the wrong direction. I will not bring her to Wikkert, and I will not be without her."

"The assembly has approved a monument to Katheryn in Aemgarde."

"I don't like gifts from politicians," Richard said.

"It's a gift from the citizens of Nordes, who will murder you if you refuse."

"From her home tribes? Then of course we accept."

"We need you in the capital, Richard," Jon said. "The Sul are not done here. They'll regroup and probe for weakness. The Hordes have plenty of warriors to waste and war-chiefs willing to die for land. It matters not that the Assembly of Parliaments disagrees, those are facts."

"That's not the issue, Jon," said a voice unknown to her. "They oppose a standing army. They fear tyranny if they give one man political and military rule. The tribes are jealous of their power and have a history of killing their kings."

Richard spoke. "I am well aware the assembly gave me the title of King for authority when speaking to the Sulerians. The tribes are afraid of tyranny, so it's fitting to split the roles."

"But it has to be you, Richard," Malveaux added. "Without the crown on your head and an army behind you, the Sul will not believe it."

"Without military unity, the army will dissolve back into the militias," Jon said. "And that will just tempt Suleria to more mischief."

The unknown voice continued. "The Assembly is adamant."

"Bah," Jon said.

"Does their offer depend on my agreeing with their strategy?" Richard asked.

"Sir, the offer is with no other condition," the unknown voice said. "Your office awaits you in Wikkert."

Her father spoke. "Good. I have a condition of my own, Peter."

*Peter from Wikkert. That must be the unknown voice.*

Her father continued. "The militias must remain under a united command. Agreed?"

After grunts of assent, Peter spoke. "I think they would agree to that, sir."

"Good," Richard said. "I resign my commission and will return to Cherbourne as King of the North. The capital will need to deal with me there."

The men grumbled and Malveaux protested. "What? No! Really, Richard, resign? Who will lead us?"

Her father laughed. "Oh, there are generals enough, Sven. You might consider such an offer."

"I'd never usurp your command! I couldn't," Malveaux sputtered.

"So, that's your answer?" Jon said with a laugh. "You can't escape them so easily, Richard. Wikkert will pester you without end."

Glasses tinkled, and Diana imagined someone pouring wine.

"General, I think I'll enjoy that, people coming to us for a change." Richard said. "Tell them, Sven."

"Of course, Your Excellency," Malveaux said, and boots shuffled away.

"Thank you, Peter, for the long ride from Wikkert. Come to Aemgarde for a visit when you can," her father said. "Jon, stay."

"Theater?" Jon asked after the others left.

"A bit. They fear me."

"And rightly so. The militias follow you rather than Wikkert. It's a dangerous strategy to relinquish command."

"It's safer than the alternative. If I abdicate now, the Sul will regard the title as a ruse and renew their attacks at the first opportunity. The Northern States will just pick an ambitious climber who will declare himself emperor."

Jon lowered his voice. "Many wish you in that role."

"We don't need that now, and I'm not so clever, even if I wanted the power. We move back to Aemgarde."

"Are you sure, Richard? The schemers will find you there. Petitioners will crowd the roads from Wikkert to

Aemgarde. You will need to build an inn and stable to house all the rascals. And recruit your own flock of spies."

"And a meeting hall and offices, I expect. See to it, Jon," Richard said.

Diana remained next to the tapestry with the muffin half eaten, and that is where Richard found her, eyes wide and smiling.

He leaned over to her, smiling through a beard now trimmed close. "Well, Princess, it looks like the Northern States will come to us."

Diana jumped up to hug him, and he took her to a couch to sit. Everything was forgiven, everything was as it should be.

"Papa, I have wonderful news. I confirmed the Book of Chaos exists. The Empress has it."

Richard's eyes turned dark. "I heard you've spent time with Garfann," Richard said, looking directly at her. "And you talked to Garfann's slave?"

*Uh-oh.* "Tina, Yes."

"And you offered to buy her?

Diana nodded.

"I was told a slave was punished for a ruckus that occurred in his tent while I was gone."

"Is she all right?"

"Do you know anything about that?"

She shook her head. *Will he ever trust me again?*

"You saw Makashti's gift to me?" he asked, and she nodded. "The body was the Emissary, Higell. He was part of the plan to kidnap you and your mother and may have withheld that from Makashti. Higell was observed mingling with Quarajii. There remains the question of how Makashti became aware that the Quarajii were the ones who murdered your mother." He paused. "Did you tell them?"

Diana gazed at her hands. *It was me who caused his death! All because I mentioned the silver-inlaid boots.*

"No," she lied and flushed bright red.

With a single word, she forever changed her relationship with her father. And her guilt and shame for lying to him, she projected onto the Sulerians, and Makashti and Garfann in particular.

She gazed at her father with tears forming, hoping to avoid his condemnation and seeking forgiveness for what she could not admit. But in his face was only the love of a father for his daughter.

Richard sighed. "Even when our intentions are noble, every decision we make has unintended consequences, for good or ill. To do good requires great care to avoid undesirable outcomes."

He leaned over and hugged her. "All that's over now. Let's go pack for home."


Pleased as she was for vengeance against the emissary, she could not contain her hatred to just one dead foreigner. With Bo in her hands, she went to her room and sat on her bed scowling at the mirror.

*So Higell's death was my fault. Good riddance to a smug murderer. But the Sulerian emperors sanctioned it, and Makashti provided the cover, witting or not. And Garfann gloats at my mother's death.*

She dropped her scowl and frowned. *But Papa may never trust me again.*

On her vanity sat a small package, and she picked it up and unwrapped it.

Her jaw dropped as she stared with horror at the contents. Inside lay her hairpin between two small toes, one with a silver toe ring.

*And this, too, was because of me.*

Diana threw up.

When the waves of nausea passed, Diana grabbed her bow and quiver and ran to the fence closest to Garfann's tent.

Garfann stood with his feet apart and hands on his hips, smirking at her. But as she nocked an arrow, powerful arms grabbed her and picked her off the ground.

"No, lassie," Sam said. "Not like this."

When she stopped struggling, Sam let go.

"Revenge is selfish," he said and took her bow and quiver. "Think of justice instead."

Diana glared at Garfann with clenched teeth. *As long as I live . . .*

"Where can I learn more?" she asked.

"Only in the militias," Sam said.

\*\*\*

After their return to Aemgarde, Diana rebuilt her sheep herd and celebrated her next birthday with friends and family. After the guests left late that night, Diana woke from the recurring nightmare of her mother's murder to find her father sitting by her bedside with Bo, now as large as a small wolf. So that Diana would not fear the new day, Richard took her hand.

With Bo at her side, Richard led Diana to Katheryn's favorite spot by a creek that fed the Alba River and Lake Ivo. In the light of the three moons at full, they made little wooden boats and wrote prayers wishing Katheryn good fortune in heaven. And as she prayed, Diana put her hand to her heart where the arrow that killed her mother had found its home.

The sun rose, and they floated the little boats down the creek to the lake, until the last boat holding Diana's vow to find the Book of Chaos and punish the Emperor.

Before sunrise the next morning, Diana packed her kit. After leaving a note for her father, she snuck off to join the militia at Le Pegre to prepare her for the dangerous journey south in search of the book.

Ray Strong

# Chapter 6
# Militia

The next spring, Diana squatted in a muddy trench with her squad, ducking arrows from the hillside above them, and waiting for the signal to attack. While waiting, she worked with indelible ink, pen, and chamois on a map to Branwyn in the South using the symbols and techniques the militia had taught them.

"And there's a bridge across the Lanshrue Gorge?" Diana asked as she put her kit away.

Dru nodded. "That's what my father said. He found a merchant who came that way from Dorreau."

"How did he survive the grax packs in the Spine?"

"He said they hunt the eastern Spine and are just rumors here in the west."

It was cold and damp in the early morning because of the late rains, and they waited in a soaking mist. Their leather armor would keep them from the wet, but the wool breeches absorbed the water like a sponge and left them shivering.

She was Corporal Diana Stewart of Cherbourne, half-past her fifteenth birthday, under a military hierarchy that could not submit to her nobility, and a warrior-king who would not intervene.

This team was hers to command. Together they were Third Squad, C Company, 3rd Militia, Army of the North; six warriors eager for a proper fight rather than the endless calisthenics and weapons training of the last five months.

Today they faced an entrenched unit of the Sulerian Army which planned to swarm into Derryh again. Their mission was clear: to take the bunker on the hilltop which defended the Sulerian garrison. If they succeeded, the rest of C Company would have a protected position from which to lead the attack tomorrow.

"Ready now?" she said. "Quint, Lisle with me, three counts after we leave, Dru, Lucy, Rollo, and Gage follow. Clear?" They nodded. "There are not enough archers to volley fire, so—"

A bugle call interrupted.

"Third Squad. Advance!" she yelled and jumped from the trench followed by Quint and Lisle. Up the hill they ran, jigging back and forth to avoid arrows.

The low brush caught her shield and tripped her. When her shield caused her to trip a second time, the rest of her squad rushed past.

"Blast!" Leaving her shield where it lay, she rose again as arrows whizzed past. Freed from the awkward shield, she outran her team.

"I am Thores the Great, unconquered in battle, and wear the wolfskin of Eldmoor!" she recited. Filled with battle fever, she dived into the bunker ahead of her team, surprising the enemy so much that one of them deserted. The defenders raised their bows as her squad jumped in behind her and drew their bronze swords.

Unable to disarm the Sul archers before they let fly, her team raised their shields. But Diana was without her shield now, and the punch from many arrows knocked her off her feet and into the mud. Before the archers nocked another flight, her squad subdued them.

While her men cheered their victory, Diana sat in the muck of the enemy fortification, her chest dripping red. But the arrows, padded and dipped in red paint, suitable for a Le Pegre training exercise, had not pierced her leather armor.

In the chow line, angered by Diana's squad laughing up their victory, the leader of the defeated team pointed to the red paint on her armor.

"Dead man walking," he said. His squad mocked her, and she blushed in shame. A head taller than her, this was the young trainee who had jumped from the bunker when she jumped in.

"Leave her alone, Sten," Dru said.

Diana scowled and stepped in front of Dru, not wanting anyone to defend her. "At least it's on my chest."

Sten's ears reddened at the accusation of cowardice. This time both squads laughed at him. He dropped his rations and lunged at her, but she stepped back with one foot and leaned back to dodge the strike. Her hand directed his body past her to crash into a table of food. His squad helped him to his feet, and he turned back to her.

"Tenshun!" Gage called, and the recruits jumped to attention and saluted.

General Jon Henlow entered, tossing an apple in one hand. The red and gold epaulets on the shoulders of his fatigues declared him a judge in the training exercise: a war-god in this battle.

"As you were. Third squad with me," Jon said and led them to a copse of trees with tables sheltered from the misty rain. While waiting for them, he put a booted foot on the bench and with a small dagger cut a slice of apple and took a bite. "Debrief."

"Sir, Third Squad—" Diana said.

Jon raised an open hand and closed it for silence. "You're dead. Who's next in command?"

She pursed her lips and nodded to Gage.

Gage stood. "Sir. Third Squad captured the bunker with three losses including the squad leader. All enemy captured."

"So, your squad lost more than your foe?" Jon asked.

Gage glanced at Diana and back to Jon. "Yes sir."

Diana raised her hand. "But we captured the bunker, sir."

Jon glanced at her. "Quiet, dead man." He turned back to the others. "Three dead is wasteful."

"It was brave," Lisle said.

Jon shook his head. "It was reckless. Without your full contingent, the Sull will wipe you out defending your position tomorrow. You must survive today to win tomorrow, and tomorrow is the point of your mission." He bit into another apple slice and surveyed Diana's squad. "You speak as if your leader's sacrifice is an acceptable trade for victory in a minor skirmish."

Dru spoke. "Sir, a leader would sacrifice herself for her team."

"No one asks for your sacrifice," Jon said. "We ask for your effectiveness." He scrutinized each of them. "You are not here to be spent on the battlefield like the arrows in your quiver. You are not here to die as heroes." Removing his boot from the bench he paced in front of the squad. "Your leader's death was unnecessary. She knew why she dropped her shield, and it wasn't for you."

Diana blushed and dropped her gaze.

"The leader is as much a team member as any other. Our history tells us battles can be won or lost through a squad leader's effective deployment of their unit. Why waste that life? Does your leader not have a role difficult for you to fill?" He returned his boot to the bench and leaned toward them. "Or perhaps you believe your leader was given her position for some reason other than merit?"

Diana's squad stared at their boots, and she frowned; they did not defend her.

Another frown crossed Jon's face. "Third Squad, let's return to your imminent demise. Tomorrow, you are too weak to hold the position you won today. The enemy will attack and annihilate you, and your battalion will fail in its mission. Alternatives to suicide and humiliation? Go." He took another bite of his apple.

After a glance at Diana, Quint raised his hand. "Sir. Retreat to the nearby hilltop and harass them."

"There's no cover on the hill," Lucy said.

Jon nodded. "Other ideas?"

Diana raised her hand, but Jon ignored her.

"Cavalry to attack the flank?" Lisle offered.

"You don't have any cavalry, private." Silence ensued, and the team appeared out of ideas.

"Attack the archers," Diana mumbled.

Jon surveyed the sky. "A voice from the grave? Well, speak to those who die tomorrow."

"Attack the archers," she said.

"Any other comments?" Jon asked, but the others stayed silent. "Why, ghost?"

"These are the Sul, not the Qu, so we face an infantry of slaves who—"

Jon made a fist and thrust it down. "Yes! The Sulerian slaves know their own archers will kill them if they don't follow orders. Remove the archers and the slaves will run. Their position will fall without a struggle. Archers can't fight in close, so you now have the advantage. That is, if you choose to attack rather than defend." Her squad smiled. "But ghosts don't speak, and this wisdom is unavailable to you now that your leader is dead. Go enjoy your last meal while I write my condolences to your families. Dismissed."

"You stay, ghost," Jon said and flipped the apple core into the forest.

Diana snapped to attention.

"At ease, Corporal."

"Sorry sir, I just outran them."

"No," he said. "You didn't trust your team to follow your orders unless you were in the fore. You outran them to lead the charge but left yourself defenseless. A shield may also be a weapon, and you dropped yours. If they had copied your bravado and dropped their shields, they would all be dead and tomorrow lost."

She stood silent while Jon paced.

"Leadership requires trust. The risks of leadership are borne by the follower, and they must trust your judgment, or they will not follow you. Be careful the entire Army does not think you as reckless as you were today." He softened his tone. "They would follow you anywhere. Don't waste their lives . . . or your own."

Diana dropped her gaze. "Yes, sir."

"And ask the quartermaster to issue you a smaller shield. Yours was meant for a taller man."

"Yes, sir."

The bugle announced the start of the afternoon exercises, and her squad would return to their positions.

"Permission to return to duty, sir."

Jon smiled. "Casualties report to the kitchen. The cooks have pots to scrub. Dismissed."

Diana saluted and turned to go just as a courier rode up.

"General Henlow!" the courier from Company A called. "Message from the King." He reached into his saddle pouch and handed Jon a letter with Richard's seal.

"Wait, Corporal," Jon said. He took the letter and read it while Diana walked back to him. "Your father has a mission for you. Pack your kit. We leave within the hour."

\*\*\*

Clouds followed Diana and her escorts all the way from Le Pegre to Aemgarde on the road home. Jon rode side-by-side with a squad from Company A behind them through the ground fog which hid much of the deep green of cultivated land.

The familiar smells of lavender and pine were their map home. Many of the flowering plants were the same in Derryh as in Cherbourne, petals of which she saved in her mother's dragon-tooth box. Throughout the trip home, except during the pragmatic moments of meals and camp, Diana remained silent.

"What brings on this mood, Corporal?" Jon asked.

"Nothing, sir."

He glanced at her from the corner of his eyes. "What was the tiff between you and Corporal Limock?"

"Sten? Our business, sir."

"Not when it reaches the ear of the camp commander. I thought you two were close."

"We were. Now I . . . I'm not sure."

"Why not?"

Diana sighed. Jon was her father's best friend, a regular guest in their home, and until months ago when she joined the militia, more like a favorite uncle. But now he was her superior officer and one of the most respected soldiers in the land.

She narrowed her eyes. "Permission to speak freely, sir?"

Jon nodded.

"I made corporal first. Corporal Limock thinks my early promotion was due to favoritism. He's jealous."

"He told you this?"

"Ahh . . . No, sir. I assumed."

"And your assessment?"

"I think my father told the commander to hold me back."

Jon frowned. "Uh-huh. Why would he do that?"

"Because he wants to make it harder on me. He doesn't want me . . . to advance in the militia."

"Another assumption, Corporal?"

"Yes, sir."  She studied Jon. "What do you think, sir?"

"I have no knowledge in this matter and am grateful I need no opinion. But it sounds to me like your pride talking. Was that the cause of the spat yesterday?"

With a word, Jon impugned her assessments as ego, and she frowned.

"No," she said. "He deserted his post when my squad attacked. I pretty much called him a coward."

Jon nodded. "Your actions were justified in self-defense. Any escalation will show on your record."

"And his."

"Certainly. But his future matters less to him than yours does to you. It does matter to you?"

"Yes, sir," she said and toyed with her horse's mane.

"Why the hurry? You hope to be the youngest officer in Company A?"

She blushed and nodded.

"Not this way. You and Limock will make excellent soldiers if you can combat your chief enemy."

"Which is?"

"Impatience. Your rush to judgment and action before thinking."

"I thought quick decisions were an advantage in a leader."

"Only if your judgment is sound."

"And mine is not?"

"You've much to learn to hone it into a weapon as keen as your impatience." He sighed. "Sten's men came to me and told me they chose him to get reinforcements, expecting him to be killed. Did they mention that?"

"No . . . sir," she said and blushed. "Did my father tell you the mission he planned for me?"

*Will that be my punishment for enlisting? And when Jon tells him I failed, will he forbid me to continue there? Without more training I won't have the skill to search for the book down south.*

"No," Jon replied. "But I doubt it includes Le Pegre."

Diana let her horse fall behind so she would hear fewer of his words, and he would see none of her shame.

# Chapter 7
# A Mission

At a cataract along the Alba River that sliced through the foothills of the Spine, Richard turned to hoofbeats.

"Reporting, sir," Jon said and dismounted.

Richard held out a flask. "Walk with me, Jon. Diana is with you?"

"Yes, sir. She went to pick up Bo."

"How is the training coming?"

Jon took a swig and whistled through his teeth. "They're children."

"So were we."

"We never enjoyed these years of peace when we were young."

"The peace is over, Jon. The Sul broke our lines at the Pelsuk, and their cavalry ride west. I've given orders to move Le Pegre west to Bayeun. They were your rear guard."

"You will send Diana north to Wikkert?"

"I don't trust them. Not all our citizens are beyond temptation. I suspect someone there conspired in Katheryn's death. Mokdar has more influence in Wikkert than I do."

"That was always a risk when you decided to stay in Cherbourne."

Richard nodded. "They like my absence from Wikkert as well, to keep my title a formality and my meddling to a minimum. But I'd make the same decision to be here with Diana."

"You worry too much, Richard. The Sul Elites are only men."

A chill breeze came with the clouds that hid the sun, and Richard turned his collar up. "They're told they fight for their place in heaven and are blessed by their god."

"Like the Hordes we defeated at the Blois."

"That was years ago, and they fought alone."

"Will you unite the army again?" Jon said and hitched his horse to a tree.

Richard took another drink from the flask. "The new assembly has not decided."

"They broke their promise to keep them under united command."

Richard nodded and offered the flask to Jon again. "They still balk at a standing army. They fear my ambition more than our common enemy. What ambition have I ever shown them but my duty?"

"Competence frightens the mediocre, Richard. But it matters not. Without unity we'll fall. You've said so yourself."

Richard nodded again. "Until reinforcements arrive, we will have to make do here with what we have. The Sul Elites landed just east of the Wye Delta. Our defense is too light for a pitched battle, and it'll take time for reinforcements from Wikkert. I've ordered Le Pegre back to defend Bayeun. I expect to confront the Sul cavalry south of Aemgarde and turn them southwest. That will give the refugees an escape route northwest to Beirn."

"Sacrifice?"

"No. But too risky for Diana. I have word Garfann searches for her."

Jon spat. "That animal?"

"He leads a cavalry squadron of the Empress's Elites."

"Not the Emperor?" he asked, and Richard shook his head. "How did this information reach you?" to which the king did not reply. "Makashti is an unreliable ally, Richard."

"Of course. And she withholds much, but she offers me this. My daughter has no strategic value to Makashti, but she's invaluable to others who want to manipulate me and the North. And her capture would remove Garfann's shame at Diana's hands."

"What's his connection to the Empress?"

"Rumor is the Empress held him hostage in Mokdar to pressure Makashti and the result is the cur we observed at Le Pegre."

"If not Wikkert, then west?"

"Royax is vulnerable to blockade by the Sul fleet. She may be trapped there," Richard said.

"Makashti again?"

"Until this threat is gone, there is no safe place for Diana here, and she's all I have."

"Then south?"

Richard shook his head. "They've just ended a civil war and settled on a new king. And I have no contacts in Capitolia or Branwyn." He put a hand on Jon's shoulder. "A refugee caravan for Bayeun is assembling at Aemgarde, and I want her on it."

"Diana will not take this separation well. That first night after Katheryn's death I feared for you both."

"Our safety?"

Jon shook his head. "Your souls. I've seen grief warp the spirit, especially in the young, and watched it fester into a wedge between loved ones." Richard nodded but stayed silent. "After you fell asleep, she watched you for a half hour. She pinched you, and when you woke, she smiled and cried. She worries for you, Richard."

They sat in silence until Richard offered him another drink.

"I want you to support that caravan to Bayeun, Jon."

"I'm better off in the field, Richard. But yes. If you wish."

"Thank you, friend," Richard said and clasped arms with Jon. "This is the hardest thing I've ever done by choice."

\*\*\*

On her arrival home in Aemgarde, Diana made a brief stop home to collect Bo and pray at her mother's rune stone, the new centerpiece of the public square.

Riding south, the peaks of the Spine broke the clouds, and she found her father at the cataract. Dismounting with her horse still in motion, she ran to hug Richard as Bo lay with his head on his paws and watched her.

"How's my darlin'?"

"Fine, Papa," she said and faced him squarely. "Father, let me return. I want to go back to Le Pegre and train."

He took her horse's reins and tied it with his. "I need to send you north with the refugee caravan."

Diana's mouth fell open. "Papa, I don't want to go. I want to continue training."

"Le Pegre won't be there. The Sul broke our defenses at the Pelsuk and race here. The militia recruits are coming home, and I've ordered the bivouac to defend Bayeun. War has come again, Dee."

She paused and then snapped to attention. "Sir, please, take me with you."

"It's not safe with me."

Diana took her father's hand. "There's nowhere on Juro I'm safer than at your side."

Richard put his other hand on hers. "Not this time."

"Papa, please."

Richard sighed. "I'd give anything to be with you. But fate gives us responsibilities from which we cannot shrink without dishonor. My place is here, yours is not."

*Doesn't he trust me at his side?* "If I must flee, let me flee south to Branwyn to retrieve the Book of Chaos."

"I don't believe in magic and less in rumor. Such a long trip is too dangerous, and I have no one to spare to protect you."

"Please, Papa."

From his pocket, he removed the semblance of a brass coin with a jagged edge, put it in her palm and closed her fingers over it. "The future is unpredictable. And whatever plans we've made may not come to pass."

*Is he talking about himself or me?*

"If you find yourself on the West Coast, show this to the head of the merchant houses to find safe harbor."

*No! He's saying goodbye!* "Papa, please."

"This is an order from your King," he said. "Jon will support the caravan. You leave for Bayeun tonight."

"Yes, *Your Highness.*" She pursed her lips, bowed with a flourish, turned, and mounted. Wheeling her horse, she stifled her tears and galloped home with Bo close behind.

As the sky darkened, Diana caught up with Jon, and they rode together.

"Is this a ruse, sir?"

"Getting you to safety is a strategic necessity."

"I want to stay with the militia like we planned. My squad has my back."

"They wouldn't be enough. Your death or capture would undo us all. In the eyes of the Sul, you alone have the value of a queen now."

"But—"

Jon's eyes narrowed. "Listen, Princess. He didn't tell you everything, lass. The militia retreat with the Sul cavalry at their heels and ride west through Derryh to Cherbourne. The Sul Elites came ashore east of the Wye Delta to block a defense of Derryh."

"Wikkert will send reinforcements."

He shook his head. "Not before the Sul reach Cherbourne and put it to the torch. And you can't be here when that happens."

At home, Diana wrote letters to her friends in the militia, including an apology to Sten. At dusk she shared a farewell dinner with her father and Jon: not king and princess and general, but family and close friend. Of her personal things she took only her mother's dragon-tooth box, and within it put the jagged-edged coin. On her father's wrist she tied a small bracelet she had woven in a pattern matching her anklet, the family pattern with a gold cord.

Tall clouds hid the moons as the three left for Aemgarde to join the caravan heading for Bayeun with Bo running at her side. Behind them rode the farmhands and a wagon with Maggie. At the edge of town, Richard said his goodbyes, and rode south to meet his troops.

After the first mile, Jon broke the silence. "It's hard to leave the only home you've known."

"That's not it, sir. He's in danger."

"He's resourceful and elusive. I'd not worry yourself too much."

She shook her head. "He doesn't want me in his world and keeps pushing me away."

"He only means to—"

"I can't help him. I can't keep him safe." She bit her lip. "And he doesn't trust me."

"Protecting a king is an enormous responsibility for—"

"If I'd have stayed in the militia, I could have made Company A."

Jon raised his hand. "Time to listen, Corporal. The role you seek is an honor few achieve. Strive for skill and a noble character and honors like Company A may be granted you. And you're a princess now with other roles to fill."

"What better disguise."

"I believe your feet are meant to fill much larger shoes than a bodyguard."

"Dancing shoes and frilly skirts in Wikkert?"

Jon smiled. "The world has many opportunities for energetic young people. And they need not wear skirts all the time."

"Like what?"

He held out his arms and smiled. "Ahh, that's what the future will tell us," he said and spurred his horse to the fore of the caravan.

In a flash of lightning, a scout raced to the caravan waving his arms. A moment later, a flight of arrows caught him, and he slumped in his saddle.

"Attack!" Diana shouted "To arms!"

"To me!" Jon shouted and circled his arms as the wounded scout galloped past. The guards joined him to form a cordon to the east as caravanners circled the wagons and ducked inside to retrieve bows and swords.

Rain fell as horsemen galloped toward them, and Jon's soldiers unsheathed swords. Diana grabbed a sword from the fallen scout and took a position between Jon and the wagons with Bo growling at her side. She was no match for the Sul warriors, but she might protect those less skilled than even herself. From behind the Sul, archers aimed for the wagons with fire arrows.

One Sulerian broke Jon's cordon and raced to the wagons. Between him and the wagons roamed a child whose father fell to a Sul arrow. Diana raced to intercept, and her horse collided with the Sulerian's, knocking them both to the ground. He jumped to his feet and raised his sword to crash down on her. But Bo jumped and grabbed hold of his sword arm and knocked the man to his knees.

Another warrior raced to the child with his sword drawn, and the mother ran in front of the child. Diana rushed to protect them and parried the strike, but his sword sliced her shoulder. The warrior turned to her and lunged, and she parried again, fast enough to defend but not strong enough to counterattack. He raised his sword to end her but paused with his blade held high. Another flash of lightning exposed an arrow through his neck as he collapsed at her feet. She followed the path of the arrow to where Sam Rickets sat on his horse, waved to her, and wheeled back to the cordon.

Jon's cordon held, and when the attack subsided, he led the squadron to chase the surviving Sulerians.

Diana turned to the circle of wagons, the nearest of which was in flames.

*Chaos. How can I stop this from happening again? It will never end unless we even the scales. What can I do?*

Diana set her jaw and raced back to Maggie and their wagon. From it, she made a kit with her map, bow and quiver, knife and sword, a change of clothes and a week of rations and stuffed them into her saddlebags.

That's where Maggie found her. "Oh my dear, you're bleeding!"

Diana glanced at her shoulder where her blood had soaked her sleeve, unaware she had been wounded with the rush of battle fever. "It's nothing."

"What are you doing, lass?"

"This must end, Maggie. Papa is our best leader, but he needs help. And I'm off to find what he needs."

"And where is that?"

"Branwyn," she said and spurred her horse south with Bo running beside her and Maggie shouting for her to stop.


On her way south, she rode the hills west to bypass Aemgarde and her home and bid her horse to run when she saw them in flames. At sunrise, the rains passed and so did the battle fever. The risks she took struck her, and her shoulder stung.

*Do I have enough food? I know the way, kinda, but not the challenges. Papa will worry anyway. Is this my impatience again?*

As the clouds broke and the sun rose, Diana spied a rider following her. She galloped to a nearby copse of trees, dismounted, and nocked an arrow. But the rider was gone.

Bo did not growl, but when a twig snapped, she turned.

"Dunna worry, lassie."

Dianna spun to the voice and found Jon with his hands up.

"Branwyn, is it?" Jon said and dropped his hands.

She nodded. "The Book of Chaos. Mother said a copy is there." She backed up. "I'm not—"

He raised a hand to stop her protest. "Fairy tale or not, I'm not taking you back."

From his saddlebag, he removed a clean shirt and tore a strip from it. After tipping the sleeve from her blouse, he took a flask from his pocket and bit the cork from it.

"This will sting," he said and poured the brandy on her wound.

"Ouch!" she cried and pulled her shoulder away, but Jon grabbed her arm and tied the bandage around it.

"The caravan is safely off to Bayeun," he said. "But Sulerians hold the ground between here and there. Distance and anonymity may give us the security we seek."


Later that day, at a clearing on a ridge, before the tall spruce announced the foothills of the Eastern Spine beyond, Diana turned around to the plains of Cherbourne. The setting sun sparkled off the raindrops and in the corners of her eyes while far to the north, her country burned.

*Mokdar will burn as well, and I will spit on the ashes.*

Without a word, she dismounted and gave Jon the reins to her horse. At the ridge, she sat and hugged her knees to her chest with Bo looking up at her as he lay by her side.

*Will I have a home to return to after this?*

When Jon sat next to her, she leaned into him, and he put his arm around her. There they stayed until the sun set and Fures rose.

"We need to be in the trees before sunrise, lass."

She nodded but did not move.

"Your father and I hunted near the Lanshrue, so that far is known."

"I have a map to Dorreau," she said.

"And Branwyn is a straight shot south from there. How about disguising ourselves as ranchers? I'll be a horse trainer, and you a shepherdess."

She tilted her head and raised her eyebrows. "Jon, we *are* ranchers."

"Well, how fortunate for us! Now let's embrace the opportunity. Our destiny is in the south, lass." He rose and held out his hand to her. "Come. This will be the adventure of a lifetime, so let's not waste a moment of it."

She nodded, and they mounted their horses on the first leg of their journey south to sanctuary. But with each step of her horse, her shoulder stung.


When Lon, set that night, and darkness washed over the foothills, Bo growled at a shadow that left its hiding place and followed them into the woods.

# Chapter 8
# Murk

## The Bridge

Snowmelt from the peaks above softened the trail beneath Diana's muddy boots and splashed under the hooves of her pack horse. The path led to the bridge over the Lanshrue River Gorge, their last obstacle to a downhill trek south. Fed from the glaciers in the heights of the Spine, the Lanshrue flowed two hundred feet below them all the way to Antona in the South and fed the Orange River.

Jon broke the boredom of the long ride at the fireside dinners with stories of his and Richard's exploits in the wilderness. And over the long ride, her shoulder wound healed in the open air. The prior night, thunder had interrupted his story and woke them early this morning. All day long as they approached the bridge the rumbling grew louder.

"These are new," Diana said, pointing to a wide-branched tree with red and yellow leaves that stood out between the tall redwoods.

"Those are stenifer," Jon said. "And the little white plants near the poppies are jenalei."

She kneeled to pick one, which woke a swarm of little wheezits that buzzed her head. In a whoosh, an alert flitterbie swooped into the cloud of fliers and escaped with a few.

"And the red berries?" Diana asked.

"Those are daemonberries."

She picked one up, squeezed it, and wrinkled her nose at a strong whiff of alcohol. "Why do they call it that?"

"They're rich in liquor, and if you eat too many, you go mad."

She smiled. "Do you know anyone who went mad?"

"Not personally." He leaned over to her. "But your father and I took a few tastes just to see."

She stopped at another peal of thunder and turned to check the sky but found no thunderheads.

*Is that what dragons sound like?*

"Where's the source of the thunder?" she asked.

"Perhaps the clouds beyond the peaks," Jon said without conviction.

Dropping her eyes to the trail behind them, a speck appeared on a switchback far to the west and she squinted. "What's that?"

He turned in time to observe the speck disappear into the woods. "An animal, I imagine."

*He's in a quiet mood.* "Bo growled again last night."

Jon glanced behind them again. "I heard."

They entered an arbor of pine and colorful stenifer branches, which masked the trail beyond the next switchback. Cracking sounds like splitting wood accompanied the thunder. Bo whimpered and slunk behind with his tail between his legs.

"C'mon, Bo," she said, but her dog did not come.

When the canopy opened, they found the wooden bridge before them, lying at the bottom of the canyon floor in a pile of rubble. A loud crack took their eyes another hundred feet upward to the destroyer, a massive glacier which spanned the canyon.

Bo ran up behind her and barked.

"Quiet, Bo."

Jon walked over to the remains of the structure and waved to Diana to join him. Together they peered over the edge to find a steep drop to the river. Behind them the gorge was not as deep, and beside the trail, an eroded gully snaked down the ravine. Melt from the glacier rained upon them and turned the ditch into a muddy chute.

She stared at the Lanshrue below them, roiling with whitewater from the glacier melt. "It's too fast to cross."

Diana reached into her pocket for the map. "Here, a wide spot where we can ford. But it's miles back up the trail."

"What other appointments do we have today? We can camp there tonight and cross by noon." He turned their saddle horses around while Diana turned the pack horses, both nervous on the narrow trail.

Bo continued to bark and run around her as if wanting to play. "What's got into that dog?" Jon said.

Another loud crack and roll of thunder startled the lead pack horse, which turned its head. It neighed, stomped its hooves in the mud, and lurched forward to follow Jon. With her hands still holding its reins, the horse pulled Diana off her feet. Now closest to the glacier, she glanced up behind her as a large wedge of ice tipped toward them.

"Run!" Jon called.

Unable to get her footing, she slipped again. The slice of glacier fell toward her but missed the trail where she lay and collapsed the remains of the bridge's foundation. Diana struggled to her feet, but the shard of glacier sliced off the slope below the trail. The ground gave way, and Diana fell into the gully.

Over fallen leaves and pine needles she slid, hastened by the muddy snowmelt from the mountains

above. The gully was not a stream but a muddy ditch
which meandered around trees and rocks. Each obstacle slowed her descent, but only after a painful impact.
Each time she stopped, she tried to regain her footing,
but the path back up to the trail became more difficult.
She slipped again and slid farther down the slope. The
gully ended ten feet from the valley floor, and Diana
flew off to land on her back on the stony beach.

Bo barked and Jon shouted, but Diana could not
catch her breath to call and only raised a hand before
passing out.

The roar of the rapids and glare of the noon sun
woke Diana with a throbbing pain in her wrist and
pounding headache. She sat up and tried to stand, but
a pain in her ankle stopped her. A deep inhale caused
another sharp pain in her chest, and she whistled instead, but only an echo answered.

The steep valley shielded the trail from her view and
it would be unlikely someone could see her in the narrow cut. And the rapids that flowed in the cut frothed
and churned and drowned out her voice. Between her
and the rapids lay a stony beach. Upstream, the beach
ended in a jam of brush and trees scoured from the
valley by the glacier. Downstream, the beach extended
wide enough to pass. Unable to climb the steep ravine,
that appeared her best option.

Limping along the beach, she found a stick to use as
a crutch to take the weight off her sprained ankle. At
the edge of the rapids, the view improved up the valley
wall, but the trees and brush still hid the trail from
sight.

When she sat, the cold glacier melt trickled between
the pebbles under her and into the river. The frigid water numbed her hand when she dipped it into the river,

so she submerged her ankle and wrist to relieve the pain.

As the throbbing subsided, a log floated past, banging from rock to rock, flipping end-over-end, and splitting in two. There would be no safety for her in the river, from the rapids or the cold.

Jon and Bo would never give up searching for her. And as the relentless pain eased, her confidence grew that she would meet them on the path up the ravine before sunset.

The river growled and swelled in volume until the hair on the back of her neck tingled, and she turned around. Not forty feet away stood a big gray wolf, head low and teeth bared inching toward her. She held the crutch between her and the wolf and drew her knife, and the beast stopped well out of range.

She was prey, injured with nowhere to go. Debris blocked her escape upstream, and the wolf her escape downstream. Even if she could dash past it, she could not climb the steep ravine. With each move to the left or right, the wolf matched her and crept closer. The river was slim hope but hope still.

Holding the stick between herself and the animal, she took a step back into the river. With another step, her weak ankle gave way. She fell into a still pool and gasped from the frigid water. At the water's edge, the beast hesitated before committing to a lunge that would bring her down but leave it in the cold rapids. It put a paw into the water but stepped back, shook its paw, and showed its teeth.

Diana's feet numbed, and she crawled sideways to bypass the threat. But on a mossy rock her hand slipped, the knife fell, and the river swept her away.

The swirling water dragged her deep, and she fought the impulse to gasp as the icy cold gripped her.

Her body tensed and shivered as she struggled to reach the surface, spun by eddies and dragged by currents. She surfaced and swam for shore. But along the bank ran the wolf, jumping over fallen logs and brush with occasional detours up the bank. Each time she approached the shallows, the predator reappeared.

The sheer cliff face on the opposite side of the rapids provided no grip. She was trapped again, and another minute in the icy cold would steal her strength to move. Fighting to keep her head above water, she gasped for breath before another falls dragged her under. All the while, the wolf kept pace ashore.

Dozens of boulders and bruises later, the beach disappeared, creating a sheer canyon on both sides of the rapids. On shore, the beast howled as Diana floated past, accelerated through the narrow gorge, and shot over the falls into the pool below.

With numbed hands, Diana grabbed the branch of a fallen tree and pulled herself hand-over-hand until her numbed feet found the bottom. She stumbled to the beach, coughed up the water she swallowed, and collapsed. It would not matter if the wolf discovered her or not: she was done.


Diana woke on the beach, helpless to stop her violent shivering and unable to call out. But if she did not clear her head and move soon, she would die here. Above the trees, the angle of the early afternoon sun told her there remained time before the river fog would rise to chill her. So she shed her wet clothing, wrung them, and laid them to dry in the sun. After painful calisthenics to warm her body, she shouted until her throat was raw.

Beyond the beach, the valley sloped more gently to the river, giving her a way up and out. But fearing the wolf's return, she found a branch to use as a crude spear, and with her good hand, sharpened it on a stone.

Before beginning her climb, she stopped to consider her options. She needed help to reach the South without harm, which meant she would need to find Jon. *Or help him find me. That means a signal fire. But not here.* The cold air above the river might keep the smoke low within the valley and not reach the trail. *I need to get above the valley floor and into the trees for Jon to see my signal. Bo can pick up my scent if he crosses my path. How much time do I have?*

*The fire should be live before sunset to keep predators away in case Jon doesn't find me.* But it might take hours to build a fire with only lichen and hardwoods she found near the beach. That left less than two hours for hiking, maybe less with her injuries.

To speed the drying of her clothes and for activity to warm herself, she took each of her pieces of clothing and waved them in the air. As her body warmed, the shivering stopped, and the pain returned to her ankle, wrist, and ribs.

*The map.* She had made the copy on chamois that survived the rough water and with ink that would not run. The map was not so detailed as to show an easy meeting point, but a dashed line paralleled the river downstream, and she guessed it was a secondary route Jon would also notice.

Unable to wait longer, Diana dressed in her damp clothing. But when she took her first steps on the trail from the beach, she turned at a growl.

Diana backed away but could never outrun the wolf that faced her. She thrust her crude spear in the wolf's snout, which forced it back, snapping and growling. It tensed its shoulders and dropped its haunches while Diana stood firm with her crude spear poised. The predator lunged, but halfway to reaching her, Bo collided with the wolf mid-body.

Her dog was half the size of the wolf, and both moved too fast for Diana to aim her spear. Bo went for the wolf's leg, but the wolf grabbed him by the neck, shook him, and tossed him aside where he lay limp. The beast went over and stood above him ready for the killing bite.

Diana jumped and struck the wolf in the side with the point of the spear to an audible crack, but did not break the skin. It yelped and hunched. She was the target again.

She hit it with the butt of her spear, and it staggered. Then she kicked it in the nose, and it yelped again. Repeatedly, she jabbed it with the tip of the spear, but it hopped away and crouched for another lunge. This time when she thrust the spear, the beast did not cower but bared his fangs, lay down and growled at her. It was as if the wolf called the battle a draw and would let her go.

*A ruse.*

When she took a step backward, it crawled closer to her. Brush rustled behind her, but she could not turn. On the next step back, her heel caught a tree root, and she fell. The wolf pounced with jaws open and teeth bared, and at the last moment, she lodged the spear in the dirt.

The wolf's chest landed on her spear and he yelped. Before it could lunge again, an arrow found its shoulder, and she kicked it away. This time, when she thrust her spear, it broke the skin of the wolf's chest, and it lay still.

"Are you alright?" Jon asked, and she jumped into his arms.

When Bo whimpered, she broke free and ran to him. As she stroked his head, he tried to nuzzle into her palm but fell back again and gazed at her.

"Thank you, Bo."

Jon came over and sat beside her. She took his hand and leaned on his shoulder.

"And you," she said and put his hand to her cheek.

Diana petted Bo's head and left her tears on his fur. After his last breath, she did not stop.

"He's gone," Jon said.

"His spirit is still here," she said and closed her eyes.

Jon left, and when he returned an hour later, Diana lifted Bo in her arms and carried him to the shallow grave Jon had dug. There, they laid him to rest.

"Seems a humble grave for a hero," Jon said. "He never tired looking for you."

"Neither did you."

He gripped her sleeve. "You're still damp."

"A swim I hadn't intended."

"You're lucky to be alive."

Diana squeezed his hand, absolving him for her trials. "You were there when I needed you most."

"Come," he said. "Let's make a fire. We can stay here tonight."

"What of the horses?"

"Tied together back on the trail." After starting the fire, he turned to her. "Now, where do you hurt?"

Jon wrapped Diana's sprains and bound her ribs. From the jenalei plants he made for her a tea with the scent of thyme and the bite of liquor. Leaving her the bow and sword, he went to get the horses that held their food and blankets. When he returned, he put a blanket around her and prepared dinner.

"The glacier is larger than shown on the map," he said.

"The map is wrong," she replied.

"Rather, I think the ice is growing faster than the maps can keep up."

Diana waited for him to explain why that might be, but he did not respond. "Why does it grow? It doesn't feel colder in Cherbourne."

Busy with biscuits at the fire, Jon did not respond.

"Where to now?" she asked.

"The ford we intended to cross is a few hundred yards downstream. We hadn't planned to get there until tomorrow."

Diana smiled. "I took the shortcut."


After dinner, Jon poked the fire and glanced at Diana. "You're not listening. Perhaps the stories of an old warhorse grow tiresome."

Diana shrugged and inspected her boots.

"What is it, lass?"

"After all my training, I'm still unable to protect myself and those I care for."

"It will take more training for you to be omnipotent." He turned to her with a patient smile. "You escaped the wolf and held it off until help arrived. Sometimes that's the best we can do, lass. Survive to fight again." He sat beside her and put his arm around her. "Come, now. The wolf weighed as much as you and was fiercer with natural weapons superior to yours. You lived, after a fight to the death. Don't fault yourself for a victory less glorious than you'd wished."

"It's not the glory, Jon. I couldn't save her . . . him."

"You're thinking of your mother now?"

She nodded as tears rolled down her cheeks.

"Your guilt is misguided, lass. It diminishes the gifts Bo and your mother gave you, as if they didn't act virtuously from their choice but by your decision. Honor them for their gifts and grieve for your loss, and I grieve with you."

"But I was inadequate."

"Now, now. You're grieving and exhausted. This is not the time to make assessments about your skills. Your life was threatened many times today, yet here you sit. And I'm glad beyond measure." He sighed and patted her shoulder. "Time for bed now."

His words had not pierced her grief, and the memory of the night her mother died came to her again. She spread her bedroll and lay on it while he stood watch.

It did not matter that they told her it was not her fault. Her mother would be alive if she had called out for help or could fight or use the bow. Her father sent her away because she could not help protect him. All her life since that night it was the same: she was too small, too weak, too unskilled; helpless to protect herself or others.

She pursed her lips. *Jon will think I'm a weepy little girl.* She made a fist and set her jaw.

*If I'm not strong enough to defend myself and others, I must make myself stronger. If I'm not skilled enough to protect myself and those I care about, then I must train harder. If I'm not perceptive to threats to myself and others, then I must become more aware.*

She turned away and swallowed the tears meant for Bo.

*Today I am not so strong, skilled, or perceptive.*

*Not yet.*

## The Stranger

At the southern foothills of the Spine, three weeks past the shallow ford on the Lanshrue River, Diana and Jon overlooked the deep canyon cut by the Orange River. Beyond lay the highlands of northern Antona. With them were three of their four horses, having lost one to a mountain lion before they could intervene.

"It should be an easy ride from here through Antona," he said, grinning, "and I expect only the usual thieves and murderers who inhabit the wilderness."

Diana rolled her eyes. "How long to Branwyn?"

"About three weeks to Dorreau and the same from there to Branwyn."

"Will we be safe then?"

"Not if our tracker stays with us."

She spun toward him. "We're being followed?"

He nodded. "I wasn't sure until this morning. With Bo gone he's become bolder. I suspect he's been following since Aemgarde."

"That speck on the trail?"

"Perhaps. If so, his interest is information rather than murder. Still, he mustn't learn our destination." Jon scanned the campsite without moving his head and stirred the embers as if breaking camp. "Stay here."

Jon rose, walked to the horses, and took the bow and quiver tied to Diana's saddle. When no one appeared from the trees, he hobbled the horses and signaled Diana to follow him into the woods.

"Where are we going?" she whispered.

Handing the weapon to her, he said, "If he won't come out, we'll need to find him."

She followed Jon who circled around their camp and back from a different direction. When they returned, they found a thick man going through the saddle bags on Jon's horse.

"Nock an arrow," Jon whispered.

"I won't kill him."

"That won't be necessary."

Diana dropped her head. "I'm not of much use, Jon. I'll stay here."

He studied her for a moment, furrowed his brow, and nodded. "Your name is Betty. Watch him." He turned and walked into the campsite with his arms outstretched. "Welcome," he said and continued to walk toward the stranger. "What brings you from the North?"

The man took a step to run, but Jon raised his hand. "No, no. You won't make it."

The intruder raised his hands. "You carry a sword. I fear for my life."

Jon removed the weapon from its scabbard and threw it behind him near the fire. "There now, is that better? Who are you and where are you from?"

The man smiled with open hands and took a step forward. "I'm a simple merchant who trades in glassware from Antona." He closed the space to Jon in another step.

"To where?"

"Corel. Have you heard of it? A half-day ride west of Aemgarde."

Jon nodded. "Ah, yes. There's an inn there, the Polecat, I believe—"

The stranger grinned and slapped his knee. "Aye, so it is, at the corner of the square."

"—owned by an old militiaman."

A squint crossed the stranger's face. "I'm guessin' you ain't been there recently."

"His daughter, Meg?" Jon said.

"No. His widow, Elga."

Jon nodded. "I remember now. And your goods? Maybe I've seen them in a shop there."

"The McCulty place across from the inn has my wares on consignment."

Again Jon nodded.

"Where's your companion?"

Jon tensed. "What companion?"

The intruder pointed toward the horses. "Not mean- in' nothing, milord, but you've got two saddles and two bedrolls. I'm only guessin' now and don't mean to pry."

After pausing for a moment, Jon waved his hand while keeping an eye on the stranger. "You can come out now, Betty. Come join us at the fire."

Diana rose from her hiding place and relaxed her bow but kept the arrow nocked as she walked toward them.

"Stop dawdling, girl, and scare up some leftovers for our guest," Jon said, and Diana glared at him. "Hurry now."

"Mighty grateful to ya. I ain't had nothin' but my horrible cookin' for weeks."

Jon leaned toward the stranger. "My Rosie wore some nice baubles in her time, Gods bless her. Perhaps you could show me your wares?"

"I'm not sayin' my little trinkets is any better, but . . ." The intruder reached into his jacket and Jon tensed, but the man pulled out a small box padded with cotton and opened it. Within it lay an exquisite sculpture of a red fox in tinted glass. He handed it to Jon.

"This is beautiful."

"Gentle now, that be my prize and will pay a week's rent for my shop in Antona and a new pair of shoes for my little Jenny."

Diana served the man a plate of stew from the pot. "You have a daughter?"

"Aye, and the sweetest little thing she is," the stranger said between mouthfuls. His smile softened and eyes glistened as he spoke of her. "All blond and curly and loves to dance."

She smiled at the man's story as Jon turned to give the fragile glass fox to her. But a cloud stole the glitter from the prize, and she looked up to see the intruder's eyes narrowed to a squint and fixed on Jon.

"Jon!" she shouted.

In that moment, the stranger hit Jon in the temple with the edge of the half-full plate, reached behind his back, and swung a ball-tipped club at Jon's head. Jon leaned back and raised his forearm to sweep the cudgel to the side and divert the force of the blow. But the weapon cracked on Jon's arm, and he fell hard. Diana jumped up, and the stranger grabbed her ankle, but she twisted her leg and pulled. Free from his grip, she scurried away and backed into the horses.

The stranger scowled and turned his back, unafraid of her. Instead, he stepped and swung the cudgel again to strike Jon's ribs. Using his right hand, Jon swept the weapon away and blended with the momentum of his attacker. But the stranger clubbed him in the head again and Jon dropped, dazed.

The stranger kicked him and picked up Jon's sword. He scowled and stood over him. "You killed my pet wolf." He raised the weapon above his head to hack at Jon.

But Diana's blade parried it.

"I did," she said and stood over Jon. The stranger swung again, and she deflected it, but his reach exceeded hers. He smiled and swung again, and this time his strength was more than she could counter, and he bumped her away with his shoulder, knocking her down.

"I'll deal with you later," he said and turned to finish Jon.

But Jon was conscious now and swept the man's legs from under him, which caused him to fall and drop the sword. With his arm hanging limp at his side, Jon kicked the weapon away and faced the man.

"That was unwise," Jon said. "You might have lived if you hadn't attacked us."

"I needed evidence," the stranger said, glancing over both shoulders. The ravine gaped behind him, and Jon stood between him and the open forest. "I really didn't mean you harm." He raised his hands. "You interrupted my—"

He lunged forward and threw a punch at Jon, but Jon leaned to the side and brushed the strike away. The man spun and aimed an elbow at Jon's temple, but Jon ducked and thrust his fingers into the stranger's ribs with a *crack*. The man gasped and stumbled backward, and even though Jon was years older and defending himself with only one arm, the attacker backed away.

In the few moments after the stranger disarmed her, Diana retrieved her bow, and when he turned to run, she shot him in the calf, and he fell. He stood again and her next arrow pierced his thigh.

The intruder limped from the camp and Jon followed, holding his arm, with Diana close behind. But the man hobbled to the edge of the cliff and a moment later the pursuit was over. The villain turned back to face them.

"I asked you who you are and where you're from," Jon said.

"They'll kill me and my family if I tell you."

"Who will kill you?"

The intruder glanced over his shoulder to the ravine below and turned back to Jon. "I dare not."

"There's a place a few days south that can protect you."

The villain scoffed. "Soon there will be no safe place in the South. No one will be able to protect me. Or you."

Diana stepped forward. "Please, just tell us who sent you. If you stop following us, we'll let you go."

Jon frowned and glanced at her.

The intruder sighed. "There's no safe place, no place they can't find me, just as I found you." He closed his eyes and leaned backward.

"No!" Diana yelled.

Jon grabbed the man's sleeve, but the intruder jerked Jon's arm away, and he fell into the ravine. The pair rushed to the brink.

"Why'd he do that?" she asked. "We would have let him go."

"He meant to avoid interrogation." Jon turned back toward their camp. "Why promise to let him go?"

Diana raised her hands, palms up. "Would we arrest him? Under whose authority? Or would we kill him?"

"Humph. The threat of it might loosen his tongue."

"What did he mean about not being safe?"

Jon shook his head and rubbed his forearm.

"Is it broken?"

"It's tender," he said. "A splint should do just in case."

While Jon awakened the dead fire, Diana dug through her saddlebag for bandages. On the ground, she found a suitable stick for a splint and bound his forearm. She tied a sling around his neck, then searched for valerian, willow bark, and plantago at the edge of the clearing.

Mixing an analgesic broth with the valerian and willow bark, she turned to Jon and frowned. "I wonder if he was telling the truth about his daughter."

Jon's voice softened. "You aren't responsible for his choices, lass. Especially the one that ended his life."

"What if his daughter has only him to care for her?"

"If true, would you have let him kill us?"

"No, of course not."

"His tale was meant to disarm us, to make us less wary, and I fell for it," he said and sighed. "As for the truth of it? The most convincing lies have elements of truth to them." He shook his head. "I was stupid. He seemed harmless enough and a simple spy. Another lesson for you, lass, not to underestimate your foe. But I expect the demonstration was more powerful than a lecture."

Jon closed his eyes and soon fell asleep, as Diana added wood to the fire. She scratched an itch on her ankle and winced at a long scratch and welt that ran along her ankle instead of her woven anklet.

*Must have caught in a bramble.*

She soothed the scratch with plantago leaf, and taking colored cord from her pack, she wove another anklet. As it had nothing but sentimental value to her and her father, she did not mention the missing anklet to Jon.

\*\*\*

Three weeks after crossing the Lanshrue, Jon and Diana stopped at the Monastery of Dorreau, a sanctuary for those whose life outside was hazardous to their health, or perilous to their soul. There, the healer checked Jon's arm, and they refreshed their stores. A separate compound welcomed women, but to avoid temptation, lived in their own community with an abbess. The monks and nuns, distinguishable from highwaymen and barmaids only by their brown cassocks or jumpers, welcomed them, happy for word from the north though concerned for the war that brought them.

During the day, the travelers traded their labor in the fields for their meals. And after dinner, the monks coached them in spoken and written Imperium, the language of the South, a task made easier due to the common structure of all Juro's languages.

After dinner on their last night, Jon and Diana sat with the Abbot and Abbess.

"Dinner was delicious," Jon said. "What did we just eat?"

"Barvost and breshk," the Abbot said.

The Abbess laughed "Meat and potatoes."

"Your vernacular has improved," the Abbot said. "But tell others you're from the provinces to explain your accent."

"What about books? Are there any here?"

"No, dear," the Abbess said to Diana. "We have only one book, and that's the Book of the One God. Other than religion, bound books are beyond rare."

"What about Branwyn?"

"Even there. The only other bound books we are aware of, are cherished by our brothers and sisters at the College of Singers far to the east. They have fragments of an ancient book of myths from which they spin their Songs. What's so special about the book you seek?"

"It's rumored to contain magic," Diana said.

The Abbot opened his arms and beamed. "I know of no greater magic than the miracles of the world that surround us every day."

Diana leaned forward. "My mother believed there was another book the Sulerian Empress uses to advantage in war."

"I see," the Abbot said. "Like the Singers, we seek knowledge of all kinds here, especially from the time before the Chaos."

Jon raised his eyebrows. "During the Darkness?"

"No," the Abbess said. "We think there was a time before the Chaos when people knew things we've since forgotten." She closed her eyes, and as if in a trance, recited:

> *There was History before history,*
> *A time before men tilled the soil*
> *And wrote the Book of the One God;*
> *A time before the Wandering when people roamed the land;*
> *And even earlier, before the Chaos,*
> *When men lived like animals in perpetual winter.*

> *There was History before history,*
> *When Juro wore our civilization like a crown,*
> *And women flew like birds.*
> *A time when we knew the ages of the stars,*
> *Before we forgot who we were . . .*

The Abbess opened her eyes again and smiled. "We call that the Old Knowledge."

"And how do you come by this?" Jon asked.

"We've discovered artifacts from before the Wandering that couldn't be created by the knowledge of that time or even now," the Abbot said. Diana opened her mouth to speak, but the abbot waved his hands. "No, not enchantments. Coins with runes we do not understand and made of unknown metals. A monk named Tobias traveled through here carrying one such marvelous artifact. And word has come of devices that move by strange forces."

"Where are these Singers you mentioned and the book they hold?" Diana asked.

"The college is many months far to the east, but Singers are traveling bards, and one may cross your path."

"And so Branwyn remains our destination," Diana said.

***

On a hillock where the North Road broke free of the forest, Diana and Jon dismounted to survey their destination. Tilled land covered the entire Branwyn Plain from the forest west to the Orange River. Late summer added a checked pattern of harvested fields, like Aemgarde in the fall, but tinged more wheat than evergreen.

Diana pointed to the rocky outcrop overlooking the banks of the Orange and the walled town and castle of Branwyn. There, pennants flew above two sets of spires to the east and west.

"Do you think they have fancy dress balls there?" she asked, imagining princesses in pretty dresses, and young officers in dashing uniforms.

Jon kneeled and dug his hand into the dirt. "There's good soil here," he said, waving his arm over the vast clearing. "Not a single acre unplowed."

"Except that plot where the forest meets the road east."

He nodded. "With land for pasture and paddock."

Before descending the grade to the valley floor, Jon gave her the reins to his horse, walked back on the trail a few yards, and sat on his haunches.

"What is it?" she said, afraid again.

He raised a fist for silence. A few minutes later, he returned and took the reins.

"Anything?" she asked.

He shook his head and mounted his horse. "Well, let's see what our silver is worth in Branwyn."

Diana mounted and joined at his side. But for the rest of the journey, whenever the hair tingled on the back of her neck, she looked over her shoulder to check the trail.

# Chapter 9
# A Carpet

Fifteen hundred miles to the east, six riders walked their horses to the watch fire on the windy escarpment of the Sulerian plateau. Three hundred yards below, a stream of migrants flowed through the narrow channel between the cliffs and the Ocean of Daggers. Still hundreds of miles north of the Spine, the trail extended to both horizons but trekked south to where the peaks of the Spine crashed into the sea. Some migrants turned west to the border of Sinefora, heading to Derryh. Others camped on the beach, and each day the camp grew larger.

Snow drifted in the bright sun as the wind billowed the garish vestments of one rider, the hooded furs of the others, and the steam that followed every breath. Nearby, a horse pawed the ground, as a liquid dripped from a carpet tied on its back leaving dark-red stains on the snow.

The man in gaudy robes glanced to the left and right without moving his head and sneered. "Chief, why are we here?"

The war chief paid no attention to the Sulerian high priest and waved a gloved hand. Other riders led the horse with the carpet to them.

The high priest squinted and frowned in confusion when they handed him a rope. "And what am I to do with this?" When no one responded, he shrugged and pulled on the rope. His tug untied the bundle and a bloody body fell to the ground—a body familiar to the high priest.

Without turning, the war chief said, "The army answers to me, not to you, priest. Take what remains of this one who sought your guidance."

He reddened, insulted by the informal title. "This is an outrage! Such men serve at my discretion!"

The hood dropped from the war chief. "And they live at mine," said High Chief Makashti Sineura, Governor of Sinefora.

The high priest bowed in his saddle. "Apologies, Your Highness. I didn't realize—" He trembled as he glanced at the others on the cliff for weapons.

"Look, priest," Makashti said, "and tell me what you see."

"I see flotsam washed up on the shore," the cleric said with narrowed eyes. "What else would you have me see in the scum drifting past?"

"I see them hungry in Tur. I see a cold winter has passed, which led to bad harvests and sickly herds. The Emperor does not know this." Makashti glared at him. "But you do."

He stared ahead as if pinned to a board. "That news was . . . being withheld for a—"

She laughed. "Spare me your lies, priest. Any fool could see the Hordes migrating south and challenging our border."

The high priest glowered. "The Qu are allies and fight for us, Chief. Why fear them?"

"I fear their numbers," Makashti said. "I fear their voracious appetite for land. The wars against the Northmen to the west have gone badly, so there's nowhere for the Qu to go. If they have no other outlet, they will devour us like locusts."

"The Emperor is grateful Sinefora keeps these barbarians from the gates of Mokdar."

"Bah," she said. "It is in our interests to keep them out and he need do nothing. The Hordes would destroy us first before going after the holy city. He can hate us and use us at the same time."

The high priest scoffed. "And Sinefora need do nothing, either. The cliffs are an adequate defense and run all the way to the Spine."

She scowled at him. With a sudden reach, she snatched a bug from the air and released it under his nose. "Even the smallest creature can scale these heights."

"But insects have wings."

"Men go where other creatures cannot," she said. "Wings or no. Men can do anything when motivated. Even defeat an empire."

"How can you doubt our strength? We have a great civilization! Years beyond counting."

Makashti shook her head. "Fool, we are old and brittle, and they're young and vital. If the Emperor had not blunted the barbarian spears on the mountains of the Spine, they'd be parading you naked through the streets of Mokdar like a dog on a leash. It's I who keeps the fangs from your throat now."

"How dare you speak to me in that tone?"

She pointed to the dead body and the blood-stained snow surrounding it. "My palace is filled with many carpets, priest. Make sure I find no more spies." She took a small vial from under her furs and threw it at him, staining his robes with purple iridescence. "And make sure you never cross my border again with the Empress's poisons, or you will taste them yourself."

The high priest trembled again and bowed in his saddle. The escort bundled up the body and rode away with the cleric.

Makashti's companion sidled his horse closer. "He's trouble."

"And a fool like the others," Makashti said. "He cares only for his whores and his dinner. Don't expect him to notice starving children or where the grass grows."

"What do you see?" he asked and pointed to the stream of migrants.

"This will break the world."

He scoffed. "A few migrants?"

"Thousands more follow. What does it take to drive thousands of people to throw themselves at the unknown?"

"Desperation. Their only other way is south through the Spine, but dragons bar the way."

"Yes, the failure at Invernell cost them dearly," she said. "But the Empress foretells another way now, and has sent her seneschal, Kalil, south with the lion charm."

He sat straight and turned to her. "To a foreigner? For what promise?"

"Troops. She's obligated herself to the Baronet of Ostia, a man called Grimes, who now resides in Branwyn."

"And the Empress, not the Emperor?"

"The Empress pretends to speak for Quesh. The old viper has imprisoned him with drugs and vice like she did your father and brother."

"I didn't know."

She raised an eyebrow. "And you still don't. If this escapes your lips, it'll be your life and mine." She turned away. "Your headstrong brother, Garfann, searches for Richard's daughter, Diana. We don't need that trouble. She's my wild card."

"Can't you stop him?"

Makashti shook her head. "Garfann listens to the empress now, not me. She speaks to him through the drugs."

"The Empress has no legitimate claim to the throne. If the people knew—"

"Don't be naïve. Power can make miracles of perception and transmute perception into reality."

He frowned and dipped his head. "I'm honored by the confidence you show in me, but the game you play is beyond me."

"The Empress aims for the South and commits forces there." Makashti raised her chin and gazed at the sky. "That's when the gods become most cruel."

"And our plan?" he asked.

"To do as she wills, when it aligns with our interests." She held a woven bracelet with a gold cord in a pattern of the far north. "The Empress asks us to deliver this to her people in the South to help locate the young princess." She threw the bracelet into the fire. "This is not in our interests."

"And then?"

"Be patient. I sense desperation in her aggression. Her overreach may present us with opportunities." She turned to her son. "With your father and Garfann under her spell, the Empress thinks she's tamed us. Until she discovers her error, it's best to defer and marshal our allies."

An icy wind swept across the escarpment, drifting snow over the cliffs. Makashti's eyes narrowed as she gazed south along the coast.

"Pity those in her path."

# Part 2 The South

*Peace reigned in the South after the barons defeated the Imperator and crowned a new king, Baron George Lombard of Alsair, now King George of Merisol. Capitolia, the center of the Imperium, collapsed under the weight of corruption and debt, and a vibrant new civilization followed the king west to Branwyn.*

*But the contest between History and Chaos was just beginning.*

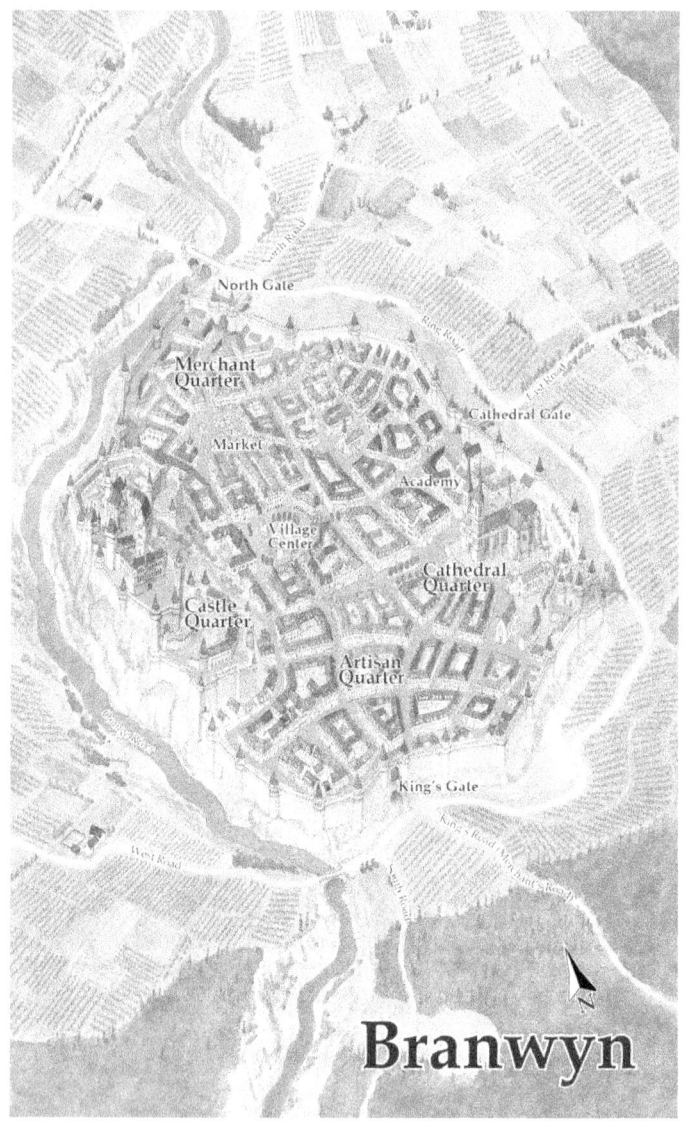

Branwyn

# Chapter 10
## Ranchers

"This is the old Reynolds' place," Tom Buckman said and handed the scroll with deed and map to Jon. "The property lines are marked here on the map. The west fence borders our farm and the east fence, the forest and the king's preserve."

Jon scanned the map and handed it to Diana as they walked the land they had scouted from the North Road the day prior. "What do you think, partner?" Jon asked, and Diana smiled.

"Three acres of good pasture," she said. "Too steep for farming and fenced for sheep and horse. We'll have to fence this back until we have the herd and flock built." She turned to Tom. "You'd be charging us twice more if you could farm this."

Tom smiled and nodded. "I surely would. The land is fertile, if you've mind for a smaller crop on the terraces."

Past the barn and stable, she turned west to the paddock fence and a sweeping view of Branwyn Valley and the walled town.

Jon leaned on the fence with a foot on the lower rail. "And a strategic view."

Diana took his arm. "We're not finished."

After a quick walk through the little cottage, Diana nodded to Jon, handed the scroll back to Tom, and they returned to his farmhouse.

In Tom's kitchen, Jon counted out fourteen silver coins and slid them across the table to Tom who passed them to his daughter, Anne. She bit into each, inspected the dents, then put them on a scale behind her. When she nodded, Tom signed the deed and pushed it to Jon to sign.

"Dinner to celebrate, neighbor?" Tom said, and they nodded.

Tom's wife, Edith, set a table with simple fare of lamb stew and bread. And when Anne's brothers joined, the conversation was brisk as Jon and Diana kept the topics to stock and farming, and away from their origin.

"And where might we buy sheep to breed and horses to train?" Diana asked.

Anne spoke for the first time. "That information isn't free," she said with a smile. "Papa knows the best stock in the valley and can steer you true."

"And what will your fee be?" Diana asked.

"I need help at the market in town."

"And you'd give me a ride to town and back?"

Anne nodded. "We leave before dawn."

"Deal," Diana said.

Anne smiled. "Good! Now that we're partners, we have bedding and towels you can borrow until you can make your own."

Diana's jaw dropped. *Make my own?*

"If it's sheep you'll be raising," Anne's oldest brother said, "you'll have a good market in town. And trained horses too. There used to be only a few goods from farms like ours."

"The Imperium?" Jon asked.

"Aye," Tom said as he set a cheese round on the table and sliced it. "The police used to spend all their time collecting taxes from us poor farmers. That left them no time to stop the bandits on the roads or the bigger thieves lurking about in fancy clothes in the town and castle. They got the silver, and we got the coppers. Now everything we make is ours. No one tells me what I can charge now. The judge enforces contracts and sends the police."

Anne set mugs of juice in front of them all.

"What dangers lurk?" Jon asked. "Brigands? Private armies?"

"The police keep the bandits outside the town now, and soldiers keep them out past the forest," Anne said. "And George disbanded the private armies of the aristos. The Assassins—"

Diana's feeling of security vanished, and she leaned forward. "Assassins?"

"Contract killers?" Jon asked.

"It's a guild licensed by the Chancellor," Tom said. "They act on edicts issued by him or his office and are well paid. I wouldn't worry. You're not likely to become important enough or violent enough to deserve a warrant."

Tom drank from his mug. "I don't much hanker for royals, but old George seems to have cleaned things up. Merisol was just a smudge at the western edge of the Imperium until the Imperator ran here during the Barons War. The barons buried him here, and with it the idea that one man would speak with the authority of God. Branwyn stands rebuilt on the rubble."

"With the corruption gone," Anne said, "Mama can even sell her extra baskets and lace without a special license." She pointed to the woven cord around Diana's ankle. "You could sell things too. I'll bet people would buy anklets like yours. Can you teach me how to make them?"

"I'm sorry, Anne, but this pattern is very special to me," Diana said, concerned that a recognizable style from the North might endanger them all. Anne dropped her gaze to the hands in her lap, and Diana took them in hers. "I can show you another pattern if you wish."

With a few straws from the floor, Diana wove an anklet with a pattern from Antona. Anne brightened, and Diana's thoughts went to where she would begin searching for the Book of Chaos, and who else might be looking for something so valuable.

Or had already found it.


Next morning before dawn, Diana shouted goodbye to Jon and dashed to the road with Anne to catch her ride to Branwyn. They hopped on the tailboard, the only room left after vegetables and cheeses, and sat together with their legs dangling.

Excited by her nearness to her goal, Diana imagined what the Book of Chaos might look like.

*Might it have multicolored characters in a strange language with arcane symbols? Or might it be within a locked binding and demand a secret word before waking the mysteries that sleep within? Would it beguile me with wonders or frighten me with consequences for invoking it? Would it fly from my grasp if I tried to hold it? Or kill me, as Garfann warned. Whatever it is, it will certainly be wondrous and inscrutable.*

"Anne, have you seen any bound books?"

Anne tilted her head. "You mean fixed along one edge? Why bound?"

"My mother told me there's a bound book that contains special information."

Anne smiled. "How special?"

Diana smiled and put her hand on Anne's. "I don't know! That's the mystery."

"Well, the only writing we see is by the tallyman and tax recorder, and those are on scrolls."

"Or the learned?" Diana asked. "Might they have them?"

"That would be the priests, most likely. Or the castle. And we're not likely to get near either. Next best thing I guess might be the aristos, but they keep to themselves, mostly."

"Where do they congregate?"

"Well, the center of town has a promenade on Sundays where the aristos strut in their finest with their noses in the air. Some of the young attend the Academy chartered by Queen Helena."

Anne dominated the rest of the conversation with fantasies about the aristos who attended the Academy and their glamorous life of fashion, balls, and handsome men. And she gushed over the aristos and Prince Eric, King George's son, who served in the army.

Once past the orchards, Branwyn reappeared as the rising sun struck the banners flying from the castle spires. The town covered every inch of the rocky point, and when they ran out of room, they built upward. Castle Branwyn stood on the highest spot commanding a sweeping view of the valley. The lords reserved the lowlands for the vineyards near the town where the periodic flooding of the River Orange kept the land the richest. And those vines gave the town its original name: Brandy Wine.

As they approached the town wall, the castle and cathedral grew larger. Diana smiled as the spires and pennants drew her eyes upward toward the heavens and the promise of a better day.

The rising sun lit the parapet of the walled town when they arrived at Branwyn. Once past the sentries, and inside the walls, Diana pinched her nose.

"You'll get used to the smell," Anne said and described the details as they passed.

Inside the east gate, the wagon entered the Cathedral Quarter, the oldest part of the settlement dating from before the Imperium. Here the walls were lower and in less repair than those surrounding the castle keep and armory. And like the town itself, access was limited by gates manned by armed guards.

"They seemed to have worshipped everything here at one time or another," Anne said. "There are bells and calls to prayer every day to some deity or another, and holidays for this and parades for that, and sacrifices, and bathing in blood, and ritual reading of entrails, and oracles, and—"

"Is there conflict between these beliefs?"

"Oh, the occasional argument at the market or the tavern, but otherwise no." Anne pointed to a shrine of a thick man with his arms crossed. "That shrine is for Apoko, the god of compliance. That was the Imperator's patron."

"Wasn't the Imperator declared to be a god?"

Anne nodded. "But King George destroyed all his shrines after the barons won the civil war."

"Which one is that?" Diana asked as they passed a three-headed shrine. One head possessed the full lips and seductive smile of a courtesan, another a matronly face and bust, and another the sharp eyes and nose of a scholar. Upon the shrine and piled around it were gifts of food and trinkets offered and received by passersby.

"That's the three aspects of goddess Junera: Harz for lust, Winz for love and family, and Joniz for cleverness."

"I think I'd like Joniz," Diana said.

Anne pointed to a massive building with windows of tinted glass and spires that reached for the heavens. Around it, men scurried on scaffolding that extended to the roof.

"That's the old cathedral," Anne said. "The bishop began rebuilding it before the Imperator came and has rechristened it to the One God."

"Where does he get the funds to rebuild such an ornate building?" Diana asked.

"I don't know, but on this side of town, he's the law and the judge. I hear the One God favors love, like Winz, which is to my liking."

"Are you taken with this new religion?"

"I'm not learned in the teachings," Anne said. "But it feels right. The Imperium's old gods are always competing and making the same stupid mistakes as humans, which seems silly. If you have that much power and live forever, why fight? Gods should be different, like the best of us, not the petty desires of humans. And they should want the best from us, not the worst."

Anne pointed to a structure in various stages of repair attached to the cathedral. "And that's the Academy there."

As they left the Cathedral Quarter, Anne explained Branwyn divided itself into quarters. The castle to the west end of town counterbalanced the cathedral and temples to the east. And along the north-south axis, merchants in the north balanced the artisans to the south. The streets would lead them to their destination north of the center of Branwyn—the market.

At the market, the bold stripes of tomatoes and apples in produce carts, contrasted with blues and greens of blueberries and cucumbers. Farmers swapped their browns and sun-bleached greens for brightly colored dresses and shirts more likely to attract buyers. And the shouts of sellers and bickering buyers kept conversations loud. Arriving after sunrise, Diana and Anne scrambled to the stall Anne had claimed with visibility and traffic.

Barbequed meats and fresh pastries cut the smell of the town and made Diana hungry, so Anne traded slices of cheese for sausage and bread for their breakfast. As Diana ate, she studied each person who passed to assess their likelihood of possessing a book. None of the shoppers appeared to have the means to own one. And the town itself seemed as devoid of mystery and magic as Le Pegre.

Anne's goods sold well and when the cathedral bell rang for morning prayer, Tom returned for the scale and unsold goods, and Diana left to explore.

Anne called after her. "Meet me here after the bell for afternoon prayers. Four rings after the chimes."

Narrow shops lined the way through the Market Quarter, each crammed with goods of a specific kind, from clothing to farm goods, services, and cabinetry. And as she passed, Diana picked out shops where she might inquire about books and magic.

In the cathedral quarter, she passed old buildings boarded up or chained shut with a sign.

Closed by order of Bishop Rochfield.

No admittance.

The Academy building that Anne had pointed out linked a rambling jumble of rooms damaged by age and conflict. Each was improved with new tiles on the roof, bricks on the fireplace, large windows, and sky-lights. Outside, Diana found a group of well-dressed teens.

"Is this the Academy?" Diana asked. After a brief scan of her, they lifted their noses and turned their backs until a round-faced boy in a brown cassock smiled at her.

"Don't mind the aristos," he said. "They're all stuffy, but some are a good sort." He stuck out his hand. "Martin."

She shook the offered hand. "Are there gentry?"

"No, just aristos and us," he said. "If Prince Eric were here, there'd be even more ladies."

*Well, that answers one question.*

Martin scowled. "It seems every young lady who attends aims to wed the prince."

Ringing interrupted, and they turned to the door where a narrow-faced man in dark blue cassock with the eyes and nose of a hawk rang a hand bell. The aristos entered, and Martin and Diana followed.

Diana entered the classroom through two tall doors of carved oak. Without fixed seating in the room, students sat on cushions or lay where they fell like leaves scattered on the forest floor.

When she entered, the priest smiled. "Ah, a new student, have we?"

The well-dressed turned with grumbles and scowled at her.

"Can't dress properly?" they chided.

"She looks like a market girl."

"What do you expect of peasants? They don't belong here."

"We know what to do with farm girls," a boy behind her said.

Diana clenched her jaw at the insults and addressed the priest. "This is the Academy?" she asked, and he nodded. "I've been told the Academy is open to all."

Someone grabbed her butt from behind, and she turned to find an aristo boy miming kisses. She closed her fist to punch him in the throat, but hesitated.

*Killing an aristocrat is a bad way to introduce myself, but I can't let them think this is acceptable.* She opened her fist, and instead of killing him, slapped him so hard he fell over, while his mates roared with laughter.

Father Dorian rapped on his desk for order. "You will comport yourselves like gentlemen in this class, or I will call the Bishop's Guard." He turned to her and smiled. "Yes, we are open to all. Welcome. I'm Father Dorian Alem, rector of the Academy. I care for your brain, not your clothing, and have only two demands: your attendance and your attention. Our purpose is practical knowledge for virtuous citizens. If that's also your purpose, find a place to sit."

"But she surely has no education to appreciate what we learn here," said one.

Diana put a fist on her hip. "I can read and write."

"You're still a peasant."

She wanted to shout she's the Princess of the North, but could not.

*I must show them.*

"What're you afraid of?" Diana said. "Is it that I'm a woman?"

The young ladies grumbled. "Women have the same right to be here as men."

The priest smiled and crossed his arms.

Diana put her fists on her hips. "Or that we'll embarrass the boys with our wit and knowledge? We can do more than needlepoint and set a table, can't we, girls."

Some girls smiled.

"Like what?" a tall aristo boy said.

"Do you know your counting skills? How many sheep can you sell if you have three pastures with a dozen sheep each?" Diana asked.

"Uh . . ."

"Thirty-six. And if you sell half?"

"Uh . . ."

"Eighteen," she said. "Or is a big powerful man afraid of being in a room with a peasant? Are you afraid peasants might know more than you?"

"That's not fair," said a pretty brunette. "I don't care about sheep."

"Then how many shoes do you have if you have five closets and ten shoes in each?"

"Uh . . ."

The priest rapped on his desk again. "That's enough. Queen Helena invited all who can attend, and we honor her charter. Make a place for her."

The aristos spread out, so the only place was in the back with Martin. But two girls glanced back, smiled, and nodded.

The lecture that followed was dry, and the students lounged and yawned as if this were their salon. Bored with the lecture, Diana schemed about how to befriend the girls to learn more about books.

At the noon bell, Diana approached Father Dorian. "Yes, young lady?"

"I'm wondering if you might help me find books."

"If it's learned thought you seek, we have many scrolls with—"

*How can I say magic but not let the beans spill?*

"No, bound books."

"Hmm. The only such books I'm aware of are spiritual in content, the Book of the One God and the Sulerian Chiniferra. Each is rare and hand-copied by the monks. I'd be glad to discuss the teachings if you like."

"Thank you. Not right now," she said and turned to go.

"I hope you return tomorrow," he said, and she waved back to him.

Outside in the courtyard, Diana waited to catch the eye of one of the aristo girls met their servants, but they all turned their backs to her, even those who smiled at her earlier.

"Don't let them bother you," Martin said from behind her. "Their parents grumble with their lost status after George denied their titles."

"They dress well."

"George let them keep their estates and their arrogance, to keep them quiet I imagine. And where are you off to?"

*An ally in my search?* "I'm in search of books, especially magic."

"Ah. Books are rare. We drown in scrolls. Books, no."

"The priest said he teaches civic virtue. And the queen supports it."

Martin sucked in his tummy, narrowed his cheeks like the priest, and wagged his finger at her. "'I aim to start a fire in your soul for learning and civic virtue,' Dorian told us. 'Because when the fire goes out, darkness and ignorance return.'"

She nodded. "And he lectures to the aristos, the ones who need that lesson most. Thank you, Martin. I'll see you tomorrow," she said and took a step to leave.

He followed. "And yet you continue your search? Where will you start?"

"I saw a goldsmith shop and an apothecary," she said and aimed for the Merchant Quarter with Martin at her side. "I seek anyone who might help me. So what brings you to the Academy?"

"My father said my nature is better suited to the priesthood than the farm. Seems I can't plow a straight furrow or milk a cow and I have four brothers who can. And I'm possessed by a curiosity not otherwise present in my family. This was my father's idea after the queen chartered the Academy. Her idea for a school to educate everyone rankled many of the citizens. Schooling most often occurs at home or the guildhall and some still don't like the competition of ideas or authority."

"And there's friction?"

"As long as the priests don't meddle in the technical or seditious, they can teach what they like. Competition with the guilds results in fines, and sedition in the gallows."

She pointed to scaffolding near the middle of town, and her eyes opened wide. "Are these gallows they're building?"

"King George is building a new Town Center and park for the citizens. And you? Why do you visit the Academy?"

"My father and I are from the provinces where the land is poor. We found good pasture for horse and sheep here and hope to make a go of it."

"And the Academy? Surely it must be more than the prince."

She smiled. "I've told you my goal. I search for books of the unusual."

"The unusual within the unusual."

"Ah, here we are," she said as they reached the gold-smith's.

A small bell tinkled when they opened the door to a narrow shop. Locked cabinets containing pendants of gemstones lined the walls. Above them, on shelves, stood kaleidoscopic crystals and silver utensils next to jewelry cases with intricate inlay of ivory and mother-of-pearl.

On a counter at the far end of the shop, two old men leaned, one bald and the other with thin hair swept over his dome like a carpet. From hooks on the walls at their sides hung chains of silver in lengths from brace-lets to ropes of every thickness and style. And behind them stood a female bust with a stunning pearl and gilt net headpiece. They were all beautiful, but Diana would not trade the entire shop for her sparkling drag-on-tooth box.

"May we help you?" asked the bald man.

"Yes," Diana said. "I'm inquiring about books."

They glanced at each other. "Of what subject? We have scrolls in the temple of Joniz holding all the learned thought that might be of value."

"Bound books only."

"There are many books of the One God floating amid the aristos, and we can procure one for you. How large and ornate do you wish? For home? Or temple?"

"Bound but not of religion."

The bald man glanced at the other and winked. "Ahh, you seek the Old Knowledge?"

Martin frowned. "She's serious, gents. Don't toy with her."

"What do you know of the Old Knowledge?" Diana asked.

The old men shrugged and alternated their replies, filling in each other's pauses.

"A young priest came through her years ago seeking—"

"Said his name was Tobias."

"Seeking such rare things. He told us of a myth he believed, that before the Wandering, and even before the Chaos, people lived in safety and splendor, but it was lost to us. He said the Chaos was not our ancient history of barbarism through the ages of ice, but the fall of a great civilization."

"Other than books, what rare things was he searching for?" Diana asked.

"He wouldn't say, fearing to engage our . . ." He tipped his head from side to side. "Our less virtuous nature."

"And what happened to him?" Martin asked.

"A nervous young man he was," the bald man said, "itching to continue his search as if he knew our answer was 'no' and wanting to ask someone else."

"Ahh, but when he talked of his beliefs, his eyes shone with wonder like he'd seen God."

"We wanted to believe just to experience that wonder."

"But the wonder didn't last. Our belief in gold and silver and things we can touch was much too strong. We are intimately familiar with hunger, and faith won't feed our children."

Diana frowned and sighed. "So you know of no other bound books?"

"No, my dear."

Martin leaned on the counter with his chin on his left palm. "That's what I told her," he said, curling a sample gold chain affixed to the counter beside a similar silver chain.

The other smith turned to Diana. "And yet you persist in your search for books?"

Diana nodded. "I was told there's at least one somewhere in town."

"It must be exceedingly rare and secret, or my partner and I would've heard of it." He smiled beneath narrowed eyes. "If something like it comes to our attention, what's it worth to you?"

She returned the smile and sensed a negotiation. "That will depend on the contents. Ask me again when you have it. You can find me at the market in the early morning or the Academy."

Tired of Martin's fidgeting, the bald man slapped Martin's hand and straightened the chain.

"This is gold?" Martin asked. "This is a goldsmith's. Where's the rest?"

"Oh, my dear sir, gold is much too rare and valuable to keep more on display. We keep it hidden with the iron. Iron is also rare but is not beautiful unless you're a swordsmith." He inspected the two of them again. "Clearly you are not in the market for either," he said, straightening the gold chain to lay parallel to the silver.

They said their goodbyes, and Diana left the shop followed close behind by the monk.

"Where next?" he asked.

She pointed across the street. "The apothecary, there."


The apothecary and the other shops Diana and Martin visited that afternoon yielded no information. At the bell for afternoon prayers, Martin left Diana at the market to find Anne and the ride home. Jon rode alongside and chatted with Tom after an adventure in town, and by the volume of their laughter, a few pints of ale.

While Diana mused, Anne wove an anklet unlike Diana's using multicolored cord bought that day at the market. However, her craft did not distract from her gossip.

". . . and I hear Timelt is very brave," Anne said. "He served with Prince Eric in the Barons' Revolt. His family has a home in every province for every season."

*Home. We've not heard from Papa since we left. Does the fighting continue? Would Papa want me back in harm's way if I come home now?*

". . . and Solange, Counselor Jerrett's daughter, is beautiful and an expert with foil and dirk . . ."

*Light weapons. A girl's weapons, her wrists fast but too weak to wield a heavier weapon. Not a scrapper, but deadly still.*

Anne raised an eyebrow to invite gossip. ". . . and she has her eye on the prince. He's only a few years older than us and a captain." She smiled at the clouds. "Maybe I'll be like Gwendolyn in the story and become famous by my virtue and steadfast love for Rowan. And he will become a king by his own hand. Any of the aristos could be my Rowan."

*What a fun idea.* "Rowan is a myth, Anne."

"Well, I hear Baron Uthir Reinhardt married a commoner. And Eric's bodyguard, Edward, is the son of Baroness Ondine and a soldier."

Diana smiled. "Or perhaps you're a princess from the faraway North who can't reveal her identity because of a secret mission. But the nobles are captivated by your beauty, and the prince defies his parents to wed you. It would be historic, a prince from the South and a princess from the North. Would the fathers oppose your union and go to war? Or ally their kingdoms in common purpose? The politics of two countries would overwhelm your naïve love, but your love will conquer all. It would be so exciting, and scandalous!"

Diana grinned at her fantasy, but Anne frowned and blushed.

"You're making fun of me," Anne said. "Do I natter on so?"

"I didn't mean to. I only meant it's fun to imagine, and—"

"You make it sound ridiculous."

Diana patted Anne's hand. "I'm sorry. You can come to the Academy with me if you wish to see more of the aristos. The queen invited everyone."

"My father would never allow it. He thinks I'd be too willing a pillow for a rich young gentleman." She grinned. "And he could be right."

"Jon and I could talk to your father. We can chaperone if you want to attend."

"Really? You'd take responsibility for me near Timelt or Edward?"

"Jon and I train horses. I think we can handle you."

Anne frowned and blushed. "No. I'd appear the idiot." She sighed and leaned close to Diana. "I can't read or write," she whispered. "I'd humiliate my father."

Diana smiled again. "I'll share a secret. Many of the aristos can't read or write either. They just talk like they can."

"How could I fit in? I'm just a farm girl."

She took Anne's hands and held them palms up, side by side with hers, both pairs calloused and stained. "A farm girl like me."

Anne beamed as if blessed by a miracle. "I accept," she said and mimicked Diana who traced the alphabet in the dust of the wagon's bed.

"I talked to some farmers in town," Jon said that night in their new home and dipped his fork into the stew. "None of them are aware of books other than religion."

Diana nodded. "The Book of the One God. I have no leads yet either."

"Tom's boy will watch the ranch again tomorrow, so I can begin my tour of the pubs for word. That should include people from the region."

"Didn't you begin today?" she said with a teasing smile.

He smiled in return. "Tomorrow in earnest."

"I have a town full of shops and businesses to query. There must be word somewhere. Any news from home?"

Jon shook his head. "You worry for him?"

"Of course. And if there's a home for us to return to."

*****

The third moon rose over their farm, and Lon's cool light lulled Diana to sleep. While in nearby Branwyn, Cirka, the mistress to Chancellor Grimes, heard of Diana's interest in books.

# Chapter 11
## The Emissary

The Branwyn residence of Focault Grimes was large, more opulent than befitted an officer of the government. Here he lived surrounded by a small portion of the wealth looted from Capitolia during the Imperium's collapse. The rest were tucked away from prying eyes in estates scattered throughout Merisol.

A spare man with narrow goatee, Grimes walked past windows where lace curtains from the deep south fluttered in the light breeze. Through the bronze-work filigree drifted the clamor of hawkers and animals from the Branwyn market below. Incense from the silver censer covered the tart smells rising from the street and diffused the sunlight to a gray pall.

As he passed the kitchen, Cirka pressed a cup of hot tea into his hands. He sipped while admiring her outfit of pantaloons with a low bodice and bare back that highlighted her sensuousness.

"Morning, dear," she said. "I hear rumors of someone with an interest in bound books, and—"

He stopped her with a raised hand. "Unless they visit our door, there will be no one to help them." He glanced out the window and pointed to a man in the market below. "See the man in the green hat? There by the vegetable stand?"

"The scruffy one?"

"That's him," he said and gave her a silver coin. "Tell him all you've found out and task him with discovering who specifically has this interest in bound books." He took another step toward his office.

"Yes, dear. And a guest from the south is waiting —"

"Greetings, Chancellor Grimes," the visitor interrupted and removed the dull gray riding cape which covered his colorful silk robes. He gave the cape to Cirka and glared at her until she excused herself. Beside the desk, on the Imperator's throne, the visitor sat.

"Ah, Kalil. Welcome, Emissary," he said coldly and sat at the desk. Two objects lay there: the lion charm from the Sulerian Empress and a cup-and-ball game. The game was the single object from his humble childhood, hand-carved by his father and sold for coppers in the streets of Ostia. "To what do I owe the honor of this visit?"

Kalil reached over the desk and picked up the lion charm. "You display the charm boldly. You don't fear charges of treason?"

"Only you recognize it. It's to remind you of your patron's promise to me," Grimes said.

The emissary returned the charm to the desk but left it on its side as if it were wounded. "We have a favor to ask."

"We?" Grimes said and returned the charm upright.

"Our patron."

"Uh-huh. Just a moment." Grimes fussed with the scrolls on his desk and moved articles from there to the shelves, occasionally glancing up.

"I'm a patient man and have no other appointments," Kalil said.

Grimes frowned and sat back in his chair. "What is it then? And be quick about it."

"We would like you to engage your resources to find someone here."

"Do I look like a lost-and-found?"

Kalil glared without speaking, as if considering which limb to flay.

Grimes persisted. "What's in this for me?"

The emissary grinned and cleaned his fingernails. "The tides of fortune can change quickly once the orbits of power are set askew as we propose. A person, no matter how influential, might need a favor in case plans do not go as expected and the pieces of the puzzle do not fit together to your benefit." He eyed a spider crawling across the desk and picked it up. "We are all pitiful creatures when left alone to struggle in the sun. A friend is often all that separates life—" He squashed the spider between his fingers with an audible *crack*. "—from death."

The emissary's threat was clear. "What would you have me do?" Grimes said.

Kalil sat on a corner of the desk with a smile to break the mood like he had broken Grimes's spirit. He took the silk handkerchief from Grimes's breast pocket, wiped the gore from his fingers, and let the stained cloth float onto the desk.

From his own pocket, Kalil removed a torn stretch of woven cord in the pattern of a northern tribe.

"If a bracelet such as this appears in Merisol, you could earn our patron's gratitude. And such gratitude is a precious thing." He placed the piece of bracelet with a gold cord in the middle of Grimes's desk. "It's sometimes worn on the wrist or ankle."

"And how are you sure the wearer is here?"

"One of our agents followed her from the North."

"And the appearance of this mysterious 'her?'"

"A young woman, brunette, is all I was told."

Grimes stared at the woven piece as if it would coil up and strike him. "I will enquire."

Kalil remained sitting on the corner of the desk.

"I will enquire immediately," Grimes said.

Kalil stood and walked to the door, his back to Grimes. "Excellent. When the resources you seek for our . . . larger endeavor become available, I'll advise you."

"Good afternoon," Grimes said to the Emissary of the Sulerian Empress and friend to Garfann Sineura.

When Kalil closed the door, Grimes went to the window to gaze at the market below. As an open-air butcher chopped the head from a squawking duck, Grimes twisted the piece of anklet around his fingers and guessed the value the wearer might have on the Sulerian slave market.

Or dead.

# Chapter 12
## Wolves

A year after they arrived in Branwyn, just a week before Diana's 18th birthday, a twig snapped under her heel. The big gray wolf dropped the lamb, turned, and snarled at her. That was her lamb, but she did not contest it.

Her vision narrowed to his bloody fangs, and the hackles rose on her neck. Blood pounded in her ears as her muscles tensed to run, but running would mark her as prey. He outweighed her and would need only a bite to her calf to cripple her. She'd be dead already if he'd wanted, but he was not the biggest danger.

Without turning her head, Diana looked for the pack. She expected to see them pacing for their turn to feed, snapping and snarling to maintain status. But rather than a pack, a beautiful white female studied her from nearby. A breeding pair, the most successful hunters, had found her woods and her flock. But there were only two.

Diana moved away from the tree to become more visible, her head held high, but did not stare at them. Without the pack, the wolves held no territory to defend, so if she chose not to challenge, she could retreat. The wolf lowered its head but kept his eyes fixed on her as she backed away.

Diana upped her pace to burn off the battle-fever, unable to run where the wolves would sense her panic. The wolves surprised her: not the reds common to the South, but big grays from beyond the mountains, larger and much stronger. A wolf like she killed in the Spine a year and a half before.

*Damn, how have I survived this long? If it'd been a pack, I'd be lunch. I should have known better; a pack would take more than one lamb and would leave more sign.*

There they were again, her weaknesses: impatience, swiftness to anger, quickness to fight. And she was so reckless she had almost shown her teeth and growled back at the big gray.

*Jon would not approve.*

Away from the wolves, she slowed her pace and cooled in the chill of the spring morning. Halfway home on a path to the East Road, she stopped to change. If the game wardens caught her in leather hunting garb with knife, and spear, they might arrest her as the poacher she sought. By a tree, she took out her bright homespun linen to change into.

Before she removed her jerkin, horses snorted, and she crouched behind a bush. A score of men rode by on horse, a third wearing the colorful silk pantaloons of prosperous merchants, followed by two wagons.

*This isn't a trade route, and they're much too slim for traders. And riding horses almost as small as ponies. Merchants would never mount a saddle if they could ride in a coach.*

Long sheaths hung from the saddle bags. Rather than the embroidered sandals of the merchants' guild, soft leather riding boots poked out from under gilt cuffs. A reflection from the sun flashed off the heel of one, the sight of which made her queasy.

*A twinkle from a spur? And why would that upset me?*

As they passed, one rider threw a chunk of meat into a thicket where a big gray wolf caught it midair and swallowed it whole. The beast glanced at her, acknowledging her presence but otherwise did not stir.

*The wolves travel with these men. Not pets, just opportunists. And well fed not to attack me.*

Diana remained hidden until the caravan passed, and the brush absorbed the clops of the horses' hooves. She crept away from the trail and changed her path home, still troubled by the merchants.

*Why would merchants who could afford silks wear riding boots? Or ride horses at all? And have wolves as familiars?*


Arriving at the East Road to Branwyn, Diana turned west to their ranch. Her sheep greeted her with bleats, and she examined an old ewe. It was a bout of the colic. They had pushed over a fence rail and snuck into the alfalfa next door.

"God, you're so stupid," she said. A small lamb came to her and nuzzled her, and she laughed and rubbed its ears. "Here I am, almost eighteen, on the adventure of my life and the eve of my majority, and I'm still looking at dumb sheep."

She took the lamb to the barn, and while brewing an elixir of dried dill weed to cure the sheep, she plotted her next move.

"Now, what will I tell Jon?" she asked the young lamb. "He'll not like that I went into the woods alone. But how could I not?" Diana took her shepherd's crook and threw her shoulders back.

"I'm the protector of my people and will vanquish every foe!" she said, brandishing the staff like a spear while the lamb bleated and backed away.

***

While Diana ministered to her lambs, Jon spent his afternoon in an apartment above the Hogue's Breath Inn. Through the window above the Promenade, a gentle breeze carried the laughter from the tables below and the hawkers on the street. In a large bed, Cindy Shale, covered by a sheet, sat watching Jon button his shirt. The soft light of the afternoon sun shone on her face that might have been the profile of goddess Winz etched into a porcelain amphora.

"It's still early," Cindy said.

"Diana will be on her way home with the Buckmans, and I want to be there. Did you get the tickets?"

"On the dresser," she said.

Jon picked up four coins marked with the stamp of the Singers, bowed from the waist, and gave one to her. "I would be most honored if you would accompany me."

She smiled and took the coin. "Of course, Jon."

He looped another button on his shirt. "And dinner here at the Hogue's Breath after for a celebration. Do you know what the Song is about?"

She grabbed his shirt tail, pulled him back into bed, and rolled on top of him. "It's about two lovers who never have enough time for each other." She kissed him. "We can watch the performance from the balcony here with dinner and wine."

He kissed her back. "It's Diana's birthday and special. I want her as close to the stage as we can get."

Cindy kissed him again and pouted. "And you leave me early."

"I want to be home when she's there. It's dangerous out by the woods and I worry about her."

Cindy sighed, rolled off, and lay on her back.

"She's my family now," Jon said and gazed at her with his head on his hand. "When I was younger, I brought to my little family what I thought was right: a hard-working father valued for my skills and respected by my peers. But kids need presence as well, and in that I failed."

Cindy furrowed her brow. "There are worse ways to fail children," she said, tracing the scars on his arms.

"I won't fail her." He kissed Cindy again, stood and buttoned his shirt. "Nothing more about books?"

"No. I heard Xorellia is buying land here with gems and iron."

"Why?" he said.

She shook her head and frowned. "When will I see you again?

"Day after next. And then the performance." He threw his leather jacket across his shoulder, leaned over, and kissed her.

Before he stepped away, she took his hand. "I know you have responsibilities, Jon, and a past you can't discuss for her safety, but will there ever be more than this for us?"

He pulled her to her feet and embraced her. "Know that wherever I go, whatever happens, I will always return to you," he said, and she kissed him hard.

\*\*\*

It was late afternoon when Diana put the potions and rags away. As she practiced throwing metal stars on a human silhouette drawn on the barn wall, she turned at the whinny of Jon's horse. Jon dismounted and walked toward her, his face almost as familiar to her as her father's.

In tunic and wool pants, a stranger could not distinguish Jon from the local farmers, except for his boots: rider's boots with narrow toes and higher heels.

*Stubborn of him to expose himself. But he'd never ride with farmer's shit-kickers.*

"Jon, we need a dog."

He grunted acknowledgment and led the horse to water.

She frowned and knitted her brow. "Oh, and how was your day, Diana," she said under her breath.

When her stars found their target, she turned to him. "Jon, why was my father the first King of the North since Thores killed Sinrall?" she asked as he unsaddled his horse.

Jon put his saddle on the top rail next to her. "The tribes don't trust leaders, especially when they invoke the wrath of heaven to justify their actions and deploy men at arms to enforce them. They took the army away from Richard before they named him king and then fettered him with a council to slow him down, just like in Wikkert with the tribal parliaments."

"Any word from home?" she asked.

"No, last word was the Sul and Northern States are still contesting Cherbourne," he said, opening a jar of leather conditioner made from beeswax and Diana's wool grease.

Diana sighed. "And Father?"

He shook his head and rubbed the conditioner into the leather.

"And your family?"

"North in Escone and out of harm's way."

"Do you miss them? And your grandkids?"

"Of course. But their parents prefer the legend to the man." He sighed. "They would like you, it's me they can't forgive."

She put a hand on his arm. "They would love you now, the way I see you."

He put his hand on hers and scanned the pasture. "Poacher?"

She turned to him with raised eyebrows.

"I can count," he said and returned to his work.

She flushed, embarrassed to admit her rashness. "Wolf. I tracked it."

"Couldn't help yourself?"

"A hunting pair. Big grays from the North."

"It's a good thing there was no dog with you, or they'd have finished you both."

"But a dog might have warned us before we lost the lamb."

"Big grays can bring down an elk," he said. "Why would they settle for a lamb?"

"They traveled with strangers headed to Branwyn, but not on the East Road. Forty or so horsemen. Others in merchant's silks but wore riding boots of soft leather. I've seen the style before, but I can't recall where."

At the mention of the boots, Jon studied her. "So you skipped searching for the book today? And the Academy?"

She nodded. "We've covered most of the town, but half is closed to us. We still don't have a connection to the castle or the cathedral grounds. The bishop still prohibits entry to any but the public buildings on Sunday."

"You might press your monk friend. Martin, is it?"

She nodded again. "But what of the royals and the keep?"

He turned back to the castle. Colored smoke rose from Branwyn's wall, dancing in the breeze and shimmering in shades from yellow to orange in the setting sun.

"Must be for the Singer this weekend," Diana said. "Everyone is talking about it. Anne says Singers' performances are legendary here, not like the tavern shows and bards at home, with a big cast and even an orchestra sometimes. And with the royals sponsoring it, the nobles will come from all over. Anne thinks they'll hold it in the Town Center. What do you think?"

Jon shrugged and closed the jar of conditioner. "From what the Abbot of Dorreau said about them, I'll bet the Singers have access to the rich and powerful."

"You know what else is this Jonday?" she asked.

He threw the saddle onto his shoulder and turned away. "Of course I do. Well, you need to get busy and secure the barn tonight."

"And what will you be doing?"

"Laying some alarms to spook those wolves of yours," he said as he carried the saddle to the barn. "When you're through, come back to the house. I brought a barvost roast for dinner, and after we'll review unit tactics with inferior numbers."

*Like me against a wolf pack. Or merchants with riding boots.*

She pursed her lips and turned to their cottage. "We need a dog."

# Chapter 13
# A Flash of Silver

## In Branwyn

In the deep of the night, Diana awoke in a sweat and sat up straight, eyes staring forward. Both hands flew to her heart, where she felt the arrow that killed her mother.

Jon came to her bedside in her small room and pulled up a chair. "Same dream?"

"Yes." The nightmares always came when her birthday neared, less often now but no less vivid: of fire, cold rain, and her mother's blood. "Did I cry out?"

"Softly."

"I remember the boots. A glint from the heel of a rider today . . ." she said. "Boots from the North. That night . . . the night my mother died."

And the images were as crisp as if the events happened only yesterday.

## In Cherbourne, Four Years Earlier

"Mother, when!" Diana asked. Today was her 14th birthday, and she'd not had a proper party in at least, well, a year.

"Soon, dear," Katheryn said. "Be patient."

In a pout, Diana wandered through their farmhouse in her stiff party dress, and dawdled about her mother's bedroom. With her arm on the dresser and her

chin on her arm, she ran her fingers over the dragon-
tooth box that lay there shimmering with pearlescence
as it caught the light—the gift to her mother from a girl
who rode the dragons.

Outside, Diana wandered along the pasture, still
green from the late spring rains. A tent erected for visiting stockmen stood next to the fence, and she snuck
in to find the farm manager, Ted, sitting in a circle of
six men. Three with rough hands and open faces were
familiar ranchers from Limint to the north. Three
strangers of short stature may have been from Derryh
in the east.

A ruddy faced man from Limint spoke. ". . . for my
son and his recent wife. We need a flock to keep them
away from the town."

His companion slapped him on the back. "And the
groom away from the tavern wenches, I'll wager."

Ted cleared his throat. "There's a lady present,
gents." The buyers turned in surprise to find young
Diana in her party dress standing behind Ted.

"Why, thank you, sir," the rancher said with a wide
smile. "No one ever called me a gent before." They
laughed again, and the man dipped his head toward
her. "Beg your pardon, missy, no offense intended."

She nodded, though not aware of what he apolo-
gized for.

"Ah, then. How long will it take?" the first man
asked. "How long before the herd will be self-
sustaining?"

"Four years," another said. "Four years for the herd
to turn a profit."

Diana shook her head. "Two."

They ignored her with indulgent smiles, and the
strangers scrutinized her again.

"Four years," the man rcpcated to the group while
glaring at her. "Three litters in four years, two per lit-
ter." The other men nodded their heads in agreement.

With a voice as loud as his, she persisted. "Two years. You start with one male and two ewes of three years. Two years on and you'll have four extra rams and one sheet of wool to trade. The males are food or wool except for the alpha. One acre will be enough to—"

The first man laughed, unable to ignore her. "Keep to your needlepoint, little girl. This is man's work."

Diana frowned and crossed her arms. Ted smiled at her pique, but the others ignored her and returned to their discussion. Infuriated, she walked to the side of the tent and opened the flap which bordered the corral enclosing her flock. She whistled, which brought her dogs running to her side.

The buyers turned at the whistle, rose, and walked over to admire the sheep. Her dogs growled at them, but she silenced them with a hand signal.

The ruddy-faced man turned to the open tent flap. "Aye, sir," he said as Richard entered. "Compliments on the fine flock you got here."

Richard pointed to grinning Diana. "If your interest is sheep, the owner stands there. But I must steal her away," he said and picked her up. "Time for your party, lassie."

From over her father's shoulder, she dodged the temptation to stick out her tongue at the astonished stockmen. Instead, she said, "Mr. Ted will negotiate the terms of sale."

But the strangers did not reply.

Near the porch, Richard set her down. "Happy birthday!"

From behind the railing, he took a bow and quiver tied with red ribbon, the same style of weapon as her father's archers bore, but smaller and without fancy decoration or flashy string and fletching.

"It's not a toy," he said. "Just a start. We can practice when I return."

She hugged him hard and kissed him on the cheek. "Thank you, Papa!"

"I'm sorry, but I need to ride to Le Pegre and will miss your party."

Noise from the gathering children reached them and Richard hugged her again. "Lass, better scoot, or they'll start without you," he said and stood to leave.

But Diana did not let go. "Take me with you, Papa."

"I'm sorry, lass."

"You're never home. Everyone here just thinks of me as a shepherdess."

"Yes, lass, you're a shepherdess. But so was the Prophet, and like him, capable of much more. Your imagination is the only limit to your future," he said with the smile she could never refuse.

"Yes, Papa."

"We'll go to the cottage when I return," he said and walked her to the door. After another hug, he kissed her and mounted his horse.

As she watched her father ride over the crest of the hill, the stockmen left the tent and walked to their horses. At the door to the tent, Ted waved to her but shook his head.

Catching a whiff of cake, Diana took a step to join the partygoers. But the bow stole her attention, and she returned to the corral where her dogs joined her.

Three yards away stood a post, and she nocked an arrow in the bowstring and raised it. The stiff bow strained her shoulders and the thin string hurt her fingers so she could not pull it to her chin. When she released it, the shaft fell to the grass a few feet in front of her.

She held out the bow and glared at it. *Papa's right, this bow is no toy.* After failing a second try, she frowned at the weapon.

She turned to galloping hoofbeats as a courier jumped off his horse before it came to a stop.

"Where's the Field Marshal?" the courier said and tethered his horse.

Diana pointed over the hill. "He just left for Le Pegre. Mama's inside. Come."

After giving her dogs a scratch behind the ears, she led the courier to the kitchen where her mother finished decorating her cake.

"There's another book," the courier said to Katheryn. "In the South—"

"There you are!" Diana's friend said and tugged her sleeve. "Everyone's here but you, and it's your party."

"Be right there," Diana replied.

She ran to her bedroom, where she glowered at the bow. "I'm not done with you," she said and hid the bow and quiver under her bed.

Hours after sunset when the partiers left, Diana retrieved her present and slept with it in her arms.


But the next day, Diana did not wake at their home, but in the arms of her dying mother in a burned-out tree stump.

## In Branwyn

Back at their Branwyn ranch four years later, Diana picked up the dragon-tooth box from her dresser and went to a chair by the fireplace. There she hugged her knees to her chest and held the box.

Jon nodded. "The Horde."

The box was her greatest comfort, more precious than anything within it. It sparkled in the firelight "like dragon eyes when they're happy," her mother once said. Her father's bedtime stories of Dragon Riders in the high mountains of the Spine were fairy tales she stopped believing after her mother died. The pearlescent box still held her most precious memories: a small silver arrowhead; rose petals from Derryh; a woven anklet in her mother's pattern; and Eavlyn's toe ring.

Jon placed a cup of hot tea in her hand and sat with her.

"I didn't want to believe it," she said and warmed her hands with the tea. "I thought all that was behind me. Do you think they've come for us? For me?"

"Unlikely, lass. Our location is unknown, and you look more native than the aristocrats."

"Then why are they here?" she asked.

"If they're in disguise, they plan to be here for longer than a murder."

"Perhaps their mission matches ours. The Book of Chaos."

"Or some other mischief. The Singer's performance would be an opportune time for trouble if that's what they intend." Jon reached for a blanket to cover her. "Time for sleep, lass. We can deal with this tomorrow."

She nodded but remained in the chair. He put his hand on her shoulder for a moment, took his sword, and went to the door.

"Think I'll have a quick look around," he said.

Diana closed her eyes and made the sign of the arrow on her chest, then turned to Jon. "Mother's memorial is Sunday. Can we go into town this year? To the cathedral?"

He softened. "Of course, lass. I'd be honored," he said and closed the door.

Diana sipped her tea and hugged the dragon-tooth box tight as she stared into the fire.

*And what will they do when they find me?*

# Chapter 14
# Castle Keep

## Chores

The rustling of servants laying out his clothing woke Prince Eric Lombard that morning. He had been a soldier since he was a boy, quite accustomed to wearing the same clothes for days, awake and asleep, and luxury smothered him. But every morning, he found his comfortable clothing cleaned and starched or replaced by new. Irritated by their fawning, he dismissed his attendants and dressed himself.

As he went to the door, his parents' voices came from the hall.

"We need to tell him before he suspects," said his mother, Queen Helena.

Eric opened the door. "Suspects what?"

"The Singer's performance is Jonday, dear," the queen said, "and we've invited many of the nobles—"

King George interrupted. "Which would be a good time for you to evaluate the young noblewomen for a prospective wife."

Eric rolled his eyes. "Have mercy, Father, not before breakfast. You make it sound like a cattle auction."

His mother frowned. "Silence, Captain, your King is speaking."

Eric exaggerated a bow. "Yes, Your Highness. My apologies."

"Bah," his father said. "You've been home for months and you're still restless. Your mother and I think it's time for you to consider your position and . . . a wife. You're my heir, but the crown is not yours by inheritance. The barons and I didn't fight the Imperium to replace a thousand-year-old tyranny with the Lombard Dynasty."

"I'm a better soldier," Eric said and crossed his arms.

"So am I, but that's not what the people need now."

Eric drummed his fingers on his arm. "Every noble family in the South knows your plans, Father. The Academy buzzes with your goal to pick me a wife to consolidate power, and they hope to gain. The Singer's performance is the honey to attract them."

"You make it sound like a merchants' transaction," his mother said.

"Well, isn't it? Father, these people are boorish and shallow and preoccupy themselves with trivial matters. The adults seem devoted to their privilege, not the good of their people."

"Not all," the King said. "Your friend Edward, Baroness Ondine's son from Belerein, is a good sort. And you haven't met Pepin who fought with me. They don't rule by corruption and diversion as in the Imperium. If they were stupid or shallow as you seem to think, they would have lost their power and their heads long ago. I call them friends, and their children, like you and Edward, were not born to privilege."

"So, should I ride circuit to find these 'normal' aristos?" Eric asked.

The King raised his eyebrows. "That's not a bad idea, but your mother thought you might get distracted on your quest. Instead, we bring them to you at the

Academy and the ball. The ball after the performance will be a suitable time to meet—"

"Where I must strut like a peacock and—"

"Grow up," George said. "This is not about you. It's about keeping the freedom you fought for. There are men with none of your virtue who would kill for the throne."

"If this is about a royal wedding, it surely is about me. I won't be a tool for your politics, Father."

"As your father. I won't force you to marry. But as your King, I hope men with your character and skill aspire to more than Captain."

His mother took Eric by the arm and walked with him down the hall. "Come to the ball, son. We won't make it about you. The performance itself will draw the aristocrats and the gentry."

George frowned. "I prefer to keep it closed to the barons, dear."

"Singers won't perform just for them, George, or just for us. It must be public. Those are Guild rules."

"What a mess," George said and shook his head.

She turned back to her son. "Wear your captain's uniform and only be who you are now. But open your eyes. Assess these men as partners. Find the substantial amidst the shallow."

"Substantial? You mean like General Alten and his brood."

George laughed. "They need a barge to carry each of them."

"Eric, measure them as you wish them to measure you: look to their character and virtue," his mother said.

"And for friends, not a wife," his father added.

"Agreed," he said, satisfied with what he wanted all along. His mother kissed him on the cheek and left to manage the castle's business.

The king put his arm around Eric's shoulder. "History opens this door for you, son. It's yours to enter or not but will not remain open forever. Sometimes these robes are thrust upon us out of necessity. Rise to them or decline, and by choice. The people need you for who you are, not for my blood. Time for you to choose," his father said, pausing, "and to attend the Cabinet meetings."

"They're hungry and grasping," Eric said as his father led him to the Council Chamber.

"The aristos here are always hungry. They all want our skins or the skins of the citizens. Only force and opportunity keep the ambitious and greedy from our throats. Leave them an acceptable means to sate their appetites and they will leave the public, and us, alone.

"Artican is sensible. As a commoner, he is more aware than others of the abuse the citizens suffered, and it is his judgment that I respect most. But listen to them all for what they don't say as well as what they say."

"And waste the morning listening to vipers like Grimes?"

"All men are flawed, son. Grimes at least is competent." He clapped his son on the shoulder and leaned toward him. "And I keep him to my left."

## At Court

Eric walked a step behind George through Branwyn Castle, past portraits and busts of famous relatives long forgotten, to a small area adjoining the audience chamber where the Cabinet met. When the Imperator ruled here, he needed the expansive hall to hold all the ministers, aristos, ladies-in-waiting, gentlemen of the court, and petitioners, each of whom flattered each other and connived for a slice of the Imperium's wealth. But George declared the only ceremony they needed was good government and canceled the audiences. He ordered the hall partitioned into smaller areas, and despite the new tapestries and furniture, the chamber smelled impossibly old.

Unseen in the shadows of the adjoining room, Eric passed the Cabinet Table where the Imperator's throne once stood. His father sat at the head of the table with his counselors sitting to both sides: Chancellor Grimes to his immediate left and Artican, the wizened old Minister of Finance, to his right. The General of the Armies and the ministers of Trade, Agriculture, and the Guilds sat in no particular order. At the far end of the table, petitioners stood to present their case.

Eric found a chair in an anteroom and placed it within sight of the king, general, and finance minister but hidden from the other attendees by tapestries. On another chair, he put his feet up and snacked on scones from the kitchen. Settled in, he caught the Cabinet in mid-conversation as the chancellor directed the petitioners.

". . . but this is change," said the petitioner, out of Eric's view.

"Death is also change," George said. "So is birth. Change happens naturally. Only the peace and the demands of the few need to be achieved by force."

Eric caught his father's eye and used battlefield hand signals to tell him to retreat: a lecture would weaken his authority.

King George turned back to the meeting. "Let's judge this by the outcome. Will the good of this benefit all? If not, then public taxes should not fund it."

The petitioner's voice thinned to a whine. "But this is an investment in our future."

Losing interest, Eric studied a scene on the tapestry of a hunt where a pack of vicious grax chased a feral pig.

"If this is an investment, who reaps the return?" croaked Artican, who slumped in his chair as if the gold chain around his neck, the symbol of his office, weighed on him like an anchor. "What gain will come to those who live on a farm but pay their taxes? Our responsibility is to all citizens, not just the nobles who build edifices to achieve immortality."

*Or absolution,* Eric thought as his eyes went to the next scene in the tapestry where the grax cornered the pig.

"We'll be doing good and benefiting the community if we support this," said a minister out of Eric's sight.

"Let me see, our funding is immediate, and the return will be that it makes *you* feel good?" Artican replied. His face turned red, his back straightened, and he rose, no more the aging minister, but a warrior.

"And what else might you want?" Artican asked. "A military excursion into Antona for more land for you to exploit? And you would petition the king to be your bully."

George put his hand on Artican's arm, and he sat.

Eric smiled as on the tapestry, the pig attacked the grax and gutted them until it faced the largest grax that would not back down.

"You have something to add, Lady Livornia?" George said.

Eric knew the woman, widow of one of the most prosperous merchants in the South, and out to build on his power.

"I'm truly sorry, milords, if we weren't clear in our proposal," Livornia said in a condescending tone. "The same genius you commissioned to design the Town

Center, Erentil the Younger, has designed our new market square. It will be exceedingly attractive and people from all over the region will come to enjoy it, bringing trade and wealth with them. The increased commerce and demand for craft and farm goods will provide a much larger economy to tax."

Artican waved his hand across the room. "Ah. And now you throw an excuse to raise taxes on the table like raw meat before dogs and watch us drool. Do you hope for material return beyond your aesthetic gratification, milords and ladies?"

The room was silent.

"Your silence implies assent," Artican said. "Then consider funding this yourselves and let the citizens decide for themselves where their interests lie."

Livornia's tone turned hard. "Your Highness?"

"Funding denied," George said, and the petitioners grumbled and walked out.

Behind the tapestry, Eric smiled at the final scene, imagining Artican as the pig gutting the last of the petitioners. He raised his eyebrows, astonished the Cabinet displayed wisdom.

He rose to leave for the Academy but stopped when Livornia spoke again.

"The aristocrats won't be pleased with this decision," she said.

George narrowed his eyes. "The aristos don't rule here. I do, as the people's protector."

"How peculiar," Grimes mumbled.

# Chapter 15
# Patterns

"Practice in ten," Jon called from the doorway.

Diana awoke in a cold house, stiff from sleeping in the chair. Still bothered by the dream and the merchants' boots, she splashed water on her face from the bucket by the door. Over her loose training clothes, she strapped on leather cuirass and vambrace to protect her chest and forearms and met Jon in the barn. Inside, she grabbed a fighting staff to match Jon's and stood in the ready position two yards to his side. After a minute of quiet reflection, they began.

Long sweeping arcs of the staffs punctuated by sudden moves at the end of each step defined the pattern: a meditation with weapons where only the whisper of footsteps and whoosh of the staff broke the silence. At the conclusion of the pattern, they returned in unison to the initial ready position. As graceful as it appeared, sweat dripped from them both by the third repetition.

The purpose of the exercise became clear when they repeated in opposition. This time Diana faced Jon in her ready stance. She executed the pattern, while he did the reverse. Jon met each of her strikes with a defense followed by counterattack, the speed determined by opportunity and vulnerability: no longer silent as one staff cracked on the other, no longer a meditation but a duel. A missed block raised a bruise, a missed parry might break a rib or a finger. Their hands stung as the force of the impact rang along the staffs, and every few steps, they improvised to hide a misplaced foot or a shoulder too high.

They ended again in the final position with a bow to each other. Without a word, Jon grabbed wooden swords, keeping the longest and throwing the other to Diana. She caught the sword and smiled.

"Jonday will be here soon," she said, hinting at her birthday again. She meant not to beg for a present nor act as if she cared. But this was important to her; she would be 18 and acknowledged by most as an adult.

"Yes, and I have something special for you, but you'll have to earn it. On guard."

He attacked without waiting for her. Diana stepped back and parried, but he deflected it and used his height and strength against her. The sword was much faster than the staff, the crack of contact louder. He forced the weapon from her hand and with a bump from his hip, knocked her into a wagon and onto the ground.

"Unfair," she said, not sure if she was angry or hurt or what portion of each.

"This is your life," he said, coaching, not complaining. He offered his hand to help her to her feet. "Use your talents, lass. You're light and fast. Don't stand your ground like a bull."

She grabbed a hoe and swung it at Jon's head, went to her knees, and swiped it under his legs.

"Channel your anger," he said, as Diana tried to sweep again before his feet landed, "but keep your intensity." This was the man from Le Pegre: militia captain, Ranger, General of the Army, unforgiving in training.

Jon jumped, but Diana drove him back with thrusts and sweeps of the hoe. Reaching for a pitchfork, he parried and thrust with the tongs. She rolled back, and grasped a scythe and as he moved in to skewer her, she chopped the pitchfork in half. The pointed remainder was six inches longer than the arc of the scythe, so its offensive value remained. But when he drew back to stab again, she positioned the blade behind his ankles, threatening to hobble him—the same as a death blow on the battlefield. He nodded and dropped his weapon, and they walked to the water bucket.

Instead of offering Diana a cup of water, he reached into his pocket, withdrew two wooden coins, and held them out to her. "Happy birthday, lassie."

"Thank you," she said, kissed him on the forehead, and examined the coins: worthless except for the treble clef symbol burned into it. "The Singer! How long have you been keeping this secret, you old coot?"

"There are two. Bring a friend."

"That would be you."

"Invite another as I have." He bowed and pulled out two more wooden coins. "Then dinner at the Hogue's Breath Inne by the Town Center. I have someone I want you to meet."

She grinned. "Someone special?"

He returned her smile. "Go now or you'll be late."

She hugged and kissed him again and ran to dress for class, grabbing an apple and a strip of smoked beef to gnaw while she put her hair up into a ponytail. This was a market day, and her concern was not vanity but economics. Customers were a bit more generous to a pretty face. *But not this face.*

From a bowl by the window, she splashed water on her face, peered into the mirror, and pouted. She experimented with different hair styles: pulled back, fluffed, braided, then rolled into a bun. With an arrogant sneer and a finger to push her nose up in an aristocratic pose, she studied herself sideways. Frowning, she let her hair down.

Pouting again, she considered which of her few outfits to wear, grateful they posed as freemen rather than nobles who took hours to dress with petticoats and stockings and chemises and attendants to help with the corsets and gowns. That ritual she had never performed, even in Aemgarde.

Gazing at the mirror, her pale image frowned back at her, and she gave her cheeks a pinch and a few gentle slaps to bring out the blush.

"Ah, there you are." For a moment, her mother's face flashed in the mirror, and she brushed her fingers over the box with dragon-tooth inlay. She smiled and rushed to dress in her blue jumper and white linen blouse and set off to Anne's for the ride to town.

"A copper and four," Diana said as she wrapped the cheese round for a well-dressed maid in the service of an aristo.

Watching them, Anne stopped reading from a scroll and sighed.

"Go on," Diana said. "I'm listening. You're doing fine."

Anne rolled up the scroll. "I heard Prince Eric has returned from service. He's a captain now. When will I be ready for the Academy?"

"Within the month, if your father approves."

Anne smiled back. "If you make the case for me. He trusts you and Jon more than me."

"Go on now," Diana said again and opened the scroll for Anne.

While Anne read, the colorful robes of merchants caught Diana's eye as they approached a building across the street. She glanced at their boots: riding boots like the merchants in the forest and not slippers.

"Anne, I'm leaving for the Academy early, if that's all right with you."

"Sure. Just meet us back here if you want a ride home."

Diana left the stall with her back to the merchants and pretended to examine apples in a cart. She side-stepped to the end of the row and confirmed what she feared. From under a cuff, the sun glinted off the silver inlay where the paint was scuffed off.

She turned away too late, and when she glanced back, one of the strange men eyed her and whispered to his companions. He waved and called out to her.

Acting unconcerned, she turned and walked away. But in the reflection of a store window, she spotted three men following her.

After rounding the first corner, Diana toppled a tower of baskets on a pair of well-dressed young men.

"Oops, sorry!" she said, and broke into a run.

Once past an intersection, she ducked into the gold-smith's shop and hid out of sight from the door but monitored the window. When the odd merchants appeared in the street outside, she ducked behind a pair of large hookahs and waited.

The two old gentlemen behind the counter smiled at her. "Morning, Miss," one said.

Diana shook her head and put her finger to her lips. From her hiding place, she scanned the small store for weapons, but none were in sight.

The bell tinkled at the door and Diana shrank deeper behind the hookahs. Her heart pounded in her ears as the floorboards creaked with footfalls.

# Chapter 16
## Alliances

"Ahem," said someone close behind Diana. "Aren't you late for class?"

Startled, she jumped to her feet and turned to find one of the young men she had showered with baskets. "And you know that how?"

"You're Diana, no?" he asked. "Martin mentioned you."

"And you are?"

"Eric."

*Eric, friend of Martin?* "Eric Lombard?"

He bowed. "The same."

"Your Highness." After a quick glance outside, she curtsied but did not offer her stained hands for a kiss. "And what brings you to the goldsmith?"

"I was on my way to the Academy, and you buried me in baskets. I thought you might need help.

"If the Academy is your destination, you're late."

"An advantage of royalty," he said with a disarming smile. "Things don't really start until I arrive."

"Right." *Arrogant, but a smile that melts the girls' hearts.* "Then we have plenty of time."

"Who were you running from?"

She flushed with anger as if he accused her of cowardice. "I was . . . evading their interest."

Eric stood in her path as if waiting for an acceptable answer, but she was reluctant to say more and stalled.

"Those merchants—" she said.

"They seemed ordinary enough."

"Have you ever seen a merchant run?"

He laughed but waited, inviting a more complete explanation.

After a pause, Diana filled the silence. "They wear riding boots, not slippers, and appear rough for traders."

Eric lifted his eyebrows and cocked his head. "Why would you notice their footwear?"

She tensed. "Coincidence. Men of the same dress and boots passed through the forest near my home yesterday on horseback rather than in coaches. Today they run rather than hide in palanquins." *How can I tell him these men are from the Horde? Eric would spot right away I'm a foreigner.*

"Why would such men be in this neighborhood?" she asked.

He shrugged. "Perhaps to meet with Chancellor Grimes. He lives near the market and meets with merchants regularly."

At another awkward silence, Diana scouted the street from the window and furrowed her brow.

"Well, I must leave for class." She curtsied again and turned toward the door.

"Since our destinations coincide, let me escort you," he said.

She blushed, liking the attention and afraid of her pursuers, but eagerness would be unladylike. And she was concerned the smell of the aromatic cheese in her pocket, warmed by her exercise, would be attributed to her.

"Apologies, Prince, but strolling with a common farm girl would be awkward for you."

"More so for you, milady. I insist."

"You flatter me, sir. I'm a commoner, and a simple 'miss' will do."

"Indulge me," he said and offered his arm.

Blushing again, she reached for his arm as a lady would but pulled back—a farm girl would not do that. She put her hand behind her back to disguise her movement and walked to the door. But Eric's grin hinted she had given herself away.

With a brief turn, she exchanged a smile and wave with the old men in the shop and walked toward the Academy with the prince at her side.

To Diana, walking at Eric's side was like walking in a sunbeam, the brightest objects on the street. All along their route, he was the focus of attention. Merchants and well-dressed aristocrats bowed when they passed or rushed to offer him samples or hand him petitions. He acted oblivious and avoided their outstretched hands or ignored them.

*He's right. This is more awkward for me, and not the obscurity I need.*

"You get lots of attention from the citizens," she said.

"I'm still novel. This is why my parents travel by coach."

"Sounds like royalty," she said.

"It's not because they dislike the citizens. My father annoys the chancellor and frightens the praetorians by mingling. But merchants and aristos always seem to be grasping. Every glance is a proposal and every courteous reply misunderstood as encouragement."

"Yes, I'm familiar," Diana said.

Eric tipped his head to one side and frowned at her, then stopped and laughed. "Yes, of course. The predicament of charming women."

"I thought royalty had guards."

"I'll meet mine at the Academy. You'll recognize them: Edward and the big blonde, Steven. My tardiness gives them a few minutes to flirt with the girls. One has captivated Steven."

"Your pardon, sir, the girls have excluded me from their company, so I know nothing of them other than their fine clothing."

"Well, they're a shallow lot. Most are children of the Imperium. Many of their parents have lost their power but not their property."

"How unfortunate for them," she said with narrowed eyes. *Eric might not run with that pack*. Pretending not to care about his answer, she changed the subject to her mission. "Do any of them own books?"

"Why, yes. Why do you ask?"

"Only that I heard about them. How rare they are. What's in them?"

"The only books I've seen are the Book of the One God. That's the only book any of the nobles have, if they have any at all. They're very expensive and hand copied."

"I thought there might be others."

"If anyone would know, it would be the monk."

"Martin?" *And if so, another dead-end.*

Upon reaching the Town Center, Eric's face brightened. Completed the prior month, the Center was a large plaza serving as the town's principal gathering place. In the middle was a large grassy park surrounded by a circle of columns. Around them, a wide mall served the restaurants and expensive shops along the circumference.

"This was my father's gift to Branwyn, his first official act as king after repairing the fortifications."

"It all seems so . . . functional."

"Have you never been here on weekends?"

"No. I'm engaged at the ranch and too busy for town life," she lied. The Center would be unusual for ranchers and attract too much attention.

"Then you must be my guest sometime."

"I'm sorry, sire. It would be unseemly for a man of your station to escort a maiden through town at night." *Or a farm girl at any time.*

Eric smiled and winked. "Sometimes I don't wear my uniform." Walking backward he said, "Jonday nights are magical, filled with people and entertainments."

He took a chair from a restaurant and put it halfway into the street and sat as the crowd passed by. "The restaurants and taverns put their tables and chairs outside in the street so patrons can see and be seen by passersby."

Reversing his position on the chair, he mimed a painter at an easel. "Artists sketch the sightseers and the contrasting castle and cathedral spires." He rose and juggled imaginary objects. "Clowns and jugglers mingle with the crowds and entertain the children."

Busy tradespeople taking a shortcut through the Center passed by and frowned at Eric's antics, while children with big smiles tugged on their nannies' hands and pointed. Those at restaurant tables tapped each other to draw attention to him, but Eric was oblivious to everything but Diana.

Eric brought the busy Town Center to life for her. Outdoor restaurants lit by torches served patrons in evening clothes who drank wine and talked of worldly events. In the promenade, young couples posed for portraits or kissed in the shadows of the columns. And in the grassy park, acrobats and magicians performed.

He took her arm without asking. "On Sunday after-noons, the Center is a promenade for the young ladies to display their eligibility," he stooped over, "and their matronly chaperones their mobility."

This was not the Captain of the Guard she expected. His playfulness charmed her, and she smiled at the fantasy of herself on his arm on her birthday.

"What do they wear?"

"It's quite the spectacle. Colorful dresses with rib-bons and ruffles, conveying whatever guise the women choose, from innocent to risqué. They pretend these are their everyday finery but are purely for display."

But of course, Diana possessed nothing suitable, and never had.

"Men wear their most fanciful uniforms and robes of office to add status to their companions."

They tried to cut through the core of the Center but found the way blocked by ropes and a sign that read "Closed for the Performance."

"A stage for the Singer," he said without emotion.

"This Jonday should be even more magical with the performance."

"Yes, yes," Eric said but his enthusiasm evaporated and broke the spell.

It was Winzday morning again, no longer enchant-ed, no longer filled with lively entertainments and in-teresting people in fancy clothes, but ordinary people hurrying about their daily business. And here, Eric turned them east toward the spires of the cathedral.

"Years before the Imperator occupied Branwyn," Eric said, "priests of the One God from Venaro took over the abandoned structures. They rebuilt the spires on the old church to make them the highest points in town. People in the area once spoke of Branwyn as a religious center worthy of pilgrimage. But when the Imperator fell, my father took the crown and added banners to the towers."

"To reclaim the authority of heaven."

Eric smiled again. "That's what he said. And he won't surrender it."

Through the cathedral quarter, they passed under gargoyles and monsters that judged her worthiness from the eaves. At the entrance to the Academy, Eric relaxed and stopped his subtle glances to the rear. Inside the gate, the aristos gathered while their servants hung about in the courtyard.

Eric stopped. "I must proceed alone now. Being seen with me might bring you harm."

Believing he was embarrassed his friends might witness them together, she turned away.

"Please don't misunderstand," Eric said. "The girls will regard you as competition. Good day, milady."

Diana stopped and tipped her head. "Why would they?" she asked, and at a distance, followed him to the classroom, passing a brood of aristo girls who glared at her.

On her way inside, Diana passed Eric, who waited with his two guards, Steven and Edward. In the back of the classroom, she sat next to Martin as he scrawled notes.

"Mornin'," she said.

"Good morning," Martin said. "Where were you yesterday?"

"Busy with wolves."

He raised an eyebrow. "And you're late today."

"I have dispensation. What's the topic?"

"The old fossil is talking about politicians and public works, specifically about the memorial square. That's on the agenda of the King's Cabinet."

"... I agree," said one well-dressed student. "We simply raze the marketplace and build a square."

"You are, of course, aware that raze means to destroy utterly?" the priest said.

"Well, I—"

"Do you own a business that will be razed?" asked the priest.

"Ahhh, no, certainly not," he said, sneering while the other students laughed. "But we would compensate the residents."

"And so you would replace a steady income that might feed the owners' families for years with a few silvers they might spend in a month?" The priest clasped his hands behind his back. "And what if they don't want to move?"

Eric and his guards entered the room without acknowledging the instructor, receiving a glare in response. But all the young women turned to him.

"Good morning, Your Highness," Father Dorian said, but Eric waved his arm as if granting permission to continue. "Again, what if the people resist moving?"

A student raised his hand and scanned the room. "If the Cabinet decides so, yes, we will move them," he replied, as if this was the only proper thing to do.

The priest smiled. "I see. You would coerce them?"

"Well ... yes," the student said with a frown and furrowed brow. "But coercion sounds so, well, negative."

The priest opened his arms. "Come, come, now. You are the leaders of tomorrow. Words have power, don't be squeamish. Would you prefer a synonym such as 'force' or a lie such as 'request'?"

Another aristo intervened, "But this action is for the good of all."

"Is your personal perception of the 'greater good' sufficient rationale for coercion?" the priest asked. "Is your perception better than that of the person whose livelihood you would destroy? Who here would speak to this?"

As Dorian waited for a response, one student who slept on the cushions betrayed himself with a snore. While waiting for the class to respond to his question, Father Dorian went to his desk for a pitcher of water.

Prince Eric leaned against the wall and fidgeted, then whispered to an aristo boy in front of him.

After a moment, the boy spoke. "Who decides what 'greater good' justifies the force of arms?"

The priest nodded. "Yes indeed, who. The evil cast their flaws as virtues, and the selfish paint their thievery as gifts." He paused, walked over to the sleeping student, and poured the pitcher of water on his face.

"And who will pay to produce this 'benefit'?" he said.

The aristos were unconcerned and remained silent except for the one sputtering under the stream of water.

"Taxes as usual, no?" another student said and scanned the room for encouragement. "An assessment on trade entering the town?"

Dorian navigated through the students observing each. "So you'd confiscate property from everyone? You'd harness the citizens to the plow just like serfs in the Imperium?"

"Surely taxation isn't the same as serfdom?"

"Please enlighten us on the difference if you remove their choice."

The room was silent.

"They're confused," Diana whispered to Martin. "They're used to getting what they want. What if they don't get it now? Children have tantrums. What do adults do who have more power?"

Another aristo spoke. "But all revenue to the crown cannot be voluntary or no one would pay."

The priest nodded. "Yes, well said. But you've confused concepts. Why do you call this 'revenue' as if it were the income of an artisan or a merchant? The artisan has no army to demand his price be paid. Muddling these terms is meant to manipulate you."

"Some Cabinet members refer to it in that way," the aristo said.

"Which should inform you of the intent," the priest replied, and some in the class grumbled.

Martin leaned over to her. "Father Dorian is criticizing powerful noblemen," he whispered.

Diana nodded and whispered back. "This newly won freedom is a blessing to everyone except the aristocrats."

Eric turned to listen, and she stopped talking, realizing he was part of the order they were criticizing.

But Martin did not see. "They're not strong enough to—"

"Anything to add, Martin?" the priest asked.

"Ah . . . no, sir."

The priest sighed and lowered his voice. "Would you celebrate your newfound freedom with confiscation and coercion as if this were still the Imperium? Judge these things by their means as well as their ends. Is a public space sufficient to deny free choice to your neighbor, or to confiscate his house and his money?"

Fearing the point lost, Diana could not restrain herself and stood. "What of the market? It's already a public good and a benefit to all."

"Leave it to a peasant to think of something beneath our attention," said Solange, an aristo girl whose sights were set on Eric. She smirked and turned her head to him, but he did not acknowledge her glance, and she pouted.

"And where do your servants get your food?" Diana said with a hand on her hip.

Solange narrowed her eyes and raised her chin. "I don't care where it comes from as long as it pleases me," she said with a flip of her hair, which produced giggles from the girls.

"You should care or someday you'll starve to death." Diana immediately regretted her response. *There I am again, too quick to fight.*

A big aristo stood and glared at Diana. "Silence, farmer, and learn your place."

Diana closed the hand on her hip into a fist. "And what place is that?"

Eric kicked the heel of his boot on the wall so hard everyone froze. In an even tone, he said, "Timelt, calm yourself. We're all citizens and equal in this room."

Solange turned to the aristo girls and whispered, "But some are more equal than others."

Before Timelt could reply, the church bells interrupted with the midday peal and a welcome break.

From the lecture room, Diana followed the aristos who gathered at the tables in the courtyard nearby where their servants waited to accompany their ladies home or to shop. But she glanced over to Eric and overlooked a foot that Solange's friend stuck out to trip her.

Diana stumbled into the mud, and the aristos laughed and taunted her.

"Just like a farm girl playing in the pigsty," Solange said, and they laughed again.

Dirty to her knees with her meager lunch buried in the mud, Diana scowled at them. Without dropping her glare, she jumped with both feet into the puddle, splashing mud on the aristo girls. After a few moments of shock at her audacity, some yelled while others cried.

Timelt stepped between them and faced Diana. "Hey! Mind your manners, farmer." He stood tall with his chest puffed out and hands on his hips but was flat-footed and unprepared for a fight. She took a fighting stance and eyed a knee as a target, but defending herself with skill would unmask her.

Prince Eric walked out of the classroom with Martin just as Diana squared off with Timelt.

"Uh-oh, he'll kill her," Eric said. "Bad if I witness it."

Martin frowned at him. "Bad for her in any case."

Waving his hand to distract Timelt, Eric walked over. "Ho, Timelt. Certainly a simple milkmaid is beneath your attention."

"She should be whipped for impertinence," Timelt said.

With both arms open wide, Eric smiled. "Come, come. This is girl business, not ours. Or are we poodles to jump when a maiden barks?"

"Eric, that was no accident, you saw what happened."

Eric dropped his smile, put an arm around Timelt's shoulder, and spoke quietly. "I saw your friends intentionally trip a girl who bested them in argument. Vengeance for something so trivial is beneath us, and unworthy of an officer to defend. Be the example they need."

"Yes, Captain, uh, Your Highness."

Eric clapped his hands on Timelt's shoulders. "Yes, *friend*," he said, raising his voice. "Let's not waste time on the triflings of women. Come, join us for a brew."

Glancing at Diana, Eric lifted his chin. When she nodded, Eric took Timelt to the tavern with Steven and

Edward, leaving the mud-spattered aristo girls seething with no one to endorse their malice.

At a rain barrel, Diana washed up, scolding herself for being goaded by Solange. *That could be me if I had been raised in Wikkert rather than on a farm, with maids to dress me and others hanging on my every word. Would I be so petty and rude, still prone to tantrums like before Mama died? Who might Solange be if she had lived next door to Anne all her life? She might even be a friend—* Then she caught Solange's glare from across the yard. *Or just a vicious little bi—.*

Martin reclined against the stone wall next to the barrel. "Timelt fought side-by-side with Eric and Steven at Glencourt. He's the wrong man to get into a fight with."

"I couldn't help it. They're so mean."

"Others will be grateful you stood up to their bullying."

*I have no grudge with them, but he still could have killed me. Where would my mission be then? Maybe I'll never be more than a farm girl, a shepherdess.* She frowned. *Even Eric called me a milkmaid in front of the others.* That stung.

Her father's words came to her. "Yes, lass, you're a shepherdess now, but your imagination is the only limit to your future."

She brightened. "Not my past," she said and punched Martin on the shoulder.

"What was that for?" he said.

"Because I can."

He shook his head and glanced over at the aristo girls huddled together, occasionally peeking back over their shoulders at Diana. "You'll hear about this."

"We need to warn Eric," she said. "The aristos long to return to a world where they have mastery or influence. Now they have wealth, but no means to exercise that power."

***

In the corner of the yard, servants cleaned up the few aristo girls who remained. One of them turned to Solange.

"Time to quit harassing the farm girl. Eric and Edward didn't take our . . . teasing warmly."

"Don't be stupid," Solange whispered to her. "This isn't about a farm girl. This is about a crown."

***

On the way to meet Anne after daily inquiries for books, a tipsy Eric and Steven met Diana and Martin at the Town Center, and the unfamiliar flutter in her stomach returned. She blushed and smiled at his attention.

But then he spoke.

"Perhaps a thank you is in order," Eric said to her.

She pursed her lips and knitted her brow, miffed he did not admit to his part in her difficulty. "I can take care of myself."

"Don't be silly, he outweighs you nearly two to one."

Though still mad, she appreciated Eric's help. *He's right. Timelt might have killed me even if I broke his knee.* She looked into his earnest face, ripe for some fun at his expense, and put a fist on her hip.

"So I'm a simple milkmaid?"

"No offense, milady, I—"

"Why would I be offended? Is there something wrong with honest farm work?"

Eric struggled. "No, of course not, I—"

"Or any less virtuous than soldiering?"

"No, milady. Martin, please, you understand what I—"

Martin raised both hands and shook his head.

She put the other fist on her hip. "And simple? *Simple*?"

"No, I meant only—"

"Am I so simple I can't hold my own in argument against my 'betters,' like Solange and her kind?"

Fully back on his heels, Eric stammered. "Really, milady, I meant no disrespect, I—"

Diana could not restrain herself and giggled.

Eric frowned. "You play me cruel, milady."

"You deserve it. And I bark?"

"Again, my words were ill chosen. But he is a poodle if the girls can sway him so."

"That poodle outweighs us both."

Eric smiled. "But I can take care of myself."

At Eric's dismissal, Diana's smile morphed into a frown, but she said nothing.

Before they reached the market, she stopped. *How will Anne react if she sees me with the prince?* "Now it's my turn to leave you. If they see me with either of you, it'll bring me too much attention." She curtsied. "Thank you again for your help today, sirs."

With a sweep of his arm, Martin bowed. "Our pleasure, milady."

"Eric, I think you should speak with Timelt," Diana said. "Martin told me the aristos lost their status when your father took the throne. Children often echo the conversations they hear at home. If their parents feel the way Timelt and others do, your parents should watch out. Polite disagreement in public could be a hint of bitter antagonism in private."

"My father commands the army, Diana."

"That may not be enough. The aristos are used to getting what they want but are fighting for relevance in your father's new order. They seek to use his power. What if your father disagrees?"

Eric nodded. "I'll speak to my father. Tomorrow then," he said, and Diana left to meet Anne.

As she passed a shop window, she caught the reflection of the young men watching her, and she blushed.

***

Walking back to the Center, Martin turned to Eric. "Until today, Diana was at peace with Solange and the other aristo girls."

"Perhaps I took too much interest in her."

"And how does a farm girl rise to the attention of a prince?"

"She listens. And she's the only girl I've met who doesn't see me as a rung on the ladder of their social climb."

Martin raised an eyebrow.

Eric grinned. "And she's pretty, no?"

# Chapter 17
# Rumors

As Tom's wagon exited the East Gate, the fresh air lifted the weight from Diana's shoulders as she composed a summary of the day for Jon. Sitting next to her on the tailboard, Anne gossiped about the young aristos, and Diana wished she could tell Richard about her struggles and about Eric. She'd had beaus in the militia and was familiar with the eyes of men in the marketplace and the Academy who would entertain a dalliance.

*Eric is the first man who treats me as an adult woman and not an object to possess . . . or use. Would Jon think me silly to note his attention? I can't confide in Anne. She'll pester me until every morsel of scandal is ripped from the idea and devoured.*

On a post by the road, a flyer advertising the Singer's performance on Jonday caught Anne's eye.

"Papa and I plan to have a picnic in the park and watch from there," Anne said. "Will you be going?"

Diana nodded. "Jon gave me tickets to celebrate my birthday."

"They're all spies and witches," Tom said from the seat. "And this troupe especially. Secreting themselves through the countryside to avoid being burned at the stake."

Anne pointed a thumb at her father and giggled. "They're certainly not going to learn much from farmers."

*But farmers might learn something from them.*

"Come, my people," Diana said regally, as she herded her sheep into the barn. The same wolves would not likely come again tonight, but others might.

One lamb bolted and led Diana on a brief chase before she caught it. As she picked it up, a wagon pulled by a long-haired barvost passed along the East Road accompanied by a dwarf and giant. On the spring seat sat a beautiful woman in plain dress who watched her struggle with the lamb.

Turning away to the barn, Diana caught the reflections of a bright blue-green flash and glanced back to the wagon. The giant and the woman on the wagon appeared motionless, stunned. But the dwarf snuck behind the wagon and picked berries from a bush. And when he smiled at Diana and put a finger to his lips, Diana nodded. A few moments later, the woman and giant woke as if no time passed, and unseen by the giant, the dwarf pelted him with the berries.

Jon's horse neighed as two horsemen in black dusters raced past the wagon heading for Branwyn. The barvost bellowed, spooking the lamb, which tore a pocket of her jumper with a hoof. Trying not to drop the lamb, Diana lost her balance and fell in a puddle.

"Jon, we need a dog!" she yelled and returned the lamb to the barn with the flock.

"We passed a poster for the Singer's performance," Diana said at the dinner table that night. "Tom said singers are notorious spics. They might be another lead about books."

Jon nodded. "Dorreau didn't mention their spying. But if they travel in the circles of the rich and powerful who can afford their entertainments and intrigues, they would have the opportunity."

She smiled and cleared the table. "A clever person might insinuate themselves into their company and enquire. This could be an opportunity."

He nodded. "Perhaps. What news from the Academy?"

"The common folk have stopped coming," she said and sat again. "The well-born girls attend to flirt with the prince, and the rest plan to marry up."

"Married or not, a child by an aristocrat is a meal ticket."

She frowned at him. "For some. It's difficult to tell sometimes what the priest is babbling about. Today the lesson was to judge by results, not intent, which is valuable enough I guess, but—"

"All they've known is tyranny, lass. Free choice is a new idea: hard to earn and easy to lose. Even one generation without freedom can kill the ability to think for yourself, and they've endured fifty. And many prefer the simplicity of the yoke to the uncertainty of freedom." He paused. "And what of you?"

Diana leaned back in her chair and pursed her lips, deciding at that moment not to tell Jon of her adventures that day. "They treat me like I'm a bug with no prospects as a butterfly."

"Good. Obscurity is useful."

She winced. As long as they needed to hide, she must remain a farm girl. She longed to have friends like the other girls, aristo or not, and it galled her to stay withdrawn. The dances in town and the balls at the castle were both off limits, even if she could find a dress. It was frustrating to sit in the back of the class and not engage the teachers in argument like she was encouraged to do at home. And the events of the day with Eric led to fantasy: an attractive fantasy to be sure, but not a destiny.

"And our mission? You're there for the location, not the lectures. The bishop guards the cathedral and your Academy more closely than the armory."

She smiled. "Prince Eric attended today, and seems accessible," she said, hiding a blush. "But he admitted he wasn't aware of any bound books other than of the One God."

"That excludes the Castle Quarter, unless our Book of Chaos hides in someone's closet. Congratulations."

Diana cocked her head and furrowed her brow. "How so? I covered all that ground and found nothing."

"But now you have so much less ground to cover."

She pursed her lips, as he quoted an old soldier's poem:

> *"And equal those who man the charge,*
> *Are they who hold the line."*

He leaned forward with his elbows on the table. "Honestly, lass, I think you're in the best place to be for information. The bishop is the biggest mystery, and the Cathedral is the most uncharted territory. From all I've learned in town—"

As if he admitted a crime, she smiled. "Ah, yes, interviews at the Hogue's Breath."

"Don't scoff. Drink loosens the lips of those with information, and taverns are where the drink is."

"We need to make a choice," she said. "The Academy or volunteering to help the performance."

"You have access to both. But Singer will only be here a few days before they move on."

She frowned. "I'll need to skip the Academy again."
*And skip meeting Eric.*

"As dry as the lessons seem, it'd be no loss," Jon said. "Clear the table, lass. You have another lesson in large unit logistics."

"Yes, sir. But we still need a dog."

# Chapter 18
## Temptations

After leaving the Hogue's Breath that night, Eric caught the King and Chancellor Grimes in the Cabinet chamber warmed by a large fire and wine in silver goblets. Above the tapestries that kept the chill from the stone walls hung pikes, crossbows, and weapons of war. And from the ceiling above fluttered the standards and heraldry of the loyal barons. From a side table, Eric poured himself a pewter cupful and sat across from them with his booted feet crossed on another chair.

"At the Cabinet meeting next Lonsday," George said, "I'll propose we break ground on an expansion to Branwyn west of the Orange, starting with two bridges to the north and south. The land there is less fertile but still productive. That will give our gentry a playground for their visions, including a marketplace."

A glare flashed across Grimes's face for the briefest of moments. "Why?"

"The aristos are grumbling, and I wish to remove their grievance."

"Your Highness, there is no power in 'Yes'," Grimes said. He stood and leaned against his chair. "Their grumbling is understandable. There is no opportunity in stability, and only bureaucrats wish for peace. The ambitious watch for chaos, and create it when it suits their needs."

"And which are you?" Eric said, eliciting a frown from George.

Grimes's eyes narrowed, but he bowed with his arms wide. "A simple minister, Your Highness, and servant of the king." He sat again. "Why not simply command the expansion? Certainly our treasury has the means, and you have the power."

"My father taught me he rules best who rules least," George said. "Not that you miser your authority, but you use it judiciously, not out of boredom or the delusion of creating a paradise here on Juro."

Grimes filled the King's goblet and added a few drops to his own. "I'm quite certain your view pleases the barons in the east and the citizens who run amok in Branwyn. However, I'm of the opinion that you exercise your authority regularly and publicly. Otherwise, like a muscle, it becomes flaccid, and people forget your strength." Grimes took a sip and reclined in his chair. "And where's the fun of power if you don't use it?"

"The civil war was about freedom, not power," the King said. "Power was the sole purpose of the Imperium, and it proved to be the power to corrupt."

As he listened, Eric cringed at a new tapestry hanging on the wall depicting the Imperator's cavalry charging a line of George's pikes.

"Counselor," Eric said. "I saw some strange men in town this morning who might warrant investigation."

"How so?" Grimes asked with a raised eyebrow.

"They dressed in the silks of merchants but wore riding boots and moved like soldiers. And, if you can believe it, they were running."

"Running from what?" George asked.

"Actually, they chased a farm girl near the marketplace."

George frowned. "Did they catch her?"

"Luckily, no."

Grimes's temples twitched. "Merchants come from everywhere now and may not behave to our ideals."

"These were toughs, Chancellor—horsemen in disguise. Really, I think you should have the police investigate."

"Yes, yes, of course. I'll look into it," Grimes said with a wave of his hand. After glancing between the two of them, the corner of a lip rose. He leaned toward George and spoke evenly. "As the prince implied, Your Highness, the people need order. They're helpless sheep and need men like us to tell them what to do. Without a firm hand to keep them from each other's throats, they'll descend into chaos." He leaned closer. "You should be that firm hand."

"People fare better when they decide for themselves what to do," the King said. "I fear you seek another Imperator."

"Maybe not. Perhaps a soft hand from the King but a firm hand from his administration. The royals would retain their popularity, while—"

George's fist boomed against the table. "The hand of the King is here!" He opened his fist, palm up. "Tyranny by committee is still tyranny."

The overhead lamps highlighted Grimes's features, and Eric glimpsed a sly smile and eyes more sinister than his words.

"One man's tyranny is another man's order," Grimes said.

"Humph. At least an Imperator is accountable," George said. "A bureaucracy is so impenetrable as to be . . ."

"What's the difference, really?" the chancellor said with a raised eyebrow.

"Do you remember nothing of the Imperium?" George said. "The capriciousness of an Imperator is visible to all, but the corruption of the state is opaque and diffuse. How can the people seek redress for the pettiness of either?"

Grimes shrugged.

Eric scanned the heraldry of the baron's above and thought of the citizen-soldiers who died to fell the Imperator.

"Rebellion," Eric replied.

Silence followed and Eric smiled.

"And redress for the mistakes of a committee?" the King asked.

Grimes yawned. "Should there be?"

"What is it you suggest, Chancellor?"

"Perhaps share power, Your Highness, if too much power is vested in one person."

Eric rose. "Father, you lecture so. How about giving power to the citizens and letting them decide?"

As Eric left the room, the jaws of both men fell open.

***

Back in his apartments late that night, Grimes took the chief of police to the balcony overlooking the market. To his left towered the spires of the cathedral and to the right the castle turrets. And in the dark streets below, rats scurried between empty crates and gutters.

"They're powerful institutions," the chief said.

Her head held low, Cirka brought them both wine in silver goblets.

"Yes, but they're nothing compared to what lies between," Grimes said. "The wealth is in the markets, the merchants, and the guilds. Minister Artican thinks he rules that, but the power is in the streets you control."

"And the king's army outside the town walls," the chief said.

Grimes grinned. "Only if they can get inside."

"George won't listen?" the chief said and sipped his wine.

Grimes shook his head. "And he plans to open development to the west."

"That would please the aristos."

"I want them surly for now."

The police chief gazed at him squarely. "Then your plan must go forward."

"Yes. George is a fine man, as is his son. They would rule weakly over chaos."

"And?"

"And they're in my way," Grimes said.

"Everyone must sacrifice something for the future they wish to build," Cirka said as she puttered about the office.

Grimes clinked his goblet against the chief's. "In a few days, this town will appear the same as it does now, but everything will be different. The crown will fall, and the riots will appear to be a popular uprising to support me, their savior."

He put his hand on the chief's shoulder and led him to the door. "It grows late, my friend, and I've much yet to do. And remember to suppress the riots the moment trouble begins. No delays, right?"

The police chief nodded and left.

Cirka sidled up to him with a hug. "You didn't threaten him with the Assassins."

"He's well aware who holds their leash," Grimes said and kissed her.

"A man waits for you, dear," she said and refilled his goblet.

"Who is it?" Grimes asked as he walked to his desk and sat.

"The scruffy man with the green hat."

"Send him in," he said. "Then warm my bed, dear."

The aroma of stale beer preceded the thief as he entered Grimes office. Once inside, the thief took off his hat.

"What is it?" Grimes asked.

"I've located the person interested in bound books, sire. A farm girl, a shepherdess with a ranch along the East Road," the thief said as he wrung his hat.

"What else?"

"Only that she works in the market in the early morning and attends the academy."

"Friends? Relatives?"

"Friends with a monk named Martin. A father who trains horses. Nothing of note, sire."

"Does the father also have this esoteric interest?"

"Pardon, sire?"

"Is the father on this search as well?"

"If he is, he's more subtle in his queries."

Grimes flipped the thief a silver coin. "Find out more about them. Where they're from, how long they've lived here, what sparks her interest." He held up a gold coin worth a month of self-indulgence. "This awaits you."

"Aye, sire," the thief said and bowed as he walked backward out of the office.

Grimes returned to the window to avoid the stack of documents on his desk that would have no purpose next week. As he finished his wine, he surveyed Branwyn with the calm of a man whose plans were in place and the eyes of a mantis viewing a bug.

# Chapter 19
# Shepherds

At Anne's stall in the market, a tiny hand slithered over the edge of the counter and reached for a slice of cheese. Diana grabbed the hand, and a little girl with big brown eyes peeked above the counter. When Diana released the hand, the cheese disappeared. A moment later, the little girl in dirty clothing appeared across the street, sharing it with her band of urchins. They were Anne's insurance against a morning of pilferage.

All morning Diana kept her head low and hid her hair under a scarf, hoping to avoid another chase by the strange merchants. And between sales, Diana considered how to find Singer and what to say.

*Would they even let me near her? She's busy and famous and might not talk to me. And if Singers are spies, would they not spy for Suleria?*

Diana turned to her right as a crone nailed a flyer to a post. When finished, the old woman leaned on a staff and walked toward their stall. From the sack on her stooped shoulders, she took another hand-written flyer and with a small mallet, tacked it to the wall near Diana.

! Join the Celebration !
Help us prepare for the performance
Jonday afternoon. We need many hands,

so please come to the stage in the
Town Center today. Seek the
giant or the dwarf to volunteer.
! Be part of the show !
No training needed! Just come and we'll
have something useful for you to do.
*Singer*

Anne leaned over to read the poster and whispered to Diana, "I wonder if the actors are cute." She called out to the crone. "Ma'am, is this only for apprentice Singers?"

"No, dear," the old woman croaked. "If you can work, you're welcome. And if you help, you'll earn a free ticket."

"Even if we're unskilled?"

"What's your name, girl?" the crone asked.

"Anne, ma'am."

"My dear, if you've ever used a mallet or a brush, you're welcome. May we count on you?"

"I'll ask my father," Anne said.

The crone turned to Diana. "And what's your name?"

The crone's eyes were younger than her posture, triggering Diana's wariness.

"I'd rather not say, ma'am," Diana said.

"No matter. Can ye help?"

"Perhaps."

"If you do, ask for Singer," the old woman said with a wink and left.

*Providence? Jon will say I was alert to opportunity.*

Diana took the flyer from the wall.

"Are you interested?" Anne said.

"I think I might go see. Will you come?"

With a crate in his hands, Tom shook his head. "There's work to be done here, girls."

Throughout the morning, Diana helped Anne sell the last of her cheeses except for the small slices they saved for lunch. When the high tide of buyers ebbed, Diana waved a slice above her head. The little urchin, whose team prepared to pinch some sandals from a new merchant, ran to her.

"Nahni, how can I reach Singer?" Diana said.

The waif smiled, held up two fingers of one hand and an open palm of the other.

Diana put her lunch in Nahni's hand, which vanished into a pocket. Anne tossed Diana an apple, after which the little girl frowned and held out her hand again. Diana shook her head, and Nahni led Diana from the market into the streets of Branwyn.

Like a fish through water, little Nahni weaved through the crowded streets towing Diana behind her, while Diana peered into every alley and shadow for a glint from silver-inlaid bootheels and worried about what to ask Singer.

*How can I get Singer's attention? What will I ask her? She's famous. But a spy should know lots about the secret worlds of—*

*Whomp!*

At Diana's feet crashed a man, and from his hand fell a red coin that rolled to a stop at her shoe. As he rose to limp away, a woman in a black cape kicked him in the back of the knee, and he fell on his face in the street with her foot on his neck.

"We need to be far from here," Nahni said with a tug on Diana's hand.

Diana back stepped as the girl pulled her. From the window above jumped a man in a wide-brimmed hat who joined the woman. Together, they tied his hands as a crowd gathered and obscured her view. None of them had silver in their bootheels, and Diana sighed.

"Come, come!" Nahni said and dragged her down an alley.

"Were those police?" Diana asked.

"No. Worse."

"How worse?"

"Assassins. That red coin was the warrant."

Diana's body tensed, and she stopped. "In broad daylight?"

"That's the law," Nahni said.

"And you know the law?"

Nahni smirked with her tiny fist on her hip. "In my business, I have to. Come," she said, and tugged again.

"Do the Assassins mete out punishment as well?"

"A delivery to the local constabulary, most often, or a beating. But occasionally the warrant is death."

"What crimes deserve the attention of the Assassins rather than the police?"

"That's up to the authorities, and I steer my mates far away from that kind of attention," Nahni said and dragged her to the Town Center.

At the stage, Nahni interrupted a man directing laborers, pulled him down to her level, and placed the flyer in his hand.

"Greggory, she's here to see Singer," Nahni said with a wink.

The stage manager turned to Diana. "You here to volunteer?"

"Yes, but—"

Greggory took Diana's arm, but Nahni pulled on his shirt again and opened her palm. The manager gave her a copper and Nahni left.

The stage manager rushed Diana to where a set of buckets of assorted colors stood near wooden panels. "What's your name, lass?"

"Diana Smyth."

"Can you paint, Miss Smyth?"

"Ahhh . . ."

"Doesn't matter. Match the color from the bucket to the patch on the panel. And keep within the lines. And hurry. It needs to be dry for tomorrow." He turned to someone's wave and stood.

"Yes, yes, be right there!" he shouted.

"Where's Singer?" Diana asked.

He hurried away and said over his shoulder, "Rehearsals."

Diana sighed and stared at the unpainted panels, then went to a paint bucket and put brush to panel.

And waited.


Diana backed away from the fairytale town ablaze, as catapults flung boulders against the stone walls and flaming tar above them. No one would survive such an onslaught.

*And what would the townsfolk do?*

She shook her head, and the backdrop she had spent hours painting lost its hold on her imagination. Grabbing another panel, she sat to paint.

A woman sat alongside and reached for a brush. As she leaned over to paint, pendants dangled from her necklace: a white and gold ring cut to sparkle like gems in the sunlight, and a half circle of a silver-gray medallion with intricate runes.

Diana put her brush down. "Excuse me, ma'am. Didn't I see you on the East Road yesterday in a wagon?"

The woman raised her head and smiled. "Why, yes. I remember. You were struggling with a young lamb. Will your father miss your help at the farm today?"

"No ma'am. I usually attend the Academy in the morning," Diana said.

"What's that?"

"It's a place of education Queen Helena chartered. The prince attends, as do some of the aristo children. I'm the rare commoner."

"How marvelous. What do they teach there?"

"Civic virtue, the teacher says. Though sometimes I can't tell if they're lessons or myths."

"Ah, myths. That's my profession."

"Are you a storyteller?"

"Yes, dear. They call me Singer."

Diana sat up straight and smiled. "Oh! I'm honored to meet you." *Dorreau mentioned the Singers might have a book!*

"And who am I pleased to meet?"

"Diana Smyth, ma'am."

"Greggory told me you were asking for me," Singer said. "How can I help you?"

"I wanted to ask where your stories come from—the ones in your songs."

"They're ancient, as old as we can imagine."

"Are they written?" Diana asked.

"Well, most are passed on orally, but some are in books."

Diana forgot her painting and turned away to hide her excitement. *More than one book!* "Have you actually seen them?"

Singer dipped a fresh brush into a bucket. "The College of Singers has a few, all ancient and tattered. They're precious to us."

Diana dropped her gaze and tried a different angle. "What makes your books so valuable? Do they contain magic?"

"In a way, I suppose. The few we have at the College are myths and stories."

"There's nothing magical about myths."

Singer smiled. "We live with magic all around us, and what you know of it, you know from those myths. They help us remember the history we do not understand and remind us how to behave, what to value, and why." She leaned forward and smiled. "And aren't as boring as lectures or sermons."

Diana's excitement ebbed. "But they're just stories and not true."

"There's truth within all the grand stories. Sometimes it's the consequences of tough decisions; in other we find the inner struggles each of us faces. Some have the power to change the course of war, like in our next performance. You will go, yes?"

"Yes. How far is the College?" Diana asked.

"Perhaps a thousand miles."

Diana sighed, and her excitement evaporated. *And beyond my reach.* "Do they have any here?"

"In Branwyn?" Singer said with raised eyebrows. "No one has mentioned such to me. I'm sure there are books of the One God."

Diana opened her mouth, but a voice behind her distracted her.

"Oh, there you are," the young woman said. "Papa is leaving."

Diana turned to find her friend and rose. "Anne, I'd like to introduce Singer."

Anne curtsied with wide eyes and a blush. "Oh my! It's an honor to meet you, ma'am."

Singer smiled. "Another volunteer?"

Anne dropped her gaze and frowned. "I'm sorry, my father needs my help."

"Well, of course, that's more important." Singer turned to Diana. "Will you come back tomorrow?"

"Certainly," Diana said, curtsied, and left with Anne for home.

***

"I met Singer today," Diana said to Jon, handing him the crone's flyer when she returned to their ranch. "She's actually seen books."

"What more did you learn?"

Diana recounted their conversation, which did not amount to much more than a hope. "Singer doesn't seem like a spy. Or carry any of the arrogance I would expect of a famous person."

"Engaging and candid?" he said, and she nodded. "Exactly like a spy. Two from her troupe came to the Hogue's Breath tonight as I was leaving."

"You didn't interview them??

"No, I'd miss you here at home."

"And?"

"Word is their capacity for drink and mischief is rather cavernous."

She folded her arms and tipped her head. "So, nothing new?"

"No. But this was just a convenient possibility. Our search will continue without them. Did you learn more?"

"Not from Singer, but I'll see her again tomorrow," Diana said, putting her dishes in the sink before leaning back against it. "The young aristos gripe about George's new regime."

"How so?"

"Their families are used to using force to get what they want and now have to petition the king."

Jon laughed. "They'd be even more confused by the governance we have at home. Sleep now, lass. I'll clean up."

"I can't sleep yet," she said and checked her sheep were safely in the barn. With a horse blanket, a knife, and the silhouette of Branwyn against the stars, she fell asleep on the chair outside.

In her dream, Eric danced with her at her first ball, surrounded by aristos who clapped with approval, while the bishop and royals smiled upon them. At the end of the waltz, Eric bowed to her as the castle and cathedral, timber by timber, stone by stone, collapsed upon her.

She awoke with a start, and on the horizon, the spires still stood.

*For now.*

# Chapter 20
# Epiphany

Hoping to run into Eric, Diana took her usual route to the Academy, calculating that Singer would not be free until after morning rehearsals. But when she arrived at the Academy, the prince was not there, and she sat next to Martin.

"Psst. Martin. I need to leave early to meet Singer. Meet me outside after."

A moment later, Eric entered class, and with a wave, acknowledged the glare from the priest. The prince stood behind Martin, and she blushed.

"And what of our lessons?" Eric asked.

Martin put the back of his hand to his mouth and whispered, "He lectures on the tribute to your father."

Eric nodded. "I understand now why tyrants seize power—their patience with consensus becomes exhausted."

Father Dorian continued. "So, Timelt, you'd destroy the Market to raise the new monument. And what of the people who live and work there?"

The young man shrugged and leaned back with his hands behind his head. "Sometimes you need to break a few urns to create the future you desire."

The priest's brows furrowed, and his eyes narrowed. "How trivial that sounds, breaking a vessel of little value. The urn's essential purpose is to hold what's inside. Take an urn of olive oil. Farmers have husbanded the olive trees for decades to produce the fruit. The oil is the result of many days' labor. But once the urn is split, the oil is spoilt."

To Diana, the urn was civilization that held the bounty of human creativity, enterprise, and community: a vessel the Quarajii wanted to destroy. But the surrounding aristos appeared confused. With a frown, Dorian turned to his desk for the pitcher and cup.

"In this pitcher I have the finest wine in the land," the priest said and filled the cup. He held out the cup to Timelt, but instead dropped it to shatter on the floor and spill. "And now without the cup, you are not refreshed by the wine."

Rather than the broken cup, Diana saw the shards of civilization and the fruits of culture and craftsmanship spilled on the floor unable to be restored.

The priest returned the pitcher to the desk. "In wrecking the urn or the cup or the market, it's clear you don't recognize their worth. How farmers conjure the food you eat may as well be magic."

"That's not magic," Timelt said. "That's mundane."

"Why? What experience do you have in farming or magic that gives you such insight?" the priest asked. "Ah, I see. You only wish to use it, but you cannot because you do not understand it. You only seek to use the people who hold that magic?" The aristos nodded. "Then be clear in the limits of your knowledge and power or you may end up under the dirt like the Imperator."

Anica spoke up. "Brother, if the *citizens* wanted the memorial, they'd build it themselves and not need government to destroy the market."

Timelt raised his hands. "Good god, we only want a new monument!" He stormed out, leaving the classroom thick with tension.

"What I want is a new dress," Solange said, and the class erupted in laughter.

Diana shook her head, walked out to the courtyard, and leaned against the wall.

*Why do I waste my time when there are no books here? To make friends?* She turned to Martin, who followed her out and smiled. *A curious monk that might help, and a prince whose interests—*

"Why leave now?" Martin said. "The teacher makes sense."

She crossed her arms and frowned. "Of course he does. It's the difference between tyranny and freedom. When he needs to teach the obvious, I don't need to be here."

"So why do you still attend?" he said, leaning a shoulder against the wall. "What value does a farm girl find in studying with aristos?"

She feigned a scowl but smiled with her eyes. "Am I less worthy to attend? Well?"

"Uh, of course not. But—"

"The queen invited us all. Is a rancher worth less than a nobleman? A girl less than a boy? A commoner less than a monk?"

"No, nothing of the kind," Martin said. "It's not about the invitation, Dee. It's why you would accept."

Before she could reply, Eric left the classroom with his teeth clenched.

"Why the mood?" Diana asked.

"I can't tell them, and it burns me. Livornia has interests with the builders and will profit immensely by controlling a new market square."

"Why not let her build in the slums near the dump and use the revenues for decent housing and a hospital."

The prince raised an eyebrow. "Interesting suggestion. I'll tell the king."

"Credit Martin," Diana said and frowned. "You still don't feel threatened by that discussion?"

"Should I be?"

"Foreigners roam your streets, and your father frustrates the aristos."

Eric furrowed his brow. "Foreigners?"

*Oops.* "Foreign to the region, you told me as much yesterday."

He studied her. "The performance draws many unfamiliar people."

She nodded. "And the crowds at the performance will be an opportunity for trouble."

Eric nodded slowly. "I've mentioned it to Grimes. The king said he'll open the land to the west of town for development."

"But that won't benefit the aristos," Diana said. "They'll have to spend their own wealth to develop it and not use the treasury."

"I'll speak to Commander Raynes about security."

Steven waved from the classroom door.

"I need to listen to my friends more closely," Eric said and backed up to return to class. "Come."

"I can't," she said. "I have a meeting with Singer."

Eric smiled. "Sunday then?"

She smiled and nodded, then frowned.

*Wait. How can he see me Sunday? A prince at the market? But—*

Martin took a step to follow Eric, but Diana kept hold of his sleeve.

"What did he mean 'Sunday'?" she said.

The monk shrugged and took a step to join Eric, but she grabbed his sleeve. "I need your help," Diana said. "We've been searching for books and the only place unexplored is the old cathedral grounds."

"The bishop has posted them out of bounds. And his guards and Grimes enforce it." Martin smiled and lowered his voice. "Just what are you planning?"

She scanned the courtyard for open ears and whispered, "Can you get the key?"

He shook his head. "Only the bishop has it, and he keeps it with him."

"You tried?"

He grinned and nodded.

"How else will we get in?"

"Do you know any criminals?" he asked.

Her frown changed to a grin. "Can you get me a cassock?"

He nodded.

"Meet me with it on the stage at the afternoon call to prayer. I can't miss my meeting with Singer."

As she walked away, she glanced over her shoulder to see Eric wave to her, and she turned away so he could not see her blush.


In a corner of the stage, Diana colored a panel of dark clouds above a battlefield with Fures tinting the scene in shades of red. Beside her, a maid of ample girth poured her a bowl of porridge and mead from a wheeled kettle.

"Thank you," Diana said as the maid dragged the kettle across the stage. There, a dwarf spoke to people so fancifully dressed they could only be bards.

"Yes, yes, Christine and Rodrigo," the dwarf said. It was the same man who passed their ranch two days prior, and now lectured from atop a crate. "Now, who can tell me what this story is about?"

A man with a colorful hat spoke first. "It's about a feud between rival clans who must come together—"

The dwarf covered his yawn with a hand and pointed to a plaid jacket. "Next."

"Virtue."

The dwarf nodded but said no more and waved toward another raised hand.

From the rear, a stout woman with stars in her eyes called out. "Love conquers all!"

"Hardly," the dwarf said. "Anyone else? Yes, it could be many things depending on what the audience needs." He paced in front of them. "But today, it's about what binds us: Rodrigo is bound by duty and Christine is bound by love . . ."

The dwarf continued, but Diana stopped painting. *Duty or love. What a horrible choice. Would I give up my mission for someone I love? No . . .*

"No, no, no!" the dwarf shouted, and Diana looked up. "It's not about what Rodrigo *says*. It's not about the *words* he speaks." He leaped atop the crate and wagged his finger. "This is not a school or a church to teach what's known or believed. If you think that, then you believe children will follow your words to war because your hero wields a sword. No. Would you plumb the depths of *Rowan* for a mere lecture? It's never about the words alone. It's about what they *evoke*."

He jumped from the crate, paced in front of the cast, and spoke to them quietly. On one student's head, he tapped a knuckle. In the middle of a young woman's chest, he touched his finger gently. The woman smiled and blushed, and when he turned away, she put her hand to her heart where he had touched her.

The cast and crew were transfixed. *He must be a Singer too. Is that the magic, the spoken word captured in their books?*

The dwarf rubbed his chin. "Now, who was with us last week at Sturmwood?" he asked and surveyed their raised hands. "Aye, good. And what was that about?"

"A heroic adventure . . ."

"A battle against fate."

The dwarf waved a hand. "Yes, yes, all those things but what fundamentally?"

"Vanquishing evil . . ."

"Courage against the gods . . ."

The dwarf put his fists on his hips. "Bah. The 'gods' in the story are mere props to clarify the motivations. Who else?"

"It's the inner struggles in preparation to confront your nemesis."

*Nemesis,* Diana thought and Garfann's image came to her.

"Yes, the journey of their entire lives was to prepare for that moment . . ."

She frowned. *And here I live in safety while my father and country are under siege.*

One bard stood and revealed a dreamy-eyed Nahni sitting by the curtain with her chin on her palms. Diana waved to her.

"I have a job for you," Diana said and whispered in the waif's ear.

The girl gave her a side-eye and nodded slowly. "This would usually be quite expensive." She grinned. "But you're a good customer," she said and extended her hand for Diana to shake. "Meet me at the Cathedral Quarter at the call to prayer."

As Nahni walked away, Singer approached, sat by Diana, and picked up a brush.

"Almost finished. Did you volunteer for the performance as well?"

"No, but I'll attend." Diana held her breath for an instant. "Singer, where did your college find the old books?"

Singer smiled. "Books again? Well, I've been told portions were found in the ruins of ancient buildings—"

"How old?"

"As old as time, from—"

Diana could not wait. "If the books you have at the College are so valuable, why aren't there more of them? If books contain such powerful myths, why are there so few?"

"Good questions, but I don't have the answers, dear. The books we make now are hand copies or wood cuts that are very hard to produce." She stood and waved to Diana to help her drag the finished panel to the stage. "Still in a decade the paper turns brown or rots, and the ink fades. Parchment does not last much longer. It seems we forgot how to make books."

Diana finished the panel. *The Old Knowledge?*

Singer lifted a corner. "Help me, please," she said, and Diana helped her drag the panel to the back of the stage.

"The word *forgotten* implies we once knew," Diana said. "How can it be that the only books are of religion and myth? How can such stories have so much power?"

Singer began a new panel and handed Diana a fresh brush. "They both speak to what's deepest in the human heart, our passions, our spirit—the things that drive us."

"Is that what the little man meant?"

Singer nodded. "Ash."

As Diana painted, another battle scene took form with pennants askew and the field strewn with the dead, and she leaned back.

"What?" Diana asked.

"Ash. The dwarf's name is Ash. And yes, the myths can express these deeper truths, like Minotaurs and mountains of gold."

"What can be 'true' about a mountain of gold?" Diana asked. "That's a fantasy."

"Sometimes the truth is deep within us."

"What do you mean?"

"Well, in the myths, gold often represents our heart's desires. An entire mountain of it means fulfillment beyond your wildest dreams. It represents our desire untethered or a temptation we can't resist. Singers tell these stories to show what people will fight for or sacrifice to appease their passions. And the myth reveals the consequences if they sacrifice for the wrong things."

"I don't want gold or power."

"It need not be gold. It may be the voice of a child or a lover's touch." She sighed and seemed to peer through Diana. "What do you desire most?"

Diana dropped her eyes and clenched her hands in her lap. The scents of lavender and pine near their cottage near the Alba River, the musty swampiness of the Wye Delta, and the wildflowers her father had sent her during his campaigns. But across the lush fields of Branwyn to her new home came a desert breeze.

"You need not tell me," Singer asked. "But what does it feel like without it?"

"Dry," Diana said. "Lonely and hollow, like wandering in the desert, thirsty all the time."

Singer sighed and nodded. "Home."

When Diana turned her head aside, Singer touched her hand.

"Is it far?"

But Diana stiffened and drew her hand away.

"I'm sorry, dear," Singer said. "Your anklet caught my eye as we passed your farm, and I was curious."

Diana tugged her skirt over her ankles. "Then it was you who came to our stall at the market."

"My disguise was so transparent?" Singer said with a smile. "Yes, I was recruiting people not afraid to work. Did they tell you I was a spy?"

Diana blushed and Singer leaned forward. "Well, they're correct, but not at the moment."

*Just what a spy would say.* Diana relaxed after the smile and admission.

After finishing the panel, Singer helped her stow it and grab a half-finished panel from the stack: a backdrop for the battlefield of Teurin.

"And the Minotaur?" Diana asked.

"The beast is what we fear most and how that fear drives each of us. It's the implacable obstacle you must confront or be forever stunted. You either face it or you die inside, your soul shrinks, and destiny abandons you. Who is your Minotaur?"

Diana narrowed her eyes at the memory of Garfann and Makashti but then frowned. *More prying.* "Who is yours?"

Singer flinched for the briefest moment and stared into the distance.

Diana bit her lip. "Tell me."

"A dangerous man. A warrior."

"Did he hurt you?"

Singer paused, her hand clasping the ring that hung from her necklace, distressed from a cause Diana could not guess. "He hurt . . . people I loved very much."

The horror of her mother's death came to her, and the anguish of the bravest man she knew, her father, when he found her covered in blood, the man who went to war to protect his country. She dropped her gaze. *And me.*

"My father told me we need to face our fears," Diana said. "The farther we run, the bigger they get; the faster we run, the more frightening they become until they consume us."

With a thin voice, Singer replied, "I couldn't face him. He was half again my size and led an army of remorseless savages with silver in their bootheels." She smiled. "So I tricked him."

*Silver inlay! Quarajii. Who is she that she would come across them?* She opened her mouth to speak but stopped. *And If I confirm who those savages are, I will unmask Jon and myself. Savages . . .* She turned away as the images of that night overwhelmed her, her home ablaze, her uncle murdered, and hiding in a burned-out tree in the rain with her dying mother while men searched for them. Bitterness still boiled in her, and she closed her fists, but her father's words calmed her.

"My father also said that what you cling to defines you," Diana said and opened her fists as if they held fragile rose petals. *Like my mother's death and my promise to her defines me still.*

Singer blanched, let go of the ring on her necklace, and gripped her hands in her lap. Her voice became a whisper. "Sometimes you need to outsmart the Minotaur."

"Is that Rowan the Brave you speak of?"

She nodded. "Rowan never sacrificed his virtue for his goal, his love for Gwendolyn, and gathered strength and skill until the Minotaur came for him."

*So she's a refugee as well and prepares before returning to confront her nemesis. But what will I return to: a country in flames, my people in chains, or Papa dead? If he's in danger, I must return soon, with or without my mother's book of magic. I'm a soldier who has dawdled too long in safety with fantasies that seduce me to idleness.*

Diana spoke for herself now. "Then you must prepare."

Singer's eyes lost focus, and she leaned on her hand.

"You're hungry," Diana said and handed her the unfinished bowl of mead and oatmeal.

Singer took a spoonful and closed her eyes. Opening them again, she blinked and focused on Diana as if she just recognized her.

During the pause, thoughts of Eric crept in, and Diana blushed. "Does Rowan see Gwendolyn as his mountain of gold?"

Singer sighed and glanced away as if taming her own dreams. "Perhaps. Through much of the story, yes, but only because he's deceived. At the start, he's naïve. At the end, he . . ." Her eyes glistened, and she paused and blinked.

"Ma'am?"

"Excuse me, dear. After Rowan defeated the Minotaur, he could . . ." Singer took a breath. "He could let go of Gwen as an unattainable object and instead treat her as the woman he loved." She lowered her eyes.

*What would cause a grown woman to react so to a story? But didn't I just blush? In her voice are Papa's bedtime stories of heroes from the Spine and the graceful dragons they rode.*

Diana smiled. "What about dragons?"

"I beg your pardon?"

"I understand mountains of gold and Minotaurs can represent our greed and fear. What do dragons represent?"

Gazing at her, Singer smiled. "Perhaps they represent themselves."

*Huh?*

Singer peered over Diana's shoulder. "Is that monk looking for you?"

Diana turned to find Martin waving at her from the curtain. She turned back to Singer and sighed. "Can . . . I feel we have more to talk about."

"Will you be here for the dress rehearsal tomorrow morning?"

"Yes, of course."

Singer put her hand on Diana's. "Tomorrow then. Ask for me directly."

Diana nodded, turned, and stepped toward Martin, but Singer called after her.

"Wait. What did you mean I 'must prepare'?"

Martin took Diana's hand and pulled her, but she turned back to Singer.

"What you fear is already here," Diana said, and Martin pulled her past the curtain.

Diana frowned, upset he interrupted her conversation with Singer, the only person she had met who acknowledged the power of books and had touched them.

*I must risk more next time I talk with her, or I'll never complete my mission.*

She crossed her arms. "What is it?"

"You did ask me to meet you here," he said and held out a cassock.

"Right. I'm sorry. I was in the middle of a conversation with Singer."

Martin's eyebrows rose. "Wow. That's her?"

"Yes. And we didn't finish."

He gave her a conspiratorial smile. "How about our adventure?"

Diana knitted her brow and turned, but Singer disappeared behind the curtain.

Diana sighed and took a last glance back at the curtain. After putting on the cassock and stuffing her hair under the hood, she took Martin's arm. "Come on. Our adventure awaits!"


They found Nahni waiting in a shadow of a cathedral buttress. Nahni took Diana's hand and led them to the run-down structures between the Academy and

Cathedral where the walls rose high, and the paths darkened in shadow.

At an alley stood another waif, who nodded and waved them past. Between him and another boy at the other end of the alley stood a locked gate. Nahni stopped and checked behind them, and then put two bronze rods in the lock and played with them. The lock clicked, and the gate swung open.

The small courtyard adjoined a large chapel with a steeply pitched roof without visible windows. A stone path led to a tall door with an unusual pointed arch surrounded by more recent stonework. Between the gate and the door, the path cut through a small cemetery. Most of the headstones were unreadable, except one that Nahni stopped at and frowned.

"Quickly, quickly!" Martin whispered.

"Is there a problem?" Diana asked.

Nahni shook her head. "This is the oldest structure in the Cathedral Quarter," she said as she used the metal rods on the door. When it clicked open, she backed up.

"Are you curious?" Diana said. "Join us."

The waif shook her head. "I have another job to do," she said and disappeared through the gate.

"We shouldn't be here," Diana said.

Martin frowned. "Of course not."

"And what will happen if someone catches us?"

He gave her a wink. "I'll just tell the bishop I enticed you here to steal a kiss."

"What about me?"

"No offense, but they wouldn't take much account of a farm girl. Me, they would expel."

*Which is worse, exposing my mission if I talk or public humiliation if I keep quiet?* "Well, let's not get caught."

Focused on their crime, the pair did not notice someone watching from the cathedral balcony as they entered—Bishop Rochfield.

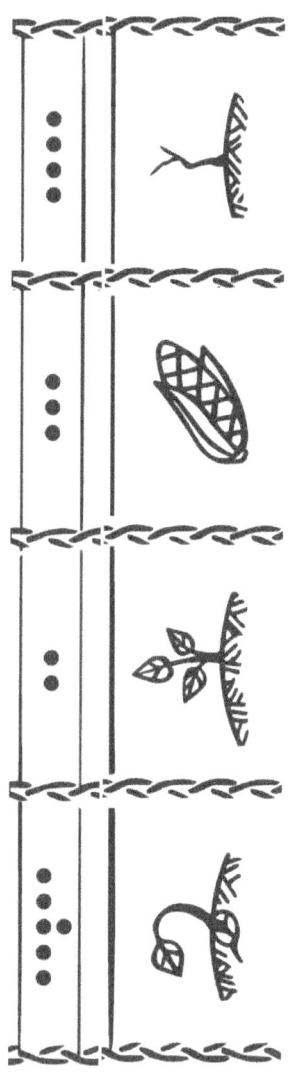

# Chapter 21
# Labyrinth

Diana entered the largest room she had ever been in. Dormers built into the high roof beamed light filtered through sooty colored glass and left the corners in shadow. Multi-colored dust sparkled in the light and tickled her nose. Columns of narrow tables and chairs filled the space like a banquet dining room. Lining walls unbroken by windows were tall cabinets with barred glass doors, some locked, holding shelves filled with scrolls. And in the center stood glass cases on pedestals.

Sneezing, Diana walked to a shelf as Martin closed the door behind them.

"Any books?" Diana said.

Martin went to an open shelf and unrolled a scroll with a ragged edge. "These seem to record the Imperator's decrees." He unrolled another. "And these record taxes. How boring that the greatest number of writings record transactions."

"I think that's how writing started," she said as she meandered through the room to the glass cases and stopped. "Martin, here!"

Inside the cases lay open books with stylized calligraphy surrounding color illustrations. Dots and bars accented a vaguely familiar alphabet, and intricate filigree intertwined with flowers and serpents bordered the pages.

His hand caressed the glass. "It's an original Book of the One God."

"It's beautiful," she said, mesmerized. "All the time spent to create it."

"It's an act of devotion," Martin said. "The monks consider it a blessing to copy them and meditate on the passages as they work." He spread his arms and surveyed the room. "Isn't this wonderful?"

"Yes," she said with a disappointed frown. *But not magic.*

Diana moved to other pedestals and studied the cases. All held beautiful hand-wrought copies of the same sacred text, each in its own majestic style.

"They're all the same," she said.

"Come, this one's different." He took her arm and steered her to a pedestal in a corner where an open book shared a case with small skeletons of bird wings and drawings of birds in flight. No ornamentation of any kind decorated the page, and the margins were unadorned. Precise symbols filled the sheet. Surrounding the case under the glass was metal filigree to prevent access.

Her jaw dropped. "An actual book! And not of religion or myth." She looked around the sides to see how to open the case.

"We have no key to the locks," he said.

She frowned. "Nahni might help us there tomorrow."

"This is better than an etching," Martin mumbled. "The characters are all perfect and identical."

Of all the fantastical images she had imagined about the Book of Chaos that would amaze her with its wonder and mystery, this was not any of them. *Something that changes the world like the Book of Chaos should be special.*

She nodded. "But it's ordinary."

"What did you expect?" he asked.

"Not this."

Martin pointed to a drawing surrounded by unfamiliar characters. The drawing showed someone blowing on a parchment figure folded into the profile of a teardrop pushed in on one side.

"They showed us this trick at the monastery," he said. "The object rises at a breath, like magic."

Diana crossed her arms. "If it's just a trick, why put it on display?"

Martin shrugged. "The priests implied the spirit moved it, but I suspect natural causes."

"Did they tell you where they found the book?"

Martin shook his head. "They didn't mention a book ever, or I would have told you."

"Why don't they teach us from these books at the Academy?" she asked.

He sighed. "I imagine the priests don't understand them. Teachers teach what they can organize, true or not, and the priests avoid controversy. I'll bet these are all a mystery to them. It might as well be magic."

The second time the monk mentioned "magic" she was fully engaged. Her eyes opened wide. *If they can make one book so perfect, why not more?*

Diana grabbed Martin's arm. "Do you see more?"

He frowned and shook his head.

As she searched, a mouse scurried along the edge of the wall and squeezed through a small hole in a narrow alcove at the end of the room. Above the hole, a diagram from the page in the book appeared on a tile with the cross section of the bird wing.

Diana crossed her arms. "What was it the priest did with the wing?"

"He blew on it, and the object rose."

"Stand here," she said and lined up his mouth to the diagram on the portal. "Now blow."

Martin blew, and the wall creaked but stopped.

"Again," she said, and when Martin blew, she pushed up on the tile as if the wing lifted, and the alcove opened to a dark corridor.

Just inside was a torch and a sparker. She lit the torch, and next to it hung a set of keys she pocketed. She turned and waved to invite him in. Before letting the door close, she checked the latch to make sure she could exit.

Down a winding stone stairway and through a narrow passage, the path led into a labyrinth of portals and tunnels. Mice scuttled past them and squeaked from beyond the glow of the torches.

The walls were damp and slippery with mildew, and the rock was not as smooth and cold as granite or marble. The floors and ceilings were straight and square, and like the walls, without seam or joint as if the masons had carved it all from a single stone.

At the end of the hall stood another metal door. To both sides lay metal armor, from helmet to sabaton. From one, a gauntlet was missing, and a skeletal hand reached for his sword.

Here in one spot was more metal dedicated to only two figures than she had seen in all of le Pegre.

Diana shook her head. "How could they afford all that metal to protect two people and a doorway?"

Like the cases upstairs, filigree and dragons decorated the door, but it glistened in the torchlight. In the center of the door was mounted a wheel that might have come from a ship except it too was of metal.

To the left of the door were three keyholes and a set of sliding levers. She inserted the three small keys and turned them, after which the levers moved with an audible click and the door opened.

Beyond her torch might have been the edge of the world, except there were no stars to catch them if they fell. A waft of cold stale air came from within, and she coughed.

After lighting torches on either side of the door, he gave one to her. "Light the others."

Light filled the space to expose a long slender room with alcoves in the walls. Extending down the center into the shadows lay what appeared to be stone coffins with figures sculpted on the lids. Shelves cut into the walls held neatly stacked bones and skulls.

"A crypt, Martin. Dead people."

"These must be the cathedral's ancient catacombs."

The crypt led to a maze of featureless stone walls and into a cavernous area twice her height with a smooth floor.

"How much further?" Martin said. "We've found nothing."

"We found hints." She ran her hand across the floor. "This isn't natural."

Across the cavern was a door without handle or knob. When it did not budge at her push or turn of the wheel, she stepped back with her arms folded.

"What now?" Martin asked. "Let's go back and examine the book upstairs."

"A door's purpose is to open, Martin."

Each side of the door was decorated with fired tiles, each one foot square, decorated with pictograms or strange runes. Below them were empty spaces from which tiles had fallen to the floor.

She sat and examined the tiles. Each bore a unique design on the front, but with dots two to five on the top margin. On the back was an array of sixteen pins the size of her little finger, some long and others short.

Empty spots on the wall matched them with sets of sixteen holes.

Looking up to the right of the door, four tiles in place broke the random pattern, each with dots: one tile with one dot above four dots, and three more with two, three, and four dots.

Diana raised an eyebrow. "Do you see the pattern?"

"Two, three, four, five. No I don't."

"One, two, three, four, five. And the five is the same as one: four plus one. The series repeats. Look around, search for tiles that might describe a sequence of four."

From those on the floor, he flipped the tiles over. The pictograms were all of farms and farm animals: sheaves of wheat, sheep, cows, offspring of each species, corn, and seasonal weather.

"Four types of animals?" Martin said. "Four types of crops?"

"What makes sense for a repeating cycle?" Diana said, picked up the four tiles of sheep, and placed them below the tiles with dots. "Animals don't repeat the cycle with the same animal."

Martin showed her four tiles of the seasons: winter, spring, summer, fall.

"In what order?" she asked, and he shrugged. She placed winter in the five-one place and followed with spring, summer, and fall.

Nothing happened.

"If five equals one," Martin said, "then that's renewal. Sounds like spring."

She changed the order and a click of stone on stone came from the wall. "Hmm. What changes with the seasons?"

"Domestic animals breed all year around."

She gathered pictograms representing the four seasons of agriculture: sowing, growing, harvest, and fallow. When she put them below the appropriate season, they clicked, and the door cracked open.

Martin smiled and went to the door, but Diana narrowed her brow and stared at it.

"What?" he asked.

She shook her head. "If that was a puzzle to keep people out, it's too easy. I mean, everyone knows the seasons and the crop cycle."

The door opened with a groan and the torches ruffled with a gust of dry air. Inside the room, they lit more torches that illuminated an enormous room. And there Diana stood with her mouth open.

# Chapter 22
# Miracles

Diana stared at a large room stacked with books of all proportions and bindings and her jaw fell open. In one corner of the room stood more armor and strange weapons; in another, delicate pottery; and in another, sculptures. Paintings of diverse sizes lay upright against the wall.

"Chermyath has been busy," Martin said.

"Who?" Diana asked once she could speak again.

"The god of the anvil and diligence."

"Are the priests aware of this?"

Martin shook his head and went to the weapons. "They guide me toward more practical endeavors," he said over his shoulder.

Diana ran her fingers across the picture frames, and they came away clean. "No dust, Martin. Like they were put here only yesterday."

Against a wall stood a large cabinet with many small drawers, each with its own strange runes.

A drawer whooshed as she opened it. Within lay seeds and a small sealed box beside a note with pictograms and writing in a strange alphabet. Each drawer revealed similar contents with seeds of various sizes and shapes.

Beside the cabinet, lay a book with an ordinary leather cover. *Could this be it? The Book of Magic? Or any of them?* She ran her hand across it and felt no buzz of magic or warning. *Will I survive a look if I open it?*

*Without the courage to look, my mission is for nothing.*

She opened the cover slowly, but nothing happened. Within, she found only color illustrations like the one upstairs. She sat with it in her lap, smiling as she ran her fingers over the smooth page. Then she turned the pages one by one, her eyes wide.

On one page she found a picture of two different pea plants of different heights with an X symbol between them. Below the illustration was a four-square grid with three boxes with drawings of one of the original plants, and a fourth box with the other plant. She stared in confusion and flipped through more pages.

"Martin, could any of these be magic?"

He shrugged. "Perhaps. But how would you recognize it?"

"Or a book from before the Chaos?"

"How could that be? People invented writing after the Wandering." He studied her. "Is that what you seek? Is that why you're interested in books?"

She nodded.

"If so, what you're searching for either can't exist, or you wouldn't recognize it if you found it."

With a simple logical statement, Martin made her search a waste of time.

*My entire trip, all my training and preparation, all my hopes, and my sword strike against the Sul had no edge*

Book by book, she searched, finding nothing special, nothing arcane. She sat on a stack of books and sighed.

*My entire mission is useless.*

She stood and smiled.

*Or maybe not!*

"Maybe the magic is the books themselves," she said. "We can't make books like these now, and someone may have just as well conjured them from a kettle."

"Magic is a myth, Diana, and may not sate your hunger."

She frowned. "Maybe you don't have enough faith."

"My faith is in the One God."

"Doesn't She perform miracles?"

"I prefer to view them as metaphors," he said.

She put a hand on his shoulder. "And so avoid disappointment when your prayers go unanswered? You need more wonder in your life." She waved her hand around the room. "And here it is."

In an alcove were swords of different shapes and Martin went to them. He took two, one of the familiar metallic brown of bronze, and another of untarnished gray. He positioned the bronze sword edge up between two books and thrust down with the gray sword as hard as he could. The gray sword cut an inch deep in the bronze sword, but itself was unmarred. He took the gray sword to a corner of the stone wall and swung again. A one-inch chip of rock flew from the wall, but the sword marred only slightly.

Diana turned at the sound. "If an army fights with swords more resilient than bronze, they'd win every battle."

"And we'd just be killing each other more effectively," Martin said.

*If the Empress has the Book of Chaos, maybe she is already developing such swords.*

Frustrated and overwhelmed by the possibilities, Diana sighed and eyed the door but sat. *The book I seek might be here, or it might not. And if I don't know what it looks like, how can I tell if I found it?* It was another puzzle, and she was tired of puzzles.

Within another book, she found more indented text with similar symbols. Drawings of stonework like that of the cathedral appeared with one page showing the pointed arch at the entrance. Another showed figures of waterfalls and water flowing through pipes. She went back to the page with the pea plants and peered at it again with a squint.

The library surrounding her dispersed, replaced by a garden of pea plants from her childhood. Days passed in seconds as the sunny days alternated with rain. Each plant grew and matured to its own height and intertwined. In cycles, the seeds were planted and grew, each within a range of heights.

A touch on her shoulder dispelled the garden in blink.

"Diana?" Martin said.

She stood and smiled but remained staring at the far wall. "It's not magic," she said and turned to face him, her eyes gleaming. "It's not magic. It's knowledge." She rubbed her hand across the page.

"It's gibberish. We don't understand it."

Taking his hand, she placed it on the illustration of the pea plants and pointed to the grid. "Here. Imagine the peas are sheep and look again."

He squinted at the picture but remained silent.

Diana frowned. "How do you get a white lamb from two black sheep?"

Martin squinted at her.

She shook her head. "You can get a white sheep from two black sheep if the grandparents were white."

Martin tipped his head and shrugged.

She pursed her lips. "Look at the peas. You know what peas are, don't you?"

He nodded but furrowed his brow.

"Sometimes when you have tall pea plants, their seeds produce small plants."

Nodding once, he glanced to the side and shook his head.

She threw her arms in the air. "Argh! Have you never been on a farm?"

"Yes, my whole life. I failed, Dee. That's why I'm a monk."

"That book upstairs, with the parchment teardrop and the bird skeletons. I think it tries to explain how birds fly."

He stared at her again. "But we know why they fly."

"Not *why*," Diana said, "*how*." She went to another stack, flipped through the illustrations, and pointed to one of a man's chest. "Not *why* we breathe, but *how*." Walking to the paintings she picked out a vibrant landscape. "Have you ever seen this brilliance of color in anything?" With a quick swipe of her hand, she knocked a ceramic figurine from a table only to watch it bounce. "Or porcelain that wouldn't break?"

"I've never seen porcelain." With one eyebrow raised, he grinned at her. "And how would a farm girl recognize it?"

*He's a sharp one.* She turned her head so he could not see her expression. "It's a girl thing," she said and went to the armor. "Have you ever seen weapons like these, ever?" After a pause she repeated, "Ever?"

"No."

Her eyes lost focus as she peered into the shadows. "From before the Wandering," she whispered. "The Book of Chaos."

"What?"

*Will he think me crazy?* "This could be the Old Knowledge, Martin."

"Those are legends, like dragons and magic."

"How can you tell it's not magic?" she said as she picked up a book of maps and leafed through it. "How can you tell if the words when spoken can conjure something, make something wonderful happen, if the words can kill or bring life?"

"Huh?"

She put the book aside and grabbed another book with pictures and runes. "What would you call someone who made the land twice as productive?"

He frowned again and shrugged. "A good farmer?"

"Five times as productive?" she said but Martin did not reply. "How about someone who made wheat grow in the desert?"

"A magician."

"What would a parent give if they could save one of their children from consumption? Two children?"

"Everything."

"And what of the person who could save them all?" She dropped her gaze. *Or save one woman from bleeding to death from a crossbow wound.*

Martin's eyes widened. "A magician. It would be magic!" He jumped to his feet. "A miracle!" He surveyed the cache as if for the first time. "There might be miracles in every book."

She nodded and put the picture book with the atlas. *Is this my "mountain of gold?" What did it cost me to find it: years of my life, the trust of my father? And what will I give up to keep it?*

"We must tell the people," he said.

"Wait. Why aren't they already aware of this?"

He cocked his head with a quizzical expression as if she did not understand where they were. "They've been hidden, buried."

"Not the books. I mean . . . I mean the knowledge. We can't do the things illustrated here. No one can make sculptures like this or even make the books that might teach us how. What happened?"

He shook his head.

"And why hide them? Who did they hide all this from? Think about the tiles outside that opened the door. Who wouldn't know something as common as the crop seasons? People who live on the ice or the ocean, that's who. And those during the Chaos who 'lived in perpetual winter.' The Wandering ended when people began to grow crops. This was meant for us, Martin. Of this age when we know the crop seasons."

"We need to tell everyone."

Diana sat on a stack of books with her chin on her hand and frowned.

"Not yet. What would our enemies do if their swords could break ours or their catapults loft boulders with twice the range and accuracy?" She frowned. "Do the priests recognize what this is?"

"None that I'm aware of, but Bishop Rochfield is crafty. He came here before the siege that felled the Imperator and survived it. Is this so precious he'd risk his life?"

"Knowledge is power."

"If this is true," he said, "then Branwyn is the most valuable rock in all the lands."

*Or the second most valuable if Mokdar has a similar cache.* She nodded. "Only if it stays safe. There are those who would burn these for their baths." Diana stopped. *I've said too much.*

His eyes narrowed. "That's absurd."

"Don't be naïve. Some resist the change that knowledge brings. Others will kill to control it." She held up the atlas and picture book. "These may be the keys to our future and our past. If an enemy was aware this was in our hands, they would capture it or destroy it to keep it from us." *As the Sulerians would surely do. And anyone aligned with them.*

She paused again. "Will you promise to keep our secret?"

"Of course, but we must tell someone. This is too important."

"Not yet, Martin. We don't know who to trust or—"

A door creaked from a different entrance behind the shelves, and torchlight flickered in a soft breeze from around the corner.

"Quick. Hide!" Martin whispered. "If we're separated, meet me at the Academy tonight or the orphanage near the market tomorrow morning." He opened a book and sat on the stack while Diana dropped the books and hid behind the shelf of weapons where she could still see Martin.

"What are you doing here?" a voice boomed as the light turned the corner into the room.

Martin stood and bowed. "I'm sorry, Your Holiness, is this off limits?" Martin opened his eyes wide and feigned innocence.

*"Your Holiness," that's Bishop Rochfield! S*he shrunk even smaller in her hiding place.

Rochfield walked over to Martin and scanned the room. "It's dangerous for novices to rout about in the ruins. Something might happen to you, and we'd never find you again."

"Yes sir," Martin said.

*Does he understand Rochfield's threat? The bishop can make anyone disappear if he wants to, and no one would notice a missing monk—or a missing farm girl.*

"What's your name, monk?"

"Martin, sir."

"And what brings you here?"

"Curiosity. My duties are limited and boring."

The bishop picked up a book and shook it at Martin. "Skill requires diligence, not curiosity, monk. And how does your mentor give you time to prowl in the cata-combs?"

"It's my day off, sir."

In a skeptical tone, the bishop scanned the room. "I wasn't aware monks were granted days off. So what've you learned here?"

"Nothing, sire, it's all incomprehensible, but the illustrations are well wrought. I can make up my own stories to fit the pictures." Martin lowered his voice and took on a childish grin. "And the crypt is creepy and mysterious."

Rochfield stared at him as if waiting for him to confess to a crime.

"Come monk, your studies await," the bishop said and took Martin by the collar from the room, snuffing the torches as they left.


Before the last of the light disappeared, Diana oriented herself to the door through which she entered and noted a route to reach it. When the other door clicked shut behind Martin and Rochfield, she was alone in the dark. After remaining still for a few minutes, she made her way to the door, where she lit a torch with a sparker and retraced her way out.

Leaving the crypt was easier than entering as each door offered no resistance to exit. At the last door she returned the keys. As soon she passed the gate, she dropped the cassock, and walked back to the Academy.

Martin was not there at the double doors of the lecture hall, but Father Dorian was.

"Your absences are troubling, young woman," Dorian said. "You attend at my discretion. If you cannot—"

"She has been on errands at my behest, Dorian," Prince Eric said.

Diana smiled at the sound of his voice and turned to see him and Steven approach.

"I'm sure you can excuse her this time," Eric said.

"Of course, Your Highness, but please advise me in advance."

"If that's in any way possible," the prince replied.

The priest smiled and bowed but gave Diana a side eye as he walked past.

"How gallant of you to intervene," she said and tipped her head away to hide her blush.

Eric bowed. "My duty, milady."

Her heart beat louder. "And what brings you here so late?"

"I came to invite the bishop to lunch with the queen. So what adventures did you and Martin have without me?"

"An exploration into the ruins, Your Highness."

*He should know about the library. But can I trust him and his parents? I told Martin to be silent until we can be sure of who has been hiding such an immense secret.*

"But I fear Martin may be in trouble with the bishop."

"I will enquire about him. Princes have few friends, and—"

She stopped listening. *Is this my excitement over the books, or . . .*

"What did you mean when you said we'd meet Sunday?" she asked with a timid smile. "The Academy is closed and a prince in the marketplace would be odd."

"A surprise," he said. "And I can't disclose it."

*For me?* "I'll be at services at the cathedral Sunday. If—"

The afternoon bell interrupted, and she took a step back. "I'm sorry, but I must leave now to catch my ride home."

"Let me escort you, milady," Eric said, stepping toward her and offering his arm.

She blushed again but shook her head.

Eric kept his arm out. "I insist."

She could not politely refuse a prince's chivalry, so first she grabbed Steven's arm and then Eric's and the three of them left the Cathedral quarter.

Diana dropped their arms before the Town Center and walked with her hands behind her back. But she could not ignore Eric's nearness: wanting to walk closer to him, wanting to be alone to sit and talk, or just be with him.

*And a surprise, for me? Uh-oh. No fantasies now. What will people say now that the prince is seen twice with a farm girl?*

"If anyone asks," Eric said, "I'll say I heard your cry for help and rushed to assist. The brigands attacked you, thinking you were easy prey." He thrust and parried with an imaginary sword. "It was a tough battle, but Steven and I bested them, and the cowards ran off." With one hand on his sword hilt, he punched Steven in the arm with the other hand. "What do you think?" To which his bodyguard shook his head.

"Eric, you don't have a mark on you," Diana said.

"Well, even more evidence of our skill." He reached down and took a handful of dirt and threw it at his breeches. Then he raised one arm and theatrically pointed to the dirt on his leg with the other. "There, see? Signs of a struggle," he said and flung dirt on Steven too, which triggered a frown.

Eric glanced at Diana. "Oh, my. You're still in shock now, yes, yes, your legs are trembling."

She played along and put the back of her hand to her forehead pretending to swoon. "Oh, my heroes," she said, smiling, and Steven prepared to catch her fall.

Just before they reached the Market, Steven stopped, and Eric hesitated a step later. "Well, I'll leave you here in the safety of the crowd. Steven beckons." He leaned over to whisper to her. "A wench waits for him, and I delay." In a normal voice he said, "Well, you're up to something, and I'll enjoy prying it out of you."

"Do your best," Diana said and curtsied. "And a surprise Sunday?"

Eric bowed and put his arm around Steven's shoulder. "Yes," he said and left.

Smiling, she turned to meet Anne. But on her first step she lost her smile at the thought of Martin in the hands of the most mysterious man in Branwyn, Bishop Rochfield.

# Chapter 23
## Shadows

"Mr. Green-hat waits for you, dear," Cirka said while pouring tea into Grimes's porcelain cup and adding sugar with a gold spoon.

The thief, unshaven in wrinkled clothing, entered the room, took off his hat, and stood across from Grimes. A sling held his arm, and a bandage covered his head.

"You were supposed to come back to me last night," Grimes said, reached into his desk, and opened a leather purse holding delicate instruments of torture.

The thief's eyes opened wide as he raised the sling. "I was indisposed, sire. I been in the hospital, where the Sisters of Mercy took care of me."

"Not looking where you were going?"

"No sire. Ran into traps on my way out, traps meant for men, not animals."

Grimes shook his head again and cleaned his fingernails with a needle designed to be driven beneath them. "Did you discover anything in your search of the girl's farm?"

"Nothing that ain't in the market right outside your door, and the cheap end at that. They live like paupers. Must have all their money in those horses a' theirs."

"No scrolls or letters?"

"I didn't find none there neither."

"You're sure?" Grimes asked.

The scruffy man squinted and straightened his back. "Beggin' your pardon, sire. I'm a professional and the value of things and their scarcity is my business, or I'd not be making a livin.' I tell you there was nothing unusual except there weren't nothing worth stealin'. Only a silver arrowhead that might be worth a night of pleasure. Nothing else worth selling in town, if'n I'd a mind to, that is."

"Well, did you find something which we might use to discover where she's from?"

"Only this, sire, and not knowing if it'll help." He reached into his pocket and threw a ring of braided cord on Grimes's desk. "Nothing else you couldn't find on any farm girl in Antona. Considerin' how stark they live, I'm surprised I found anything a'tall."

Grimes examined the woven ring and pursed his lips. Sitting, he slid a gold piece to the edge of the desk but kept a finger on it.

"Wait," Grimes said when the thief reached for the gold coin. He frowned and twirled the colorful woven band between his thumb and forefinger. He stopped, and his jaw dropped. In haste, he rummaged through a desk drawer, spilling the contents on the floor. Within he found the braided anklet that matched the one in his hand, the one given to him by Kalil, the friend of Garfann Sineura.

Grimes jumped to his feet. "The girl this belongs to, where is she now?" Grimes asked and took the coin back.

"Unknown, sire," the thief said. "But her father, Jon Smyth, haunts the Hogue's Breath."

Grimes scribbled a quick note. "Cirka!"

Cirka leaned in from the adjoining room. "What is it dear?"

"Take this to the sheriff. It's an order to arrest this Jon Smyth person and bring him to me. And send the merchant who waits downstairs here. Hurry!"

He flipped the gold piece to the thief. "Go with her and identify this man."

When Cirka and the thief left, a man in merchant's silks and riding boots entered the office, where Grimes gave him one of the woven anklets.

"Ride to Kalil and tell him I've found the girl they've been searching for."

The scullery maid passed the merchant on his way out. "Dinner, milord," she said. "Beggin' your pardon, soup tonight."

Grimes glared at her and tapped his fingernail on the desk where the maid placed the tray of food.

"I'll take these old dishes," she said and collected the tray from lunch.

Grimes waved his hand. "Out with ya now."

The maid curtsied again, left, and closed the door.

A moment later, Bishop Rochfield entered as Grimes slurped from his spoon, guarding the bowl with his other hand as if the bishop might steal it.

"Greetings, Your Eminence," Grimes said without glancing up from a scroll. "And what brings you?"

"Chancellor, we may have a problem."

Grimes took another slurp of soup and waved his hand to hasten the response. "Yes, yes, go on."

"Her Majesty invited me to lunch."

"And?"

"She also invited Singer."

Grimes inspected the bishop over the rim of his glasses and returned to the scroll and his dinner. "Decline or delay until she leaves. She's a spy from the Order of Ancients, and we don't want her finding out about our treasures."

Rochfield paced in the office. "Of course, but there's more. A young monk has discovered our . . . project."

He sighed and slurped another spoonful. "Isolate him."

"I think he may have told others."

Grimes examined Rochfield again and paused with the spoon in flight. "*Which* others?"

"A young farm girl who attends the Academy," the bishop said.

Grimes grinned, nodded, and finished the spoonful of soup.

"They're friends of Prince Eric."

The chancellor's eyes narrowed, but he remained silent as he returned the spoon to the bowl.

The bishop continued, "We must tell the royals and end this secrecy. It's been long enough. A luncheon with the queen would—"

Grimes rose from his chair and smiled. "No, my friend, we discussed this years ago." He went around the desk to hover near the bishop. "We must keep our prize away from the clumsy and ignorant, especially the royals and the Singer, who might expose it during the performance." He put his hand on the bishop's shoulder, his voice smooth as honey. "No, no, my dear friend. Something so valuable as the secrets of the ages must remain with people like you and me. Only people of learning and intelligence can appreciate its true value and employ it for the betterment of all. Aristocrats and entertainers will only use this for their selfish interests."

Rochfield lowered his eyes and pursed his lips but nodded. "I'll occupy the monk with other duties. And what of the farm girl?"

"I'm taking care of her," Grimes said with a smile and patted the bishop on the shoulder.

# Chapter 24
# Threats

## Red coins

Diana's excitement from the day's adventures migrated to her fingers that drummed on the tailboard of the Buckman's wagon.

*Somewhere in that trove of information may be the means to keep the Sul and Qu from our lands. Once I find it, I can go home.* A thought of Eric came again, and she smiled. *But not too soon. And the opportunities that the cache could provide to citizens like Anne and Martin.*

"The Academy can be good for you," Diana said. "Beyond the chance to meet rich friends."

Anne looked up from reading a scroll. "Like?"

"As a scribe or a tallyman."

Anne pouted. "I already know my numbers, and tallying is boring."

"But it can support you and a family. People won't care you're a woman if you have skills."

Anne smiled and stared back at Branwyn. "Like Gwendolyn and Rowan?"

"Yes. And it's off the farm. There'll be lots of opportunities as the market grows."

But Anne scrunched her face in effort. *She's not listening.*

"The letter f is curled at the top," Diana said as Anne's hand traced the letter. They were hands like her own with chipped fingernails and stains which never washed off, hands just as calloused and stained as when they considered her royalty back home. It hit her again; the fantasy of being more than friends with a prince. But her childhood was no preparation for the intrigues of the aristocracy here, regardless of her father's title. She sighed. *This caterpillar must remain a bug*.

Anne sighed, and Diana guessed her line of thought.

"The aristos aren't who you imagine, Anne."

"Oh, and you're so familiar with them?"

"No, but I've watched them at the Academy. They're like everyone else: some are petty and some nice, others are stupid or dangerous."

Anne grinned. "They look so luscious."

"The perfume and fancy clothes may hide it, but they bathe as often as the stable boys. They just don't worry about food as much."

"I don't worry about food either." Anne shimmied and added a wink. "What a glamorous life it'd be to be a princess."

Diana laughed. "It might not be as exciting as you think."

"And now the royals confide in you too?"

"A guess. Anne, the young aristos may care about us, perhaps even love us, but their parents would never let it be."

"Are they so special?"

"No. We're not special to them. For their families, marriage is economic and political to protect their property and privilege. We add nothing. Like your father tills the soil, their parents till the field of society for opportunity. Their ways are as mysterious to us as ours are to them." She glanced away, realizing she was talking about Eric.

*And what could I do if he were interested? I can't expose myself. Is Eric the only acceptable man for me? Is there no one else in the land who's smart enough, civilized enough, man enough?*

"You'd be special," Anne said. "You're so pretty and smart, you'd have an easy time with them if you tried."

"Beauty is in the heart, not the eyes, Anne. And you've plenty for any man who's looking for it. Patience. Love will find you."

*But what about me?*


When Diana arrived home, she ran to find Jon to tell him about the cache of books, but Jon was not there. The sheep were still in the pasture and his sorrel mare was gone. Inside the small cottage she found it as it was earlier that morning.

Almost.

On the floor in front of her dresser lay a small, dried flower petal; a petal her father once sent her from the battlefront in Derryh. She opened her mother's dragon-tooth box. The silver arrowhead was there with the broken coin from her father but not the braided anklet. *No thief would leave silver behind, and Jon would never touch my things. Who was here?*

She ran outside at the sound of galloping hooves to see dust billowing from the dirt road that caught the fading sun. When Jon turned the road to their ranch, she waved and called to him.

"Jon, I've found something wonderful!"

He jumped off while the horse skidded to a stop. "Buy it quickly," he said and hurried to cool down the mare.

"Don't you want to—"

"Pack up, lass. We need to leave," he said, removing the saddle bags and throwing them on a fence rail.

"No, we can't. We have too much left to do."

He loosened the girth on the saddle and led the mare to the paddock. "It's not your choice or mine. The chancellor advised me that the Royals don't want a peasant for a daughter."

"What? That's absurd!"

He felt the horse's chest. "Not according to Grimes."

"That fool prince just noticed me this week."

"Princess, who are you to this boy?" Jon said, as the mare snorted with impatience.

*Princess?* She took a breath. *This is serious.*

"He's not a boy. He's a captain in the Praetorian Guard and the prince." She caught Jon's frown which made her angrier. "And you're not my father."

"I'm your father when he's not here."

"Then please act a little less like him," she said and went to get water from the trough. "I liked it better when you called me 'lassie'."

He turned to face her. "And what of this prince?"

"I've kept no secrets from you. He's the royals' only surviving child. They've most likely been trying to wed him since he got back from the war, but certainly not to a farm girl. I'm sure he has enough maidens to amuse him, but I seem to be the only one who doesn't go all weak in the knees at his smile." *Though maybe I want to.*

Jon removed the saddle and left the horse to cool off in the corral. Slinging the saddlebags over his shoulder, he stormed into the barn and put both hands on a stall door. He raised his eyes after she closed the barn door behind her. "And . . .?"

She rolled her eyes. "Oh, gosh! Well, he's sooooo cute in his uniform, and he's sooooo smart and he's sooooo strong, he's so . . ." She placed the back of a hand on her forehead and pretended to swoon.

"Princess, this is serious."

"He's a friend, I thought, and not . . . interested in that way."

"Chancellor Grimes thinks otherwise."

"Refuse him. We can't go now. I have something wonderful to tell you."

"It wasn't a request. He arrested me today and ordered me to bring you to him tomorrow. There's a warrant out for you." From within a saddlebag, he removed a small pouch and threw it on the table. "We've been paid, and he'll double that when we see him."

Gold and silver coins spilled from the pouch when she picked it up. "Too much for this ranch," she said. "Even with the livestock."

"He hopes to encourage our cooperation. We're simple ranchers here and any resistance is—"

"This isn't the Imperium. Freemen have a voice here."

"Perhaps. But who will hear it? The chancellor has the ear of the King and commands the police."

Diana examined the coins and spread them around. "Jon, what if . . ." She stopped mid-sentence and backed away, as if a viper slithered among the coins. At the bottom of the pile lay two red coins, contracts of the Assassins Guild.

Her heart stopped. "What are these for?"

"More incentive. They're for us, unless we see him tomorrow. Or if you try to contact Eric again or the Royals. The chancellor made a point of showing them to me before dropping them in the bag."

"And if we appear, he may imprison us."

"Or kidnap you. His true motives may be hidden."

Diana shook her head. "The king and queen wouldn't do this."

"Then who?"

She shrugged. "The aristos detest me . . ."

Angry again, Jon said, "And how does the daughter of a simple rancher rise to their attention?"

". . . and the priest dislikes me," she continued with her head down.

"Lord, girl," he said, exasperated, "have you posted a sign in town of your mischief?"

His bad news swamped her good news, but she persisted. "Please, Jon, there's something I need to say, something I need to tell Papa."

"What, lass?"

"There is no Book of Chaos."

"Just as well. We needn't risk your safety by staying here."

"No, there's no 'Book' anywhere."

"Then we return home."

"No, it's not *a* book, it's *books*. There's an entire cache of them here under the Cathedral, many hundreds, and no one understands them. The texts are all written in different symbols, and no one holds the key to unlock the meaning."

He paused and rubbed his chin. "I see. Yes, we must inform your father."

"We can't bring all the books with us. We must tell the royals."

"How? We're not invited to court."

"The prince."

Jon flipped a red coin. "This is too much of a coincidence. Who was with you when you discovered the cache?"

"A monk named Martin."

"You were seen?"

"The bishop caught him, but—"

"Demons, girl! Now the bishop? Who else have you angered? It's a wonder they didn't hang you on the spot."

"I left unseen."

"Someone saw you together, lass."

"Perhaps the chancellor acts on his own without license from the King."

"Regardless, you're not anonymous anymore, which puts you at risk. We must leave or you'll be in danger."

"I would never tell anyone of our mission, even under torture."

"Your Highness, it's not the information I aim to protect. It's your life."

She warmed at his concern and softened her voice. "But our task is not complete."

"We have enough, lass, and our assignment must continue elsewhere. Now we must run. We leave tomorrow morning to get a head start on the assassins."

"I want to stay, Jon. We only need to find a key—"

"My primary responsibility here is your safety. I won't endanger you for all the books in the land."

She frowned. "Then all our searching was for nothing?"

"By no means. If your assessment of the cache is correct, you found exactly what your mother hoped and confirmed what she feared about the Sul. To complete both missions is rather extraordinary."

She hoped for another possibility, but he shook his head.

"I'm sorry, Your Highness. We must leave."

Dropping her eyes, she nodded and walked outside.


While Jon finished brushing down the mare, Diana sat on the bench beside the barn door as the sun's shadow climbed the banners of Branwyn Castle.

When she first arrived in the South, she prayed they would find the book and return north to Aemgarde without delay. She never imagined she would miss

Branwyn or make friends and never expected any boy or man to pay attention to her. Now she wanted to stay.

*Damn, kill that fantasy, girl!*

Jon stabled the mare and sat next to her.

"My birthday is tomorrow," she said.

"I'm sorry, lassie. It's too dangerous." He put his hand on hers. "We'll celebrate on the road."

A howl echoed from the deep forest to the east and a bleat took her eyes to the sheep crowding near the gate. She rose to herd them into the barn and wiped the tears from her eyes.

"The wolves will be hungry," she said.

## Cabal

Martin followed Bishop Rochfield through a rear door to the cache into the cathedral proper. The bishop gave him no reason for the private audience, and that aroused all the murky corners of Martin's imagination. Unaware of punishments that might await a wayward monk who dug too deep and knew too much, he feared the worst. But since the bishop could find him anywhere in town, running would be fruitless.

"Your curiosity intrigues me, Martin, and I thought we'd have a private chat. I call the cache a reliquerium, reliques stored . . ."

Martin conjured a vision of the bishop's opulent quarters in the shadowy spires of the cathedral. Decorated with the finest treasures from the crypt, the bishop hoarded the magic and kept its bounty from the people. And there, the evil genius used the secrets of the cache to advance his nefarious schemes, in league with the forces of darkness to reap their souls.

These fantasies distracted him from confronting even worse fears until they reached the bishop's private quarters. Opening the door released a cloying aroma that addled his senses.

Oil lamps threw shadows across the room, and wisps of incense danced with images of Jinns and spirits. As his eyes adjusted, and the fumes cleared, Martin beheld a sight more astonishing than anything he feared.

It was ordinary.

In front of him lay only the pragmatic furniture of the cleric and executive who lived here, with stacks of scrolls on every flat surface.

Martin frowned. *A man with the power to remove God's grace, sanctify a marriage, or crown a king should live in splendor.*

Three books with similar drawings but different text lay open upon a table as if they were ordinary scrolls not priceless artifacts. Above them hovered Bishop Rochfield without his formal robes and instead a threadbare brown cassock.

The bishop turned, and on a hook by the door hung a ring of keys with filigree that matched the locks in the cache of books.

"Martin. Sit, please." Rochfield paused for the briefest of moments to clear away scrolls from a chair. "You've shown a unique curiosity and initiative about the contents of . . . the cache which I want to harness." He paused and leaned over with his palms on the desk. "I invite you to help me and a precious few others in our investigations."

Martin's jaw dropped.

"You realize what an honor this is, monk. Only a few priests have access to the reliquerium. Never have I granted a monk, much less a novice like you, such a privilege. What have you to say?"

Martin raised his eyebrows. "Why have the town folk never heard of the cache?"

"Good! The inquisitive mind starts with a question. Why? Because the texts must be kept hidden and secret."

"And why is that?"

With his hands behind his back, the bishop paced. "We're afraid this knowledge will frighten the powerful and superstitious. They may claim it's the devil's work that will corrupt the people and destroy it before we understand what's in it."

*He thinks like Diana. But who's "we"?*

The bishop leaned over the table again. "Do I have your oath to silence?" Moving another scroll, he exposed a copy of the Book of the One God.

Without hesitating, Martin put his hand on the book. "Yes, of course. I swear I will tell no one."

*But such a vow cannot bind my prior conversations with Diana. And if he asks, I must lie.*

As if using his mind to claw out Martin's secret, the bishop squinted and stared at him. Rochfield sighed and nodded, then came around to Martin's side of the table. Leaning against the edge, he opened his hand in front of the three books laying there.

"Do you realize what lies before you, monk?"

Martin shook his head. "Books with pictures, printed by some device other than hand, in text I don't understand, like those in the crypt."

"Based on the illustrations, I think these three texts address the same subject. My theory is people today speak a language similar to that transcribed here, but we can't interpret it. Our written languages are distinct." Martin nodded, and the bishop continued, "This is your new duty, monk, to make sense of this."

"How am I to do that?"

The bishop raised his hands in the air. "I can only guess! Perhaps search for some used words or series of characters within the words."

Rochfield spoke with eyes wide and face open though not smiling, like a child at play. At that moment, Martin found it impossible to believe Rochfield conspired for his soul.

"Why not hunt for a book with only pictures and captions?" the monk asked.

"We've been searching for something like that but haven't discovered it."

*But Diana did, right off.*

Martin inspected the books with printing so precise that individual symbols were not just similar but identical.

"Is this the Old Knowledge?" Martin asked.

The bishop studied him as he paced near his desk, then walked to the open window through which the three moons shone and recited.

*"There was History before history,*
*When Juro wore our civilization like a crown,*
*And women flew like birds.*
*A time when we knew the ages of the stars,*
*Before we forgot who we were . . ."*

Rochfield turned to him. "Show me what you know of the moons."

Martin opened his mouth, but the bishop silenced him with a wave of his hand. "Don't tell me. Show me."

The monk scanned the room and found three cups and a dinner plate left from lunch. He placed them on the table with the plate in the middle and the cups a few feet away. "This is our world here," he said, pointing to the plate, "and the moons circle it. Lon is the largest moon, furthest away and slowest. Elein is the next largest, and her brother, the War Moon, Fures, is closest and fastest."

"Round, or flat like the plate?"

"All round, like river stones," Martin replied.

"Yes, that's splendid. Now, how did you come by this understanding?" He crossed his arms over his chest and grinned.

Martin lifted an eyebrow. "What do you mean? Everyone knows."

The bishop came near and leaned against the table again. "*How* does everyone know? What principle guides the motion of the moons?"

"Principle?"

"What rules say the moons should move around our world? And what information do we have that our world is round like the plate?"

The questions had never occurred to Martin. "The scholars reasoned this out?"

Rochfield laughed. "Martin, no one can be more wrong more often than a scholar. What evidence can you cite that the world is round or that the moons move around it?"

"Perhaps God directs them?"

"In the holy books," the bishop said, "both here and in Suleria, they're mere discs in the heavens whose positions are ordained by God, like the kites of children. Some in the far south say our world is flat. And what's to prove them wrong?"

Martin pursed his lips. "Perhaps I'm just ignorant."

"No, Martin," the bishop said with a generous smile. "*No one* knows how we know. *No one.*"

Martin gave Rochfield a blank stare.

"We believe these things, but we don't know where the belief came from. No one has the skills to tell us if they're true or not. How did we find out? Where's the evidence?"

Martin shrugged.

The bishop resumed pacing, his eyes wide. "It's my belief we once possessed such evidence, but we lost it.

And we forgot the methods to gather the evidence. And because we forgot, we can't build upon it to something greater. We struggle here with sickness and starvation and war and pestilence. Yet we have no weapons to fight them, no building blocks with which to build a better world."

Rochfield gazed at his closed fists. "We once held it, here, in our hands, the means to understand, to treat disease, to avoid starvation." The bishop stared at Martin and opened his hands. "This was God's gift, and we let it slip through our fingers."

*Rochfield speaks from his heart, but not to me. Perhaps to God. If this is a conspiracy, I want to be part of it.*

"To answer your question, Martin, it may well be the Old Knowledge. I'm not sure. Old, it certainly is, and preserved by great effort. As a young monk, I searched the entire South for artifacts like those in the reliquerium after a rune coin intrigued me. They called me Tobias back then. Over all my travels, I found nothing to match the miraculous artifacts here. I'm sure people of this age did not create what lies within. And I'm certain this is knowledge."

"Knowledge of magic?" Martin asked with a glimmer in his eyes.

"No, no, Martin. Nothing so small. The power of magic is limited by the spell or the wizard who casts it. But knowledge can build upon itself forever. And that's what I think we have here. I'm convinced it's comprehensible, and I need your help to make sense of it." He pulled up a chair and sat with his hands folded in his lap. "Martin, you've shown more initiative in the last weeks than my gaggle of priests have shown in years. Join me."

Martin was not sure if principles or the hand of God guided the motions of the sun and moons. He was a farm boy who failed so miserably his poor father sent him away. He doubted his ability to help the bishop fulfill his dream to make the reliquerium comprehensible.

But Diana believed it was knowledge, and Martin believed in her.

"Yes, of course," Martin said.

"Good. These are your duties now, and no hanging about the Academy anymore. This project should occupy all your time and attention. I expect to see you here at this desk unless you're at meals, prayers, or in bed."

Martin nodded. He had found his purpose.

And Rochfield had found a way to keep Martin away from Grimes's assassins.

# Chapter 25
# Whirlwind

## Deception

*It's my birthday, but I can't tell anyone,* Diana thought as the sunrise shone through the window. She threw a jerkin into a carpetbag, sat on her bed, and sulked.

*I'm eighteen today and should be in my full power. Now my party is canceled, and I must run like a dog. I have real friends now, and how can I leave without telling Eric about . . .*

She dismissed the fantasy again with a wave of her hand.

*. . . about the cache of books.*
*It's not about Eric.*
But it was.
*It's not about an impossible romance.*
But it was.
*And I will miss the surprise Eric teased me with.*

"Argh, Grimes!" she said, fuming that a bureaucrat could drive her away.

She stood and threw another blouse into the bag but paused. *But why does he demand I report today and need assassins to guarantee it? Two farmers can't be that important. So what's this about?*

She frowned, knitted her brow, and paced her room. A minute later she stopped, and her mouth fell open. She hurried to Jon who packed the wagon in the barn.

"Jon, I think Eric and the royals are in danger. We must warn them before we leave."

Jon did not stop packing. "We're ranchers, lassie, without influence at court. And as far as we know, we're under a death sentence from the people we would petition."

"I think this is all Grimes's doing."

He stopped and frowned at her. "Say more."

"The Royals and Grimes must know Eric is not interested in me beyond friendship. All they'd have to do is ask him."

"We can't be sure until we know who commissioned the red coins. So why? And why now?"

"It's the cache of books. You're right. All this can't be a coincidence. The bishop knows about it, and he meets with Grimes. But the royals don't."

"They told you somehow?"

"No, but learning is a pet project of the queen, and if she knew she'd make it public. And Eric's aware I'm looking for books. Why would Grimes have us report today and not tomorrow or the next day? He must surely be busy with the performance."

"The cache again."

She nodded. "The royals don't know about it, and Grimes doesn't want us to tell them today. Why?"

Jon paused and narrowed his eyes. "Because it won't matter tomorrow."

"Right. He's planning something tonight. You yourself said that the performance is a perfect time for trouble."

"He can't do it alone. The public seems fine with George's rule."

"But the aristos grumble, and Grimes commands the police. The horsemen with Quarajii boots hang around Grimes's residence near the market. The royals are in danger, Jon, and we need to warn them before the performance."

Jon leaned against the wagon and folded his arms. "It's dangerous to insert ourselves into the middle of a revolt, lass. We still don't know the intrigues which ensnare the royals. And we don't have Company A on hand for protection."

"We can ask Eric to determine that first."

"Sons have little sway in politics, lass."

"He's also a captain in the Praetorian Guard. Once they grant us an audience, I'll announce our roles as emissaries."

"An audience could mean an execution," Jon said. "How can we trust them? You've never met them. They're from the Imperium and have no history of freedom. Without a tyrant to command them they can't tie their own shoes."

"Eric's folks were barons from the west, not the sheep of the Imperium."

"The chancellor said he acted in their name."

She crossed her arms and furrowed her brow. "I know the prince and don't believe his virtue arose in a poisoned family."

"Diana, I'm sorry, this is too risky."

Her face reddened, and she stomped her foot. "This is not your risk to take! I am the emissary of King Richard and of age now. I'm your princess and will make my own decisions." She recognized her imprudence and took a breath to calm down.

"Is there a conflict between my father's wishes and mine?" she asked.

Jon laughed. "No. My duty is clear. I have the king's charge to protect you. When he relieves me of that responsibility, I'll bow to you despite your petulance. My authority comes from your father, not you, and does not require your consent."

"Jon, I'm—"

He paused for a moment and then bowed from the waist. "It's your life that concerns me, Your Highness, not your obedience. I'm your guardian, and I am here by choice in the service of our king. In any fight I am your ally, not your commander . . . or your subject."

She blushed, shamed by his sincerity, and she dropped her gaze with guilt for her rashness. "I'm sorry, truly, Jon. I was rude and spoke in anger. But I do intend to warn them."

Jon smiled. "Your will seems up to this adventure. Well, if we are to enter the lion's den, we'll need a plan we can survive. Finish up and we'll chart our course."

When Diana returned to her bedroom to finish packing, Jon went to a cabinet, and with a damp cloth, covered the cake that Anne's mother had made. The box of candles, ribbons, and bunting he placed in the cabinet beside the wooden tiara he whittled for her and meant to celebrate her maturity. The present from town, he placed in his pocket to give her when there might be idle time to celebrate her eighteenth birthday.


As noon approached, Diana and Jon took the East Road to Branwyn in the wagon drawn by their two best horses. In the event their plan to warn Eric did not work, they packed the essentials needed for the road and left a note with instructions for Tom and Anne. But Diana was confident she and Martin could contact Eric, either at the castle or the performance.

Along the road, shadows from the towering clouds swept over colorful tents pitched in newly cleared fields. Above each tent, pennants snapped to announce the nobles from far away who would attend the performance and the ball.

"George wouldn't tolerate the nobles squatting on farmland," Diana said.

Jon nodded. "They must be wealthy to pay for the crops the farmers lost." He raised his eyes to the sky. "Let's pray the rain doesn't cancel the show and drive the royals back to the keep."

He turned to her and smiled. "And next time you give a command, Princess, presume obedience. Don't stomp your feet. It looks like a tantrum."

"Yes, sir," she said quietly and raised the hood of her cape over her head as a rider approached. As he passed, she noticed the epaulets of a royal courier, who unbeknownst to them, headed to their farm.

At the Branwyn gate, Diana smiled. "The lion's den. Here we are, under a sentence of death, and I just might have my birthday party yet."

Jon glanced at her and returned the smile but did not confirm her hope.


Diana tracked Martin to the orphanage near the market. There he tried without success to wrangle a pack of ill-behaved children who screamed and ran from him and then pulled his cassock from behind. After drawing his attention with a wave, he led her to a corner, where they hugged.

"I worried for you when you didn't return to the academy," Diana said.

Martin glanced at the door and lowered his voice. "Don't tell anyone you found me here. The bishop wants me working in his offices and I snuck out."

"The bishop didn't punish you?"

"It turns out he's as curious as we are about the books and invited me to help him. This is a great opportunity for us."

"It is. But I might not be able to accept."

"What do you—"

She touched his forearm. "Martin, I need your help."

"Wait." He turned round to reach for a satchel. "I have something wonderful to show you."

"Later. First, I need a favor." She showed him her tickets. "I need you to escort me to the performance today."

He blushed and dropped his gaze. "I think your invitation is meant for another."

She replied with a coy smile. "Perhaps, Martin, but I have no way to reach Eric. Please, I need your help desperately."

"Anything."

"Will you be my companion?"

He nodded. "Of course."

"Second, I think Eric and his folks will be in peril tonight and I need to warn them," she said and outlined her fears for that evening. "How can we contact him?"

"I'll send the monks to locate him and give him a message where to reach me."

"Good," she said and gave him an envelope. "Third, I need you to manage the contents of this envelope for me and execute the instructions."

"What lies within?"

"That's not important just now," she said and spun her cover story. "My aunt is sick, and our family calls us away with short notice. Our neighbors . . . you've met my neighbor, Anne Buckman?"

He blushed again. "Yes. In the market."

"I left a note for Anne and her father to tend the ranch in our absence, but there are other matters. If you don't see me at the Academy or in the market next week, open the envelope and follow the instructions."

"You say that as if you might not return."

"I only expect to be gone a few days, but she might be sicker than they think." She smiled and took his hand. "Please don't worry, but you must promise to follow those directions. Promise me."

"Yes, of course, I promise. About that, I found something," he said, trying to wedge his way into her string of requests. He turned to the cloth satchel at his side and reached into it.

She nodded, but a man in the colorful silks of a merchant distracted her. Below the hem of his pantaloons appeared the cuffs of leather breeches and boots rather than embroidered sandals. This was where similar men in riding boots had chased her earlier that week. A pretty woman opened the door, scanned the street, and put a finger to her lips.

"There's an odd couple," Diana said. "Whose door is that?"

"It's to Chancellor Grimes's apartments. That's Cirka, his mistress. She helps here in the orphanage."

Cirka turned, squinted into the sun, and walked their way.

"A pleasant lady, really, and—"

Diana jumped to her feet and raised her hood again. "Tell no one I was here. Don't forget. This is vital: It must be the prince, and it must be before the performance." Martin nodded, and she hurried away through the back door.

Diana collided with a noisy jumble of people at the Town Center. Tables and chairs surrounded the fronts of taverns and inns, which narrowed the torus between them and the central park. And the performance drew the clowns and street vendors, turning the promenade into a turbulent crowd.

With the hood of her cape over her head, Diana elbowed her way through the crowd to the best guarded of the private seating and guessed it was meant for the Royals. She headed to the benches nearby and sat with other people to not appear alone and draw unwanted attention. Optimistic about her success, she smiled and waited for word from Martin.

While she sat, the benches filled, and the open seating area packed to the ring of columns. The noise increased with the chattering of excited adults and children, and each peek of the sun through the darkening clouds was a turn of the hourglass as the time to speak with Eric ran out.

It struck Diana that contacting Eric and getting protection from the royals was not much more than a hope. Still she clung to that hope, that her 18th birthday might be special, that her luck would change, and she could stop hiding and live a normal life.

Because of her indiscretions, they were running for their lives again, this time with a plan that depended on chance. Still, Jon supported her. The man who traveled a thousand miles and crossed the Spine with her; the man who took years from his life to protect her, stood by her. Indulging her hopes, he helped her create a workable plan, not because it was his duty or because he believed it would succeed. He helped her because he cared for her as only her father had.

*And because he couldn't stop me.*

*Whatever happens tonight, I can depend on Jon. Yet just this morning in anger I insulted his judgment. There I am again, unable to hold my temper or my tongue.*

A rumble of faraway thunder brought her eyes skyward, where tall clouds masked the afternoon sun. She crossed her fingers to hold back the rain that might drive the royals indoors and dash her remaining hope.

The first bell rang, and Diana turned around to spot Martin elbowing a path toward her with the satchel slung from his shoulder and a small bag. Hope sparked briefly until he shook his head, and the creases returned to her brow.

"I couldn't reach him," he said. "They're keeping the entire household sequestered. They won't even forward a message to him. I still have friends trying to contact him, but I'm afraid this possibility is closed to us." He opened the bag. "Want a roast chestnut?"

She shook her head. "Perhaps we can reach him during the show." *But if I do, will the royals take me as the threat Grimes warned about?*

\*\*\*

From a private platform opposite the stage from the Royals' box, Grimes and Cirka met with the tall man in the wide-brimmed hat.

"What do you mean she's not there?" Grimes said, jaw clenched and eyes narrowed.

"We searched the farm and found no one," the man said. "The wagon and horses are gone."

The chancellor paced with a hand behind his back. "They must have run early." He had converted a liability into an asset, but the asset slipped his grasp.

The cathedral bell sounded as the wind picked up.

"South and east are open country and their most likely path. Send your men now to retrieve them."

"And if they resist?"

"You have the contract," Grimes said and threw him a purse. "Here's an incentive for speed."

The assassin opened the purse, smiled, and turned to go, but Cirka whispered in Grimes's ear.

"Wait," Grimes said. "Bring the girl to me alive."

## Chaos

A bell rang at the Town Center where Praetorians surrounded the royals' box and hustled the king and queen within. Prince Eric followed, and Martin stood and waved his arms, but a nearby guard threatened him with a spear. As the sky darkened with thunder clouds, ushers lit the torches, and the crowd found their seats.

The second bell rang, and the crowd hushed. Diana smiled as Ash, the dwarf, appeared wearing a jester's costume with bells jingling on his hat and shoes. To the front of the stage he pushed a tall stool, squeaking and scraping across the floor, and climbed it. When he reached the seat, quiet returned. With one hand on his heart and the other hand opened wide, he cleared his throat and spoke.

"Welcome to the land of Granloren. Open your hearts to a time not so long ago and a place beyond the hill where two young lovers changed the world forever." Behind him, the curtain opened to a party scene with scores of dancers in traditional dress, but frozen in place.

"Welcome to a place called Teurin!" he shouted. The stage erupted with folk music and dancing, as stage-hands picked up the ladder and dwarf and hustled them off the stage.

Entering from stage left came Singer, arm-in-arm with a handsome young man, two lovers caught between feuding families and a war for survival, to begin the Tragedy of Christine and Rodrigo.

And Diana's time to contact would end before the performance.

A flash of lightning and boom of thunder brought her attention to the sky. There, above her to the opposite side of the audience, stood a man and a woman.

*Cirka! Then the man next to her must be . . .*

She spun away and cowered.

"What is it?" Martin asked and Diana pointed her thumb at the platform.

"That's Cirka," Martin said and turned away as well. "With Chancellor Grimes."

\*\*\*

From the private platform, Grimes sat with Cirka standing behind him, observing the show. Below, in the front of the stage, the dwarf reappeared in a change of clothes as the director. On stage, Singer led her dance partner to a corner where they schemed to elope to escape their feuding families.

But Grimes's interest was the royals' security.

Along the thoroughfare between the royals' box and the castle keep, stood armed praetorians. Swordsmen lined the street, and archers kneeled on the rooftops.

"It won't matter," he said and smiled.

He stood and waved his arms to direct his own performance. Lifting his hands as if conjuring demons from the earth, he said, "Chaos in the crowd to block your escape." He brought his hands together and made one into a fist as lightning crackled through the clouds above. "Then caught like a fish in a net." He turned to the south, extended his arm, and brought his hand to his chest as thunder boomed. "And a tidal wave that crashes upon the walls, rushes through the gates, and swamps the town before anyone can stop it."

He sat again with a smug grin, and Cirka put her hands on his shoulders.

"And I'll save them all from drowning."

"Who's that sitting with the monk?" Cirka asked, but Grimes dismissed her with a wave of his hand.

\*\*\*

In the audience below, Diana was at the edge of panic.

*It should've worked. I would enjoy the show and talk to Eric and his parents, and they would protect us. Now every move I make is under the gaze of the man who contracted for my death.*

Eric sat in front of her and to her left, but he would need to turn around where the glare of the torches would hide her. In her imagination, she tested methods to get Eric's attention without her arrest and subsequent surrender to the Chancellor. And she tried each.

A guard refused a note which Martin tried to pass. Diana stood once to wave, and another time stumbled through the benches, attracting only the annoyance of their neighbors. Her options faded as the clouds brought an early evening.

On stage, the scene shifted to Rodrigo delaying his escape with Christine and volunteering to fight in the defense of Teurin. But Diana could not escape until she contacted Eric.

At the end of the bench closest to the box seats sat a merchant dressed in silks but leather breeches and boots below the hem.

*This can't be coincidence.*

"Martin. Work your way down the bench near the aristos. If you approach them, the praetorian will stop you—"

He furrowed his brow. "Or kill me."

"—and you can catch Eric's attention."

"But if the guard kills me."

"Be resourceful."

"What if Grimes sees us?"

"We're out of options, Martin. Move."

"But if—"

Lightning flashed and thunder boomed as the play reenacted the Battle of Teurin on stage. Diana and Martin would now need to compete with both the weather and the performance.

As they worked their way down the row, two more oddly dressed merchants moved up from farther behind. A momentary gust of wind fluttered the robes of one and exposed his boots and the paint scuffed from the heel—riding boots with silver tooled in the heel. She froze. Martin glanced at her, but she shook her head and pushed him forward into the aisle next to the boxes and the guards. Approaching the praetorian caused him to put his hand to his sword hilt, and she paused so as not to startle him.

"Sir, aren't weapons banned from the audience?" She tipped her head and glanced over her shoulder.

Following her gaze, the praetorian caught the glint of a metallic edge under the silks of the merchant and walked over to him. As the praetorian approached, he signaled the robed man to stand. The merchant smiled and opened his arms to show he was harmless.

But when the praetorian was a yard away, the merchant drew a dagger from his sleeve and stabbed the guard in the chest repeatedly. The victim was too shocked to cry out in alarm, and the attacker caught him before he fell. The battle on stage was loud and riveting, and only she and Martin witnessed the murder, him with a hand to his mouth, and her looking for a weapon.

From beneath his robes, the attacker pulled a crossbow and whistled, whereupon a score of phony merchants stood and approached the royals' box. Unable to stop them all, she grabbed the bag of nuts from Martin's hand and spilled them on the ground, tripping six into each other. She pushed the nearest attacker into the crowd, which spoiled his aim and caused other patrons to rise and protest. His companion grinned with broken teeth just before he punched her in the face and she fell, stunned. The public nearby stood to escape the scuffle, which was all it seemed to be, and made it impossible for the killers to get a clean shot at the royals.

"Alarm, alarm!" Martin yelled, and praetorians scrambled to shield the Royal Family from the melee.

Still on the ground, Diana could not escape the killer above her who aimed his crossbow and smirked. In that moment, a blinding blue-green flash lit the Town Center like a lightning bolt: the same kind of flash that stunned Singer and the giant while riding in a wagon as it passed her ranch.

*\*\**

On the platform, Grimes smiled when movement appeared near the royals' theater box, but he soon frowned. There in the middle of the fray stood a girl and a monk who matched the description given by the thief and Bishop Rochfield, a girl who was supposed to be gone. This was not the climax he had planned.

"That's her!" Cirka said.

A blue-green flash lit the audience, and the girl and monk disappeared. The melee subsided, and the praetorians resumed control. But when Grimes scanned the royals' box, the Soria family from the performance sat in the places of King George, Helena, and Eric.

"A pox on that girl!" he cursed, turned to the assassin, and took him by the lapel. "I don't care if the Empress herself wants her. Find the girl who wears this." He thrust Diana's ankle bracelet into the man's hand. "And exercise the contract. Now!"

# Chapter 26
# Hunt

At the blue-green flash, everyone who saw it froze. But Diana did not see the flash and remained unaffected. On her hands and knees, she scrambled between the forest of legs, stood, grabbed the monk by the collar, and ran for the exits.

Diana dragged Martin through the crowd along the Promenade, aiming for the Marketplace to meet Jon. That required crossing the thoroughfare which led to the Castle, but there she ran into a thick knot of people. Boring her way into the crowd, she confronted a line of uniformed guards.

"Not this way," the guard said and pushed her back with a thick baton. Above her, archers manned the rooftops, and behind her, the killers forced their way through the crowd toward her.

*Trapped.*

Just then a cordon of praetorians rushed past and at the fore ran Prince Eric.

"Eric!" she shouted.

He turned his head but did not stop and turned away again before she waved.

"Nuts," she said and pushed Martin to the edge of the street and into a crowded tavern: the Hogue's Breath Inne.

Through a sea of pipe smoke and liquor fumes, Diana dragged Martin. As she passed the bar, Martin slipped on spilled ale and fell on his face at the feet of a beautiful woman. The woman turned to the commotion at the door they came through and signaled three burly men who rushed to the door. She leaned over to help Diana with Martin, and they locked eyes.

The woman smiled as she helped Martin to his feet. "Hurry."

"Thank you," Diana said and tugged Martin to the back of the tavern.

Outside the back door, she threw her cape in a trash pile and blocked the door with a board. Running south down the alley, they checked each door they passed and opened those they could to leave false trails. When they turned the corner, Diana stopped in a shadowed doorway to assess their situation while Martin caught his breath.

Her eye was swelling shut and her cheek ached. With every step it throbbed with pain, but they could not stop now.

"Better drop the satchel," she said.

"No, can't," he gasped and shook his head.

"We'll never elude them with you exhausted so soon." *I can escape alone to meet Jon, but Martin will never make it.*

"You go. Leave me," Martin said.

"No."

"Then where?"

"Nowhere, Martin. The police report to Grimes, which makes them untrustworthy. And he works for the king and queen, so we can't trust them either."

"The Cathedral," Martin gasped.

She nodded. The labyrinth of alleys and hidden places would give them the advantage. But to get there they would need to run past the killers and back through the crowded Center. And she did not trust the bishop, so sanctuary might be a trap.

During a flash of lightning, she saw the barbarians turn the corner to the alley and investigate the open doorways.

"We won't make it," she said. "We need to hide."

She nudged Martin beyond the thoroughfare and into the Artisan Quarter, where they would have a better chance of hiding. After a quick diversion through a small park, she pushed the wheezing monk up the outside staircase to the roof. There they could avoid the street crowds and put more distance between them and their pursuers. But as they ran across the rooftops, lightning flashed and exposed them.

*But where to hide?*

The gathering winds carried the applause and shouts of encore from the Center. But they could not stop. They reached the far end of the block of buildings, and Diana led him down the stairs and into another building. Within the complex was a puzzle of small shops, offices, and warehouses, and within it they found an open door to a shop and the scent of glue and pine.

"We saw no other monks tonight," she whispered. "You'll need a change of clothing."

On the second floor they discovered an office with a closet which stored the dusty aprons of artisans. To one side hung the ornate and colorful robe of a Master Cabinet Maker.

In each hand he held aprons with many pockets and stains. "These are not for the street," he said.

Diana nodded, and they returned to the corridor, checking each door until they encountered another unbolted. This was a tailor's shop with racks of clothes of various styles and sizes.

While selecting their disguises, boot heels sounded in the hall outside. It was too soon and impossible to escape. Desperate for a place to hide, they scanned the room.

In a burst of lightning and crash of thunder that rattled the windows, Martin spotted an enormous wardrobe with a ring of keys hanging from the latch. He removed the keyring, and they rushed inside to find it full of furs and capes.

Martin fumbled for the key, found it, and locked the wardrobe from within. As soon as the lock clicked, the shop door opened, and boots walked the racks. The pair put their backs against the sides of the closet and pulled their knees in so as not to be visible through the crack in the doors. It was stifling underneath the long robes and furs, but like deer in a thicket, they needed to be motionless and avoid the flight response that would drive them straight into the knives of their attackers.

Boots walked to the door of the wardrobe and paused. The door handles turned slightly, but the lock endured, and the door remained closed. After a moment, the door shook, but the latch held. A long dirk glinted as it slipped between the doors and thrust to the back of the cabinet.

As if it were a snake with a life of its own, it moved upward from just above the latch. When the blade encountered the tug of a fur, it struck deeper. After the weapon hit the top, it withdrew and reentered below the latch. When it reached the bottom, the dirk retired, and the room was silent.

Through the crack in the door, beads of sweat glinted on Martin's forehead and collected on his chin until one formed. When the tiny drop reached the floor of the cabinet, a boom louder than thunder came, and the cabinet shook.

Splinters fell on them as the point of a sword poked through a fresh hole in the door. After the weapon withdrew, a sliver of dim light showed through the hole. Again and again the thick door shuddered as the searcher tried to hack his way through the thick cabinet doors. And with each whack, more light slipped in. It would be only a matter of time before the door fell to pieces.

Diana prepared to turn the key and kick the door open to startle their pursuer when the thuds of running boots echoed from the hall. The thuds stopped, and a heavy accent filtered through the holes in the cabinet. "Nidokx saw them down the street. Let's go."

The hacking stopped and quiet returned, after which footfalls left the shop and drifted to silence.

Martin reached for the lock, but she grabbed and held his hand to stop him. After five more minutes sweltering in the wardrobe, boots sounded inside the workshop again. There had been two searchers, this one more suspicious and diligent than the other. The boot heels walked the length of the shop and back and faded away.

After a few extra minutes of stifling heat, she stood behind a cloak, hoping the heavy fur might lessen the impact of a crossbow bolt. She unlocked the closet door and stepped outside to a cool draft and empty shop. Without delay they changed into their disguises: the green robe and hat of a healer for Martin, and the faded black dress with white apron of a kitchen maid for Diana.

While killers searched for them in the streets below, Martin waited with his back to the wall to let the sweat dry. Opposite him, Diana gazed west through the window at the castle spires, not knowing how Eric faired after the attack.

# Chapter 27
## A Balcony

From a balcony far above the streets, Prince Eric looked east across town to the artisan quarter as the breeze on his face cooled the buzz from the wine and the sweat from dancing. The post-performance ball was fun, but something was missing—or someone.

Waltz music rising from the covered courtyard below caught his attention, and he dropped his glance to the dancers. Held within the castle walls, the ball after the performance continued. Steven had kept him out of trouble, coaching him which girls schemed to wed him or bed him, and made sure he was never alone with either.

The king, red-faced from brandy, approached him. "Break your plans tomorrow. The lockdown will extend another day or so. The kitchen remains off-limits, and praetorians will deliver our meals."

Eric nodded. "Why did they hustle us from the performance?"

"Precaution. Praetorians found a crossbow in the audience near a dead guard."

"And the perpetrators?"

George shook his head and leaned a hip against the railing. "I remember when the maidens sought me the way they did you tonight. One of those was your mother and wedding her was the best decision I ever made."

Eric smiled and raised an eyebrow. "That was your decision?"

"It amuses me to think so. You seemed distracted at the ball."

Eric did not take the bait.

"There's talk of a farm girl at the Academy."

"A friend. I've sent an invitation to her home to join me Sunday at the promenade," Eric said with a smile. "A carriage will meet her at the cathedral."

"No, no," George said. "They'll brand her a trollop. Invite your friend to dine with us, publicly, and soon, or rumors will spread that will tarnish her reputation." George patted him on the shoulder and walked back to Helena. "Tomorrow then? Tea?"

"Do not meddle in this!" Eric called after his father.

At the door, George laughed. "Tell that to your mother."

Eric guessed at the effect of inviting Diana to the castle after the enormous expense for the Singer's performance and the ball.

*"Mother, guess who's coming to tea."*

But he smiled that though unasked and undesired, his father, the king, had given his permission.

"Prince!" Ash called from the doorway followed by Singer with a praetorian at her side. "More trouble is afoot!"

# Chapter 28
# Birthday

In the tailor's shop, under windows that rattled in the wind and rain, Diana touched her swollen cheek. She guessed her nose and eye were a dark purple, but that's not what hurt most. She was embarrassed. In her excitement at the performance, she forgot her stance, and the attacker had caught her flat-footed.

Martin squinched and pointed to her eye. "Does it hurt?"

"Only when I think about it," she said as the clouds that loomed all day hammered rain on the roof and thunder pounded against the walls.

*"In a fight your body chemistry takes over unless you control it," Jon once said. "That's why we train, so that our training overcomes our emotions." But I forgot my training.*

"What language did the killers speak?" Martin asked.

She knew but shook her head. He opened his mouth, but she changed subjects to throw him off again. "Well, I think I can tell you now, but you need to keep it a secret."

"What?"

"Today is my birthday," she said.

"I'm sorry it was more exciting than you planned. Oh! These are for you." He reached into the satchel that slowed him all night and handed her two books. "Happy Birthday!"

These were the books she had picked out in the cache, and her mouth fell open.

*I have something to show them at home now, some proof that Mother was not delusional. And just maybe, somehow, I can wake it to become the weapon I hoped to find.*

She pursed her lips, blinked back a tear, and kissed him on the cheek. "Thank you, Martin. This may change everything."

After a long hug, she sat to leaf through the smallest of the pair, the picture book with large print.

Still blushing from the kiss, Martin said, "I think you found the key, or at least one small key. See, here." He pointed to a picture of a hawk, below which appeared symbols like the works in the reliquerium.

She nodded and glanced at him with a smile, then browsed the pages for common symbol sets that matched the pictures.

He took the other book and opened it. "This is the scary one." He turned a page with a familiar map of the land. A fanciful image of a wingless dragon split North from South and left its backbone as the mountainous Spine. It emerged from the Ocean of Scythes in the west and submerged in the Ocean of Daggers in the east, leaving its vertebrae as the archipelagos on each coast.

"The Worm of the World," she whispered.

"What do you see?"

She frowned and examined it more closely. The rivers and mountains were in about the right locations, but the coastlines were unfamiliar. Martin pointed to the east edge of the land where the peaks blended with the Eastern Archipelago. She squinted: a thin but visible path showed between the cliffs and the ocean which the maps at Le Pegre said did not exist. At this scale, the strand would be miles wide.

"The map is wrong," she said.

"More."

She ran her fingers along the brown border which faded to a pale yellow near the center of the page. The corner of the page crumbled in her hand.

"It can't be over twenty years old," she said. "Singer said we can't make paper that lasts any longer than a decade."

Martin took her hand and led her fingers along the sheet. "Feel it. It's not paper."

She held a sheet to the window, where torchlight from the street outside shone through the page. "Parchment?"

"Close."

"Vellum?"

"Perhaps. And still it's only brown with age. There are scrolls of vellum upstairs dating to the founding of the Imperium that are in worse condition than this."

She ran her fingers over the surface again. "Then it's older than the founding, more than a thousand years old."

He nodded.

"Then the maps don't represent what *is*. But what *was,* long before the founding."

She sighed as she studied the page. "But we can't be sure, and why would anyone care? Just being old and different doesn't make it magic or useful."

As she examined the map, the room dissolved into a sea of clouds and the edges of the map grew to east and west to both horizons to envelop her. From the heavens, she descended to the Alba River and what should have been her home. Instead, Aemgarde was a snow-covered forest, and a colony of domed huts appeared at the north outlet of Lake Ivo. A scattering of marshy islands dotted the Inland Sea, and she shivered at the ice that grew between them and the men who—

A loud snore broke the spell, and her vision evaporated. Sedated by the steady rain, Martin snored, leaving her alone with her regrets.

They had missed Singer's finale tonight, the famous lament where Christine wished Rodrigo had not been bound by honor but had taken her far away from the feuding families and the war. But his honor and selfless duty to the citizens were reasons Christine loved him, and she felt responsible for his death.

Eric slipped into Diana's thoughts again. *The prince's position is so lofty he could not, or would not, respond to warnings from his friends. If we ever were friends. I'm still a simple farm girl to him. And I have a contract on me which might endanger him as well. Better I leave and take the threat with me.*

*Was his surprise for me more than good wishes? No, that just was my hope. A birthday gift? No, he didn't know.*

And whatever fantasies remained of a life in Branwyn vanished.

A year ago when she first arrived in Branwyn, her dreams had been nothing grand, just a lucky find of a magic book that would help her people. But since then, those dreams changed to those of a young woman. Now, she had friends she could count on. And she had tasted the possibility of a genuine relationship, and she wanted more of it.

But her discovery was much bigger than her dreams, with consequences that could affect the entire world and bring it into balance or force it into war. And the personal cost was even bigger: an assassin's contract on her and Jon. And again, she was on the run.

*Jon will wait for me and then come looking and risk himself for me again. I've put him in danger because of my schemes. And it was all to see Eric and presume I could oppose the second most powerful person in the land.*

The steady rain ebbed, and the mist rose from the street, reminding Diana of another birthday. At this time four years ago, barbarians attacked her home and killed her mother, the night after her party. A pang of guilt shot through her that all day she had not a single thought about her mother.

She glanced at her friend, a simple monk who stood by her, put her hand on his sleeping arm, and kissed him on the forehead.

"Martin, I don't want another birthday party. Ever," she said between his snores.

The events of the day overwhelmed her, and she cried softly. When the tears stopped, she turned back to gaze west to the castle and wrote a brief note to Eric.


At the entrance to the street, Diana and the monk ducked back into the shadows when a pair of drunks stumbled through the fog and rain, singing a bawdy. She doused the lantern and wrinkled her nose at the smells that rose from the rain-wet streets.

Martin handed her the satchel with the books. "You know the way home from here?"

Diana bit her lip. *Glaciers block our path across the Lanshrue, but he means the cottage.*

"Yes."

"There's a gift in the satchel that might help."

She nodded, presuming he meant the maps. "Where's the envelope I gave you?"

"Safely hidden."

"Give the package to Eric. And this." She handed the note to Martin. "Say only they're from a girl he met in a goldsmith's shop. No more."

After a long hug, Martin left. When he turned a corner, Diana checked in both directions and made her way through the alleys and lingering crowds to the Merchant Quarter.


"I failed to warn them," Diana said when she found Jon waiting for her in the market. The wagon and its contents were gone, and their horses stood ready with saddlebags filled. Without delving into the why, he treated her black eye with a cold compress while she summarized the evening's adventures.

"How did they fare?" Jon asked.

"I don't know."

He put a hand on hers. "I'm sorry, but we can't tarry here any longer."

She nodded and led her horse beside Jon to the main street leading to the North Gate. There, crowds of people trying to leave stopped them. Jon found a praetorian while Diana ducked behind the horses.

"The king has closed the gate," Jon said when he returned.

"Why?"

"The guards wouldn't say and offered no opinion. East Gate?"

Diana nodded, and they led the horses back to the Cathedral Quarter.

These were familiar streets to Diana. Tonight they were empty, and they rode past the Academy. But when they approached the thoroughfare, praetorians ran past them toward the East Gate and citizens ran away from it. A crowd of people surged behind them, pushing them toward the street.

"What's the panic, mate?" Jon asked, and the man pointed up.

Above them, flames rose from the roofs of the buildings. Diana glanced back at the streets they had just ridden, now blocked by burning debris.

"Look out!" someone cried from the crowd as the wooden cornice of the adjoining building collapsed in flames, and a stone gargoyle crushed a wagon bed. The shower of embers blocked the thoroughfare, and the trapped crowd panicked.

The only break in the walls was the service entrance to the Academy, and Diana ran to it. She shook the handle on the heavy door but found it locked. A shoulder on the door did not move it.

"Jon, help me!" she called, but the two of them could not move the door.

"Here!" called a man who grabbed a companion and added more shoulders to the door.

From the damaged wagon, a father and son stripped a sideboard and joined them at the door. The six of them, using the board as a battering ram, broke the lock. A cloud of smoke billowed from the open door, and they backed away, but the smoke ebbed to a wisp that crawled along the top of the doorway.

"I know a way through," Diana said as she grabbed her horse's reins and prepared to lead it inside.

"You sure about this?" Jon asked.

"Do you see another way?" she said.

Jon took two shirts from his saddle bags and threw one to her. "Cover her eyes," he said as he tied the shirt around his mare's eyes, and Diana did the same.

"This way," she shouted. Still, no one followed.

Jon removed a rope from a saddlebag and tied it to his saddle horn. "Take her," Jon said and gave her the reins to his mount. "I'll bring the rest."

Diana entered the building as Jon enjoined others to go.

"There's no future for you there!" Jon shouted to them. "Follow her if you want to live." He held the rope out. And as they took it, Diana led them into the Academy.

With smoke burning her eyes and lungs, Diana led them through the labyrinth of rooms and halls by memory. A wall collapsed and she found an alternative route. A hallway in flames blocked their path and she found another way. And when she entered her classroom, the smoke cleared, and the followers rushed past her through the large entrance doors and into the open courtyard.

As Diana tied the horses' reins to the fountain and removed their blindfolds, some survivors helped pull the rope for the stragglers while others praised her and hugged her before washing up at the fountain. But Diana's only thoughts were for Jon.

"Will you come with us?" one asked.

"Not yet," she said and continued to pull the rope.

But Jon did not come. And when the end of the rope appeared, charred and burned through, she stopped.

"No, no, no!"

*Here I am again. Someone I love is in trouble, and I stand here helpless.*

*No more.*

She tore her skirt into rags and dipped them into the fountain. One she put over her mouth and tied behind her head to filter the smoke. Others she laid on her head and draped from her shoulders to shield her from the heat. Then she grabbed the brass ladle, a stone, and returned to the classroom.

"Jon!" she shouted and coughed. The smoke burned her throat when she called, so she banged the rock on the ladle, but there was no response.

She went deeper into the Academy, but when the wall they first escaped through collapsed, she stopped.

"Jon!" she called again, coughed again, and banged the ladle. "Jon!" she called again and again, but he did not answer. She fell to one knee. "Jon," she whispered.

She put her hands together. "Whatever gods live here, please, help my friend," she said and banged the ladle on the wall until the handle bent.

"Here!" Jon called from the other side of the wall.

Diana banged on the door, and a moment later, Jon broke through with a rush of more smoke. In his arms, he held a child, and hanging onto his belt were a woman and two more children.

"This way," Diana said with a raspy voice, and led them back to the courtyard.

At the fountain, Diana hugged him and would not let go. "I was so afraid for you. I thought . . ." She couldn't finish and buried her head in his chest.

"My, my," he said. "This is a different mood from this morning."

"I can't lose you," she said and coughed again.

The woman and children kissed them and hugged them and stopped fussing only after Diana promised to visit their home. After more thank yous, they said their goodbyes. With nowhere to go, Jon and Diana sat at the edge of the fountain as the husk of the Academy collapsed.

"You're sad," Jon said and put a hand on hers as she frowned at the burning buildings.

Diana glanced over those rescued from the flames, each grateful for their life, but still preoccupied by their nearness to death.

She shook her head. "The town is unaware of what they lost, Jon." She ripped more cloth from her skirt for a bandage to wrap his burned hands. "They tried to teach us how to think. And 'when the fire goes out, darkness and ignorance return.'"

He nodded. "The cache is safe?"

"It's surrounded by stone and should be."

"Well, so much for our plans," Jon said as Diana washed his burns with cold water from the fountain. "With no way out, the assassins will find us here."

"We need a new way," she said, which triggered a memory of Martin. She searched in the bag, and there at the bottom was an ornate passkey tied to a map.

She held up Martin's key. "I have a way."


Following the map, they used the key to enter the courtyard above the reliquerium. Opposite the door, she found a rusted gate that opened with the same key.

Jon made a torch from a stick and weeds that, once lit, shone past the gate into a dark tunnel.

"How much do you trust this monk?" he said as he stared into the black that seemed without end.

In answer, Diana smiled, took the torch, and entered.

Under the buildings and the town wall, they led their horses to another gate. After clearing the heavy brush that hid the gate from the Ring Road, they joined the others heading north, all lit by the fires still burning near East Gate.

*** 

Diana coughed. "I heard them speaking, Jon. It sounded like Quarajii," she said when they stopped along the North Road to care for their wounds. After rubbing salve on Jon's burned hands, she wrapped them with strips of clean cloth. "What are Qu doing this far south?"

Jon shook his head.

"It was more dangerous than I expected," she said. "You guessed this?"

"No."

"Why'd you let me go?"

It took a moment before Jon spoke. "Could I have stopped you?"

She dropped her eyes.

"My role is to shield you from harm, lass, but not from your life. Sometimes it's hard to assess whether the risk will overwhelm you or strengthen you."

"That's what my father said."

He nodded. "My goal is to prepare you for those challenges so you can overcome each and grow stronger from the experience. I assessed you were trained and clever enough to outwit the challenges I could foresee, including Grimes. But the coup attempt was . . . unexpected. I suspect much of Branwyn was in danger tonight and we were swept up into it."

"But I failed."

He smiled. "Failure is not the lack of success. Failure is when you stop trying. We have an alternative in your friends for all you wished to achieve here. You're speaking of the cache, right?"

She blushed.

"I see," he said with a smile. He reached into his pocket for the birthday present he had placed there, but found the pocket torn, singed, and empty.

"What is it?" she asked.

"Another time."

The North Road became lonely when the last of the crowd from town peeled off to their homes. Jon doused the torch, and they rode alone in silence. Fures rose to join Lon, and Diana recognized the hilltop where they first viewed Branwyn Valley years ago. There at the edge of the Northern Forest, she did not look back at the fires that still burned in Branwyn. Instead she thought of the journey to Antona and sanctuary in the North.

But the dark road bore dark thoughts, and she frowned.

*Without Papa's safety, my mission has no purpose.*

\*\*\*

On the parapet of Branwyn's eastern fortifications kneeled a figure in a black cloak. Rain dripped from his wide-brimmed hat as the fires burned near the East Gate. The politics and opportunities had changed that night. But it mattered little to him, for he knew someone with his skills would always be in demand.

From his pocket, he removed two red coins and rubbed them together, but after a moment, he stopped and squinted into the dark.

Exposed by the crackles of lightning to the east, two horses and riders appeared from the wall below and joined others on the Ring Road. He returned the red coins to his pocket and stood.

"Time to go to work," he mumbled.

# Chapter 29
## Enigma

On Lonsday morning, two days later, while the Academy still smoldered behind him, Father Dorian rang the handbell.

Steven turned to Eric. "Solange isn't here."

"Her mother backed the coup attempt," Eric said.

"And the monk and the farm girl are absent. Did they have anything to do with it?"

Four different monks reached Eric that morning with urgent messages to contact Martin the day of Singer's performance. Their messages were now two days late, and Martin was missing.

The prior day, the praetorians and police detained all the conspirators they could find, but Grimes had escaped. Commander Raynes planned to keep the royals locked inside the castle, but Eric would not stay cooped up. To protect him, the king assigned personal guards under Steven's command.

"I don't know," Eric said and called the two guards over. "Sergeant, inquire about the monk named Martin," he said and turned to the other. "Go to the marketplace and ask about a farm girl who answers to the name Diana. Be discreet. Don't harass them or draw attention to them. Return here before noon, sooner if you have news of them. Go." He put a hand on Steven's shoulder, and they joined the students.

No word of Martin or Diana arrived during class, and when Eric's guards returned, he gave them another mission.

"Ask Raynes to search the town for the monk," the prince said. "And send a rider to the farm of Jon Smyth, on the East Road near the forest. Tell me what you find there."

"Princes rarely concern themselves with milk maids and monks," Steven said.

Nodding, Eric turned back to the guard. "If anyone asks, tell them Steven Dumont inquires after their health," he said with impatience and waved him to leave.

Steven grinned. "They'll think I pursue the maiden. Perhaps I should." But the prince frowned and walked away.


A tavern owner found Martin the morning after the performance in a pile of trash and thought him to be sleeping off a drunk and a mugging. He now lay unconscious with the Sisters of Mercy in the Artisan Quarter. Eric ordered the praetorians to post a guard on Martin's room. On Furesday morning the day after, he woke and told Eric what had happened.

After leaving Diana, Martin reached the Cathedral Quarter. But the attackers found him and interrogated him about her: why she was following them, how much she knew, and all of which he knew nothing. He fell out a window trying to escape, and next opened his eyes in the hospital.

Martin gave Eric the location of the hidden envelope, and the prince sent a courier to retrieve it.

"We tried to get your attention during the show," Martin said.

"The praetorians hustled us away early as a precaution. So the ruckus masked the intent?"

"I think the target was your parents. And you."

The prince nodded. "A guard was killed."

"I saw. There were at least ten other attackers in the audience."

"It was a coup attempt," Eric said. "They planned a fire and a riot as an excuse for Grimes to declare martial law. We had to defend the gates against an external attack. Some aristos allied themselves with Grimes and are in hiding now. They murdered Artican, the Minister of Finance." He sighed. "Did she know?"

"Diana? I can't believe she would cause you harm. She alerted the guard." Martin paused. "The first shot would have struck one of you if she hadn't interrupted them. She saved your lives, Prince."

Eric nodded and pursed his lips.

"They chased us through the town," Martin continued, "And . . . oh! She left a note for you."

Martin handed him the note he had stuffed into his sock, and Eric read it.

*Dear Eric*

*My father and I are forced to leave in circumstances we cannot disclose. I had hoped to discuss this with you in person but failed. We will not be returning.*

*The false merchants we saw from the goldsmith's shop wore boots of the barbarians, one of the Quarajii Hordes. These men caused the raucous and killed a guard. I'm sorry I could not warn you sooner.*

*Also, ask Martin about the priceless treasure we found. It can change the course of history, and you must protect it. There are those who would*

*destroy it if they cannot control it. Please tell only*
*your parents, but at the first opportunity, disclose*
*it to the public. Until then, protect it.*
  *Farewell,*
  *The girl in the goldsmith's shop.*
  *p.s.: Tell Martin . . .*

Eric stopped and stared hard at the letter as if a secret message would appear.

"Why the subterfuge?" Eric asked. "Why not just
sign it with her name?"

"Perhaps she fears for you, or for herself," Martin
replied.

"What of the merchants with the riding boots?"

The monk frowned. "We saw them with Cirka at
Grimes's office near the market and again at the performance. Hard to say if they were the same men, but
the clothing was similar. They killed the guard and
tried to kill you."

"Grimes attempted a coup using foreigners," Eric
said.

Martin shook his head. "Diana couldn't have been
part of that, Eric. She was desperate to warn you and
seemed lost when we couldn't contact you. The merchant with the crossbow, or whoever he was, surprised
her. I'm sure of that. He might have killed her." Martin
softened his voice. "It could have been much worse if
she hadn't intervened."

Eric nodded, but frowned.

"Why the look?" Martin asked.

"I sent her an invitation to the promenade on Sunday."

Martin raised an eyebrow. "My, my."

"The courier who delivered the invitation found
them gone. I missed my chance, and she may be in
trouble."

The courier entered with Diana's envelope and gave it to Martin. Within it he found the deed to the Smyth farm and instructions to dispose of the property.

"Did she tell you what forced her to leave?" Eric asked.

"She only repeated the same story about visiting the sick aunt, but that can't be true."

"They were running, Martin. Why?"

"She didn't say, but she was running for her life."

Without saying, they both understood why Diana had tried so desperately to contact him.

Eric frowned. "She hoped I would protect her," he said and shook his head. "And I was at a party."

"There was another reason she wanted to reach you," Martin said.

Eric handed Diana's letter to him. "There's a note here for you."

*p.s.: Please ask Martin to take personal responsibility for the continuing education of Anne Buckman. She is a motivated student and wishes to attend the Academy. But she will need supervision in the presence of aristocrats, especially the males. Her farm is along the East Road near ours. You can find her in the market most mornings at a booth selling cheeses.*

Eric smiled at Martin. "So who is this creature, my young priest?"

The monk blushed beet red. "I've not taken my vows, prince."

After a long silence, Eric spoke. "So what's this treasure she wrote of?"

"Eric, you won't believe—," he began and sat upright in bed with wide eyes and a grin. But he cringed with pain and groaned, his hand went to his forehead.

With a hand behind Martin's back, Eric helped him lie back down. "Easy now."

"I won't do that again."

"And the treasure, Martin?"

"Oh, yes. Eric, we found something marvelous!"

\*\*\*

Later that day, Eric held a private audience with his parents. With a strategic view through windows in four directions and crossbows on the walls, Eric recounted Martin's story.

"There's more treachery if she had to run, Father. Martin witnessed the phony merchants implicated in the coup attempt visiting Grimes."

"Send soldiers to search for the girl," King George said.

Eric turned to leave. "No, father, this is my task. And I won't be delayed by a company of soldiers."

Concern etched Helena's face. "Stay, son. Let the army find her and protect her. There are still killers at large."

"We were fixed targets with a known agenda, Mother," Eric countered. "I'll be safer far away from the castle in disguise."

The king nodded. "Don't forget our invitation to dinner," he said as Eric left to hunt for Diana.

But Eric did not smile as he rushed to the stable, hoping to reach Diana ahead of whoever hunted her.

# Chapter 30
# Hostage in Orbieto

The Barbarian was too slow to stop the guarded point of her foil from poking into his chest, a chest half as broad as she was tall.

"Score," she said and backed up along the long carpet, returning to her ready position.

The hilt of the foil was small in his big hand and the moment he raised it to ready, she whacked his bare arm and he glared at her.

"That was for fun," she said with a smirk. He slashed his weapon at her, and she parried with her dirk. With the foil in her other hand she smacked the back of his hand and knocked his weapon to the ground.

Solange took off her face mask. "Clod. Take off your mask, this is no sport at all." She longed for her ability to hector her servants without respite. "Mother, get me a decent fencing partner. He's tireless but no fun at all."

Her mother, Lucrezia Jerrett, studied her scrolls. "He's the last swordsman who speaks our language."

Her opponent smirked. "Perhaps, young one, we might play with my sword, not yours." He nodded toward his leather armor and longsword, a weapon that would shatter her foil at a touch and chop her in half.

"Out with you, cur," Jerrett said. The brute squinted, picked up his things and left. She turned to her daughter. "You might be less confrontational with our allies."

Solange went to the basin to splash the sweat from her face. "Calling them 'cur' is your best example?"

"They despise weakness. I need to exhibit my authority lest they think me weak."

"And what of my authority?"

"In their world, you have none."

"And you have it all? Mother, we're prisoners, not allies."

Her mother remained silent.

Solange shook her head, took a drink from a wooden cup and sighed. "Wood instead of silver, drafty canvas instead of brick walls, camp chairs instead of cushions. Mother, what have you done to us," she said and stormed out of their tent.

She walked through the camp as she might in Branwyn, unafraid of the commoners surrounding her. But the barbarian warriors heckled her in their strange tongue and threw scraps of meat at her feet for the dogs to get in her way and trip her.

A large man smirked as she passed and seized her. "Ah, dessert." He hugged her close, lifting her off the ground and pinning her arms.

"Let me go!" she shouted. "I'm the daughter of Counselor Jerrett, emissary to Baronet Grimes and Prince Senekx. How dare you!"

"Ha! What can Jerrett do? Bring her with next time. We may like a taste of her as well."

Solange writhed in his arms and beat her fists on his side while the brute stared with uncaring malice. She banged her forehead into his nose, but when it bled, he laughed. He held her out at arm's length and eye level. "All you need to do to save yourself is to say yes."

"To you?"

"To any of us."

She surveyed the crowd: men with broken teeth, unshaven and rough. The fear hit her that what she saved for a prince she would lose to a barbarian. Nausea rose as she considered what might happen, and she stopped struggling.

He spoke to her alone. "You all bore me so. The only fire in your belly is contempt. You can't see yet, sprite, but you may soon, and when you do, come find me. I am called Voreckk."

He let her go, and immediately she kicked him in the leg. He laughed and before she could kick again, he placed his hand on her head and pressed down so hard she could not kick and remain standing. She swung and could not reach him.

In a language she did not understand, a man taunted her from the crowd. Then he said, "Grimes can't help you here."

"It's not so much fun when you're not beating your servants, eh?" another said.

With a push, her captor released her, and she fell on her butt in the mud. The men laughed at her and ridiculed her. No one in the camp would protect her, not even Grimes.

Voreckk sneered at her and said, "Let her go. I claim her."

She did not understand what he meant, but the scowls and bared teeth panicked her. She rose and backed away into a man who laughed at her.

With a brush of his hand he dismissed her, mimicking the same brush of the hand her mother used. "Run, chicken, run," he said.

In her torn and muddy dress, Solange ran away through brambles to the bank of the Orange River. Under a willow tree between the bank and the bushes, she found a hiding place and tried to soothe the cuts on her legs. There she sat with her head in her hands, and cried, trembling from the chemistry of fear.

Sixty miles south of Branwyn, there was nowhere for her to run. Certainly not back home, where they would accuse her of treason regardless of her lack of involvement. Grimes was here with them, and he would be of no help.

*To Voreckk, I owe my life—or my virtue. And what will they do with us? Ransom? Who are we valuable to now? No one.* The despair overwhelmed her, and she cried until the sun dropped below the trees, and she ran out of tears.


"No!"

A girl's cry woke Solange, and she rose to investigate. Thirty yards along the bank, where the cold fog and insects were certain to add to the misery, sat a girl in a cage, her hair so dirty and matted Solange could not tell its natural color. Two little barbarians stood outside the bars, and one tormented the captive with a stick.

"Kinutha sen," the first said in Quarajii and punched the other in the arm. "Illuna Senekx Kurakk." They laughed.

He poked her again and whacked her on the shoulder.

"Leave her," the second said in Imperium. "She needs to be able to talk."

"Which leaves many entertainments between now and death." He rattled the stick against the bars, tossed the stick into the brush, and walked away with his companion.

Afraid the guards might discover her, Solange threw a few stones to get the captive's attention. But the girl was absorbed in her own misery, holding one bruised hand in the other and rocking forward and back, her shoulders shaking with sobs.

Solange crept closer. "Psst."

The girl turned and Solange recognized her dirty, tear-stained face and frowned.

"Did they hurt you?" Solange asked and gave her a bowl of water from the nearby bucket.

The girl raised two fingers from her left hand, swollen and red. "I . . . I think they're broken." She returned her hands to her lap and rocked again. "But I think they'll hurt me worse when they come back."

"Why? What did you do?"

"I don't know! I'd tell them, if I knew anything."

Solange shook her head. "How could you? You're just a stupid farmer," she said, but for the first time, among all the times she felt and said the same thing in the past, the words tasted bitter.

"What do they ask about?" Solange asked.

The girl lowered her eyes and her shoulders shuddered. "They keep asking me about my anklet. I told them I made it, and they kidnapped me. Right off the street."

"In Branwyn?"

"Yes," she said wide eyed, "Can you help me? Please. Help me!"

Solange put a finger to her lips. "Shhh, quiet."

"Help me! Please!" The girl reached out for her, but Solange backed away, afraid the guards would see her, and sneaked into the trees.

On the way back to her tent she evaded the soldiers to avoid not only their threats but their contempt. *They despise weakness, and we are weak.*

Back in her quarters, she sat on her bed to pout. This was not their luxurious apartments in Branwyn, but a tent in the wilderness, drafty and cold.

*There's nothing separating me and Mama from that girl in the cage except bars. What can I do that would help? Nothing. What might I do to hurt them?*

An idea came, and with it, a smile.

Inside a chest were the skeleton keys which once helped her mother steal so many secrets; secrets used to blackmail others. *This was an essential part of our life, something Mother was forced to do to survive in a man's world. She had no choice but to lie and betray.*

She shook her head.

*No longer. Mother's life was a decision, the path she chose for power and influence. But she reached too far and reduced them to a tent surrounded by animals.*

"That life and this one aren't for me," she whispered.

Along with the ring of keys, Solange took smoked meat from the larder and a dirk and snuck through the cold mist back to the cage.

When the guards left again, Solange tried various keys until one worked. Opening the door, she put her hand over the mouth of the sleeping girl, who lay curled up and shivering. She woke with panic in her eyes.

"Shhh," Solange said. "Listen. Can you swim with your injured hand?" The girl nodded. "Cross the river and follow it north. Stay near the river for fresh water but cover your tracks. Don't go south." She gave her the dirk and dried meat. "Branwyn lies three days north. Don't stop for anything."

The girl hugged her and waded into the water.

A twig cracked behind her, and Solange spun around. Voreckk, the same big barbarian who had humiliated her earlier that day, stared at her with narrow eyes. She reached for her blade but had given it to the captive. She sighed. In her anger she had not considered the consequences of helping the girl escape. *This is it*. Resigned to her fate, she turned her back on him.

Across the river the farm girl crawled up the opposite shore, turned, and raised her hand, but stopped. She took a step back to the river, but Solange waved her away, and she ran along the bank searching for a break in the brush.

Solange turned back to Voreckk. *The life I was born to is over forever*. "Will you kill me?

"No. But others will die for this."

"What of my mother?"

"You may save her yet," he said but made no move.

Her shoulders fell. *I know what he wants. But what would he want more than my body?* She took a chance and stood tall. "That's not the girl you seek."

"Say more."

"You seek the girl who wears the anklet?"

The barbarian squinted and nodded. "Then where is she now?"

"My information is not free."

"I'll need a token." He reached for her arm, but she pulled away.

Without instruction, she entered the cage and handed him the ring of skeleton keys but remained standing tall. He nodded and locked the door and waited with her until the girl with the anklet from the North, Anne Buckman, disappeared into the woods.

# Part 3 A Princess Returns

*It was a time of unrest in the world, and the fall of Empires was not enough to sate the Chaos. And again, the unrest aimed for Cherbourne.*

# Chapter 31
## Along the Orange

### The Woods

"I'm sorry we missed dinner at the Hogue's Breath," Diana said and put a hand on his. "And sorry I missed that someone you wanted me to meet. Was it someone special? I don't mean to pry, Jon, it's just . . ."

A fortnight's ride north of Branwyn, Jon prepared the campsite and cooked dinner while Diana unsaddled the horses and hobbled them.

"It's fine, lass," he said. "Yes, she's special. Cindy, Cindy Shale, the owner of the Hogue's Breath. She's a widow with grown children, a former tutor. You'd like her. She's the first since my Rosie died."

"You left Cindy for me, to protect me."

"Of course," he said as if no other choice was conceivable. "And there's no place else I'd rather be." Leaning over, he patted her hand. "And don't worry, I will see her again." He stood with his bow. "I'll take first watch."

While Jon took a position on a rise just beyond the edge of the firelight, Diana cleaned up and made her bed just behind the lean-to. Within it, she made two more beds, stuffed them with grass, and covered them with blankets. Her bow and quiver lay beside her, but she slept with the dirk.

With a sword on his lap and bow to his right, he listened to the owls and sounds of the night as the fire burned to embers.

Jon flexed his hands, still healing from the burns. As he unwound the bandages, the crickets hushed and he tensed. The next sound was the crackle of a leaf, followed by the reflection of firelight in an eye. One shape moved slowly, circling toward him. Jon tracked it with an arrow, but the shape made no move toward Diana. Instead of killing the tracker, Jon worked around behind and placed a knife to their ribs.

"Your heart is not in this, Berta," Jon whispered.

"I didn't know it was you until I recognized your horses, Jon," the assassin said. "My apologies."

"How many with you?"

"Four others," Berta said with a tremor in her voice, sweating visibly in the moonlight.

"I appreciate your warning," Jon said. "But it will still be much simpler to kill you. You understand, I can't trust you."

She nodded.

After tying and gagging her, Jon whistled a short nightingale song. From behind the lean-to, Diana rolled out, leaving two other beds within it. Jon crept over to an open spot and kneeled, put four arrows in the dirt in front of him, nocked another, and waited.

Three blackened arrows hit the blankets, but the angle of entry left a clue to their origin. Jon rose, drew the bow, closed his eyes, and whistled again.

A flare arced over the campsite and lodged in a tree, throwing long shadows and illuminating black shapes stunned by the harsh light. Moments later, Jon dropped two with arrows and a third after a brief fight. The fourth remained missing. Jon whistled once more.

"Here, Jon," Diana called from across the camp and Jon went to her voice.

"Drop your weapons."

"Closer," she said, standing in the open with arms wide, and empty palms facing him.

"Slowly."

Behind her stood a large shadow, indistinguishable from the night, except for the left hand tight against her throat and the knife held in it. He hid his right hand, which might hide another weapon. A professional, and much too big for her. And she was the lure to flush Jon into the open.

"Stop," she said. Jon was too far away to act, and the man was too close to Diana for an arrow or knife. Slowly, he cast off every visible weapon that would be useful at this range. The outcome depended on her now.

She whimpered softly.

Jon nodded at her signal, but still he dropped the last of his weapons.

"Show him the tokens," Diana asked.

Untying the bag of coins at his belt, Jon removed the red coins and held them up.

"Drop them where you stand," she said.

Jon kneeled to put the tokens on the ground. "We have wealth far beyond your contract, and if—"

The shadow laughed. "Your bounty is enough, and my life, worth nothing if I accept your bribe."

When he laughed again, she jammed her booted heel on her attacker's right foot, crushing his instep and causing him to loosen the blade from her throat. In one move, she dropped her chin to his wrist and raised her right shoulder, then trapped the knife with both hands. He yelped with pain as she stomped on his right foot again. Ducking, she rotated and drove a knee into his thigh, spun, and rolled away. The shape fell to one knee and swung the crossbow hidden behind his back, the weapon he meant for Jon.

Jon slipped the knife from his belt buckle and threw it, hitting the man in the chest. Diana kicked him in the face, and he fell back.

Grabbing his sword, Jon ran to them. "Turn your back, lass," he said, and ran his sword through the assassin's neck.

When Diana moved to scratch an itch on her cheek, her fingers came away bloody.

Jon put a hand on her shoulder to keep her seated. "Do you feel that?"

Her eyes widened. "No."

"The battle fever dulls your pain." Tearing a strip from his shirt, he pressed it to her head. "Hold this tight. You did well, lass."

"I think not," she said.

"Perfect. Confidence now would be arrogant. Remain hidden." He left to search the area for more threats, found nothing but the assassins' horses, and took those to the camp.

After walking back to Berta, Jon removed her gag. "I'm disappointed."

"The farm is failing," she said. "The mule kicked Jake and put him on his back for a month. I thought I could feed the kids this way." She dropped her gaze. "I couldn't tell them or Jake."

"Who took the contract?" Jon asked.

"The big guy. He didn't say who it was from."

"Chancellor Grimes commissioned the contract."

She shook her head. "Then my family is doomed."

"You can't go back. The Counselor will have a contract on you as well to keep you quiet. "

"And he surely will if we don't return," she said and dropped her gaze. "Finish me quick, and free my family."

"Jake would never forgive me," he said with a slight smile. He untied her, and she sighed.

"We need to run, Berta. Take the bodies and their horses to the Monastery of Dorreau a few days north. Tell them of us. They can bring your family safely to you. Tell no one else and remain hidden."

"They're monks, Jon. What can they do?"

"The Guild can't touch them," Jon replied, "or anyone under their protection. Do this and you may live to see your husband and children again."

Diana and Jon saddled their horses, packed light, and rode north.

"Berta was a good woman, lass, and may be again," Jon said.

"And yet she accepted a contract to kill us," Diana said, her forehead smarting from the assassin's knife.

"It's the way of the Assassins' Guild to repay debt with blood. To guarantee a contract, they hold your family as bond until the deaths sear your conscience away. It's business to them: life and death reduced to a transaction. And vulnerable to corrupt officials like Grimes."

"She's a participant in a corrupt system."

"Aye, but gave us warning as redemption." He sighed.

They rode in silence, and Diana guessed his mood. "Jon, it's not your fault."

He nodded but frowned. "The ferry at Chelmsford will be best to shake off other assassins."

## The Ferry

Three days after their trouble with assassins, they approached Chelmsford Crossing, miserable. A drizzling rain soaked them in the morning. When it stopped, clouds hid the sun and could not dry them. Midday resembled twilight, and night fell, the air thick with fog and a chill that cut to the bone. And more often than she wished, Diana thought of Eric and what might have been.

The crossing was about an eighth of a mile downstream of the Turno falls. For miles upstream, the Gruen River narrowed, confined by high cliffs on both sides with no bridge.

The wide shallows made Chelmsford the only suitable crossing on a fast river. Here the Orange widened and slowed, too deep to ford but steady enough for a reaction ferry.

In the mist and creeping darkness they approached the ferry. Jon spoke with the ferryman and told him to warn the town that assassins were coming and might destroy the ferry. When the ferryman left, they led their horses aboard.

Jon shifted the control cable to the right side of the ferry and undocked. The ferry drifted into the river and rotated counterclockwise, moving left powered by the current alone.

In mid-river, just before they lost sight of the shore, a horse and rider rode out onto the dock. The roar of the rapids drowned out all sound, and the fog distorted their view. The rider dismounted with a bow in his hand. Diana squinted and tried to move forward, but Jon pushed her back.

"Behind the horses," Jon said.

The rider moved his arms, but they could not tell what he was doing, and Jon took his bow. "Who would pursue us other than an assassin?" Jon asked. "The local sheriff?"

"The monk would have warned Eric if he were able. Maybe the royals enquire as to the events at the performance. Was that a wave?"

Jon nocked an arrow, but she put her hand on his arm.

"He doesn't raise his weapon," she said as the fog closed in.

At the Skipton side of the river, Jon detached the control cable and let it drift free to take it out of service and give them a half-day lead.

But a half-day lead would not be enough.

# Chapter 32
# The Gruen

## Keelboat

After riding east, Jon and Diana rested their horses and changed their bandages.

"With the Lanshrue bridge gone, the fastest way home is by sea along the west coast from Venaro," Jon said. "And the fastest route to there is along the Gruen River."

"Our horses aren't bred for long distance racing," Diana said as she added salve to his burns. "And we may not be able to stay ahead of assassins."

"How about a boat? The Gruen is a fast river and flows all day and night while horses must rest."

"We don't have a boat," Diana said and wrapped a fresh bandage around his hands.

"We might crew a river boat that serves the towns along the Gruen. I saw one docked in Skipton."

"Mid-stream is no place to hide."

"But it's easier to defend and easy to escape to the opposite side of the river if needs be."

"We'll bring the horses along?" Diana said, and Jon nodded.

"Then we circle back to Skipton, and this will be our false trail."

The *Shiela Reine* was a big keelboat, almost the length of a barge, and took up much of the Skipton dock. A spacious cabin ran along the mid-plane so large it would accommodate their horses as well as crew quarters and tiny galley.

Summer to winter, thirty-odd men might pole the keelboat upstream or pull it from the shore using ropes. Only six were needed now on the downstream leg, with the four stops from here to Petra and eight more to Venaro.

They found the captain and owner, Seizu Clagett, at the pub with the crew celebrating their last down-stream run before the rains made the river too fast to pole back upstream. There, Jon signed on as a pole-man and cargo handler and Diana as a tallyman and cook with a cash incentive to Clagett to leave that night.

After casting off and floating down the Gruen, Diana was free from pursuit for the first time in weeks and slept peacefully.

Clagett and the light crew were friendly the next morning, having low expectations for meals on board. Preferring to eat and especially drink at their ports-of-call, Diana used the time to reflect.

*Was that Eric? If not, who would let them escape without even a shot at their horses? Was Martin right: was Eric interested in me?* Dismissing that idea as ridiculous, she went to find Jon.

"Jon, I think it was Eric at the ferry," she said and unwrapped the bandages on his hands.

"Perhaps, lass."

"If Martin reached him, he'd tell him about the cache and the attempt to kill him and his parents." She finished unwrapping the bandages and applied more of the salve. "I think they should air heal now. Just keep applying the salve so they don't scar."

"Why would Eric follow us?"

"If it wasn't him, why didn't he shoot? An assassin would have at least wounded one of our horses to slow us."

"Would Eric suspect you were part of the treachery?"

"Martin would convince him otherwise."

Jon sighed. "Lass, your feelings for him—"

Diana opened her mouth to protest, but he raised his hand and shook his head.

"Feelings for him as a friend or more, maybe you're not sure yourself. But if he comes, we need to assess if he's a threat." He leaned over. "He might be acting as an agent of Grimes—"

She interrupted to protest. "Eric is his own man and wouldn't answer to Grimes."

"—or investigating the attempt to kill his parents. In which case he's unlikely to travel alone."

Diana sat straight and stared at him. "You wouldn't hurt him!"

"I wouldn't let him harm you or take you." He leaned back, smiling. "Don't worry, lass. He most likely comes as a friend, even if we can't guess why."

Dropping her gaze, she frowned, uncertain why Eric would be here, but hoping it was for her.

He patted her hand. "Perhaps we are simply a mystery to a curious and energetic lad."

Diana walked back to her bunk, still confused about Eric's motives. *Is it me that interests him? To him, I'm a farm girl and plain as a post compared to the aristo girls with their fancy dresses and makeup.* Shaking her head to clear the fantasies, she went to her satchel to look at her presents from Martin.

She opened the atlas again and studied the maps marking the familiar continents, rivers, and mountain ranges in about the same places. This time she examined north of Cherbourne. The maps she had studied at home showed sea ice near Xorellia and glaciers in the mountains of Nordes and Bouveil. But on this map, the line of ocean ice and glaciers appeared much farther south at the same time the strand was open along the east coast.

*Is the map of our past or our future?*
*Or both?*

\*\*\*

Three days from Skipton, a crewman shouted, "Port ho!" and the crew prepared to exchange goods at Remsford.

The dock was a long wood walkway that extended two hundred feet along the shore. Parked along it were five flat-bottomed river skiffs and three other keelboats riding high at the end of the season. Across the dock road was the main street along which stood a dry goods and produce store and between them, the Twin Harlots Inne. Overfull, the tavern crowd spilled onto the tables set on the front patio.

As she passed the tavern, the smoke, stale-ale, and cooked meat bouquet caught her nose, and she turned. At a table sat a man in a duster and wide-brimmed hat hunched over a tankard with his collar up and face in shadow, and she quickly turned her face away.

When she entered the produce store, three wiry men joined the duster. They did not follow when she left the store, but when she boarded the *Shiela Reine*, they watched her from the tavern.

Full night was Jon's shift to watch the shore, and hers to sleep. With only the dim light from Fures insufficient for reading, her thoughts drifted first to home and then to Eric. *What would we do if he appeared? Could I tell him everything now that we are leaving? What if the king and queen felt betrayed and saw me as a foreign spy? And if they captured me and executed me, would Papa start a war? IIow horrible to be remembered that way, but, oh, how exciting! Would Singers write Songs about us?*

As she drifted off to sleep, a shadow in a wide-brimmed hat entered the common cabin and rifled through her gear.

## A Dark Night

The *Shiela Reine* drifted sideways to the current, and Captain Clagett walked back to chastise the tillerman. Instead, he found five strange men throwing the unconscious crewmen into a skiff tied to the stern.

\*\*\*

Diana woke at a nicker and opened her eyes to find the covers removed from her foot and her anklet exposed. In the shadows, a dark shape searched her belongings and found the pouch of gold and silver coins from Grimes. After removing the red coins, he put them in his pocket and tied the pouch to his belt. Grabbing an empty grain sack, the shadow approached her.

Realizing the sack was about her size, she jumped from bed and took a fighting stance. "Don't come any closer."

The shadow ignored her, opened the sack, and raised it, but she kicked his hand and leaped out of his way.

The shadow reached for his knife but grunted. "You're worth more alive," he said, grabbed a short stretch of rope, and moved toward her again.

Diana kicked him in the stomach, and he dropped the rope. On deck above them, Jon called out in alarm.

"But not that much more." He unsheathed the knife and backed her into the wall away from the door. She would run out of space soon and struck.

One kick knocked the blade from his hand, and another struck him again in the side of his knee. When she ran past him up the stairs to the deck, he lunged for her and threw a punch. She raised her forearm to block, but he was too strong and punched through it, hitting her on the side of her head and knocking her into the wall. Dazed, Diana rose on shaky legs one step out of his reach, knowing his next punch would kill her.

*** 

On deck, the thieves were not prepared for Jon, who tore through three skinny men and threw them overboard on his way to Diana. Encouraged by Jon's fighting skill, Captain Clagett armed himself with a bronze skillet and chased another man over the side. That left Jon with the last, but the man stood and towered over him.

The giant was clumsy but strong. Jon kept out of his swing but could not reach in to hit him. The captain grabbed a pole and struck the giant repeatedly, but he covered up in defense. When the big man had the opportunity to hurt them, he did not.

The giant was an unskilled fighter, but was too hefty to go down. Even together, they could not defeat him without the weapons stored in the hold. Still, the giant stood between Jon and Diana.

\*\*\*

Below deck, the shadow lunged for Diana, forcing her to find high ground at the top of the stairs. Her arms were not long enough to punch him, and he parried or ducked each of her kicks. *He's a killer, not a thug, and enjoys my struggles. And he'll kill me if he can.*

In the torch light on deck, his face became clear—the cold man at the tavern in the duster—as he crept toward her. She aimed a kick as he climbed the stairs, but again he deflected her strike.

The weapons were on the opposite side of her attacker, so she improvised with a board. He swung to punch her, and she blocked the blow with the board. But when his punch struck it, her arms folded with his power, forcing the board back into her chest and knocking the wind out of her. Stunned, she fell back hard against the cabin.

In the moment it took to catch her breath, the shadow closed the gap and put both hands on her throat. It was over. He could break her neck or crush her trachea, but instead, he gloated as she struggled.

"Silly little girl," he said with contempt.

Struggling, she could not reach him. She tried to raise her feet to his chest and push, but he tightened his grip painfully, forcing her to stop.

*He's going to kill me.*

*No! It's not my time to die.* And with that clarity, she stopped struggling and centered herself. *There will be a moment, an opportunity.*

The villain misunderstood her relaxation as unconsciousness and moved his head closer and sneered.

*Almost . . .*

***

Though preoccupied with the big man, Jon worried about Diana. When he reached for a barrel stave to use as a weapon, the big man turned and ran to the back of the boat. When they caught him, he turned and pushed them both into the crates. But when he looked across the deck, he stopped in his tracks.

"Stop!" the giant shouted.

Just then, the captain hit the giant on the head with the skillet, and he collapsed like a felled tree.

***

A thundering voice shouted "Stop!" which was enough distraction for the shadow to take his weight off Diana, and for her to focus her remaining strength. With her hands together, she thrust upward between his arms, using her shoulders to push his elbows out. This loosened the hands around her neck and brought his head closer. As she took a quick breath, she cupped her palms, smacked him in the ears, and grabbed them with her thumbs to gouge his eyes. He relaxed his grip more, and he stepped back.

Taking another quick breath, Diana crouched and sprung, striking his chin with the heel of her hand, knocking his head back with his throat exposed. With her knuckles, she struck his windpipe. He collapsed to his knees, holding his neck, eyes wild and gasping for breath. She grabbed a belaying pin, but before striking him, she reached into his vest pocket to retrieve the red coins.

When she reached again for the bag of gold and silver coins, the shadow grabbed her wrist and glared at her, red-faced and gurgling through his ruined throat.

She let go of the bag, which spilled its contents into the river. But unable to pull away from him, she slammed the pin into his temple with a loud *crack*. He released her wrist, and she kicked him over the side.

As the shadow drifted away face down, his duster billowing on the surface, Diana collapsed.

*** 

Jon freed himself from the crates, rushed to her, and kneeled.

"I came as soon as I could," he said, his voice echoing as if in a cave.

But Diana stared into the dark, her eyes bloodshot, and bloody welts and bruises rising from the punches. She trembled, overwhelmed by the battle fever that had nowhere to go. Opening her shaking palm, she gave him the red coins, which he put in his pocket. When she tried to stand, he gripped her shoulder to stop her.

"No, girl, not yet." He moved a crate for her to lean against. "How are you?"

No sound came when she tried to speak. She squeaked out something unintelligible, and Jon held up his hand to stop her.

"Shush. Use hand signs," he said. "Can you breathe?"

She nodded but winced in pain.

"Is your name Diana? How many fingers am I showing? What day of the week is this?"

She replied in sign, but when hand signs were inadequate, she tried to croak out responses before giving up. Nodding gave her a headache, so she resorted to thumbs up or down.

"Now it's important we find out where you're hurt." Jon touched her shoulder, and she winced. "You won't really feel those bruises until tomorrow."

Trying to speak, the words would not come. With her face contorted in pain, she slammed her fist to her chest and then on her palm.

"I don't understand, lass."

Diana wheezed. "This I feel now."

He paused, realizing what she was struggling with. "Yes, Princess, death is different now, closer, yours and his. Put that aside. Our concern is for you now, not him."

"Is this like combat?" she croaked.

"Sometimes. If you're lucky and survive."

She tried to rise again, but he put his hands on her shoulder.

"Stay," he said, "I'll be right back."

Jon called to the captain, who was binding the big thief. "Please bring us bedding for the girl. I'm afraid to leave her."

Clagett returned with blankets and made a second trip for bandages and salves. Jon applied salve to the cuts and scrapes and gave her willow bark to chew to relieve the pain. But her jaw hurt too much, so the captain brewed tea from the willow bark for her. The remedies soothed her discomfort, and exhausted, she slept.

Waking in the night, she found herself in a lean-to that Jon made as a windbreak. Warmed by a brazier to keep off the river's dampness, she took his hand in hers and went back to sleep. But Jon kept his eyes on the night and the dangers in the dark.

Diana's first moves when she woke in the morning also woke all her painful bruises. Each breath was agony and the black eye and headache pounded with every beat of her heart.

Nearby, Jon spoke with the captain.

"How's the girl?" Captain Clagett asked.

"A day or so will tell," Jon said with creases between his eyes.

"Why'd the giant help her?" Clagett asked, but Jon only shrugged. "You called her Princess."

"A nickname, nothing more," Jon said.

Satisfied, Clagett returned to the tiller.

Diana's throat was tender, but she still spoke.

In a raspy voice she said, "I'm sorry, Jon."

"For what, lass? You're alive and whole."

"I've been holding back," she said, "in all those practices. And last night, I didn't use strikes that would kill."

"Until the last."

She dropped her head. "He came with a sack and a rope first. I thought my skill would be enough."

"He held the advantage in size and weight."

"I didn't want to hurt him. Until . . ."

"That must change. You're a sheepdog, not a sheep." His face softened. "You are blessed, lassie."

"Yes, to have survived. Thank you for—"

Jon shook his head and smiled at her. "No, Princess. You're blessed with a reason to live that's larger than yourself." He paused. "Your father embraced such a mission."

She nodded. "Cherbourne and the North."

"No, lassie. You."

She remained thoughtful while he checked if her eyes could follow and focus and tested her balance and reflexes. When satisfied there were no internal injuries, he sighed.

"I understand your attacker, Diana, but not the big guy."

Jon called for Captain Clagett, and when Diana retrieved her sword and throwing stars, the three of them went to talk to the giant.

"What's your name?" Jon asked.

"Name's Fell," the giant said with a long sigh, "from Langston, upriver."

"And your companions?"

The giant watched the riverbank pass before him. "Cousins, except for the man in black."

"Why us?" the captain asked.

"Easy pickings: light crew, rich cargo," he said and paused. "We've done this before: throw the crew overboard, take stuff that's easy to carry, leave the boat moored downstream, and disappear. No one gets hurt. My lazy cousins wanted to turn this into a business and quit their menial jobs. A score here would set them up."

"Which of you picked us, picked this boat?" Jon said.

"The man in the wide hat. He said there was a strongbox on board."

"Tell me about him."

"A mean one," Fell replied. "My cousins vouched for him, said he could pick locks like yours here, but I didn't know he was a killer. When he came aboard, he said 'the girl is mine.' That a girl was on board was a surprise to me."

"He's not from around here?"

"No," Fell said. "Yesterday was the first I laid eyes on him."

Jon rubbed his chin. "And you, Fell, why a thief? There are easier trades."

"Look at me," Fell said. Unable to free his hands, he turned around and showed them, palms up, fingers twice as wide as Jon's. "What trade is suitable for these hands? Jeweler? What shop would fit this body? There are no schools on the river, and I by nature am not the most industrious." He glanced at his shoes and paused. "It's been easy so far. No one hurt except my cousins."

"Why'd you help the girl?" Jon asked.

Fell glanced down. "He was killing her."

"That's all?"

"Isn't that enough?" Fell said.

Jon took Diana to the other side of the boat. "He seems innocent enough."

"He saved my life," she said in a raspy whisper.

Jon frowned. "Perhaps. But without him, I would have reached you much sooner."

"What are we going to do with him?" Diana said. "The sheriff?"

"We need him to disappear."

"I won't see him killed," she said.

"Nothing of the kind." He pulled her close. "I have an idea."

As Fell wiggled in his ropes, the captain whittled, aware the struggling would only make the bonds tighter. But he tapped his knife on the skillet at his hip as a warning, and the giant stopped.

Diana rejoined the captain, and Jon stood in front of Fell, hands on his hips. They were eye-to-eye though the big man sat.

"We are Rangers from the North," Jon said. "You helped the girl, so we spared your life. Now you have a choice between life and death. We travel in secret, so if we're discovered or tracked, we'll find you and kill you."

The giant and captain both raised their eyebrows and glanced at Jon, then Diana, and back.

Fell laughed aloud. "Hah, boogeymen." He grinned. "Rangers. From the North, yet. These are fairy tales." He laughed again. "Spare me, old man."

Showing no emotion, Diana reached into her breast pocket and flicked her wrist. The bronze throwing star clipped Fell's ear and stuck deep in the cabin wall.

"Will you bet your life?" she croaked.

The big thief stopped laughing and lost his grin but did not respond.

She glanced at Jon. "He chooses death now," she said and reached for her knife.

"Sorry," Fell said. "I'll keep your secret."

With a raised eyebrow, Jon grinned. "You're right, death is simpler."

"No, no, wait! Really, I promise not to tell anyone."

"Why should we believe you?" Jon asked.

Fell did not speak.

"Who holds your bond?"

The giant furrowed his brow.

Jon sighed. "Who guarantees your promise?"

Fell shook his head and glanced down again. "If the word of a thief depends upon a third party, I am lost," he said. "Father Estaban at Langston might remember me. I was once a very mischievous attendant during services."

Jon frowned. "Then your life is your bond, and we hold it. Endanger ours and yours is forfeit. And what of your cousins?"

"They never saw her . . . and it'll be to my everlasting joy never to see them again."

Without smiling, Jon nodded and led Diana to the cabin. When they were out of sight, Jon smiled at her. "That was a dramatic throw."

"I was aiming for the door," she said with a big smile, a target a foot away from where the throwing star landed.

After a brief word with Jon, Clagett steered to shore.

"If you want a better life," Jon said as he untied Fell, "go to the Monastery of Dorreau." He scratched something on the throwing star with a nail and handed it to Fell. "Give them this. If you're willing, they'll teach you a trade and to read. If not, they're in need of a strong back. And if you're honest, they'll speak for you."

After he jumped into the shallows near the bank, Fell glanced at each of them. "Why do you help me?"

"You helped her," Jon said.

"But my friend would've killed her."

"He wasn't your friend."

Clagett polled the keelboat from the shore, and as they drifted away, Fell smiled for the first time, a wicked smile.

"You'd trust a thief in a monastery?" Fell said.

Jon laughed and called out. "The monks have nothing to steal but virtue, so take all you can carry!"

# Chapter 33
## Reunion

"Ahoy there!" came a shout from shore the next morning.

"Stay below," Jon said to Diana as he peered out the shuttered window of the cabin to see a horseman riding parallel to the boat. Captain Clagett maneuvered the keelboat to shouting distance from shore and set it adrift as Jon came on deck.

"What's your business?" Jon called.

"I'm inquiring as to the health of a young lady named Diana Smyth from Branwyn, who might be in your company."

"Who are you?" Jon asked.

"Eric Lombard, son of George, King of Merisol."

"Eric! Jon, stop the boat," Diana whispered from below.

"He's not my king," Jon shouted to Eric. "And why does the girl concern you?"

"Her friend, Martin, was hurt during serious trouble in Branwyn," Eric said, avoiding Jon's bait.

"Is he alone or with company?" Diana asked, referring to their test of Eric's intent.

Jon turned to her within the cabin. "With company," he said, teasing them both now. He turned back to Eric. "Is that your only business with this Diana person?"

"There's more," Eric said. "She has information from . . ." He paused before continuing, "Information about our history that may affect the present."

"Who rides with you?"

"Steven Dumont. Officer in His Majesty's Guard. Only him."

Jon turned to her. "Is Steven Dumont known to you?"

"Yes," she said. "He's Eric's bodyguard and a soldier. He's always been a gentleman with me."

"We'll pick you up," Jon said and went below to fetch Diana.


Eric boarded and took Diana's hand in his. Even through the bruises, she could not hide her blush.

"Are you all right?" he asked. "I came to help."

"You're a day late, lad," Jon said with a slight grin.

"That was our fault," Diana said and smiled. "Eric, this is Jon, my guardian."

Eric and Jon shook hands, but the captain interrupted.

"Excuse me, Prince," Clagett said, "but we can't idle here. Please let us drift, and your man can ride along shore."

After a word with Steven, Eric returned and sat with Diana on side benches near the keel.

"What of Martin?" Diana asked. "You said he was hurt."

"Bruised but recovering. When he told me the story, I came as soon as I could, well as soon as I could catch you. When I saw that mess in the woods, it confirmed my fears."

*He came for me!*

He took her hand in his and she blushed again. "Martin said you distracted the assassins who targeted the king and queen. They offer their heartfelt gratitude. And mine. Princes have few real friends, and each is precious."

Diana's pulse raced, and she hoped her excitement was not obvious.

"Did you get those bruises at the fight in the woods?" he asked.

"No, I—"

"What happened?"

"Thieves!" Clagett said. "Aye, and what a battle it was, Your Grace! Five there were, and a giant and a killer . . ." But Eric and Diana were concerned with each other.

"I couldn't believe it was you, Eric," she said. "That was you at the ferry dock, no?"

He nodded.

"Why'd you come all this way?"

"To make sure you were safe," Eric said. With a blustery voice he added, "You're a friend of the prince, and your harm would reflect badly on Branwyn."

His official tone stung, and she removed her hands from his.

Eric's voice softened. "But mostly because I was worried about you."

The blush returned, and she wanted him to take her hand again.

"Why'd you rush away?" Eric said. "You should have come to me."

"We tried but ran out of time. The Chancellor paid us to surrender to him and intended us not to speak to you."

Jon showed him the red coins.

"Grimes, that snake," Eric said and told them of the coup attempt that began at the performance and ended at the gate. "And what of you? Those bruises are fresh. The thieves attacked you or the boat?"

"Both," Jon said. "An assassin came for her."

Diana broke a pause in the conversation. "I'm glad you're here." Unable to wait any longer, she surprised them by taking Eric's hand. "I can't stay, Eric."

"You can't leave with so much mystery surrounding you," he said. "I won't leave without knowing who you are."

"What do you mean?" she said.

"The fight in the forest. Who are you two to best four attackers?"

"Five," she said with a smile.

"Ranchers could not have done that. And why'd Grimes have any care for you at all?"

She turned to Jon. "I think we should tell him." Jon nodded, and she addressed Eric. "Prince Eric, let me introduce you to Jon Henlow of Cherbourne, General in the Army of the North, and advisor to Richard Stewart, King of the North."

Captain Clagett's mouth fell open. "Well I'll be a . . ."

Eric glanced back and forth between Jon and Diana. "Ahhh . . . pleased to meet you, General. From the North you say?"

She leaned forward. "You have news of the war?"

"You've not heard?"

"No," she said. "And fear no news is bad news."

"The Sulerians have swept to Royax on the coast—"

She took a deep breath. "That's what Father feared."

Captain Clagett interrupted. "When I left Venaro last spring, I saw a fleet set sail north."

"You say a king rules the North," she said with crossed fingers, hoping for good news. "Do you know who?"

"No."

"There's hope still," Jon said as Diana paced with her hands across her chest.

With a tear in her eye, she turned to Jon. "There may be a new king and puppet of the Sul."

Eric leaned toward her. "Why do you worry so, Diana?"

Jon turned to Eric. "Prince, let me introduce Her Royal Highness, Diana Stewart of Cherbourne, Princess of the North."

Clagett smiled and shook his head while Eric raised his eyebrows again.

"But how . . ." Eric stammered. "A princess . . ."

"Don't fuss," she said, "We're ranchers caught up in events. And as for princess, that's only if my father still rules."

Eric frowned and lost his good humor.

She glanced at Jon who nodded, rose, and took the captain's arm, leading him away to leave the two royals alone.


"Grimes was behind the coup attempt and the Sulerians and Quarajii were part of it."

Diana nodded. "The phony merchants I mentioned were Quarajii. That's what we tried to warn you about. My father said the Qu dream of a home in the South and kick at the corral their neighbors have built to contain them."

"The corral may already be broken if they defeated the Northmen."

Diana's eyes burned. Eric referred to her home as if it were a mere point on a map, a token in a contest between states that did not endanger her father and tens of thousands of people.

"They once tried to cross the Spine to get south."

"Apparently, they're already here," Eric said. "Capitolia has fallen to darkness and the entire eastern coast lies undefended. Steven brings me orders from George to rally the barons. And Martin said there was another worry to the east."

Removing the hide wrap from the atlas, Diana pointed to the land passage along the eastern shore. "The Horde may have a way to invade the south. If not now, then in the future."

Eric studied the map. "It's real then. Is this the proof Martin wanted to warn us of a land invasion?"

"Perhaps," Diana said. "The map is of our past, and he fears it may also be our future. If the strand opened up before, it may again."

"This would be like removing a cork from a bottle. The South couldn't absorb a mass migration, and the barons won't accept a troublesome neighbor. But only my father takes the invasion threat seriously."

Diana gripped Eric's hand. "You must make them listen. These are the Hordes and won't relent until their mission is complete. Chaos is to their advantage, and the barons are their obstacle."

"Why'd they attack Branwyn if there's a path open to the East? And why continue to war with your people if there is a path south?"

She shook her head. "The motives that might help us predict their moves are confused by time and distance and culture." *And the Empress's magic.*

He nodded. "We need to verify the Strand before we can take the threat seriously. That will be a job for the barons when I meet with them."

"Eric, if the reliquerium is what the Horde sought in Branwyn, then you must protect it. This could alter our future. The Sul would burn it for their baths if they can't control it. Tell your father."

"I've spent weeks chasing you, Diana. I won't be dismissed so quickly. I've . . ."

Diana stopped listening. *I will wait no longer.*

She rose and pulled Eric to his feet. But at the stairs to the cabin, she stopped and glanced back where Jon watched her, his face expressionless.

*Is what I desire now appropriate for a respectable woman? Is what I want of him suitable for a chivalrous gentleman?*

*I don't care.*

*But Jon will kill him.*

*Would Eric think less of me for what I want, or I think less of myself after?*

*I don't care.*

*But Jon will kill him.*

*We're both mature adults.*

*But Jon will still kill him.*

She sighed. *I do care how they regard me. And I do care how I regard myself.*

*I can wait.*

And with her hand still holding Eric's, she returned to the bench and smiled.

"Tell me of your home," she said.


Diana idled the afternoon with Eric, she talking about the North and he about his childhood in Alsair. He relayed the worrisome news of the shorter growing season in the North and the darkness falling over the far South. Over dinner, he and Jon compared campaign stories during which she remained quiet. And over tea, she talked about Venaro and their destination home, but not the means to get there.

After dinner, they sat alone again, and she took his hand.

"Eric, when Jon announced my station, you seemed disappointed. My title does not encumber me."

"But they obligate us. For the last years I've been avoiding a royal matchup because the politics would mire it down. But you—

"I would mire you down?"

He shook his head. "I don't think anything could mire you down. I've never met anyone like you, and I don't want to leave you just after I found you." He sighed. "But I must."

She took his hand in both of hers. "You won't lose me," she said softly.

"I must ride east on a mission for my king," he said.

"And I must head north on a mission for mine."

"I must be off tonight. Every hour we drift adds two hours to my mission. How will I reach you?"

"Jon and I will try to establish a communication channel through Venaro." Before the prince spoke again, she handed Eric a note. "Please ask Martin to decode these symbols."

"Why?"

"I think they're dates on the atlas. If so, the maps have a bigger story to tell." She frowned. "Something's coming, Eric, something larger than the Strand to the east, changes that will affect us all."

"What is it?"

"I'm not sure," she said. "I just have a sense of it."

Jon approached to signal their parting was nigh.

Eric stood. "I can't leave you as magnets for assassins."

"The red coins mark us," Jon said.

Eric rubbed his chin. "Assassins aren't chartered here in Antona. Do you have the warrants?"

Jon handed him the red coins.

"You have now surrendered yourselves to the crown," Eric said. "Steven and I will visit the sheriff at Remsford to alert any passing assassins that your contract has been closed. I'll have a courier ride to the Guild offices and alert the assassins. When Steven returns to Branwyn, he will petition the king to void Grimes's warrant and impound the deposit."

"And we'll request asylum in Venaro," Diana said.


The rowboat put to shore again, and Steven rode closer leading Eric's horse. Diana went ashore with the prince to say goodbye.

"Diana, I . . ." Eric began but took her hand. "I wish I could visit Venaro with you."

"Perhaps in the future."

"Perhaps if I finish my mission early," he said, but that was unlikely. "Safe journey." He took her hand and kissed it, turned, and walked away.

Their parting and his formality saddened her, and she cursed herself. *Why do I hang on his every word! Must I be less of a lady?*

Eric stopped, turned, and marched back to her. She took a step toward him, ready to speak, but he spoke first.

"Damnable royalty. It would be so much simpler if you were a farm girl. Now my mother will aim her sights on you."

"Would that be so bad?" she said with a smile at his discomfort.

"You have an invitation to dinner at Branwyn Castle," he said, "and I damn well mean for you to attend even if I have to come to the North get you myself."

She dropped her gaze. "An invitation from your father?"

"From me," Eric said. He took her cheeks in his hands, closed his eyes and kissed her full on the lips, pinning her to the spot.

Shocked, Diana's eyes were still open. She melted into the kiss and closed her eyes, feeling the strength of his arms, the softness of his lips, and the heat of his chest. But all she heard was her beating heart.

When he leaned back, he smiled, and she looked into his eyes for only a moment before jumping into his arms and kissing him back, hard and long.

"I accept for my father," she said with a big smile.

As Eric and Steven mounted their horses, Diana boarded the keelboat and took Jon's arm.

"Well, your mood has improved, Princess," Jon said.

"Uh-huh. I'll see him again, won't I?"

"I'm sure of it, lass."

\*\*\*

"Finally," Steven said after mounting the saddle. "I was going to hit you if you left without kissing that maiden."

"Turns out she's a princess."

"What difference? She's a woman," Steven said as they wheeled their horses back to Remsford.

\*\*\*

Diana watched as Eric and Steven rode away. After a bend in the river, she lost them and turned to Jon.

"He has big boots to fill," Diana said.

"Eric?"

She nodded. "There are only two men in my life, other than the boys in the militia. My father and you," she said. *Fierce, skilled, responsible, kind.* "And how can he live up to that?"

"We're the wrong models," Jon said. "We've had a lifetime to slay the dragons within us. Eric is still young. Judge him for what he'll become. If you're serious, the future is where you'll be spending most of your life."

"And what of love?"

He smiled. "Certainly. But I think we acknowledge that possibility, at least for you."

She gazed downstream at the river and the horizon brought closer by another bend in the river. "How can I tell what he's becoming?"

"By his actions."

"Not what he says?"

A slow shake of his head emphasized his words. "Never."

"And what do his actions tell you?"

Jon glanced away for a moment. "He's skilled in combat and leadership. He respects his men and has none of the arrogance of nobility."

She frowned, but he turned with a smile to face her.

"And he rode for weeks to find you to assure himself of your safety. He did so not for a princess, but for a farm girl who helped his family. He speaks to you with courtesy and respect. There's no commission in that, only chivalry. He leaves you now only for his duty and the orders of his king. And he left you no doubt regarding his intentions. I'd say his arrow aims true." Jon turned back to the river. "For the two of you."

The possibilities for her future and the love of a prince warmed her, and for a few moments, she did not worry for her father and her country.

Ray Strong

# Chapter 34
## City of Lights

Downstream of the granite of Antona, the *Shiela Reine* slowed as the Gruen River opened to a lush marshy delta and patchwork of small islands. Bordered by mangrove and willow, the soft soil supported only low buildings, some on stilts to survive the tides and annual floods. No army could cross this landscape with its cavalry and trebuchets, as the Imperium discovered. But legions of smugglers and insects thrived.

Clagett was in no hurry as the keelboat approached Venaro from the East, but Diana was. Since Eric's hints of the heightened conflict in the North, her father's safety burdened her again. A few miles upstream from Venaro, Diana sat beside Jon, who tended the tiller while Clagett checked the currents at the bow.

"We're safe, Jon," Diana said and took his hand.

"Perhaps, but it's not time to be incautious. It will take days for news to reach the guild and more days for the guild to notify their members. And there may be agents on the road now who will not get the news. Let's keep our watch."

"Tell us of Venaro, Captain," Jon asked as Clagett returned.

"If'n I might, General. What's your purpose there? Perhaps I can steer ya true."

"We'll be looking for a trading house to help us with the next step in our journey."

"You'll be dealing with pirates then," Clagett said with a side eye and a grin.

Jon sat straight. "How so?"

"The free traders and pirates was run outa' the old ports near Capitolia," Clagett said, climbing onto the cabin. "And they scurried here to these islands. Success tamed them, and they smuggle everywhere they can't trade openly." On the roof, he furled the little sail and the ship slowed. "They founded the trading houses and have a Compact they call the Scythean League."

"Does the League rule Venaro?" Diana asked.

Clagett harrumphed at the course of the boat, jumped from atop the cabin, and took the tiller from Jon. "No. At least not publicly. But I'm a riverman, milady, and a native of Antona."

"Antona broke the Imperator's back."

Clagett nodded. "With Venaro's help, and I won't speak ill of 'em."

"They came for Venaro's wealth?" Jon said.

"Who knows what tyrants want except 'more'," the captain said and spat over the side.

"Why are we slowing, Seizu?" Jon said.

"A surprise, milord."

Diana smiled as the *Shiela Reine* neared the masted ships on the way to the mouth of the Gruen. "What's that ship there?"

"That's a sloop," Clagett said. "And the fat one there is a barque: wide boats for cargo and narrow for speed." He pointed to the tallest ship with masts reaching for the sky. "And the clipper there is for the open ocean."

Farther west, the masts competed for the heavens with the ornate spires of the temples. And as they drifted to the dock, the lights of the city came on.

Diana's mouth fell open with a word half-formed on her lips. At the starboard side of the boat, she leaned over the gunwales with wide eyes and a big smile.

This was the captain's gift, to observe Venaro turn on its lights, like pearls lining the wharf and diamonds studding the buildings. The city was young and vibrant and dressed for the evening.

Captain Clagett docked the keelboat and arranged for longshoremen to unload and stable their horses. After recommending a nearby inn, they said their goodbyes.

On Jon's arm, Diana walked through an immense warehouse in dim torch light through puddles and the smells of cedar and cinnamon and old fish. A wagon preceded them as they neared the far end away from the dock, and tall doors opened to a well-lit street and a sea of bustling people and palanquins.

She stopped and smiled. Across the thoroughfare stood a square lined with shops open and restaurants and taverns with tables set on the streets, like Branwyn Town Center.

Their goal was the inn across the square, but to reach it they must pass through the crowd of men and women out for the evening: men in long capes and colorful robes of their guild, and women in vibrant colors and ornate hats with feathers from peacocks and parrots.

Almost to their destination, she stopped when a man and woman approached them. So provincial and out of place, wearing clothing so tattered and drab, she pitied them. But this was her reflection in a shop window. She blushed with shame and hurried Jon on their way.

At the inn, they obtained rooms, cleaned up and dressed, and went to dinner inside the adjoining tavern. Diana yearned to sit near the street as the citizens in their colorful clothing passed by. But though she changed into her best dress, her simple attire embarrassed her.

At a table outside the inn, a young girl in a frilly dress caught her eye and Diana smiled, imagining a party cake topped with a spray of tiny flowers. The young girl's escort, a handsome officer in uniform, suggested a winter faire ornament with shiny brass buttons and polished leather. Diana put her elbow on the table and chin on her fist. *They must be on a date, and she's just old enough to be without a chaperone.*

"How much would a dress like that cost?" Diana asked, dreaming of what she would look like in the dress, arm-in-arm with Prince Eric in full dress uniform.

"We have enough," Jon said with a gentle smile. "But not the occasion."


The next morning, Diana ran the back of her hand along a smooth and shiny fabric whose touch made her smile.

"That's a new weave they call satin, and a stunning choice for you," the assistant said and took her arm. "Come, I'll show you dresses of it in your size."

The innkeeper had directed them here to a clothier where they might find attire more likely to blend in. These would be Diana's first proper dresses rather than the farm girl jumpers or militia uniforms she had spent her life in. Designed to expose more of her feminine assets than she was accustomed, they were exquisite but the common style in Venaro.

Nervous and awkward, Diana studied how other women held themselves and walked. High heels that let them reach the height of men were the fashion, but not needing to compete with them, she chose hard-soled slippers. In the mirror, she tried on different expressions with a curve of her lips or a tilt of her eyebrows: aloof, proud, snobby, but settled on confident.

While waiting for her, Jon selected a rather ordinary day-suit and dressed. More accustomed to uniforms or overalls, she had never seen him in town clothes before: tailored clothing that fit his body well but was much too small for his character.

"Suitable camouflage," was all he said, but he did so with confidence.

Standing in front of the mirror, she admired her dress as if she were a manikin, but then recognized how out of place she was within it. Unlike the delicate white-skinned attendants and women at last night's dinner, her skin was deeply tanned. And unlike their polished nails and smooth hands, her nails were broken and knuckles dark with stains that scrubbing could not remove. She covered her hands immediately and leaned over to the clothier.

"Is there something you can do about these?" Diana whispered and gave her a quick peek at her hands.

"Certainly dear," the owner replied with a wink, "Jack across the street." She glanced behind her. "But tell him nothing."

As she spun in her frilly dress, Diana told Jon about their next stop at Jack's. "Does this not totally transform me?"

"Not to those who know you," Jon said.

She frowned and dropped her gaze. "Is the farm girl still so obvious?"

He took her by the shoulders. "To the contrary. These clothes only hide the most beautiful young woman in the land. Except for my own darlings, of course." He smiled and offered her his arm. "Now, let's go complete your disguise, Milady."

Diana dragged Jon to the beauty shop where a uniformed man more polished than the officer from the night before opened the door for them.

The salon was spacious, filled with well-dressed matrons in chairs, some in long curls and others in hair the size of beehives. A squad of maidens attended each woman, working from toe to eyebrow like construction workers remodeling a building. One elderly woman with thinning hair sat next to a table holding a wig being primped and coddled as if it too possessed a soul.

In the middle of it all, a man directed as if conducting an orchestra. While the matrons glowered with disdain, he smiled when Diana entered and greeted them with outstretched arms.

"An exotic and her captain," he said with a glance to Jon and then to her hands. "Oh, my!" He snapped his fingers, and a team of young maidens whisked her into a chair and fussed with her without delay.

He presented himself to Jon and offered his hand. "I am Jacques," he said with his nose in the air as if this were a title of royalty and took Jon's arm to seat him by the window. He leaned over to Jon's ear. "Fear not, she's in the hands of artists."

Another snap of his fingers brought a charming young lady with refreshments and company for an impatient Jon. And after putting his finger to his chin, he frowned and whispered to an attendant who rushed out the door.

After smoothing her calloused palms and removing the stains from her hands, two attendants manicured her nails, while the others inspected her for other areas to improve. Finding none, they frowned with fingers to chins. And Diana, having never been so pampered, found it all amusing.

One attendant prepared to cover her tan with a lighter shade of makeup, but Jacques waved his hands and came over.

"Accent her natural radiance, don't hide it." He wagged his finger and pointed to complements for blush and lipstick.

"Now the hair," Jacques mused, his hand on his chin.

Diana scanned the women in the shop, with hair done in lofty edifices.

*There I will not go.*

"Milady, I recommend . . ." He moved behind her and brushed her hair back to highlight her high cheekbones and upward slant of her eyes. Then he braided it loosely, leaving a long ponytail. Dancing back around in front of her again, he gave her a hand-mirror. "I recommend . . . nothing." He flung his hands out again and stepped back with a smile.

The attendant returned with an outfit she hung on a rack, and a dress, off-white to complement Diana's tan and much less ornate. When Diana put on the dress, she was no manikin intended only to display a garment. Instead the gown accented her natural beauty without contrivance. Diana stood at the mirror, and the shop hushed. She turned around, and the attendants admired her and Jacques like they were ready to applaud, while the patrons glared. Smiling, Diana blushed at the attention focused on her as a woman, not a farm girl.

She smiled in the mirror. *This is the dress I should wear on Jonday night with Eric at the Town Center.*

"My work is done," Jacques said, putting his fingers to his lips and kissing them. With a tear in his eye, he bowed with his arms outstretched.

As they prepared to leave, Jon went to Jacques. "A word, sir?"

Jacques signaled a girl who came to attend Diana. "Excuse us, milady," he said, and took Jon to a corner. "Yes?"

"We need to meet with the head of the trading houses," Jon said. "Who might that be?"

Jacques gave him a sly smile and turned away from the shop window. "I believe you mean House of Fontana. At the south end of the docks."

"Thank you," Jon said and turned, but Jacques took him by the arm.

"If I may," Jacques said. "If your destination is the docks . . ." From a rack behind him he took another outfit and draped it over his arm. "I suggest a simpler dress. We can send the one you are wearing to your lodging, and you can save it for dinner."

Diana turned to Jon who nodded, took the outfit, and went to change again.

"She's unaware of how beautiful she is," Jacques said as Diana changed. "Keep it that way and don't spoil her."

Jon frowned at his suggestion and spun to walk away, but Jacques stepped in his path.

"No offense, sir. She's in danger."

Jon eyed him with suspicion, but Jacques rolled his eyes.

"Come now," Jacques said. "I'm a beauty consultant, not an assassin."

"Tell me more."

"Someone has been searching for your . . . ward."

"Who?"

"I don't know. Yet." He showed Jon a woven bracelet with a gold cord similar to Diana's, this one untorn.

"How did you come by this?"

Jacques leaned back in surprise. "Come, come. I'd have to be an idiot for this not to find my hands. The bounty is sizeable. Advise your ward to burn her anklet or wear it as a garter, but for her safety make it less obvious."

"We may be the target of assassins."

Jacques rolled his eyes again. "No, not those cretins."

"How long?"

"More than a year."

Jon furrowed his brow, "That can't be Grimes."

"The powerful have a long reach," Jacques said and turned as Diana left the dressing room.

Diana's new outfit, a jacket over a white blouse with dark floor-length skirt, was more businesslike than the dress and shouted wealth. She spun to show it off and kissed Jacques on the cheek.

"Who are you?" Jon asked Jacques as Diana took his arm. "Certainly not a humble beauty consultant."

Jacques smiled. "Humble? Don't be absurd," he said and led them to the door.

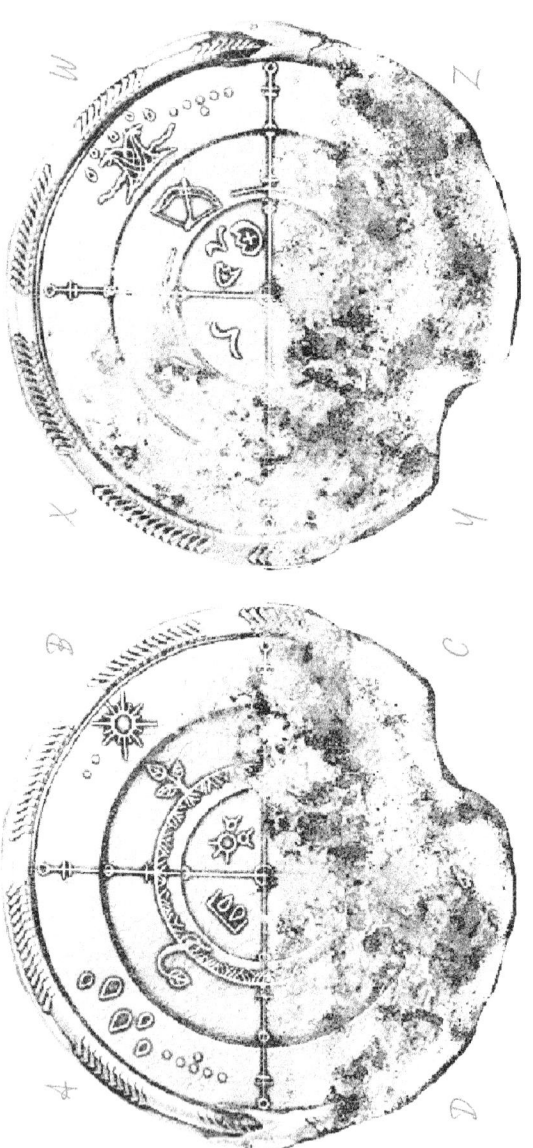

# Chapter 35
# House of Fontana

At mid-day, Jon and Diana wound their way through the bustle of sailors, wagons, and longshoremen on the docks, all smelling of old fish and olive oil. Deep within the warehouses and wharfs, behind stacks of crates in the oldest part of Venaro stood the trading houses.

House of Fontana's doors faced the docks, and a beefy doorman armed with sharp eyes and a cudgel let them inside. After a brief word with a clerk, they followed him through rows of desks and copy boys with heads low, making notations on parchments and scrolls. The smell of ink and sardines surrounded them as the clerk led them down a long hall and up two flights of stairs. There the clerk opened double doors to an expansive office lit bright by the mid-day sun.

Furnished with dark leather furniture, the room highlighted the engraved woodwork of etched glass cabinets lining two walls. Ship models in full sail from skiff to clipper stood on them as if they would fly off the edges. And between the cabinets nestled tall porcelain urns. West-facing windows extended the length of the room and overlooked the docks. Two floors above the scents of old fish and manure, doors opened to a balcony with a fresh salty breeze and the calls of longshoremen and clops of horses on the wood dock. Beyond the tall masts outside lay the open ocean, and

Diana imagined how fantastic the sunsets and how frightening the storms would appear through these windows.

The man behind the desk reached for a cane, rose, and went to greet them. Tall, and gray-templed, he was middle-aged, but his sun-etched face and fit body proclaimed an active man who spent most of his life out of doors.

He wore the more pragmatic breeches of a ship's captain rather than the robes of a merchant, and a silk shirt hiding a scar that began behind his ear. He may have been a handsome man at one time, but still his eyes gleamed with fire when he glanced at them and extended his hand.

"I'm Jones," he said. "Just Jones. And you are?"

"Jon and Diana Shepard," Jon said and shook his hand.

Jones raised an eyebrow. "My clerk mentioned you held something of interest for me."

"We seek safe passage north," Jon said.

Impatience crossed Jones's face. "You can see the clerk downstairs about that. If there's nothing more?" he said and raised his hand to the door.

"And asylum from the Assassins Guild," Diana said.

Jones returned to his chair and leaned his forearms on his desk. "The Guild has no charter here."

"The bounty is large and . . ." She glanced at Jon. "There may be others as well."

"Without a charter to sanction your murder, our police will arrest your attackers . . . *after* commission of the crime. Assassins and contractors skulk about in the shadows, so I'd say you're not safe. But here in Venaro we have more . . . experience with criminals and extra-legal activity than Antona. Our police can help, but the risk remains." He leaned forward over his desk. "Then the passage you seek must be discreet?"

"Yes," Diana said. "Our identities and our destination must remain a secret."

Jones stared at them with narrow eyes as if recalculating the fare with every word. "Xorellia?"

"Royax."

Jones went to the window, breathed deep the scent of the sea and the docks, and turned to them. "Are you certain? Our fleet recently broke the Sulerian blockade there."

Diana gripped Jon's hand. "Was the North victorious?"

Jones shrugged. "If you can call it victory."

"And Cherbourne?"

"Roughed up by the Hordes I heard, and the army that chased them out. East of the Royax Docks I cannot vouch. If safety is your goal, I recommend a different destination."

She squeezed Jon's hand even tighter. "Who rules?"

"The North still rules itself," Jones said. "If that's what you're asking."

"Any news about the King of the North?" Diana asked.

Jones smiled. "Of that I can say nothing. Royax is it? What you ask is exceptional and quite expensive." He pursed his lips and inspected them both. "So, what am I to make of you?"

*We'll lose him unless we do something.*

"Perhaps this will persuade you," Diana said. Into Jones's hand, she put the segment of brass coin Richard had given her before their journey south.

"We hope—" Jon began, but Jones raised his hand.

"Patience, Mr. . . . Mr. Shepard, did you say? A moment, please." Jones took an envelope and spilled a score of similar coin fragments on his desk, each painted with a unique symbol. Putting on a pair of narrow gold-rimmed spectacles, he attempted to match them to her fragment.

As Jones worked, Diana toured the room, examining the ship models and noting the many knickknacks posed in the glass cabinets. In one lay a small ivory disk with an intricately carved likeness of a schooner. Next to it stood a tooth as thick as her fist and a fang as long as her forearm. On top of the case stood a model of a three-masted ship in full sail: a replica so detailed she could make out the ropes wrapped around the belaying pins and the pegs in the deck planks.

Another cabinet held a carving in translucent blue stone of three mermaids and a boy riding a fish, all jumping from the water at the same time. On the shelf lay clay, wood, and metal coins of all shapes and sizes with strange markings, but she recognized only those from the North and Branwyn.

In a glass-topped case with its own lock lay six red assassins' coins next to a medallion with a pair of serpents. Nearby lay the distorted fragment of a silver-gray coin with what might be a snake or worm eating its tail around the edge. Etched on it were symbols and runes like those in the reliquerium.

And in one of the locked cabinets, she caught her breath at the sight of a dozen bound books yellowed and damaged by age. *And what magic might be in these?* She opened her mouth to ask about them but stopped, not wanting to seem too eager and expose them. *Patience, girl.*

Jones found a match to her coin fragment and leaned back with his eyes wide. "Ah, here we are. Our friend in the North told me you might come, Miss Shepard."

Jones scribbled on a slip of parchment and pulled a cord on the wall. "Please be my guest while arrangements are made."

A handsome clerk came in to take the note and, after a brief exchange of glances and a polite bow to Diana, promptly left.

"I have no spirits here during the day," Jones said. "But may I offer you water?"

They accepted and Jones filled crystal goblets with a clear liquid from a pitcher behind his desk and offered it to them. "It's flavored with fruits from the far south."

Jones joined Diana as she admired his knickknacks. "The souvenirs of a young adventurer. This one I especially like." He pointed to the translucent blue sculpture with mermaids. "It's a fantasy of sailors. He rides a dolphin we only see in the deep ocean."

"It's beautiful," she said.

"Perhaps you've seen something like this before?"

"I'm a simple farm girl, sir. And unfamiliar with such fine things."

"Ah, yes. So you mentioned."

Struggling to disguise her excitement, she pointed to the books behind the glass case. "And these?"

"These are my treasures from a more recent adventure," Jones said, "and of little interest to most."

"May I see one?" she asked.

Jones opened the cabinet, removed a book yellowed with age, and opened it. "Gentle. They're fragile."

She noted the same strange symbols as in the books in the reliquerium. "What does it say?"

"We don't know," Jones said. "At one time the priests came here regularly to copy them, but I won't part with them. These few might be more valuable than all my treasures. When I first showed them to a young priest, he left to start a monastery in Branwyn."

Jon sat forward with surprise. "Rochfield?"

"Yes, a bishop I hear now. Of course you'd be aware of him," he said with no hint of how he might have such information. "Do you have a particular interest in artifacts?"

With a wide smile, she raised her eyes to Jones and opened her mouth to tell him of her discovery in Branwyn. But she glanced at Jon, who shook his head. Saying nothing, she handed the book back to Jones and changed the subject.

Jones caught the exchange and smiled.

She pointed to the rune-coin. "And this one?"

"Another mystery," Jones said. Unlocking the cabinet, he took out the object and gave it to her. "This was found near a body in the mountains partially thawed from a glacier. The priests couldn't figure this out either. The coin is exquisitely wrought and more resilient than Xorellian iron, but the man's clothes were rags. Half of it is smashed, perhaps by a rock-fall or the ice. It's not clear if we could understand it even if we possessed an intact copy."

"The characters appear to be the same as in the book you showed me," she noted.

Jones smiled. "How perceptive."

"I've seen another like it," she said.

"Where?"

"It belonged to a Singer who recently performed—"

Jon cleared his throat.

Ignoring him, Jones scribbled a note and pulled a sash that hung on the wall. The handsome clerk entered, grabbed the note, and left without a word.

The coin intrigued her, but she feared Jones might dismiss them before telling her about the other items. She pointed a finger at two bronze balls connected by a chain, each about the size of her head. "What's the purpose of this?"

"Yes, well, when the Imperator found Venaro as a prize to steal, we were already strong. It was the cost of his attempts to subjugate Antona and capture Venaro that put the final nail in his coffin."

"The South blooms without him," she said.

"All but Capitolia, which is lost to darkness. Venaro needs neither the barons nor an empire to prosper. With freedom we can do what we imagine."

"And what of this?" she said, still interested in the bronze balls and chain.

"Oh yes," Jones said, "a gift shot from a catapult by the Imperium's navy during a sea battle just off the coast." He whacked his leg with his cane with a loud crack. "The price for that memento was my leg."

A knock came from the door. "Here we are," Jones said, then louder, "Enter." His clerk entered and gave him a flyer. Jones read it, nodded, and handed the flyer to Jon: a bulletin recruiting sailors.

"Report to First Mate Fortier at the Dancing Dolphin tonight before we post this tomorrow morning," Jones said. "Go together. Tell him you served on the *Poppy*."

"Thank you, sir," Jon said.

Jones bowed to each and shook their hands again. "My pleasure. Regarding your request for asylum, Browne here will coordinate with the police for your protection and help you navigate our city."

Jon reached out his hand. "Mr. Browne."

"Just Browne," he said, shaking Jon's hand. Browne tipped his head, and Jon and Diana nodded to the introduction. "I'd be pleased to give you a tour if you wish."

*Maybe in his twenties, with the square shoulders and direct gaze of a soldier. Blonde hair to Eric's brown . . .*

When she raised her eyes to his face, his smile told her she was staring. "That would be delightful, thank you, sir," she said and averted her gaze. He smiled, and she blushed.

"Milady, Milord," Jones said. "It was a pleasure to meet you, but we'll not meet again on this trip. Give my best to our friend in the North."

They said their goodbyes, and Browne led them to the door.

"One more thing," Diana said. "Can you show us the way to the Moretti house?"

"I think you mean House of Moretti. Are you sure?" he asked, and Diana nodded. "They've fallen on hard times after—"

"After Sulerian Corsairs kidnapped the family."

Jones studied her and nodded slowly. "They have a small office farther down the docks. You will need an escort," he said, and Browne nodded.


Led by a burly clerk assigned by Browne, Jon and Diana headed to Moretti's. At each dock they passed, a flag waved of the house that owned it. Some docks moored sea-worthy ships, while others hosted skiffs and tenders that serviced the largest of the merchant ships anchored in the harbor. And at the far end lay a small merchant ship flying the Moretti flag.

Outside House of Moretti sat a guard with an eyepatch, his legs across the doorway. After inspecting them and a nod to the clerk that accompanied them, he asked, "Your business?"

"I'm here with a message from Eavlyn," Diana said.

After another scan through narrowed eyes, the guard opened the door and led Jon and Diana inside. Under dim lamps, clerks occupied only a few of the score of desks, and the hubbub and bright lights inside House of Fontana were absent.

"Says she has a message from your sister," the guard said to the first clerk and returned to the door.

The clerk frowned and peered over the rim of her glasses. "Say more," she said, and Diana showed her Eavlyn's note.

"How came you by this?" the clerk asked.

"This note enveloped a silver bracelet she wished me to get to her family."

"And the bracelet?"

"Taken by the man who holds her."

"Then how am I to believe this is from her?"

When Diana gave the clerk Eavlyn's toe ring Garfann had given her, the clerk gasped and closed her eyes. When she opened them again, her eyes glistened.

"Pardon my suspicion," the clerk said. "We often get ransom demands from grifters. Come." Without asking, the clerk took Diana's arm, and led her to a small dark office that adjoined the warehouse.

"Brother, we have news!" the clerk called, and a tall young man with a captain's cap and another woman joined them. The clerk showed them Eavlyn's note and ring.

The other woman ran to hug Diana as the captain and clerk lit lamps to brighten the office. "Sit, please, and tell us everything."

As graciously as she could, Diana described Eavlyn the last time she saw her and her condition. And the family sat on the edge of their chairs and listened with wide smiles and tears.

"Yes, she's a slave, but a house slave and cared for, though she longs for freedom."

"Where did you meet her?"

Jon gave Diana a side eye that Diana ignored.

"In Derryh," Diana said, "held by a prosperous Sulerian visiting from Sinefora."

"So far away," the clerk said and looked up. "Excuse me, please. I've been rude," the clerk said and introduced them to her sisters, Judik and Merik, and their brother, Captain Jorgen. Diana and Jon introduced themselves only as travelers from Branwyn.

"And how do our parents fare?" the captain asked and poured drinks for them.

"They were alive when I spoke to her," Diana lied. "But I was not told their condition."

The captain raised his cup, and they all drank. "We can't thank you enough for this news. We expect bad news if any. The Sulerians made a ransom demand, and we sold our ships to pay it, and still needed donations from other houses. But the Sul, damn their eyes, reneged after taking our gold. As you can see, we've been struggling since."

"What can we do for you?" Merik said. "Are your accommodations here in Venaro to your liking? Is there anything we can—"

Diana frowned. "We hadn't expected any consideration for this, really. I hoped to free Eavlyn myself but failed, and would have bought her if I could." She dropped her gaze, lost in the memory that Eavlyn was crippled further because of her attempt to help.

Judik hugged her again. "Thank you."

As the sun left the docks in dusk, Jon interrupted. "I'm sorry, but we have another pressing engagement tonight and must take our leave."

Jorgen shook Jon's hand. "We can't thank you enough for your news. If you need anything while you're here, please contact us." He put an arm around Jon's shoulder and spoke quietly. "And when you can, please give us your real names so we can provide you a similar kindness."

Outside Moretti's, Diana took Jon's arm. "I caught your look. Was I too candid about meeting Eavlyn?"

He shook his head. "No. It concerned me, but you said nothing that would betray you." He turned to

Browne's burly clerk. "Please escort us to the Dancing Dolphin."

"Of course, sir," the clerk said. "This way please."

As twilight settled on the docks, the clerk led them through narrow and dimly lit streets past the open windows of taverns advertising their allure by the volume of the crowd. And as they passed, the occasional dock worker or sailor traded nods with the clerk.

At the far end of the docks from House of Fontana, the tavern burrowed itself into the warehouses. It was late when they arrived for the interview.

"I'll wait at the bar," the clerk said.

Jon nodded and took Diana's arm. "Stay close, lass."

At this hour, the Dolphin was loud and crowded with colorful characters from the docks and young gentlemen out for an adventure. Thick smoke filled the room and burned their eyes, and the floor was slick with spilled ale. Noise pretending to be music came from a group of men and women in a corner of the tavern. Their songs of the sea and bawdies with lyrics caused her to blush even after months of militia training. Here she was underdressed for a lady and overdressed for a floozy.

When they entered, a tavern wench of ample girth nodded to the clerk and came to Diana with a scowl.

"Out with ya, girl," she said. "We got enough satin weavers here."

"What, I—," Diana stammered, not understanding.

Jon interrupted. "We're here to see First Mate Fortier."

The barmaid frowned and pointed to a man in a dark corner but never lost her scowl or took her gaze from Diana as they walked away. "See to it ya don't mingle," she said to their backs.

First Mate Fortier was a tall man with steely eyes. "I understand why you're here," he said. "What about her?"

"She's a cook's assistant," Jon replied, handing him the recruiting poster.

Fortier perused the flyer and squinted at them as if considering when to slit their throats.

"We crewed on the *Poppy*," Jon continued.

The First Mate raised an eyebrow, inspected them both again, and rose. "Come with me," he said, led them upstairs, and knocked on a narrow door.

"Enter."

Fortier opened the door and waved them into a small room. Behind a desk sat a woman in a dark blue uniform with white epaulets studying manifests and scrolls.

"Excuse me, Captain. Two new recruits," the first mate said as Jon and Diana stood at military at-ease with hands behind their backs and feet apart. The captain did not raise her eyes, and after a few moments, Fortier placed the bulletin next to her scrolls. "They claim service on the *Poppy*."

The captain stopped and read the flyer, raised her eyebrows, and without raising her head, scanned Jon and Diana one at a time. She nodded to the first mate who saluted and left.

"I am Greit, and you will refer to me as Captain, ma'am, or sir. I do not care who you are or where you're from." She tapped the flyer. "You earned your berth a day before this will be posted. That means you're valuable to a friend, and that friendship binds me to silence. But my silence is of no value if you unmask yourselves, so from this moment on you are crew and you must comport yourselves as such."

Greit inspected Jon. "You, sir, are a brawler or a soldier; I don't care which, but stay away from the grog." She moved her gaze to Diana, "Girl, can you boil water?"

"Yes, ma'am," Diana said with a frown.

The captain squinted and inspected her more closely. "You girl, I need you to respect my crew."

"Of course. I understand, and—"

"No, you don't," Greit said, but with a hint of a smile. "My officers are gentlemen. They will look out for you but have no time to hover. Do not tempt the crew or risk events where they cannot protect you." Greit scanned Jon and then Diana. "Your companion appears a competent bodyguard but can't be with you all the time. You will sleep in the cabin boy's stall next to my quarters. Lock the door behind you. Bind your hair and keep your eyes to yourself. Do not be alone, ever, and don't unpack your skirts." Greit stared at her. "Are we clear?"

Diana nodded.

The captain paused and leaned back in her chair. "When we undock, I am the law, the judge, and the hangman. My officers are my police, and you will do as they say. Understood?"

"Yes, ma'am," Jon said.

Diana nodded again. "Yes."

Captain Greit remained silent.

"Yes, ma'am," Diana said, and the captain nodded.

Greit returned her gaze to her scrolls. "You two are a marine and a cook's assistant. Your ship is the *Razor*, Dock 12. Report onboard to Fortier before daybreak next Lonsday, day after tomorrow, one duffle each. Your trunks will be baggage. If you have horses or live-stock, they will ride along as cargo. Everything but your sea bag will be inaccessible during the voyage. We sail with the dawn with or without you. Dismissed."

*** 

The next morning, Jon and Diana met Jones's handsome clerk Browne at their hotel for a tour, the first stop at Dock 12 and the *Razor*. Along the way, Browne pointed out the larger ships and their purpose: from the broad cogs for coastal ports and the galleons for warfare. Every ship was armed in some way with ballistae, catapult, or firing platforms.

They found the *Razor* dwarfed between two broad merchant barques, and she smiled. It was sleek as an arrow, a lightly crewed corvette, built for maneuverability and speed with two masts square-rigged and the mizzen gaff rigged. It seemed it would rush away if not moored, and she took a step toward it, but Browne kept them at a distance. The ship was undergoing repairs to the bowsprit.

"Pirates?" Jon asked.

Browne nodded.

"I was told Venaro was the home of pirates."

"Piracy inhibits trade and is outlawed by the League. But there are always opportunists and Sulerian slavers."

"She's a beautiful ship," Diana said.

"Yes, a favorite of the House," Browne said. "The ships that can defeat her can't catch her, and the ships that might catch her can't defeat her."

After viewing the *Razor*, Browne took them on a tour of the city, traveling as much by water as by foot. The canals were the city's thoroughfares, navigated by slender boats and propelled from the stern by a single oar. Flowers decorated the hundreds of bridges that crossed the canals which, from the boats, appeared to be hanging gardens.

They walked through crooked streets between tall buildings more like alleys and too confined for wagons. Each of the neighborhoods reveled in its own flavor, some with colorful painted houses and others with ornate facades. Small squares punctuated the jungle of streets and facing each was at least one temple and a café. And each neighborhood carried distinct scents from fruits and pastries to liquors.

*How nice it would be if Eric could explore this with me as he wished.* But every time her thoughts drifted to Eric, the handsome Browne interrupted.

At Santarini, the new trade and finance center, they climbed the bell tower, to view all the islands of Venaro and ten leagues inland. The view took her breath away. And each time she glanced at the magical city, she turned to Browne and his smile.

"You have a natural defense from an attack by land," Jon said as he looked east.

Browne nodded. "And we're masters of the sea. Each supports the other."

"But you have no navy to control these, as you say, opportunists," Diana said.

"The League has chartered privateers to protect our shipping lanes and ships flying our flag. The Sulerians have something similar they call corsairs."

"Privateers are not a navy?"

"Not really. They rarely coordinate their activities through the League."

"And they attack competitors?" Diana asked.

"Occasionally," Browne said. "Their charter is rather . . . broad."

Jon considered this and smiled. "What's the difference between your privateers and pirates?"

"I admit the distinction is somewhat vague," Browne parried and turned to Diana. "How do you like our city?"

She smiled. "It's beautiful, especially at night."

"Yes, it is," Browne said. "Visitors see the lights as decorations rather than the energy of the city itself. A free people built this. No one orchestrated this. No one voted for it. No one commanded it."

"Where can we see one of these privateers?"

"You sail on one tomorrow. The *Razor* is such a vessel."

On the return to their hotel, Diana stopped at the stairs to a basement with a colorful sign "Satin Weavers Wanted. No Experience Needed."

"Is there a shortage of weavers in Venaro?" she asked Browne.

Browne peered at her with a strange smile. "No. Why do you ask?"

She recounted the words of the barmaid, and Browne let out a quick burst of laughter before calming himself. She frowned at her foolishness and his sense of humor at her expense.

"Apologies," he said. "She complimented you, milady. It was a warning that the working girls in the tavern did not want competition from an amateur for the . . . attentions of men."

"Working girls . . . Oh . . . I see," she said, blushing brightly.

Jon smiled, amused by the subject but said nothing.

"But why satin weavers?"

"Well, it seems the members of congress and their spouses can't condone public immorality, but they haven't been able to put an end to it. So instead, they classify them as satin weavers with a special tax and turn their heads away. The block we just passed has the highest density of satin weavers in the city and produces more tax revenues than the docks."

Jon laughed out loud, which led Diana to punch him in the arm in a very unladylike fashion.

When Diana returned to her hotel room, she found a long cloth bag holding two exquisite new dresses. The attached note read:

> *With compliments from House of Moretti. Our best wishes for a most enchanting evening.*
> *Jacques.*

Within the hour, Browne's aide arrived and escorted her and Jon to a café, one of many lining the largest canal in Venaro with a view of the bridge that arched over it. Browne took them upstairs to the second floor and a private table on the veranda. The awning folded back for the evening, giving full view to the spires of the cathedral and the bell tower at the Santarini Center. Elein at full, the brightest moon, and a few candles lit the table, and in the warm offshore breeze from Antona, Venaro turned its lights on.

"You'll have clear sailing the next few days," Browne said as he pulled her chair from the table.

"This is exquisite," she said and sat. "Thank you."

"I thought this setting would be more familiar to you, milady."

But it was not, and the fine table set before her was as unknown to her as the names of the stars.

Upon the embroidered silk tablecloth lay crystal goblets cut with intricate patterns of flowers and rimmed with gold. Around the porcelain plates lay the familiar knife and two-pronged fork. But the setting also included engraved utensils of unfamiliar style and purpose.

Browne acted comfortable here, treating the finery as if it were pottery and pewter on a kitchen table. But Diana was very conscious of it.

"Excuse me if I brag a bit," Browne said, "but these are all merchandise traded by the House." He held up a small plate. "The dishes are made from a clay that's mined only in Auxiere and are glazed here in Venaro with a pigment that includes colored glass." He raised a fork. "The tableware is from Xorellia." Flicking a fingernail on the wine goblet in front of him produced a sustained ring. "And the glassware from Bouveil."

All were in the far north. She imagined they ate like this at the capital in Wikkert, but she never had, being much more familiar with a cold dinner at a kitchen table. And now Browne assumed that this was her regular fare.

Diana panicked. *He referred to me as "milady," an improper title for a farm girl. What did he suspect? Is his flattery part of a seduction? Or a test? Will I appear the fool if I act with certainty and grab the wrong fork? Or seem too primitive and offend him that my upbringing is less lofty than his.* She struggled to recall Maggie's lessons on how to hold a glass and the proper use of each utensil. *Let's see, appetizer fork in front, small fork to the left, . . . large fork . . . But I'm only a farm girl and shouldn't know such things.*

When the server laid salads of fresh fruits from Antona in front of them, Diana froze. Jon smiled at her and picked up the small fork. Following his lead, she took the same utensil but hesitated and glanced at Browne who copied her and smiled.

She pursed her lips. *He had waited for me to mask any embarrassing mistake I might make.* His thoughtfulness made her blush, and for the first time in weeks, her thoughts of Eric vanished.

"Your freedom is admirable, Mr. Browne," Jon said, "but free towns don't seem to remain free for long. Mertor is the recent example."

Browne nodded. "Yes, freedom grows easily in the absence of tyrants. And lasts until a tyrant arises to enslave it."

Diana's heart drummed in her ears, and she wished for a fan to cool herself as she struggled to reengage in the conversation. "But Venaro has prospered for a hundred years."

"The people created this land," Browne said. "And the people aim to keep it."

"But you're all ruled by your congress, no?" Diana said.

A smile crossed Browne's face. "The people rule the congress, milady."

"And if your congress decides not to respond to the people?"

"Then the people replace the congress," he said matter-of-factly as if this simple idea did not threaten every aristocrat in the land.


As the evening waned, Diana did not want to go, enjoying this time with Browne, but Jon intervened.

"Well, this is our last night in Venaro, and we must rise early," Jon said. "Thank you and please give our regards to Jones."

"It's my pleasure, milord, milady," Browne said. "Jones has asked me to give you this small remembrance of your visit." He reached into his jacket and handed them each a small package with elegant wrappings.

She unwrapped her present to find a plain wooden box. Within it lay one of the silver-gray rune coins that caught her eye in Jones's office, with a pin to wear as a brooch. It was exquisite, hardly a farm girl's accessory, but neither was the dress she wore.

"I must say, that's a surprise," Browne said. "Jones never parts with his trinkets."

Jon prepared to open his gift, but Browne shook his head. Jon stopped and put the package in his pocket.

"And Diana, please accept this from me," Browne said, laying a black cloth in front of her. He unfolded the cloth to display a necklace with a pendant, a delicate version of the translucent sculpture of mermaids and dolphins. She could not control her blush and tried to divert his gaze by holding it up to the light, but her diversion did not work.

"Let me," Browne said and rose. "My father said the original fascinated you." He took the necklace and stood behind her to place his gift around her neck. In her new dress, the pendant hung right to her cleavage, and the heat rushed to her face so fast she feared she would melt.

Jon grinned at her discomfort, and she glared at him.

The server stopped at their table and gave a small token to Browne, who nodded and stood.

"Excuse me, please," Browne said and went to the stairs, where Jacques waited.

Diana smiled when she saw Jacques and waved to him, after which the stylist smiled and bowed with his arms extended as if she were royalty. But his smile vanished as he spoke with Browne.

She caught Jon's smile. "What are you smiling at?"

"Youth, lass. I admire your bearing. And it's a pleasure to see you enjoying yourself after so many years."

"It's fun here."

"And it appears you've made another conquest," he said and tipped his head to Browne, who now spoke to the server.

"What do you mean, you old goat?"

"Jones is head of the Scythean League, lass. Browne might as well be a prince."

Browne returned to their table but did not sit. "Our friend brings word that ruffians are restless, and he fears for you. Time is short, so I've taken the liberty of having your things packed and moved to the *Razor*. The ship is more easily defended in case his fears are realized. Please wait here with me until my men arrive to escort you."

"Of course," Jon said as Browne went to the balcony and watched the street.

A few moments later, Browne went to pull Diana's chair back. "Ready now."

At the door to the street, a team of ten marines, men and women both, armed with swords and crossbows met them, each in blue shirt with a red stripe on their pants. Outside, ten more followed to guard their rear. On the short walk to the docks, Diana's eyes followed Jon's that glanced up to the rooftops. There, more men kept pace with their group.

At an alleyway, one marine fell from the rooftop, and two in the fore were taken by crossbow bolts.

"This way!" Browne said and led Jon and Diana down a flight of stairs to a satin weaver shop with racks of clothing and shelves of accessories. There Browne stopped and spoke to the marines.

"You two with me, I'll meet the rest of you at the docks and warehouse K4," he said, and the marines raced back up the stairs. One of the two remaining threw aside a curtain and slipped into a dark hall.

"Is there a way out?" Jon asked.

Browne nodded. "This is *my* town. Stay close and follow me," he said and followed the marine into a dark narrow hall.

With Diana between Browne and Jon, they raced through a labyrinth of tiny rooms and cubbies. From each ran partially clothed women frantically screaming and within, men hurried to cover themselves.

Up a flight of stairs, they entered a small theater where scantily clad women danced in front of small tables where well-dressed men and women watched with drinks.

Through a side door stormed thugs with swords drawn who ran over or pushed aside patrons that stood in their way. Browne's marines engaged them before they reached Diana and Jon. But from behind the melee, attackers shot small darts that whizzed over their heads and toppled more of the patrons who had not found a place to hide.

Up another flight of stairs, Browne led them through lounges hazy with smoke, but not so foggy as to miss the young women on the men's laps and the young men entertaining older women. But Diana was beyond blushing.

At the end of the lounges, through an ordinary door, Browne led them to a walkway that linked to the dock's warehouses. Across the bridge and down the stairs again, they met a dozen marines who split to the front and rear as they ran to the *Razor*'s boarding ramp.

Another score of blue-shirted marines met them on deck, and Browne posted them as lookouts. When done, he escorted Jon and Diana to the captain's cabin.

The cabin was compact, with all the furnishings but the chart table built into the walls. To the stern were narrow windows cracked open to the sea breeze and a large door on the opposite wall. On the ceiling was a skylight of frosted glass.

"These are stealth killers," Browne said as he unlocked the captain's sword locker. "Cowards, and not much good at a stand-up fight."

"We'll see," Jon said and helped himself to a sword and dirk.

With a cutlass and crossbow, Browne turned to them. "You are guests in my town, and I promised your safety. Please stay here until the fighting is over."

A moment later, they heard boots running on the quarterdeck above, and Jon rushed out the door. Diana ripped off the bottom of her gown, exposing her knickers. She grabbed a dirk and a scabbard with its saber, and ran to join him, but Browne met her at the door.

"Please remain inside," Browne said, frowning at her knickers. But as he swung the door closed, Diana saw two men in dark clothing jump Jon.

"No!" Diana shouted and kicked the door, but Brown locked it, and all her pounding could not open it. "No!"

*I will not remain idle while someone I care for is in trouble!*

As she searched the compact cabin for a key, a draft chilled her and she turned to the windows, where an attacker crawled through one. He spotted her attention and with only one arm through the window, pointed a small crossbow at her and fired a dart. Grabbing a wooden tray from the chart table, she ran to the window. Before she reached him, he shot again, and this time four darts cracked the tray in half. With the pieces, she knocked the little crossbow from his hands and pushed him out the window into the water.

Another dart whizzed past her ear, and Diana ducked below the chart table. When the thug climbed through a different open window and set a foot inside the cabin, Diana charged and knocked the woman into the wall and the built-in vanity. Sitting on top of her, Diana blocked the darts with the water basin and hit the attacker on the forehead until she lay still.

Sounds of fighting came from outside the cabin, and Diana tried the door again without success. She ran to the stern windows and looked out, but pulled her head back in when a dart flew past from another thug climbing a rope. After locking the remaining stern windows, she took two crossbows from the weapons locker. With the scabbard and crossbows over her shoulders, she pulled the chart table below the skylight.

The quarterdeck was empty when she peeked out. Opening it, she climbed out to see chaos on the main deck. There, dark-clothed attackers fought a score of marines with red stripes on their pants. Jon fought off two attackers with his sword and dirk, and Diana ran to him. With the crossbow, she took out one, and with the other, killed a thug climbing over the gunwales. But she did not have time to reload and dropped them.

As she climbed down the stairs to the main deck, she slipped on blood and fell hard on her back, seeing stars with the wind knocked out of her. An opportunistic attacker swung his cutlass, but she rolled away. Before he could reach her, she drew her saber.

This sword fight was not like Jon's training. She had never engaged someone in a fight with blades before, where any missed parry might mean her death. The thug's offense overwhelmed her cautious defense, and he backed her against the gunwales and the stairs to the quarterdeck. But she slipped through a gap between them and under the stairs.

*Don't wait until he's ready to kill you again!*

With a flurry of thrusts and slashes, Diana backed the attacker against the door to the captain's cabin. And when she saw the cold look in his eyes of the assassin on the *Shiela Reine*, she sliced his sword arm and ran him through.

A dart whizzed past her ear, and she turned to see two more killers running toward her. She grabbed her victim's sword and took a stance to meet them, but having never sparred with two swords, she was outmatched.

Over the gunwale, a dark-haired streak rushed and knocked one attacker to the deck leaving Diana to fight the other. When the killer rose again, the dark streak, Judik Moretti, joined her, and back-to-back they fought until both attackers dove over the starboard side. There, skiffs with Browne's marines fished them out.

When Diana checked the port side, guards blocked entry to the *Razor's* dock, and among them stood Judik's brothers, Merik and Jorgen, who waved to her.

With the attack over, Diana rushed to Jon, whose arm bled from a cut, sat him down on the stairs, and bound the wound with a cloth strip from her knickers. On deck, Browne saw to the dead and wounded.

"That was reckless, to join us in the fight," Jon said, but Diana ignored him.

After a brief stop in the captain's cabin, Browned joined them and smiled. "It seems I wasted an asset by locking you up," he said and handed a cut crystal bottle to Jon.

Diana intercepted the bottle and with closed eyes took a big swig to let the brandy burn her throat. "You'll find another body in the cabin you locked me in."

Browne raised an eyebrow as Judik accepted the bottle from Diana, and drank deep of it.

"I can't stay," Judik said. "I need to tend to our wounded." She kissed Diana on the cheek and shook the hands of Jon and Browne. At the gunwale, she turned and waved. "Safe passage!" she shouted and returned to the docks and her brothers.

"What's the toll?" Jon asked.

"A dozen dead and five arrested. Seven of our marines are injured, plus two of Moretti's. It seems they underestimated us." He held up a dart with a purple tip. "The darts were poisoned. And meant for you."

"Assassins?" Jon asked.

"Contractors, most likely."

"Paid by whom?" Jon asked, but Browne shook his head.

Diana took the bottle again. "Ow!" she said when the liquor spilled on a deep cut on her palm masked by the battle fever. Browne took his handkerchief and bound her hand.

Between Browne and Jon, Diana sat and drank with them as the marines tended to the wounded and carted off the dead. A thump came from the quarterdeck and the three jumped to their feet with their hands on their weapons.

"Sorry," a marine said as he picked up his scabbard.

"The crew will return before dawn to scrub the decks and repair the ship," Browne said and stood. "And I will need to report to the captain and the police."

Diana took his hand and rose. "Thank you. And give our thanks to Jacques."

"The captain will come aboard at dawn, and you will need to be crew by then. If you ever find yourself in Venaro again, or need anything, please call on me."

She gazed up into his eyes, almost expecting a kiss, but then he broke the spell.

"Ah . . . or House of Fontana," he said, kissed her hand, and walked away.

As she watched Browne depart, Jon dug through the slop-chest by the boarding ramp and threw her the linen shirt and tattered pants of a seaman.

"Your new disguise," he said.


At the wash basin in the captain's cabin, she removed her makeup and nail polish. And to be more believable as a ship's cook, she bit and scratched her nails and scrubbed her hands raw. In the loose-fitting shirt, wide-legged pants, and hair tucked under a cap, she could almost be confused with a boy.

Almost.

As she collected the pieces of her new dress, the feelings of a young woman that possessed her earlier that night returned as if a distant memory. She stowed the pieces away in her trunk with the other dresses, and with a sigh, admired them one last time before closing the lid.

But their spell had already been cast.

# Chapter 36
## Corvette

Still unwinding from the battle-fever, Diana went on deck to the forecastle as the repair and clean-up teams came and went. At the edge of the docks and ramp to Dock 12, a score of marines stood guard. While still dark, the crew boarded, each with worn sea bags. Captain Greit and First Mate Fortier arrived, each with the same type of sea bag, and went below. And at the first glow of dusk, the city woke, and the docks came alive.

Venaro at dawn was not as beautiful as the evening they arrived. The docks were the muscular end of the city and more like the Branwyn market than a candy store. Here only an occasional gold leaf or gold tooth replaced the weathered browns and grays. And only the spire from the Aliós Cathedral and the dome of the Town Center rose above the masts.

On the docks and the ships, gulls fought each other and jostled for positions with the pelicans and the four-winged targalans for the bait of the fishing boats that sailed out into the harbor. And on the *Razor*, with few words from Fortier, the crew, including Jon, busied themselves loading the last of the cargo and preparing to leave.

Past the pier, the *Razor* raised the kedging anchor and dropped sail, agile enough to maneuver away from the docks on her own. Buoys marked the narrow deep-water channel that led between the smaller islands that served as parks and cemeteries. Two tall lighthouses and the defensive fortifications guarding the city stood on spits of land at the mouth of the harbor. They, and the change from port chop to deep water swells, confirmed the transition to open ocean.

"Aye, slacker," first mate Fortier called from the deck. "Enough sightseeing, you're here to work."

The cook limited Diana's duties to garbage disposal and potato peeling. With only one chief cook and three shifts to feed, those tasks filled her time. And as a sailor, she passed her first test early.

Carrying a pail of kitchen waste, Diana went on deck to the gunwales. At the sight of her, gulls and targalans fought each other for positions downwind and below her. Behind her, the idle crew observed, chuckled, and traded bets, and behind them stood the cook.

Wetting her finger, she stuck it in the air to check the wind direction, and then threw the waste overboard to be caught mid-air by the sea birds. She turned to laughter, coins exchanged, and a few gripes of disappointment. But the cook nodded, and Jon smiled.

One of the crew scowled at her and groped her as he passed, and the cook slapped him on the back of the head.

"Pay us no mind, dearie," the cook said. "They were betting if you'd check the wind before tossing the peelings overboard. Pitt there lost."

Diana put the bucket down and watched the sea with her elbows on the gunwales.

"It's beautiful," Jon said as he joined her.

"Yes. I can imagine a life with this view every day," she said.

"You might wait until bad weather before choosing," he said. "And your day?"

"This was my first break. The cook doesn't trust me with anything but peeling potatoes and garbage duty."

He nodded. "Fortier makes no distinction between marines and sailors. I spent the day scrubbing the fo'c's'le." He pointed a thumb to the bow of the ship above the sail locker. "Did you notice the other ships?"

She shook her head.

"They seem to chase us but veer away when they get close enough to see the flag of the House of Fontana."

She nodded idly. "Jon, on the keelboat, you said I was blessed to have a mission larger than myself."

"Yes."

"I was thinking about that. Having a mission simplifies things, doesn't it?"

He smiled. "Yes, lass."

"Your priorities become clearer; decisions come more rapidly."

He nodded. "With it comes clarity and courage, as long as you remain true to that mission."

She stared out to the horizon as Jon continued. "Most people can't rise above their self-centeredness or fear to grasp their larger destiny, and they sour for the lack of it." He paused and looked out to sea. "That's what your Eric yearns for."

"Thank you," she said and took his hand. When he walked away, her hiding place turned into a trap when Pitt blocked her escape.

"Let me pass, please," she said. But Pitt took her courtesy as an invitation and groped her. She cuffed him hard in the ears with her open hands to communicate her disinterest more clearly. Surprised, he backed away but glared at her, and a knife glinted from his boot. When he lunged for her throat, she did not hold back.

Moving inside his reach, she grabbed his shirt and kneed him in the groin repeatedly. After his legs buckled, she spun to one side and smashed his face with her knee. Then she stepped behind him and kicked him in the back of the head. His face hit the gunwale, and he fell unconscious, nose bleeding on the deck. It was over in moments, and it took the crewmen more moments to realize what happened before they cheered.

"Hey, Fortier!" one sailor shouted. "We have another marine onboard." He laughed, and the others laughed with him, expressing no concern for their fallen comrade or Diana.

"All a ya, back to work!" Fortier shouted and came to her. "Go to your quarters and clean up, Cookie." He leaned over. "He deserved it, lass, but don't get caught alone again."

Jon stayed, leaning against the stairs. On the way to her berth, she stopped and took his hand.

"Are you well?" he asked.

"Yes," she said, but her hands shook with fatigue and battle fever.

Jon chuckled and put a hand on her shoulder. "We need to recalibrate your response to threat, lassie."

The next morning, with the crew on deck, the *Razor* sailed an eighth mile out from a harbor town south of the Spine and the Western Archipelago.

"You are accused of attacking a shipmate with intent to harm," Fortier said. "What say you, Seaman Pitt?"

"I admit to the altercation, sir," Pitt said. "And I was mighty surprised at her skill. But ain't this a big deal for a little tussle? And why ain't she up here too?"

Greit threw the knife that the seaman kept in his boot, and it stuck between Pitt's legs. "She wasn't armed."

Pitt glanced to the left and right. "She came to me, sir, and offered me a deal to trade a night of pleasure with her if I smuggled hanta root into Royax. When I refused, she attacked me with—"

Laughter from the crew erupted and drowned him out.

"And she would ask you to smuggle the drugs you already hid in your kit?" Greit said.

The seaman glanced at his kit as Greit removed a bag of the drug and threw it at his feet.

The crew mocked him. "And you risk prison for a little cooch," a sailor shouted, and the crew laughed again, but Diana blushed.

"She planted them! I'm innocent," Pitt shouted over the laughter. "And she offered me Fortier's post if'n I joined her and her marine in a mutiny against our fair captain!"

Jon chuckled, and the crew laughed even louder. But Greit raised a fist and they quieted.

"A petty fight and some bruises we can tolerate," Greit said. "But drug smuggling is the gallows."

Pitt's jaw fell open.

"When you break the law, keep a lower profile," Greit said and scanned the crew, who looked away or inspected their boots. "You have a choice now, Seaman Pitt," the captain said. "Three days on the yard, or swim to shore."

"Captain, ma'am—"

"There's no appeal. Unless you want to make your case to the constable in Royax."

Pitt scowled at Diana and reached for the bag of drugs, but Fortier put his boot on it. A crewman put Pitt's duffle on a sealskin float, threw it over the gunwale, and Pitt followed it.

Greit tipped her head to Fortier and left for her cabin. The crew dispersed, and satisfied by exposing a criminal after their scuffle, Diana smiled and turned to the galley.

First Mate Fortier shouted to her, "Report to Captain Greit, Cookie."

At the captain's door, the cabin boy glowered at her. Since Diana took over his quarters, she was not his favorite crewman, but still he knocked to announce her.

"Cookie to see you, ma'am," he said and opened the door. Inside, Diana snapped to attention, while Captain Greit stood at a table with a compass and ruler concentrating on charts.

"Cook's assistant reporting, ma'am."

Greit did not raise her head. "Until yesterday your admirer was an able seaman, and we have no more to waste. See to it we have no more such confrontations or you and your marine will be the next to swim ashore. Dismissed."

"But he . . ." Diana began, but Greit raised her head with a steely glare that stopped her cold.

"Dismissed," Greit repeated.


That evening after scrubbing the pots and plates, Diana returned to her tiny cabin, judging it to be the place least likely for trouble to find her. Having no outlet for her worry for home and father, she distracted herself with the rune coin gift from Jones. As the sun set, her tiny window lost the light, and she lit a lantern to inspect the coin in the hard shadows.

The size of a coat button, the coin was small for the details crowded onto it. The symbols were precise, unlike the money coins of the North and South that were stamped onto soft metal. Using a water drop lens, she magnified the markings and copied them to parchment.

Etched on the periphery wound a cross-hatched ring and the mouth of a fangless snake or a worm eating its tail.

"The Worm of the World," she whispered.

Quadrants marked both sides, each split into three concentric segments. The coin was damaged and only two of the quadrants were readable on one side, and one quadrant on the other. Below the serpent were dots in the undamaged quadrants, two dots, and another with four plus one, or five dots, like the puzzle outside the reliquerium door.

On one side, the dots and pictograms matched the symbols for the seasonal weather and agriculture. The innermost circle showed two runes which in the children's dictionary meant spring and summer.

*So one side is the cycle of weather and agriculture . . . like the puzzle tiles at the entrance to the cache of books.*

Flipping the coin over revealed the same serpent eating its tail and dots in the same location as the opposite side. *So this must be a cycle as well.* But only one quadrant and part of another was undamaged. On this side, opposite the raindrops, appeared the five dots and one dot above what might be a tree underwater in the rain. And below it, a pictogram of a bow and arrow.

*If they represent similar things, perhaps spring is flooding, and food is supplied by hunting.*

Without the whole coin, she could not tell if these were simple decorations or meant something. *Perhaps Singer's fragment showed other quadrants and could solve this puzzle.*

She sat back on her bunk. None of it made sense. *And why would Jones want me to have this? The Ve-*

*narians are seafarers. Is there a connection to the sea?*

"Argh! Damn, girl! One question at a time."

Returning the coin to its box, Diana took out the atlas and opened it to a map of the northwest where the North Sea ice touched Nordes. The walls of her little cabin faded away, and she sailed between towering ice castles where ice should not be. Her ship shrunk to a small boat, one of many, where men in heavy furs broke the ice and fished with harpoons.

*Captain Griet should see what I see.*

A hypnotic melody drifted above the crash of waves and squawk of seabirds, as if a chorus of women serenaded. Diana smiled as the melody became louder with complex harmonies, and in her small boat, she stretched her arms out in the cold and closed her eyes.

The *Razor's* bell sounded "all hands to stations," and Diana woke to the clomp of boots running past her cabin and on the quarterdeck above. Jumping from her bunk, she reached for the door latch, but a sudden lurch of the ship slammed her into the bulkhead. Instead of visiting the captain, she turned to the doors to the deck as the mesmerizing song changed to a beastly roar. Opening the doors, a splash of water hit her in the face.

All the sailors and marines were above decks, half in the yards reefing sails and half, including Jon, manning the ropes on deck. Ropes strung along the gunwales port and starboard helped sailors navigate the lurching deck. As she staggered to the starboard stairs leading to the quarterdeck, the three moons at full showed her why.

Just off the gunwales to both sides, tall peaks rose like spires from the ocean—the Western Archipelago—the Scythes—the vertebrae of the Worm of the World that formed the Spine of mountains that crossed Juro. Surf crashed against the rocky shore of the spires that would shred to splinters any ship that drifted too close. The winds that whipped the surf growled through rocky outcrops that would tangle a sail or snap a yard that heeled over too far. Snaking through the spires, the gusts carried surf spray to wash the deck and her face again.

"Hard to port!" Fortier shouted and the *Razor* lurched again, throwing her into the railing. "Below decks might be safer, miss, and dryer."

Leaning against the bulkhead for support, Diana made her way back below decks to the captain's cabin, where the cabin boy knocked for her again.

"Beggin' your pardon, Ma'am, but Cookie wants a word," the boy said.

Greit's voice sounded from within. "Enter."

Diana entered and stood at her best military attention, and when the cabin boy closed the door behind her, they muted the angry roar of the Scythes.

"At-ease, Cookie," Greit said without looking up, and Diana relaxed her stance. The ship lurched again, forcing Diana to shuffle like a drunk while Greit seemed to bend with the ship.

"You heard the mermaids call?" the captain asked.

"Is that what they were?"

"The sailors like to think so. The voices seduce us into thinking the archipelago is inviting us rather than aiming to kill us. Many ships have lost their way and sailors their lives following those voices."

"You're not concerned?"

Greit shook her head. "No. There's a fine crew in the yards and first officer at the helm." As she spoke, she worked over a chart with calipers and parallel rule. Diana had stared at the maps in the atlas long enough to grasp that the charts there on the table did not depict their course to Royax. These were maps of Xorellia and the North Sea, near Nordes province.

Greit looked up, followed Diana's eyes, and rolled up the charts. The ship pitched and Diana grabbed a handhold.

"Charts and knowledge of the weather are competitive advantages to merchant sailors, Cookie." She stowed the maps away inside the table. "My competitors would kill for these."

"I understand, ma'am," Diana said. *Am I too naïve? The information I seek may be too valuable to disclose.*

Greit returned to her desk and leaned back in her chair. "Well, what is it?"

"I have a question about the weather, ma'am."

"Will the answer affect your duties aboard my ship?"

"No, ma'am. It's for my education."

"Hmm, well, carry on. Your question?"

"Do you sail east to west through the North Sea?"

With a raised eyebrow, the captain studied her. "You board my ship with a marine in tow and beat one of my sailors unconscious. And now you ask me a question I told you might be a trade secret. What am I to think, girl?"

Diana blushed but continued. "Coincidence, Captain."

"Well, ask your question, but I don't promise an answer."

"As a child I was taught a northern passage by sea between east and west is free of ice year-round. Is this true?

Greit rose, leaned against her desk, and folded her arms. "Yes, historically the North Sea has been free of ice, even in winter."

"Is that still true?"

The captain raised an eyebrow. "And why would it not be?"

Diana pursed her lips but pushed on. "It's just an intriguing question from a friend in the South, ma'am. But someone with your intimate knowledge of the sea might be more likely to have an answer than we who are bound to the land."

"I understand. Please tell your friend when the geographers change the maps, we'll all know at the same time. Dismissed, Cookie."

"Yes, ma'am," Diana said, returned to her tiny cabin, and locked the door.

"Well, what was I expecting, the charts themselves? But—"

She sat on her bunk and frowned. *If the ice was the same as I was taught, she'd have no reason not to confirm it. But she didn't, so something has changed.*

*So how bad is the ice?* she thought and shivered at what might befall them.

Sailing day and night in a fast ship, Jon and Diana covered the longest leg of their journey in the shortest time, and within three days the *Razor* anchored at Royax. They packed their kits and loaded them, their trunk, and their horses on the tender that ferried them to the dock.

"Royax has grown since I was here last," Jon said and pointed to the new docks and warehouses under construction. "It used to be a small dockage with a deep-water harbor."

"We've joined the Scythean League," the ferryman said. "Those are for House Moretti. And this is just the start."

Diana pointed to a block of burned-out warehouses. "What happened here?"

"Ain't you heard?" the boatman said. "This is where the Sulerians were turned back in the war."

"We'd heard they blockaded the port."

"Oh, my word, yes sir, they did. The Hordes rode all the way to the ridge of hills yonder."

"Not the Sulerian Elites?" Jon asked as they tied up the tender and unloaded the horses.

"They was there all right, but the barbarians led the way, flyin' banners of the Silvan and Desert Hordes. We could smell 'em from the docks."

"Was Richard here?" Diana asked and tapped her foot.

"Patience, girl. As I was say'n, the Sulerian warships lay just off the coast here, lobbing firebombs on us from their catapults and ready to land troops. Why, most of the town was burned to the ground. But at mid-day, galleons from the League sailed into the harbor, sunk half the bastards, and drove the rest off. By the gods, it was glorious!"

"Good timing," Jon said.

"Not an accident, sir. When the galleons arrived, the militias attacked from the north—"

Diana sat hard on a barrel and pursed her lips.

". . . and chased the Hordes back across the Wye River," the ferryman continued.

She took Jon's hand as her eyes glistened.

"It was that close?" Jon said.

"Why, yes it surely was, sir, Lenore and the kids and I were heading for the hills there when the militias charged past us. Without the League, we woulda' lost Royax, and the Sul dug in permanent."

"Who led the militias?" Diana asked.

"Dunno," the ferryman said. "They left a contingent here, and the rest chased them damn hordes back east."

"Thank you," Jon said and turned to Diana. "Our answers will come within a fortnight."

After saddling their horses and packing the saddle bags, the *Razor*'s first mate ran to them and handed Diana a letter from Captain Greit.

"Thank you, Mr. Fortier," she said and smiled.

He bowed slightly. "Milady, the captain requests you leave a note with the harbormaster for House of Fontana if you wish to return to Venaro." He bowed again and left.

Diana opened the note before mounting.

*Cookie.*

*Regarding your friend's intriguing question, passage in the region of your interest is now limited in certain seasons. Your friend may also have questions about the tides. Please regard this information as confidential.*

*I hope your journey met your expectations and hope to see you again in different circumstances.*

*Captain V. Greit*

Diana smiled. *Clever. "Certain seasons," most likely means winter. And the "region of your interest," the North Sea. So, yes, ice is growing and blocks passage where previously it was open all year. I need to tell Martin and Eric. But what's this about the tides?*

She handed the letter to Jon and mounted her horse. "No one could understand this unless they overheard my conversation with Captain Greit."

Jon mounted and raised his eyebrows. "You must tell me more of what you fear."

# Chapter 37
# The North

In the afternoon two weeks from Royax, Diana rode past a group of wagons that turned off the road to another village razed by fire. As they rode, Jon fiddled with a small object, gazed up at the sun, and back to the object.

"What's that, Jon?"

"It's Jones's gift and came without instructions. I'm trying to figure out if it's one of the artifacts he spoke of, or a child's toy, or just what it is."

"What makes it so mysterious?"

To her, he gave a cylinder the circumference of her middle finger touching her thumb and almost as thick as her hand with a glass top. Within was a disc marked with four quadrants on top of which a needle balanced on a pin.

"What does it do?"

"It seems to be limited to one thing only. It seems to always point north."

"We can already find north based on the sun during the day and the stars at night."

"But not if it's cloudy. Jones is a seafaring man and would know the value of such. And a soldier lost in the fog? You can't stop sailing or marching just because the weather is unsuitable."

She handed the object back to him and he put it in his pocket. He reached back into his saddlebag and handed Diana a small package wrapped in tissue. "I lost your birthday present in the fire."

"Thank you, Jon," she said and accepted the gift. Within the tissue, attached to a white cord lay a small engraved ivory disc like in Jones's office. But the shape etched into the surface was none other than the *Razor* at full sail. Tears came as she closed her eyes and smiled. She reached out and Jon took her hand.

"It's to remind you of our adventures together. It's not as precious as the gifts from Jones or Browne—"

"This means more to me than anything they could give me," she said and squeezed his hand.

As she put the necklace around her neck, she said, "We should send a message to my father of our arrival."

"No. It's too dangerous."

"Why? We're in Cherbourne now, and the armies are far to the east. Why do we continue to hide? In just a few days we'll be home and surrounded by friends."

"You're still hunted," he said.

She stopped her horse and frowned. "You tell me this now? How did you come by this?"

"Jacques," Jon said and wheeled his horse to face her.

"In Venaro? Sure, that's where assassins roamed."

Jon shook his head. "He told me he'd known for months, so it couldn't have been Grimes or his henchmen. Someone else has been combing the entire South for you, and for some time now."

"How could Jacques know?"

Jon held up the copy of her anklet. Her hand jumped to her thigh, but her anklet was still there. "Garfann?"

He nodded. "Or the Empress."

"If that murderer is here, this is where I should be," Diana said with narrowed eyes and walked her horse to his.

"He's too violent to confront."

"I won't live in fear in my own land. No one will have that much power over me again, ever."

"I don't counsel fear, lass, only caution," Jon said as they continued on their way. "You don't appreciate your value yet."

"I won't run from them again."

They reached the Alba and turned north to Aemgarde, and along the way found the ruins of their summer cottage. Two men were busily dismantling the charred chimney stones as Jon rode to them.

"Say, are you Jan Yerid's kin?" Jon asked.

"Aye, sir. Name's Kurfa. And you?"

"Jon Henlow of Cherbourne."

"I heard a' ya," he said, brushing his dirty hands on his pants and offering one to Jon. "Much pleased to meet a hero such as yourself, sir."

"What of the residents?" she asked as Jon shook Kurfa's hand.

"Still up north, I'm guessing, lass. Most evacuated with Richard to Bayeun and beyond."

Diana caught her breath. "Any word?"

"Not since they chased the devils back east. There's a bivouac up north, but they're army and kinda quiet about their plans after that sneak attack. Those Qu bastards took my girls captive, and I followed them west. Happiest day of my life I can tell you when I saw the Cherbourne Militia ride east chasing the Horde.

The bastards dumped the captives off. Slowed them, it seems."

"Your daughters are safe?"

"Aye, and back at home now, thank the Gods."

"And Richard?"

"Ain't heard nothing since the evacuation."

"Thanks, Kurfa. Are any lodgings still standing?"

"Aye, the Inn of the Stags still has a roof. It's a half day's ride along the Alba."

Jon nodded. "I'm familiar with it. Many thanks."

They followed the Alba north to Aemgarde, silent about what worried them both: would her father be alive to meet them?

Along the road to Aemgarde stood the Stags. There Jon and Diana sat facing the door with their backs to the wall after a long day's ride and a late dinner.

"Jon, Captain Greit reported that sea ice is farther south now than it has been."

He nodded. "And Cindy said Xorellia is importing food. Perhaps it's getting colder, and the cold is moving south."

She smiled, relieved he did not think her crazy.

After a drink of ale, he added, "Perhaps we've misjudged the Qu. Perhaps the Turajii farther north are pushing them south."

"That would explain why the Sul have helped them."

"If for no other reason than to keep the barbarians out of Suleria," Jon added. "But let's be careful we don't let a good story tranquilize us into thinking these are facts."

The next morning Diana was quiet as they readied to leave.

"You're thinking about the old maps again?" Jon asked.

She nodded and threw her saddle bags over the back of her horse. "The old maps show glaciers even larger than now, with ice as far south as Wikkert. We have vineyards along the sides of the mountains there now."

"That surely would be bad," he said. "Wikkert can't enjoy their harvest holiday without wine. So, if there's pressure on agriculture in the north now, it may get worse."

"Much worse," she said and tied the bags to the saddle.

Cresting the ridge of hills separating the Aemgarde valley from southern Cherbourne, Diana stopped and smiled. Their rural village, once not more than a clearing in the woods, was now the dominant feature on the landscape.

At the top of the hill, in front of the small hut of their old neighbor, stood uniformed men. Sentries, Jon guessed, but they did not stop them and simply waved. Passing atop the hill, a ditch appeared parallel to the fence, a feature hidden from charging horses. Jon stopped and smiled.

"What, Jon?"

"A trap for cavalry. The farm and village are defended. Finally."

A few minutes down the road, Diana's joy at returning home ended at the charred ruin of the tower stronghold from the night her childhood ended. And only the remains of the chimney stood from the old farmhouse.

But just over the trees drifted smoke from a taller chimney.

*And yet there's still hope.*

# Chapter 38
## Home

"Hello, miss. Who lives here?" Jon asked a young shepherdess near a fenced pasture adjoining a barn and large new house.

"The king and his daughter," the girl replied.

Diana closed her eyes and put a hand to her heart. "What's the king's name?"

The girl peered at her as if she were an imbecile. "Why, Richard Stewart of Cherbourne, of course."

A big smile crossed Diana's face, the tears came, and she leaned over in her saddle. When she sat up again, Jon took her hand to help her dismount and led the horses to the stable.

"Why do you cry?" the girl asked.

Diana could not answer. "What's your name?"

"Judith, ma'am."

Diana pointed to the lamb following her. "That's a fine lamb you have there."

"He's my favorite. Papa promised I could keep him if he lasts the winter."

"Whose lamb is it?" Diana asked.

"That one there," Judith said pointing to a stubborn old ewe eying down the sheepdog.

"Hiccup," Diana said.

"How do you know her name?" the girl said with a frown of suspicion.

"And that one there is Ginger and the old man there, that's Burps."

"How do you know?" Judith said again.

"They used to be mine," Diana said with a smile.

The girl stared at Diana with mouth open and curtseyed. "Milady, ah, Your Highness." She turned and yelled to the man nearby, "Papa! Papa! She's home!"

He stopped, took a step toward them, but turned and ran to the house and then the stable. A moment later he galloped away on horseback toward the village.

"Oh my, Princess!" Maggie called as she left the kitchen and waddled to Diana. She curtsied stiffly, and with a gravelly whisper, choking back tears, said, "Welcome home, dear."

Diana kissed her forehead and hugged her. "Maggie, I'm so glad to see you."

Maggie blushed at the informality and smiled warmly. "We worried about you so, dearie . . . we'd not heard from you until the Venarian . . . Oh my dear! Where did that scar come from?" she said in a breathless dash of words between sobs and sniffles, scarcely waiting for an answer before the next question. "Come, come."

Diana stopped at the porch. "I'll wait here," she said, and when Maggie sat by her side, Diana rested her head on Maggie's shoulder. There, Diana nibbled on the remains of her fingernails.

*How tolerant will he be with a disobedient child who left without permission . . . twice?*

*He suspected I played a part in Higel's death, and he didn't punish me. I joined the militia early without his approval. And I left for Branwyn against his orders. Should I confess and throw myself on his mercy? That sounds dramatic.* She smiled. *Would that amuse him and defuse his anger?*

Diana pointed to a plot of green shoots with red berries. "I thought daemonberries only grow in the Spine?"

"Your mother brought them from Derryh. They fruited for the first time this winter. She said the—"

A horse and rider galloped over the hill and past the gate, and Diana ran to meet them. Without a word, Richard dismounted, scooped her up, and swung her in circles. Trying to bury her face in her father's chest the way she did as a child, she found his shoulder instead. Unable to help herself, her eyes glistened.

"Papa."

"Let's look at you," he said and held her at arm's length, his eyes sparkling. "My, my, a woman returns to me."

She gazed at him, grinning with eyes wide and gleaming bright. "We have tales to tell, Father."

He held both her hands in his. "Not yet, lass. How are you, girl?"

In a softer voice, she said, "Fine, Papa."

Richard ran a thumb across her forehead. "A recent scar, but healed." He smiled. "And your heart?"

"Unbroken, but not untouched."

Hugging him again, she put his hand to her cheek and touched his wrist where the bracelet she had woven for him hung in tatters.

Inside the house, Richard took Jon's hand with his right, and his forearm in his left. "Thank you, friend. I couldn't have hoped for more."

Jon bowed his head, keeping his smile.

"Now, tell me everything. Maggie, bring out our best," Richard said, and Maggie poured three glasses rather than two.

"You say there are even more wonders?" Richard asked as he flipped through pages of the atlas and picture dictionary.

Diana nodded and snacked from Maggie's dinner fixings, pacing the kitchen amid pots and pans that hung from the ceiling and ovens and pantries that could feed scores.

"We must send an emissary south to meet this King George."

Diana smiled and crunched a carrot. "We're fortunate to have an invitation to the castle from the king and queen."

Her father leaned back and raised his eyebrows in surprise. "How opportune."

"And another from the prince," Jon said with a wide grin as Richard caught his daughter's blush.

To move the focus away from her and Eric, Diana flipped a page in the atlas.

Richard raised his hand. "Let me ask this first. Your mother mentioned the Book of Chaos and the magic it might contain. Did you find anything that would lead you to believe what you found contains magic?"

Diana frowned and shrugged. "I can't recognize spells or incantations. But what we saw in the cache isn't possible today."

"Let's presume your books aren't magic. Then what's their value that gives the Sulerians an advantage?"

"The knowledge in the cache may be the same thing." She turned a page in the atlas. "I may not have the right books here, Papa," she said and pointed to the strand along the eastern ocean. "But look. It shows a migration route from Tur to the South. This would be invaluable knowledge to the Empress."

She had their full attention now and grabbed a stalk of celery waiting for their response.

"The Quarajii have been pushing to get south since before you were born, lass," Richard said. "This would give them the easy path they seek."

"If the Qu have a way south, why attack us here?" Jon asked.

Richard nodded. "Their push west was a surprise. And they're still poised across the Wye to invade. Why?"

Diana wagged the stalk of celery at them. "It may simply be the goal of the Sulerian Empire. They want all the North, and the Qu are their weapons. Our real enemy are the Sul."

"Perhaps the Empress tempts the Qu with a way south without telling them where or how," Richard said.

"Or perhaps they're being goaded," she said.

He raised an eyebrow. "How so?"

Diana nodded when Jon glanced at her again.

"By the cold," Jon said. "We have reports Xorellia is growing colder."

Excited now, Diana spoke. "And Captain Greit said ice blocks the North Sea in winter."

"Greit?" Richard asked.

"Captain of our ship from Venaro," Jon said. "Jones is your man?"

"An ally," Richard said.

"You knew him before the invasion?"

"Yes. Good man. Royax is a member of the Scythean League, and they came to help us." He paused. "You said Xorellia is importing food? Nordes and Bouveil have shorter growing seasons and poorer crops. They think this is temporary. But if the freezing persists, Suleria will push south as well as the Quarajii."

"If the northern sea lanes are closed by ice, the Sul will need access to the western ocean overland—"

Richard nodded. "Or the Inland Sea."

"And we're in the way again," Diana said and snuck a handful of radishes. That earned her a side-eye from Maggie, and Diana returned those uneaten to the bowl.

Richard frowned. "The Sul have come to negotiate a treaty, and the Cabinet is debating this now."

"Those talks are a sham, if the cold is driving the Sul," Jon said. "Our war is not yet over."

"Wikkert is tired of fighting."

A smirk crossed Jon's face. "How inconvenient for them. That makes us all vulnerable. I hope you oppose this."

"Of course. Derryh is ours," Richard said. "But we don't have the strength to take it back."

"Prince Eric gathers the barons to defend the East," Diana said.

Jon scratched his chin. "He may be too late. Barbarians roam the South now."

Richard poured himself another glass. "In force?"

"Hard to say, but confident enough to attack the king in Branwyn."

Jon scratched again and Maggie turned to them. "I'm not gonna have you two smelling like the horses at my table. There's hot water enough for both of ya. Now scoot."

"Maggie," Richard said, "When you can, ask Killian to stop by. We need direct communication with Branwyn and Venaro."

As Diana passed on the way to her room, Richard took her hand. "You like him?"

"Who, Papa?"

"This young prince. Eric?"

She blushed and dropped her gaze. "Yes."

"And a future?" he asked.

"Perhaps. But fifty score miles lay between us."

Richard took her other hand in his. "We can close that quickly when the opportunity arises, lass."

She leaned over to hug him and kiss him on the cheek, then went to her room to clean up.


After a quick bath, Diana found nothing to wear. Her trunks with her new dresses from Venaro would not arrive for days and would be too fancy for a meal at home. She found clothing in her closet, new and stiff and beautiful, and she hated them all.

Her comfortable old clothes were there in a trunk, but they did not fit anymore. With them lay her old hunting outfit, and with a glance at the stiff new dresses, she wondered how they would feel after a drag through the mud. Instead, she borrowed a cotton jumper from Maggie to cover her last clean shirt.

While fastening Jon's birthday present around her neck, she toured her father's rebuilt house. There in his office, she found a map of the North and frowned.

As she studied the map, the North gradually grew until it filled the room, no longer a map, but an entire world surrounding her. Stars from the sky fell as snow, and she stood in deep drifts at the foot of the Spine where men with spears left a cave in three groups of five. She shivered and entered the cave where breshk and jenalei grew tall in the light of oil lamps while potato leaves withered. Deeper within the cave, women and children in furs prepared animal skins and cooked slabs of meat beside a fire whose smoke escaped through a hole in the cave roof. The children turned to her with gray complexions and hollow cheeks, and she gasped.

A hand touched her shoulder, and the vision dissolved like fog in the morning sun.

"Are you all right?" her father asked.

"I'm fine, Papa. It's just . . . the atlas has unsettled me."

"Can you talk about it?"

"I have no words for it yet."

Maggie called, and Richard put his arm around Diana.

"Come, then," he said and led her to the dining room.

At the new formal dining table the length of their little Branwyn cottage, Maggie had set each place with cut crystal and hand-painted porcelain plates arrayed with forks of various sizes and shapes. She sat Richard at the head of the table with Diana to his left and Jon opposite her. But the table was too long for Diana to reach her father's hand, and uncomfortable, Diana fussed.

"Certainly you don't eat alone at this table every night," she said.

"No. I'm rarely here," Richard said. "They have an even more massive banquet table at the formal residence in town where I'm expected to entertain. But my presence there is a secret while the negotiations are ongoing."

Maggie served each of them, but unlike the free-flowing discussion earlier, the talk was stiff.

Diana sighed and stood. "My apologies, Maggie. You've set a beautiful table, and I'm honored. But we're family, and I can't do this." She took her plate and glass and moved it to the small kitchen table.

After a moment of stunned silence, Richard and Jon smiled, and flummoxed Maggie helped Diana move the other settings and the food. From the crystal goblets, Diana poured the wine into fired clay mugs. After setting a fourth place for Maggie at the same table and setting her down, Diana went back to herd the men into the kitchen and sat them.

Dinner was plain, chicken, dumplings, and vegetables, and the conversation just as plain. In the casual setting, the talk was spirited and the mood light, as Richard recounted the battles for the North and their victory.

The Sulerian and Quarajii cavalry had taken the fore, while the Sulerian Elites protected their northern flank and the Sul engines of war. Together they pushed almost to the coast. They put farms and villages in their path to the torch and scoured the land for forage like a plague of locusts. And they took many of their countrymen as slaves.

The Army of the North could not stop them, so Richard gave the invaders their head. The Sulerians' headstrong young leaders were greedy and galloped too far ahead of their supplies in their rush to the western ocean.

At Royax, rather than reinforcements from Suleria, Richard's troops and Venarian ships met them. Richard left them hungry with no place to rest and harassed them along their retreat east until they freed the hostages. They drove the allied Sulerian and Quarajii forces back across the Wye River. And in Cherbourne, the Sul engines of war, the catapults and trebuchets meant for the siege of Bayeun and Wikkert, stood abandoned. What survived the crossing into Derryh was only a remnant of the invasion force, but until the victory at Royax, it was a close thing.

"The combined force is still just a few days' ride east?" Jon said.

"Aye. And I expect they're waiting for another opportunity to attack," Richard replied.

"Why do they wait?"

"Our forces are larger now and united again. And last time the low banks east of the Wye Delta made a landing easy. The cliffs along the western shore protect us as they have for centuries."

Jon raised his mug. "From everything except smugglers."

Diana frowned. "Are the cliffs still patrolled?"

"Always," Richard said.

"What means do the smugglers use?"

"If we knew, we'd stop them. Wikkert doesn't like competition for the wine and tobacco trade." He raised his glass. "And just where did you get this wine?"

"Brought all the way from Branwyn," Jon said.

"If Wikkert finds out about this, they'll go to war to stop the competition. You should get an exclusive right for this."

Jon waved a fork. "Things seem peaceful enough here."

Richard scoffed. "Rather a deadlock and a poor one at that. The Sul squat in Derryh now and the fields lie fallow. That's been our breadbasket and compensated for the poor harvests in Nordes."

"The Quarajii are unlikely to farm it."

"Aye, the Sulerians mean to keep it from us," Richard said. "Our troops at the Wye prevent them from crossing, and if they do cross, we have cavalry reinforcements at La Pegre."

"What if that's not enough to stop them?" she asked and both men turned to her.

# Chapter 39
# Dark Passage

Diana woke, shivering in thin rags in an old barn, in the outer layer of a tumble of children huddled together for warmth. It would be another hungry morning among weeks of hungry mornings, and without food the barn would be their grave. Facing them was another day searching for sustenance in the relentless snowfall on the road to Aemgarde and safety.

She had lost her horse a month prior, and the icy cold ground crept through the holes in her shoes as she walked with the children. With her emotions frozen by exhaustion, all her dreams collapsed to the survival of her troupe. Starving and trembling, they dug under the snow hoping for a bean plant or melon but found only dead sticks and shriveled skins.

The villages and farms they passed were all empty of people and resources that might help. And behind them, hungry wolves trailed close, waiting for a child to fall behind.

Along the road they traversed a forest of frozen men, armed with spears and swords. Invaders or defenders, their allegiance did not matter. All were dead, with wolves tearing at the occasional ankle or hand freed from the ice. Just beyond the army they passed a graveyard with caskets laid upon the surface because no one could dig graves in the frigid ground.

The falling snow cleared as they entered a village, but this too was deserted and frozen, the houses and shops empty of food.

*How could God forsake an entire country?*

They trudged to the town center, and Diana's heart stopped at what appeared in front of her, and she fell to her knees.

*This is my mother's rune stone. This desolate village, frozen for years and everyone dead or gone, is my destination, my home—Aemgarde. There's nowhere left in the North for us to go. Then where?*

She led the children south to find the mountain pass that she and Jon had taken years earlier on their escape to Branwyn. But glaciers blocked the pass and forced them west. And along the west road, they ran into a solid forest of ice. Not a glacier, but an ocean of refugees heading for Cherbourne, frozen in mid-stride. There was no place left to go now, no safe place to lead the children.

What would she tell the helpless young ones who followed her? When she turned around to tell them she was sorry and to not give up hope, she found thousands more children had joined. Like her, all were shivering and starving, and she cried out.

\*\*\*

Diana jerked upright in her bed, trembling in their Cherbourne house and blinked, disoriented. A hand took hers, and she turned to her father's worried face.

"There, there, now," Richard said.

The atlas lay open in his lap, and she glanced at it.

*It touched me. Has it driven me mad?*

After a blink, she looked at her father. "Are you in my dream?"

"You're home," Richard said and put another blanket on her. "Back to sleep, lass."

She took her father's hand in both of hers and held it tight. The frayed bracelet he still wore on his wrist caught her eye again. "I need to make you a new one."

"Plenty of time tomorrow," he said.

Lying in bed with her eyes open, she stared at him and smiled. In time, she blinked and fell back to sleep.

When Diana woke early the next morning, she discovered her father asleep in the chair next to her. The atlas lay open in his lap and his hand on the bed where her hands had held his. In her dresser she found the distinct colors of cord and went to work weaving the new bracelet in the family pattern.

After finishing the bracelet, Diana found Maggie in the kitchen with a fresh pot of tea. Richard joined them with the atlas, and Diana gave him a big hug and took his wrist to tie the new bracelet around it.

On a map, Richard pointed to the island to the northwest. "I noticed many symbols prevalent on Xorellia that are rare elsewhere in the maps. I think these are metals like iron." He placed a finger just south of them in the foothills of the Spine. "And the same symbols here."

Diana nodded. "There may be another reason the Empress wants Cherbourne."

With his free hand, Richard pointed to a symbol that crossed the Wye River, -)||(-. "Do you recognize this? There's no bridge or ford there."

Diana shook her head. "It's not in the picture dictionary or the map key. There's a similar symbol near the cliffs along the Inland Sea, but I don't know what they signify. Is there a cartographer in Aemgarde?"

"No. Ours is with the militia at Le Pegre."

She turned to him with a crease between her eyes. "Papa, when you were examining the maps last night, did you have a dream about them?"

"No, dear," he said and took her hand. "Jon told me about the nightmares."

"This one was different," she said and described the dream to him.

"Triggered by the atlas?"

She nodded. "The glaciers on the old maps keep bothering me."

He looked at her expecting more, and Diana went to his office. There, she removed the map from the wall, returned to the kitchen, and laid it next to the atlas page representing the same regions of the North.

"Compare the old map to the new map," she said. "On the recent maps, the glaciers cover less area, and the sea ice is farther north. And so we expect further warming and longer growing seasons for agriculture."

"That makes sense with the history we're taught," Richard said. "Our civilization developed after the Chaos when we struggled in perpetual winter, and it's been warmer since."

"But that's not what's happening. From Xorellia, Nordes, Captain Greit to the Lanshrue bridge, everyone is telling us it's getting colder, not warmer."

Richard leaned back in his chair as Maggie poured them fresh cups of tea and listened with the pot in her hand.

"How much colder will it get?" Richard asked.

Diana shrugged. "Maybe cold enough to resemble the old maps. Maybe that's our future as well as our past."

Deep creases appeared between Richard's eyes. "I studied the maps last night. If the old map is our future as you suggest, we'd lose more than three quarters of our crop land. Derryh, Cherbourne, and Sinefora would be the only viable land. It'd mean mass starvation, unless there was time to adjust."

The image came from her dream of the cave the day prior of the thriving breshk and withering potato plants. "Or find substitute crops." She sat by his side. "How could we adjust to such a catastrophe?"

Richard shrugged. "People are resourceful. There are folks that thrive on the ice floes near Xorellia, and others who live all their lives on the sea."

Jon joined them, flipped a chair around to sit on, and Maggie poured him a cup of tea. "The Turajii follow the reindeer herds north of the Qu where it thaws for only a few months."

"If the Sulerian Empress has a similar book," Richard said, "That explains her hunger for Derryh. Derryh and the South will be how she saves her people from starvation. And if—"

Diana leaned over the table. "And the invasions and the Empress's assassins who killed my mother were all because of the coming cold?"

She slammed her palm on the table and stunned them to silence. "I don't want to blame the cold for my mother's death. *Men* killed her and the Empress told them to do it. I want them punished!"

Diana stood, slammed her chair into the table, and stormed out.


At the pasture fence, Richard came to Diana and held her hand without speaking.

"I'm sorry," she said after a time. "I spoke in haste."

"You spoke from the heart," he said. "And that's always welcome." Without a word, he opened her hand and within it placed a flower petal as he had the day he left for war.

She leaned into him and let his shirt take her tears. "I miss her."

He nodded. "Every day."

When the sun rose high, Richard put a hand on her shoulder. "Come back inside. You've been pondering this longer than us and we need your insight."

She nodded, and on the porch stairs, it struck her, the question that nagged at her and was so hard to put into words.

"Papa, what if ice eventually covers even more land than these old maps show?"

"Colder? Go on," Richard said and held the door open for her.

"We can't make books like the atlas now or those in the reliquerium, books that can last more than a thousand years. That means the civilization that made them collapsed *after* they made the books."

Richard nodded and sat at the table opposite Jon. "The history we're taught tells us all our technology was developed after the Chaos and Wandering when we had nothing at all. Your book proves that can't be true."

At the table, Maggie put fresh cups of tea in front of them.

"What you're holding may be the Old Knowledge," Jon said.

"But what happened to the rest of that knowledge?" she asked and leaned over with her elbows on the table. "No one remembers anything but myths the Singers tell of."

They were silent.

*What if they think I'm crazy? Is it worth the risk? But who else can I trust with this?*

"What if it got even colder than the old map shows?" Diana said. "If the atlas is a product of the Old Knowledge, then civilization collapsed *after* they made these books. The cold may have become worse before people could adjust and civilization fell. And over centuries of perpetual winter, people forgot."

*Is this the thought that destroys those who read the book?*

Richard leaned back and raised his eyebrows. "And to us now, it looks as if we started from nothing."

"Except the old books and artifacts are evidence to the contrary," Jon said. "Interesting speculation. What might do that? A collapse of civilization, barbarism, total loss of agriculture?"

"Maybe all three, and the memories of what really happened were lost over time." Her hand touched her rune coin. *Perhaps this is a record. Or a clue.*

"Go on," Richard said.

"That's what's bothering me so much," she said. "What if the cold came too fast, and they couldn't respond in time, couldn't adjust, were insufficiently resourceful . . . and fell behind in the food supply or suffered through a series of poor harvests—"

"Starvation, riots, barbarism," Richard said. "Chaos."

"How could they let it fall?" Jon asked. "How could those charged with defending their civilization let it fall?"

"Maybe it began gradually," she said. "And they didn't see it coming until it was too late to respond. Like now, everyone maneuvers for advantage, settling old feuds, and using all their resources to secure arable land that may only last a few decades. And while they fought with each other, it got colder faster than they could prepare for it."

Jon spoke as a cool breeze drifted through the door. "What if the wars now are echoes of the past, fighting for shrinking farmland, and we're unaware of what's coming."

Diana paused and her gaze lost focus. "Short-term scheming and fighting combined with a lack of appreciation for what kept their civilization going, the technology, trade, agriculture—"

Her father raised a hand and broke the spell. "Lass, you need to keep quiet about these speculations and not commit to them. Keep them between us and your monk friend."

She frowned. "But why? If—"

"If people hear you talking about the Old Knowledge and times before the Chaos and a coming catastrophe, they'll burn you for a witch."

"But if it's true, we must prepare," she said.

"If, lass. But we'll not get the chance if you're ridiculed, and opinions harden. We need to position your role as a courier rather than an oracle."

*And not called mad.*

"Papa, I'm only concerned if we divert all our attention to war and don't prepare, civilization may fall to barbarism again, and—"

Jon interrupted. "If the Qu and Sul cross the Wye River again, barbarism will come even sooner."

Richard stood. "Speculations won't get action from politicians unless it aligns with their goals. They'll need something concrete. And we can't claim the books are magic."

"But this is knowledge we don't have, knowledge the Empress may use against us. And if she has a similar book, maybe she found a cache like in Branwyn that unlocks other wonders. There's a sword in the cache that's almost unbreakable, and—"

Richard shook his head, "It won't matter if we have one unbreakable sword if we can't make more. It won't matter if we have an enchanted book if we can't use it to make bread, or weapons, or a better life for ourselves. That's where we are in our struggle now."

Diana stood and crossed her arms "Then all our searching and risk was a waste?"

"No, no, lass. Nothing of the kind. What you've found may change our future entirely and save us. But information must be useful to be valuable. And that is your mission now, to tell us why this knowledge, here and in Branwyn, are not just clever ideas, but of strategic consequence."

Diana sighed and gazed out the window. *But how am I to do that?*


While Richard bickered with the ministers the next morning, Diana visited her mother's rune stone, the centerpiece of the new public square in the rebuilt Aemgarde. There she told Katheryn's spirit everything that happened since she had left, and especially about Eric and Browne. There she prayed to find useful information within the books.

"I might have found what you sought, Mama," Diana said. "But my work is not done until your death is avenged. And I can't do that until I find value in my discoveries."


That night, the squeak of the corral gate woke Diana from a fitful nap near the fireplace waiting for her father to arrive home. She closed her eyes again, safer than she had been in years, but troubled by the secrets she held from her father for years and his trust in her.

When the stable door closed, Diana opened her eyes again and rose. His room was empty when she peeked in. In the kitchen, she found a covered dish on the table and opened it to find a plate of cold mutton and potatoes for Richard. Into the oven she put the dish to warm and sat at the table nibbling on a bun, waiting for her father.

Richard entered and hung his cloak by the door. "Evening, Dee. You stayed up for me?"

"I woke when you stabled your horse," she said as she took the dinner from the oven and set it on the table. He sat in front of the plate of mutton, and she sat opposite with her cheek on her fist.

"Simple fare for a king," she said. "Wikkert would be shocked at how modestly you live."

He nodded, and while he ate, Diana chewed her cheek as she prepared her confession.

"Is there something you want to say?" Richard asked.

"I need to apologize for my defiance these last years," she said. "That I ran away to join the militia and crossed the Spine to Branwyn against your orders."

He smiled. "I'm only glad you've returned to me whole."

She pursed her lips. *And this is the hardest . . .*

"What troubles you?"

*This is my king, my father, a wise man whose judgment I trust. Just say it!*

"I'm the reason Makashti killed Higell," she said. "I snuck out to meet Garfann and confirmed it was Quarajii who murdered my mother. Before you returned, he said his mother killed Higell to 'even the score.'"

Richard nodded.

"You knew?"

"I guessed," he said. "You were the only one . . . involved with motive. But you aren't responsible for his death. That burden falls on Higell and Makashti."

"What is your judgment, sire?" she asked with respect.

Richard tipped his head. "The issue is closed. The Sul would have killed him before reaching Suleria. And the information you gleaned was valuable. No need to reopen this."

She inhaled deep as he lifted from her the weight of guilt and betrayal she had carried since Le Pegre. But her brow furrowed at the memory of her responsibility for the events that caused it.

His voice deepened and he put his hand on hers. "But you are an adult now, a royal, and a public figure. The next time you decide to defy the law, or your king, the consequences will be different. The politicians in Wikkert are not our friends and may tie my hands."

"Yes, sir." *My king pardoned me, and my father forgave me with a warning. More than I hoped. And he gazes at me like all he cares about is me.*

And at his gentle smile, tears formed in the corners of her eyes.

"Have you thought about your plans, Princess?"

"I hope to rejoin the militia and continue my training," she said. "Jon has been coaching me, so I've kept up to date. But, for now, I like it here. A Singer in Branwyn reminded me of how much I love it." The dryness in the pit of her stomach came, and she took a drink from his glass.

"What did she sing?" he asked between bites.

Diana smiled and rested her chin on her hand. "It's not an activity but a title for the guild of entertainers in the South. Everything from a tavern song to a production of hundreds with stage and orchestra. People come from miles around to watch their performances."

"We'll have to invite them north."

"You might reconsider when you hear more. Rumors are that Singers are intriguers, and one Singer admitted to me she was a spy."

He pushed the plate away and leaned back in his chair. "They'd find plenty of opportunity for intrigue in Wikkert. And perhaps we can use them."

"I think they study the Old Knowledge for the stories they tell."

"Do they know about the cache in Branwyn?"

She shrugged. "Perhaps now if Eric told them."

"Have you learned more about the cold?" he asked. "Or heard from your friend?"

"No. I sent a message to Martin with Captain Greit, but I don't expect a response for weeks. Do we have pigeons to send?"

Behind Richard, Maggie came to the kitchen doorway but stopped and smiled before leaving.

"They need to travel via Royax as well. The Spine is too cold and desolate for the little birds to traverse. I'll write Makashti to ask if Suleria is experiencing the same cold."

Diana's jaw dropped, and she stared at her father. "Makashti? Garfann's mother? You deal with our enemies?"

"We aren't allies, lass."

Pain etched her brows. "But yet you bargain with her."

"We have mutual interests, and it—"

"For years I blamed myself for Mama's death because I couldn't protect her from those animals, and here you deal with them? Her people killed my mother!"

Richard winced as if struck. "I don't believe Makashti was behind the attack on—"

"Based on what? Her assurances?"

"One of those mutual interests is you. She warned me Garfann was searching for you."

Diana stood. "And you sent me from home on that caravan north on the word of our enemy? How deep can you cut, Father?"

"She was right, lass."

Before his protest was complete, Diana was already halfway up the stairs. There, she locked herself in her bedroom, stared out the window, and cried.

There was a knock at her door. "Diana, please. It's not as you think."

Her retreat, the one safe place in the entire world she could go, had been violated. Suleria's long reach corrupted even her home.

"Go away."

The next morning, she rode beside Maggie's wagon to the center of town to pray for guidance at her mother's rune stone. A reflecting pool now lay around it bordered by a rim that served as a bench. She sat, unable to escape the memories of her mother's death and her hatred of Sulerians.

"Why do you cry, milady?" Maggie asked.

"It was my fault," Diana said.

"For what, dearie?"

"That I couldn't save her. I carried a weapon and was too—"

Maggie's jaw dropped. She stood and turned her back to Diana, and when she turned back around, she wore a disappointed squint and a tear in her eye.

"Milady, I'm afraid that I must leave your service. Please tell your father—"

"Maggie, no!"

"I'm sorry. I must insist."

"But why? If I said anything wrong, I—"

"No, ma'am. For what I'm about to say."

"Please speak. Who other than my father and Jon can I speak to so frankly?"

Maggie put a hand on a hip and shook a finger at Diana. "I thought I'd left that self-centered little brat who ran through the house like a tyrant when your mother died."

"I'm sorry I was—"

"Not was, still are. You've not dropped that millstone after all these years? Find another purpose in your life than guilt for something you couldn't have changed. And stop blaming your father."

"But I don't blame him. I—"

"You still think the world revolves around you? That a little girl could have stopped the forces of an empire? If so, then you're back in the magic world of omnipotent children. You're a princess who would rule the North. And now you behave like a child, and in front of me?"

"You're disappointed?"

"I'm hurt that all the guidance your father and mother and Jon gave you was not enough. And you believe your childish opinion of events is the one that should govern the actions of your king."

"But, Maggie, I—"

"Who was it that might have been strong enough to save your mother that night?" Maggie said.

Diana dropped her gaze. "My father."

Maggie nodded. "That's what you can't face. Your father had the power to influence the outcome, and even he couldn't change events. And he never forgave himself for your mother's death or the risk to you. Every act you take or word you say that tries to take that burden on yourself, you as a little girl, he takes like an arrow in his heart. This is his burden, girl, not yours."

Diana turned to her with tears in her eyes. "I want to carry some of it for him."

Maggie sat next to her and put her arm around her, and Diana laid her head on Maggie's shoulder.

"He knows, dear," Maggie said, her voice soothing. "And he knows you can't share his burden. It's you who must drop this guilt and delusion of power and be grateful for the gift of life your mother gave you."

"But I might have called out and saved her," Diana said.

"You would save your mother and in saving her, lose everything she fought and died for?"

"What do you mean?"

"You're older now and a woman. Have you not thought what a vicious and all-powerful empress would do to a female child in Mokdar? What your future would be if you had saved her life, but they captured you both? Concubine to a beast or worse. And your mother enslaved as well."

*Eavlyn.* "Father mentioned . . ."

"Yes, your father knew this. You asked him if he would trade her life for yours. And you knew the answer but couldn't face it. You remember his reply?"

Diana's tears fell freely. "Yes. He agreed with my mother's choice."

"Your life and your innocence are your mother's gift to you, and the burden of responsibility is your father's. These gifts are not free. *Your* burden is not guilt but *gratitude* for their wisdom and their love for you. These are gifts you honor by living a full life."

Diana raised her eyes to Maggie. "I need to see him, to find out what he sees in our enemy."

"You're ready to talk now?"

Diana stood and unhitched her horse. "Yes."

A narrow gaze and furrowed brow crossed Maggie's face. "He's your king and need not defend himself to you."

"He's my father," she said and mounted her horse.

Diana galloped to the council chamber, and her horse skidded to a stop. The filly was young and wanted to run almost as much as she did and turned in circles. She dismounted, handed the reins to a squire, and stormed inside.

"I'm here to meet with the king," she said to the guard at the door.

"Beggin' your pardon, Your Highness. They're taking lunch in session."

"Then tell the king I want to see him."

"Sorry ma'am. I have orders they're not to be disturbed."

He could not put her off. "Who do you report to?" Diana asked.

"Me," declared a voice behind her.

Turning, she glared at the officer who approached but raised her eyebrows.

"Well I'll be, Di . . . Princess," he said and bowed.

"Ensign Gage," she said. "An officer now, I see. And worthy of the bars?"

Gage appeared uncomfortable. "If you would please accompany me, Your Highness." He raised his hand to the hallway, and she followed him into an office.

"Can an officer be hugged?" she asked.

Without reply he opened his arms, and she jumped into them.

"I heard we lost you," he said.

She shook her head. "Just a different mission."

"You've come to see your father?"

Diana frowned and nodded. "He's busy, and the endless talkers and climbers never seem to let him go."

"Come with me," he said and took her through the hall, through a narrow door and staircase to the second floor. A slender balcony circled the Council Chamber below, and when she stepped onto it, she walked into the powerful fumes of smoke, perfume, body odor, and sausage that collected near the ceiling. In the chamber below, guards stood at the corners and doors, and within sat the council and a chair for Richard. The majestic throne of elk horn and fur he had sat on when he argued with the Sulerians was absent, replaced by a simple chair like others in the room, intended to convey the equality of the tribal ministers in this room. But on that chair, he sat like a king, the center of the conversation. Next to him on the desk was a satchel holding the book of maps and picture dictionary from the reliquerium. And when he spotted her, he gave her a slight nod

*What could I say to Papa that will make this better? Maggie was right. Maybe I have been blaming him and not been able to face it. But it wasn't his fault. What can I say? I'm not a diplomat with words always at the ready* . . . An image came of Makashti's cold eyes as she faced Richard so many years ago. *He must have a reason to trust her, or at least listen.*

Gage joined her as she leaned over the railing to listen. It only took her a minute to follow the squabbling between unfamiliar men and women.

". . . and the Sul and Qu are a spent force that will take years to recover."

"But they hold Derryh."

"The Sulerians are petty, driven west by greed for the wealth of the North."

"A greed dampened by their recent heavy losses."

"The location of Derryh as a buffer between Cherbourne and Suleria means nothing to Wikkert a thousand miles away."

Richard nodded. "Derryh is the breadbasket for Cherbourne, Beirn, and Aquilla because we're shipping our own crops north to feed Wikkert."

"And paying us poorly for it."

A man stood in the back. "Doesn't Wikkert care?"

"Not if it means a renewed conflict," said an over-dressed man with a nose pointed so high on his narrow face he might trip at any moment. He stood and strutted in front of Richard. "Wikkert complains the resources you request to oppose Suleria are too high and a constant drain on the North. Perhaps an accommodation can be made that—"

Richard's eyes narrowed and his brow furrowed. "Accommodation with Sul slavers? No. They must be defeated and prohibited from land where our citizens walk."

"Some in Wikkert say you're offended by their religion, that your prejudice blinds you to—"

"It's not their beliefs that offend me, it's their behavior," Richard said.

"But—"

"I don't care a whit if their god tells them we're beasts, I care they *treat* us that way. They steal our children and enslave them. And I will not tolerate it."

"*You* will not—"

"The resources I request are not to feed my prejudice, but to save *your* neck. If the Sulerians run through Cherbourne, Wikkert is next. And if the cold is driving them—"

"*If* the cold," a stout minister stood and waved his arms. "What has changed? So what if the vineyards in Auxiere have moved south a few miles? They're still productive and prosperous."

*What a weasel. And if it continues to get colder, they'll be picking those grapes in the Inland Sea.*

Richard put his hand on the satchel with her books and glanced at her before turning back to the ministers. "I will invite emissaries from the Northern States, Xorellia, and Venaro. They can provide more insight into what's happening to the North. And advise Wikkert they deny my request at their peril. The forces here are not sufficient to hold back a second front if the Sul invades."

*That will take months.* "We might not have that much time," she whispered.

Smiling up at her, Richard tipped his head as if to say, "What can I do?"

"Just say 'to hell with you' and walk out," she whispered. But they would not let him go, and she sighed, remembering Eric's remark that tyrants arise because they tire of building consensus.

"How can he be so patient?" she whispered to Gage.

"We're still a Republic, Princess. And we're at peace for now. They delay until forced to act."

"By then it might be too late."

*And here was her father, just a man who opposes an empire to protect his people. And who protects him? Company A. But a company is not enough to thwart an empire.*

She smiled. *But I have magic!* Blowing him a kiss, she tapped her ear to signal she wanted to talk and returned to the hall. There at the secretary's desk, Diana wrote a note to her father and took her place at the balcony. Gage delivered the note to Richard, who read it and nodded. And as he interrupted the session to pen a reply, the ministers scowled up at her.

When Gage returned, she smiled as she read her note—

*Your Highness, my apology for my lack of understanding of your question. You asked if the books are magic. I don't know any better definition of magic than the miracles we do not understand.*

And Richard's reply,

*Then find those miracles for us all.*

Diana turned to Gage. "Do they still patrol the coastal cliffs?"

"Yes," Gage said.

"Under whose command?"

"They're regional. The Beirn Home Guard patrols those north of Bayeun."

"Who patrols the coast to the Wye?"

"Cavalry scouts from Le Pegre," Gauge said. "Say, I'll be escorting General Henlow to review the Le Pegre cavalry. Why not come for a visit? Most of your old squad is there, Lisle and Rollo."

*Le Pegre, where the cartographer might decode that odd symbol.* "And Dru?"

"Yes, yes. Dru as well."

She blushed. "Are they all officers now?"

"Most. Rollo is engineering, Lisle's infantry, and Dru cavalry. A hard ride and we can be there tomorrow. What say you?"

"I'll need to ask, but yes," she said and ran to her horse and rode to meet Jon.

# Chapter 40
## Deceit

Into the midst of senior chiefs of the Sulerian Elites camped on the east bank of the Wye River strode a young cavalry officer as if he commanded them all. And though a junior officer, he wore what they could not: a white and silver ribbon of a courier of Empress El-al that hung from his belt.

"The Empress grows impatient with your progress," Garfann Sinura said as he threw a letter onto the table strewn with maps and weapons.

"It's Richard," a war-chief said. "He's resourceful and escaped to attack our rear at Royax."

"I've been to Wikkert for the treaty negotiations," another said. "The Northmen are all mewling kittens and drooling opportunists. Only Richard has the fortitude to oppose us."

"If you value your heads and your families," Garfann said, "don't return home without victory. The Empress gave you the resources you asked for to win, and she expects victory."

The room was silent.

Garfann poured himself wine and pointed to the letter on the table. "The Empress has consulted the Book of Chaos and proposes a plan."

"Bah, magic."

"Scoff if you like," Garfann said. "Her information has proved to be of strategic value before. Let's hear your plan instead."

When no one spoke, Garfann swept all the drinks and weapons off the table, leaving only the campaign map that included their current bivouac, Beirn, and Aemgarde.

"If Richard is the boogeyman holding you back, then we capture him. Wikkert will sue for peace to save their skins, but we will own Cherbourne as well as Derryh and secure our route to the western ocean."

"We've tried many times, and . . ."

Garfann waved him to silence. "Our target is in Aemgarde, a lightly defended town. Two squadrons of cavalry can defeat all they have, and a regiment will secure the town."

The high-chief raised his hand. "Come, come now, my youthful friend. Le Pegre and the reserves are between us and them. We can't get to Aemgarde without going through them."

"There will be no resistance," Garfann said, and the war chiefs grumbled.

"By what miracle . . ."

"No miracle," Garfann said and slammed his fist on the table. "Speed and boldness! We draw the strength of Le Pegre to the Wye River where they can't cross, while our army waits on the other side.

A chief laughed. "They can't cross the Wye without our knowing, but neither can we."

"Yes, we can," Garfann said and held up the letter. "And that's the gift of our empress. Two squadrons attack Le Pegre. They will think we have crossed undetected, and they will rush to buttress the Wye defenses. Another light cavalry unit will travel by galley from here." Garfann put his finger on a spot on the map east of the Wye delta. Then he slid the finger across the map to the cliffs of Cherbourne. "Across the delta to land west of the Wye and rush to Richard unopposed."

"And the Empress has given you the means to cross the Wye invisibly and level the cliffs?"

Garfann nodded. "Yes. I will lead the attack on Le Pegre and draw the reserves to the Wye. Then we'll race back to defend the landing along the coast."

The high-chief leaned on the table. "The bulk of our army, the looming threat to Cherbourne, stays here unmoved, while strike forces hit behind their lines?"

"Yes," Garfann said. "As soon as my courier arrives with word of our attack at Le Pegre, you can cross the Wye. And with news of Richard's death or capture, you can march into Cherbourne unopposed to secure the territory we've won."

"And you will lead the assault on Le Pegre?"

Garfann nodded. "Yes. And War Chief Forekx will ferry his units by galley to the cliffs east of the Wye delta."

"And the empress has also provided you a means to defeat the cliffs?"

Garfann waved the letter. "Yes."

"When?"

"I can leave tomorrow. Shallow draft galleys await you on the coast. I expect to meet War-Chief Forekx on the cliffs in Cherbourne in five days."

The high-chief stood straight. "It seems you take most of the risk while the bulk of the army prepares to march." He scanned the room. "Any objections? Then make it happen."

Just outside the command tent, Garfann winced and stumbled. There on her haunches sat a beautiful woman dressed in a silk sheath with gold trim meant to impress the officers, but with her ankles in a hobble chain.

Eavlyn stood and caught him before he collapsed. From his pocket, she took a small packet of powder and poured it on his tongue.

"That'll be the death of you," she said with pity in her eyes. He leaned on her more, and she braced herself against the tent pole.

"It will be a good death," he said. "And I will be reincarnated as an emperor."

Eavlyn shook her head. "You will be reborn as a bug for the crimes against my family, and I will step on you."

Still shaky, Garfann smiled. "How will you know which bug?"

"I will step on them all."

He smiled at her, stood straight, and turned to go.

"Wait," the high-chief said and put his hand on Garfann's shoulder. "I'm aware King Richard's daughter has returned home."

Eavlyn's eyes widened, while Garfann's narrowed.

"Yes," Garfann said.

"I don't want you distracted by a personal grudge. You may hold the key to the north here with this gambit. Don't let a skirt divert you from your goal."

"I'm not going after her. I'm going after what she loves. And in this, my goals align."

# Chapter 41
## Le Pegre

### Le Pegre—Now

What Diana intended as a fast jaunt to Le Pegre with jerky and blanket in her saddlebags stretched into another day. But Jon dismissed her casual plans with enemy forces camped across the Wye delta another day's ride east. He insisted five of the King's Guard escort them. The troupe and Maggie's meal plans meant a wagon and supplies and the slow draft horses to pull it. Diana's only joy was when she recognized the same species of flower her father had sent to her during his campaign.

At the top of the hill she stopped. Le Pegre sprawled in front of them, a trip line to an invasion of Cherbourne. The camp announced itself with the familiar scents of horses and barbecued meats that came with the easterly breeze and the fife and drums as a unit drilled on the parade ground below.

"Only the location changes," Jon said. "The layout is as constant as the moons, and a touchstone in our lives."

Gage nodded. "And an essential ingredient."

Diana smiled at the memory of her arrival three years ago, and she sat with her back straight and shoulders squared.

*I am a soldier, and my mission is to fight for my king and country.*

*I am a soldier . . .*

## Le Pegre—Three Years Past

Sergeants pushed the female recruits into rows at the Le Pegre training camp. Like Diana, most were teens who volunteered at their first opportunity after their fifteenth birthday. A senior sergeant with her hair brushed back tight marched up and stood in front of them.

"You will address me as 'sir,'" the sergeant said. "As you will all your superiors. And you will respond to all questions with a resounding 'yes, sir' or 'no, sir'. Are we clear?" The recruits were silent. "I didn't hear you."

"Yes, sir," they said.

The sergeant put her hand to her ear. "Are you babies or soldiers?"

"Soldiers, sir!"

She paced in front of them with her hands behind her back. "I will say this once and it's your responsibility to remember everything as if they were commandments. I will not shout but speak with the voice of God and whisper in the wind. And you will hear me and respond immediately with the thunder of a thousand men, or you will go home. Are we clear?"

"Yes, sir!"

"On these grounds, there are no titles, only rank, and you, boot, have none. Everyone is your superior. Are we clear?"

"Yes, sir!"

"You are not women in this camp, you are soldiers. You are killers. Whatever you think about beauty, or love, or sex, you leave outside the gate. Are we clear?"

"Yes, sir!"

"Remember, this army doesn't need women. We need soldiers. The moment you can't carry your weight, you will be gone. The criteria for you to stay are the same as for you to survive combat: to have the skill, strength, and the will to defeat our enemies and support the soldiers who fight at your side. There are no other criteria. Are we clear?"

"Yes sir!"

"The militia needs no one, man or woman, who puts themselves and their needs above their brothers in arms. Young men have issues with controlling their emotions and their biology, just like young women. And a goal of this camp is to confront those needs and subvert them to the needs of completing your mission and saving your life in combat. You will need to confront your issues in the name of discipline and order just as they do. Are we clear?"

"Yes, sir!"

"You are soldiers. There is no consolation if you can't keep up the pace: your country falls. There is no solace if the backpack filled with rations is too heavy for you to carry: your brother in arms starves. There is no forgiveness if you drop your weapon: your brother in arms dies. Are we clear?"

"Yes, sir!"

"You are soldiers. And the moment you act like a woman within this camp or in combat, you will trigger your fellow soldiers to forget their duty and protect you. They're chivalrous, like all honorable men, and concern for your weakness will bring them to their doom.

"You are soldiers. And whenever you act without self-respect with a wink or wag of your bum, you declare yourself deserving of no more respect than the whores who follow the camp or the tramps at home.

"You are soldiers. And whatever happens outside this camp, your brothers will remember when they return. If you act with dishonor, your brothers will not trust you with their lives. Are we clear?"

"Yes, sir."

"And if you ever reply to your drill sergeant with that pansy-assed 'yes, sir' you gave me, they will send you home. Are we clear?"

"Yes, sir!"

"Drill sergeants report!" she commanded, and sergeants lined up beside her. "Recruits, when you hear your name called, sound off and line up behind your sergeant."

"Diana Stewart!" a sergeant shouted, and Diana called out loud enough to get a nod from her sergeant.

## Le Pegre—Now

"I am a soldier," Diana whispered.

Jon glanced at her upright posture and smiled. "Your Highness?"

"Sir?" she said and noticed the sentry who stood at attention and held his salute. The sentries had honored Jon and Gage with salutes as they rode past. Without a crown or uniform, Diana thought of herself no more noticeable than the cook. But when Jon made her presence known, she returned the salute.

"As you were," she said, and with an attitude that outranked her, she dismounted and walked beside Jon to the camp commander's quarters.

Though at a new location, the mobile bivouac was the same, dusty and brown as dirt, cut into quarters by function: residence and mess; cavalry training and parade ground; infantry training; and archery. At a corner of the parade ground with a view of all quadrants sat the commander's tent.

"Where is everyone?" she asked Gage, who walked beside her.

"On watch at the Wye River or on missions. There's movement, and we're concerned the Sul prepare for mischief. We patrol more frequently now."

She turned to Jon. "Do you really need me, sir?"

"Yes, Your Highness. It would be unthinkable for the princess to attend the camp, regardless of how dressed or attended, without notifying the commander."

"Please, spare me from reviewing the troops."

He smiled. "No promises."

She frowned but followed, and after a few minutes of courtesies, the commander smiled at her fidgeting.

"Well, I expect you want to find your old team, Princess," the commander said. "Why don't you leave us old warhorses to our stories."

"Sir, may if ask if there's been any activity along the sea cliffs?"

"No, Your Highness. We patrol regularly. The last will return tomorrow." He smiled. "The cliffs have been our ally against the Sul for hundreds of years and they're not ready to crumble yet."

"And the defenses on the Wye?" Jon asked.

"Commanded by General Fredricks. We're their logistics center and plan a supply run later tomorrow. Want to join, General?"

"Yes, sir," Jon said and tipped his head to Diana.

She stood and saluted, ignoring her title. "If you'll excuse me, sir."

Outside, she found Gage waiting for her. Together they went to the duty officer to locate their old friends and found them in the mess.

*Everything is as it should be, with natural defenses and patrols to alert us. Then what's bothering me? The cliffs and the tides. Until I know for sure . . .*

The Le Pegre mess was a large semi-permanent tent to shield the soldiers from the rain and snow, but not the heat or cold. And there Diana and Gage found Rollo.

With a wide smile, she greeted her friend, but when she went to hug him, he backed away.

"Ensign Brandeis to you." He stood as if waiting for something. "Where have you been, Corporal?"

She snapped to attention and saluted. "Sir!"

"Active or inactive?" he asked.

"Unassigned, sir."

"At ease, Corporal," Rollo said, smiling. "Now let's have that hug." After the hug, he picked a table by a tree, ordered refreshments, and the three talked about the exploits of her old squad and what she missed.

"So where are they now?" she asked.

"On patrol. They'll be back soon. Lisle is never late for dinner."

"Attention!" a sergeant called, and they snapped to.

Dru joined them. "As you were."

She grabbed his arm. "Give us a minute," she said to Gage.

"Ensigns, you're on duty," a lieutenant said.

"Yes, sir," Dru replied.

"Stay Dru, I want to talk . . ." she said.

"I have one more watch before I'm relieved," he said. "Say, we're heading out to the cliffs tonight. Can a princess join the militia for a party?"

She smiled. "No, but an unassigned corporal can."

"There will be twenty or so and some town folk."

"I'll need to escape my escort. Will I be the only girl?"

"Some girls from the fishing village will be there. And Jeannine and Lucy, you remember?"

She smiled. "The Garter Club?"

"Yeah, but don't remind them until they've drunk some grog. They both outrank you now. I'll meet you at the bower's to the west of the camp."

"See you there," Diana said and headed for the cartographer.


The cartographer's tent was almost as she had left it years ago with barrels of rolled-up maps and crates of scrolls. Over the table leaned an old man with mussed gray hair.

"Excuse me," Diana said.

Alcore spun around in his chair, inspected her from over thin glasses, and nodded in place of a bow. "Your Highness."

"You remember me?"

"Of course. You once asked for a map of Branwyn. What brings you?"

Diana unfolded the parchment she had copied from the atlas with a detail of the Wye Delta and laid it on the table. The cartographer squinted and frowned and then inspected it with a jeweler's loupe.

"Where did you find this?" Alcore asked.

"It's a copy from a cache of the Old Knowledge in Branwyn that—"

He laughed. "You're making fun of an old man now?"

"Truly."

He looked up with a big smile. "And where's the original?"

"With my father. I'm sure he'll let you examine it if asked."

"I most certainly will. And how can I help you?"

"There are symbols here I don't understand." She pointed to the symbol -)||(-. "There are no bridges spanning the Wye River. What could this be?"

"The military doesn't use such symbols. But engineers use a similar symbol to designate a drainage culvert or a path beneath a natural stone arch."

With a finger to the -)||- symbol, she said, "And there's a similar symbol here along the Inland Sea."

Alcore scratched the stubble on his chin. "Hmm. Perhaps the same. The shore occasionally has odd features scored into the cliffs by the waves." He took a caliper and divider, measured the distance between the Wye and Alba Rivers, and then the distance to the symbol.

"About forty miles from the mouth of the Wye," he said. "Your map is very old and the distances—"

"How do you know this?"

He fumbled through a stack of maps, pulled one out and laid Diana's fragment next to it. "See here? Similar, but not the same. A beach shows on your map."

"Perhaps the tides?"

"No. The Inland Sea doesn't have tides more than a few inches, and the three moons cause them to appear randomly over the day."

"Why do the tides depend on the moon?"

He shrugged. "It's what we're taught. I hear that once the Inland Sea supported trade between Suleria, Auxiere, and Nordes, but now is too shallow."

"Your map doesn't show a beach," she said.

Alcore shook his head. "We make our military maps from the land, not the sea. The cliffs and lack of beach make it too hard to survey." He stared at her. "But the wider beach in your map implies the water level was much lower."

"Thank you," Diana said.

"I look forward to seeing the rest of your map," he called as she left for her quarters to prepare for the party.

*** 

A ten-minute ride north of Le Pegre, Diana and Gage reached the cliffs and the first thing she did was ride along the edge, assuring herself the water had not receded like the strand along the eastern ocean. To the north spanned the blue green of the Inland Sea that separated the Northern States from Suleria. Eastward lay the delta at the mouth of the Wye River and marshland that could swallow an army. To the northwest, cliffs fell straight to the water below except for the occasional smugglers' trail etched into the rock.

*The cliffs remain our bulwark.*

She sighed as if a burden was lifted. "I can't remember feeling this way. My father is safe, my country safe, and the worst of my fears are far in the future." She stared at the reflections from the moons. "I should be able to relax."

"Maybe you forgot how," he said. "Come. Let's begin your retraining."

They walked their horses to the picket line over patches of scrub brush, salt grass, and succulents that lay between the expanses of sand, all lit by the three moons in full. The largest and slowest moon, mother Lon, waited near the horizon for its smaller children. When all three set in a few hours, they would be in total darkness.

"Dead man walking," Sten said and stood a head taller than her. His jacket and shirt were open, and he wore sergeant stripes on his sleeve. She recognized the team behind him from her last day in the militia, all grown into men.

He walked over to her. "I heard you deserted."

"Leave her alone, Sten," Gage said.

"Different mission," Diana said. Sten did not respond and glared at her. She jumped to attention. "Different mission, sir."

"At ease, Corporal. Rumors say you ran to avoid the action."

That hurt, but she did not want to be baited into striking a superior. "Not under fire. You still have that target on your back?"

Sten frowned and took off his jacket with his rank giving her permission to strike a superior officer if she chose. He lunged for her, and she dodged him. Gage folded his arms and Rollo just shook his head, but neither of them intervened. Sten lunged again, and she diverted his punch with her right hand and spun into him so he could hug her if he chose. Instead, he flipped her, and she landed on her back with the wind knocked out of her.

"Target on your back, *sir*," he said with a smile. "You're getting slow, Dee," he whispered and reached out to help her rise.

"You got my letter?" she said, and he nodded. She grabbed his right wrist with her left and spun under his arm, twisting it behind him. But he was much stronger than her, and her hammerlock would never hold. She tried to push him away, but he being twice her weight, she instead pushed herself backward to where one of Sten's crew caught her before she fell.

He smiled and put his arm around her shoulders. "Buy you a drink, tough guy?"

"Sure," she said, returning his smile, and put her hand around his waist.

The two teams went to the bar for fruit punch where Dru joined them. Under Sten's other arm slipped a village girl who kissed him hard on the lips and glared at Diana.

"Are you happy?" Diana asked, took Sten's arm from her shoulders and put it around the girl's.

Sten smiled, nodded, and kissed the village girl again.

"Well, he's recovered," Diana said to Dru, clinked her mug against his, and took a drink.

"Did you see action when the Sul overran us back then?" Diana asked.

Sten waved a hand. "Bah. The seniors treated us like infants in swaddling until we reached the mouth of the Alba. Malveaux lined us up to divert them from Bayeun and it worked. We made it hard for them, and they rushed west, where Richard crushed them."

Dru moved closer to Diana, and she leaned into him.

"Remember Scottie?" Sten said. "He died there in a skirmish. I got this." He pulled his sleeve up to show the scar of a crossbow bolt along his biceps. When he flexed, his girl took his arm and kissed it.

Diana pulled up her sleeve to expose the scar from the Sulerian sword. "I got this at the caravan that rushed to your protection."

Sten smiled. "And the Sul?"

"Died with an arrow in his neck."

Sten raised his mug to hers. "Bravo. So, what's your plan, Corporal?"

"I hope to restart training after a brief vacation in Aemgarde."

Sten frowned.

"Why the look?" Diana said.

"You're off the path now, Dee," Dru said.

"What do you mean?"

"I mean you're eighteen and most of the recruits are fifteen like when we arrived."

"Jon was training me. I won't be behind."

Sten raised his eyebrows. "General Henlow?"

Diana nodded, and Sten whistled.

"If he trained you, you'll be too advanced for your squad. And you're untested with a team. So where are they going to slot you?"

That had not occurred to her. She had put her militia training on hold expecting to return. Now with Jon's coaching, she was in better shape and better prepared with weapons, tactics, and strategy. But Sten was right. Where would she fit in?

"You'll have to prove yourself all over again," Sten said.

She stared into the night and sipped her fruit punch. Without combat experience Company A would be out of her reach. Though she was back in Le Pegre, her plan to protect her father was even further from her reach than when she left for the South.

She sighed. *Focus, girl. You're here for a miracle that might find justice for Mother.*

Sten raised his mug again. "And when you prove yourself, as I'm sure you will, you'll always have a place in my unit."

Dru joined him. "And in mine."

After the toast, they downed their drinks, and Sten began a bawdy limerick. Diana's team followed the local girls who danced to a guitar and flute played by two village boys. One girl fell into Gage's arms with her skirt in the air. But Dru stayed near Diana, which kept the rowdies away.

"I missed you when you left Aemgarde," Dru said and poured her another punch.

"We were kids," she said.

"I thought it was more than that."

Diana put her head on his shoulder and gazed at the stars. "Your family already picked out your fiancée."

Dru smiled. "They would've traded up for a princess."

"It would have been dishonorable."

"That wouldn't stop them," he said.

"You didn't marry?"

"My fiancée traded up, and her parents bought off my folks. It's better this way. I have a girl in Wikkert, a merchant family with interests in Royax. Your father talked to a few of us about a Navy in alliance with Venaro, and I might switch services."

*Is Captain Greit recruiting?* "If that's your plan, I met people you should speak with."

"And you?"

She blushed. "I met a man in the South," she said. *Or two?*

"Serious?"

"I hope so. But it's not even a relationship yet."

"Then he's a fool."

She lowered her gaze. "He has duties."

"More so the fool."

Before Diana could change the subject, a tall blonde woman walked to them with two drinks and a villager in tow. "Hey there, shy ones."

"Hi, Jeannine," Diana said.

The local boy stood by Jeannine with his hands on his hips, staring at her ample cleavage. He grinned, blinked twice, and fell on his face.

"Well, he's done," Jeannine said and rolled him aside to sit next to Diana. "I need a mount with more stamina." She hugged her. "Lucy and I missed you, girl."

Thirsty from the salt air, Diana accepted the offered fruit punch.

"Water?" Dru asked.

Diana nodded, and he left.

"Is it always like this?" she said.

"Every weekend," Jeannine replied. "We're soldiers with nothing to fight. We had a taste of battle and like it. Now we're racehorses locked in the stable kicking at the door. So where did you go?"

"Mission," she said, and Jeannine opened her mouth. "I volunteered."

Jeannine glanced at Dru at the water barrel. "You need to put him out of his misery, girl."

"He has a love interest in Wikkert," Diana said. "He'll be fine."

"Yeah, right," Jeannine said and took a swig of her drink. "You keep telling yourself that."

Diana smiled. "He was my first kiss."

"Damn, girl. You need another milestone. We're soldiers, and life is short."

Diana's eyes followed Dru's back, but the world tilted, and she leaned on her friend.

Jeannine gave her a sly smile. "Oops. I should have warned you. We spiked the punch."

"But I . . ." Diana protested.

"You were always too high-strung, girl. Time to relax."

Diana lay back on the warm sand, her last sight being Dru returning to sit with her.

"Dee?" he said from a thousand miles away. "Dee?"

But Dru and the cliffs disappeared in blackness.


"Dee?" Diana heard again. It was Dru.

Diana sat up and squinted from the hammer of a headache, with each beat of her pulse a mallet on her forehead. His jacket lay around her shoulders.

Only a dull glow remained of the fire, and the revelers slept around it. And of the moons, red Fures remained in view as it neared the horizon leaving the silhouettes of sentries against the stars.

He smiled. "You're not used to this."

"No," she said, woozy.

"Seems wherever you went for the last years, you had adult supervision."

She nodded. "Ouch." Her head throbbed, and she squinted. Just over his shoulder, a glint in the dark caught her eye. "Sorry. I nccd to pcc."

She staggered through the scrub for a quiet spot and took care of her business. On the way back she tripped over something soft. Even at night she could tell what it was. A body.

"Dru!" she called, and he rushed over.

It only took a moment for him to identify the body: the Le Pegre cavalry scout assigned to patrol the coast.

Diana frowned at a glow on the eastern horizon. "It's too early for dawn." She jumped up. "Le Pegre!" she shouted and ran to her horse.

# Chapter 42
## Feint

As Diana galloped to Le Pegre, the glow brightened and resolved into fires. Riding through the smoke, dead sentries met them at the gate while horsemen rode through the camp, slashing the recruits with scimitars. At a gallop, she raced to the command tent to check on Jon. But when an attacking horseman charged in front of her, her horse reared and threw her from the saddle.

On the ground, Diana grabbed a unit pennant and rushed the horseman, knocking him to the ground where a recruit hit him on the head with a barrel stave. "Where's your sergeant?" she asked, and the trainee pointed to a man lying on the ground with his throat cut. Around him other recruits, all teens, stood leaderless.

*Too young to have learned how to be effective alone. Then they must fight as a unit. What are they likely to have learned by now? Only the simplest formations and tactics.*

"To me!" Diana shouted and waved the pennant. "Grab a weapon and shield and form a square. Archers in the middle. Pikes and spears to the perimeter. Hurry!"

When the square formed, she ordered the archers to volley fire on groups of attackers so their combined arrows might find one target, while the pikes kept the horsemen away. In the distance she found what could be the command tent by the flurry of nearby fighting.

"Advance!" she called. "Column of threes, archers in the middle." The square moved toward the parade ground with archers picking off Sul as they passed. A white and silver ribbon flickered in the firelight, and she looked up to see the rider, a ghost from long ago, in front of her rallying his men: Garfann Sineura. She stopped with her mouth open, and her unit stopped with her while the archers kept firing until Garfann rode away.

"Ma'am?" a recruit asked.

"Forward!" she commanded, and her unit cleared a path to the parade ground and similar formations of recruits led by Gage and Dru. Together, they marched to the command tent.

"Halt. Form a picket and defend this location with your lives!" she shouted and ran into the command tent. There, Jon stood with blood dripping from his cutlass above the dead camp commander, whose neck was pierced by an arrow. Around them lay a score of dead Sulerians.

"How bad?" she asked and pointed to the blood running down his sleeve to his hand.

"Minor," Jon said. "Just need a bandage."

"Where's our cavalry?" she asked.

"On foot. The Sul scattered the horses first."

In the light of the fires and torches, seniors and training officers led the survivors to form a defensible cordon around the command tent. As the archers found their marks within the raiders, a trumpet sounded, and the Sul cavalry left the field of battle.


Le Pegre moaned with the wounded as Fures cast a red tint on the dirty faces and grim expressions of the survivors who gathered near the ruins of the commander's tents.

"You're senior officer," the master sergeant said to Jon.

"What do we have left?" Jon asked as a medic wrapped a bandage around his forearm.

"The reserves are on maneuvers and intact," the sergeant said. "The casualties are mostly the juniors, the teenagers."

"And worthy enough for revenge," said an officer.

A sergeant threw a curved sword on the ground in the middle of them. "Scimitars. The curved blades don't affix themselves in the flesh, so they slash, not stab, to slice men down and clear a path for infantry."

"But no infantry followed."

"To avoid the burden of prisoners but still remove Le Pegre as a threat. Every injured fighter is a burden on the healthy."

"Assessments? Motivations?"

"This was a raid, not meant to finish us," a training sergeant said.

"How could they cross the Wye without our knowing?" the master sergeant asked.

"Good question," Jon said. "If there's an unpatrolled ford, we need to find it. Sergeant, send the juniors to gather the horses. We'll need them by dawn to rally the reserves and bolster the Wye."

"Aye, sir," the sergeant said and left.

"Ensigns Lorentz and Wilmette," Jon said to Gage and Dru. "You'll lead the others back to Aemgarde. Who's senior?"

Dru saluted. "I am, sir."

"Wilmette, collect your units. We march at sunrise. Lorentz, find a fast courier and alert Aemgarde to the threat and return to your unit."

"Aye, sir," he said and saluted.

When the men left, Diana stayed.

"Well done with the juniors," Jon said. "Your officer friends noticed as well."

"I saw Garfann," Diana said, and Jon narrowed his eyes. "We must stop him."

"You can't confront him and risk us all to quench your thirst for vengeance."

She spoke with confidence. "It's not vengeance, Jon. We can't leave you with an enemy at your back. And we can't permit an invasion force a day's hard ride from the king."

He smiled. "'We'? I don't hear you say that often."

"About that unknown ford, I spoke with the cartographer about a symbol on my map that might show a secret cave or tunnel under the Wye." She pulled out the map and unfolded it below a torch. "About twenty-five miles south of here. Just upstream of the Mintek Falls."

"Copied from the atlas?" he asked, and she nodded. "Close enough for a surprise attack. And why haven't we found it before? I'll send a scout ahead when we're on the move."

"There are similar symbols northwest of here along the coast," she said. "If they can cross the Wye without us knowing, maybe they can defeat the cliffs as well."

Jon pursed his lips and nodded.

"The most vulnerable point for a landing is there, between Le Pegre and Aemgarde."

He nodded. "We can't split our forces."

"I agree, sir. And the present danger is the Wye. I'll go with Gage, and we can check for a weakness in the cliffs on the way."

Jon smiled. "Action and prudence in the same decision. Finally. Well, see to it. But remember, Princess, you're a courier, not an oracle. And if you're exploring, you might need this," he said as he gave her the north finder. "I'll meet you in Aemgarde."

\*\*\*

Two days hence, Gage rode beside Diana on the coast road to Aemgarde. Three miles behind them, Dru led the Le Pegre forces Jon left behind, some on horse but most on foot. The food and injured followed in wagons.

"What we're looking for could be anywhere at the scale of your map, Dee," Gage said.

"Within five miles of here," Diana said. "But you're right."

"If smugglers are using it, they'll hide it well," a sergeant said. "So what do we look for?"

"I'm not sure," she said. "If it'll support an invasion, that means horses, so nothing too steep. If it's a cave, the entrance here above the cliffs should be against a hill. And there should be a path leading from it."

That afternoon, they circled each hill or vertical feature, and into the hanging vines or thick foliage they poked spears or sabers. But as sundown approached, they had found no doors or cave entrances.

"The caravan will catch up soon, and it's getting late," Gage said. "One more hour and then we need to quit."

In an open clearing, Diana circled her horse and called out. "Here!" When Gage caught up, she pointed to the ground, and in the low sun appeared the shadows of two parallel lines of bent grass. "A wagon passed here."

Gage followed the trail to a hillock on which a copse of trees stood. "A rabbit warren?"

Diana poked her spear into the hillside, and at a spot where it went through, she dismounted and pushed the vines aside. There she found a crack in the rock wide enough for a wagon and two horses abreast.

"Light the lanterns, Sergeant," Gage said as he dismounted. "And leave one here with a pennant to show the caravan where we are. We're going to explore."

Diana glanced up at the setting sun and frowned. "Which way to the cliffs?"

The Sergeant pointed. "Maybe a quarter mile that way."

Removing Jon's north finder from her pocket, she oriented north to the sergeant's arm. In the last hint of sunlight, she entered the cave holding the lantern, north finder, and reins of her horse as rabbits skittered from her path.

"If the horses shy, it's unsuitable," Gage said, drew his saber, and followed.

The cave opened to a cavern stocked with empty barrels and bottles that smelled of liquor.

"Smugglers," she said. "They might have to carry things here from the beach."

At the first fork in the path she stopped. A pool of standing water obscured the smugglers' path and three choices presented themselves, each of which disappeared into darkness.

"It will take us days to explore each possibility," Gage said.

"The path should be down and north of here," she said and checked the north finder. The needle pointed to the right of the three paths and they followed it.

"Sergeant, leave markers to show us whence we came," Gage said.

The cavern meandered through rock, sometimes narrow, sometimes so wide she could not see the walls.

Occasional pools collected water dripping from stalactites that hung from the ceiling. Iridescent green glowed from the walls as they passed. At each fork she consulted the north finder. But all along, the path was flat or covered with stones or wood and wide enough for a horse and cart.

An hour later they reached the widest and driest part strewn with barrels of wine and fish in salt or oil.

"This is how they compete with Wikkcrt in the wine trade," Gage said.

Above them, soot covered the ceiling and absorbed the light like a moonless night while insects and minerals reflected the lanterns' light.

On the walls in dark-red pigment were simple paintings of animals and runes like in her picture book. Small alcoves like sleeping areas had been chipped from the rock so a hundred people might stay here. In one Diana found stick figures drawn that might be a family.

Littering the floor were stone chips that might become arrowheads, wood shafts the size of arrows, hemp to be woven into rope, and a boat frame with the leather skin dried and rotted.

"People lived here," Diana said.

Gage nodded. "Smugglers."

"No. Fishers, people of the sea," she said and held up a line of fishhooks carved from bone.

Farther on, squawking gulls echoed up the cavern walls. The floor became sandy, and the rising sun peeked through vines that shielded the entrance. When she pushed the vines to the side, the rising sun reflected from symbols in the stone: symbols like on the rune coin for 'winter' and 'fish,' and above them dots.

Outside the cave was a beach wide enough to land a score of galleys, the shallow surf of the inland Sea, and the coastal fog.

"I figure a cavalry company could pass this way every ten minutes," Diana said.

"That could mean seven hundred men and horses in an hour. More could land in the night and disappear in the dark, enough to overwhelm Aemgarde."

As she turned back to the cavern, a flash of light through the fog caught her eye and she squinted into the sunlight. There above the slow rolling fog were the masts of ships.

"Fishing boats have no need to lurk," she said.

"Smugglers?"

"No, a fleet. Gage, this cavern could be the 'magic' path the Quarajii assassins used to sneak into Cherbourne and kill my mother." *And Father is there again now.*

She waved Gage closer. "I have a state secret you're not to disclose."

"If it's—"

"No, listen. I have no rank or authority with the troops that follow. You do. And what I will ask of them cannot come from me."

"We all saw your skill at Le Pegre," Gage said.

"That won't be enough. I can advise, but I can't command."

"Go on."

"We need to defend this path from the possibility of a landing by Sulerian cavalry."

"We can send seasoned troops here when we reach Aemgarde."

"No. Tonight."

"There won't be enough time to—"

"I know," Diana said and summarized her conversation with Jon. "The Sul may land nearby, and if they do, they mean to attack the king. I need you to back my bid to stop it."

Gage nodded slowly. "You guessed the caves were here?"

She grinned and narrowed her eyes. "I have the same magic as the Sulerian Empress."


Back on the cliffs, while the caravan set camp for the night, Gage and Diana updated Dru at a meal with the officers and senior sergeants.

"With Le Pegre reinforcing the Wye, there's a weakness in our defense of the coast," Dru said. "A path leads to the sea that can support an invasion. General Henlow's assessment was the raid on Le Pegre might have been a feint to bring the reserves to the Wye and leave this section of coast undefended. It will be our mission to defend it. Thoughts? Speak freely."

"We don't have a fighting force here, Sir," Sergeant Stone said. "These are recruits, camp cooks, and wounded. Having us caught between a force on the beach and the land, we risk a potential massacre. Best to ride to the bivouac in Bayeun for seasoned troops."

"The threat is now," Diana said. "Not next week. Our lands may be invaded. The enemy prepares to tie up our forces at the Wye while they attack Aemgarde. I think your question should be how to stop this."

Stone turned to her. "Our force is too small. Less than seventy seniors and two hundred and fifty trainees, some injured."

"Send the injured to safety and let the rest of us stop the invasion."

Stone faced her squarely. "Pardon, miss. May I inquire as to your rank?"

"She knows the terrain and speaks for me," Gage said.

"I'm a corporal, sir," Diana said. "But I speak from knowledge, not rank: an invasion that threatens Aemgarde must be stopped."

"And what knowledge would that be? Aemgarde isn't strategic, and the Sul would do nothing more than burn it to cinders again. Troops at Bayeun will limit any attempt to expand the front."

Diana bit her lip and glanced at Dru, who nodded with a slight smile.

"Your king remains at Aemgarde with a skeleton force," she said, "locked in secret negotiations with the Sulerians. General Henlow said a landing here by light cavalry would leave us the most vulnerable. They used a similar ruse five years ago that led to the death of Katheryn Stewart."

Stone narrowed his eyes. "And you know this how?"

"Because I was there. I'm Diana, daughter of Katheryn."

"Beggin' your pardon, Your Highness." Stone said and bowed his head. "I meant no—"

"I claim no authority here amidst combat veterans and defer to your judgment. But if you leave, I will stay and defend this place, alone if I must. I will not leave my king vulnerable to a surprise flanking maneuver."

Stone nodded and smiled. "Then I'll stand with you." He turned to Dru. "With your permission, sir."

"Granted. Any other discussion? We stay."

"And our plan, sir?" Stone asked. "We don't have enough experienced soldiers to halt an invasion or re-take a fixed position."

"Correct," Gage said. "But they're not helpless children either."

*Diana remembered Singer's admission and smiled. "I couldn't face him. He was half again my size and led an army. So I tricked him."*

"Can we control the cave entrance with the resources we have?" Diana asked.

"I think so," Stone said. "But not against a force of thousands."

"Those thousands haven't landed yet," she said.

Dru nodded. "And it'll take hours to land the main force."

She turned to Rollo. "What would it take to stop a landing?"

"Overwhelming presence on the beach or the cliffs would discourage them," he said. "But we don't have that."

"When will they land?" Stone asked.

"At night, most likely," Dru said.

Diana nodded. "All they might see are fires and unit banners."

Creases appeared in Dru's brow. "What are you thinking?"

"If an army will stop them, we bring an army," Diana said.

Gage laughed but quieted when she did not smile.

"But we don't have an army," Stone said.

"If we did, what would it look like from the sea?" she said.

"But—"

Dru nodded. "I understand what she implies."

"What if they charge like in Le Pegre?" Gage said.

Rollo smirked. "I have something for that."

"And they could flank a fixed position," Dru said.

"I think I have something for that as well."

"We have the day to prepare. Rollo, let's hear your defensive plan."

# Chapter 43
## The Cliffs

Near sunset, in leather armor with shields at their sides, Diana and Dru waited. At the cave entrance on the cliffs, a score of senior sergeants with pikes and spears stood with two score archers behind them. Inside, another score of archers and infantry prepared to defend from the beach. Two recruits waited there to shoot a fire arrow above the cliffs if the ships landed. And the rest of the juniors poised along the cliff edge waited for their signal.

"You really think they'll invade?" Dru asked.

Diana nodded. "If not tonight, then tomorrow night."

As the sun neared the horizon, horsemen rode from the forest and stopped, forming a line a hundred wide.

"Ready archers!" Dru shouted.

Garfann's cavalry rode toward the defenders and stopped just out of range. Boldly, Garfann rode closer and turned along the line of seniors, his sword and the rivets on his leather armor gleaming in the setting sun. He sat tall in the saddle, unafraid of the Le Pegre archers, unaware of the juniors with lances and bows who stayed out of sight behind them.

"Time to surrender!" Garfann shouted. "I'll be merciful and let you walk back to Le Pegre."

Dru turned to Diana. "It's too early. Rollo needs more time." He waved his arm to signal Rollo.

Diana stood. "No!" she shouted back. "We stand."

"And who are you, little girl?" Garfann asked.

"The little girl who spared your falcon."

Circling his horse, he squinted into the failing light to see her, but from the corner of his eye, he caught the glow of flames. A brush fire raced toward him as fast as a man could run, drawn by the onshore breeze.

"Bitch!" Garfann yelled.

Horses nickered behind Garfann. Waiving his scimitar, he shouted orders in Sulerian and galloped back to his men. A flight of arrows caused the defenders to raise shields, followed moments later by the thunder of charging horses.

As the cavalry raced to attack the defensive position, the seniors lifted pikes and palings to break the charge. The horsemen dismounted and engaged.

But the fire intended to split Garfann's force and panic his horses stalled with a shift of the wind. If more cavalry joined the invaders in the melee, they would overwhelm the seniors. That would be their end.

"No!" she cried and ran for a Sulerian horse.

"Dee! No!" Dru called after her.

Ignoring him, Diana jumped on the horse and raced west to the stalled edge of the fire.

There, Rollo tried to restart the blaze, but without luck.

She tied a rope to the last of the burning branches, mounted, and galloped east.

Focused on the front, the horsemen were not prepared for an enemy in their midst. Through the middle of them Diana raced, dragging the flaming branch through the dry hay and lamp oil Rollo had spread earlier. Behind her, the flames grew to engulf both sides, spooking Garfann's cavalry and splitting them in two. As she raced through them, the tip of a crossbow bolt pierced her leather armor to vex her. Stopping at the east side of their defenses, she dismounted, drew her saber, and joined the melee.

Caught between a fire behind them and the pikes in front, some of Garfann's horsemen escaped to either side, only to gallop over the cliffs in the dusky light. But there were still more than enough of Garfann's men to win, and the fire behind left them nowhere to go but to engage Dru and the seniors.

As dusk ebbed, only the shadow play of fighters against the grassfire was visible, but the shadows did not reveal whose side they were on.

"The signal fires! Stop them!" Sten shouted when two Sulerians ran toward the kindling stacked near the cliffs. Diana and Jeannine joined him and together they fought side-by-side.

More Sulerian soldiers attacked, and Sergeant Stone joined. But Sten fell with a slash to his neck and Stone with a spear to his chest. Diana and Jeannine held the last soldiers off from the fires. But one Sulerian grabbed a second scimitar, overpowered Jeannine, pierced her side, and she collapsed. Before he could hack her head off, Diana's saber found his neck.

Feinting a parry from another Sulerian, Diana moved inside his reach, hit him in the temple, ran him through, and kneeled to her fallen comrades. Sten and Stone were dead, but Jeannine still breathed in ragged breaths. Diana placed a compress on the wound while the rising Lon accented the lines of pain on Jeannine's face.

"I'm sorry," Diana said, putting her hand to her comrade's cheek.

Diana surveyed the field where the small group of seniors battled the Sul. *Sten and Sergeant Stone lie dead because of me. And Jeannine may join them.*

Jeannine's eyes widened, and she opened her mouth but could not speak.

Cold metal bit Diana's throat, and a thick arm locked around her shoulders.

"I thought I'd have to dig to find you," Garfann said, smirking. "But here you've come to me."

With raised hands, she spoke. "You've grown into your sword, War-Chief."

"And my titles, but you've yet to earn yours. You ran from me."

"I had an opportunity I couldn't forgo," she said and squirmed to assess his balance.

"And I have the opportunity to capture the daughter of the King of the North."

He held her arms so she could not reach his eyes. She maneuvered her hip to get under his center of gravity for a throw, but he shifted his weight. She raised her foot to crush his instep, and he moved it. All her moves were amateurish and clumsy, and he expected them all. He dragged her backward toward the cavern to the beach, keeping her off her feet.

Garfann laughed and put the knife closer to her throat. Instinctively, she grabbed his forearm and wrist, but she was not strong enough to pull it away.

"Time to surrender," he said.

*And forget my mother's sacrifice? Papa will suffer less with my death than my capture.*

Instead of pulling away, she pressed the sharp edge to her skin and cut, the blood tickling as it flowed down her neck.

Garfann struggled with her to keep the blade from cutting deeper. "Stop! Do you wish to die so soon?"

"I'm not afraid to die."

"Why would you sacrifice yourself for your father?"

"This is no sacrifice."

He repositioned the blade from the artery to below her chin, and she relaxed.

*He doesn't aim to kill me, at least not right away.*

"Your people tried to kill me with your poison. Why do you hesitate now?"

"In Venaro?" he said. "The darts were not to kill you but make you question your senses, to fill you mind with visions and make you more pray for capture. I have the elixir to remove the curse."

"If you don't plan to kill me, then do you mind?" She pointed a thumb to the tip of the crossbow bolt still stuck in the back of her leather armor. With a wiggle, he removed the remains of the bolt, but with each move, she winced as the cut rubbed against the torn leather.

"You've lost, war-chief," Diana said. "We blocked the beach and we hold the cliffs."

"Hah. A bluff. Only a few remnants from the camp aid you. You can't stop my force when they land."

"*If* they land. Look. They don't approach. Your signal fires are cold. Even if you kill me, you won't make it to the beach with our contingent of archers."

"Nonsense. The invasion will succeed, and I will own your people."

She squirmed again, but Garfann remained wary.

"Go, now, war-chief. Tell your men to stand down. I'll let them go."

"Don't be absurd. I'll delight to throw you at the foot of the Empress. Then you will know real suffering."

"Like Eavlyn?"

He laughed. "You'll never have it so good."

*What will stall him? Flattery?*

"It doesn't matter," she said. "You and I are alike; our bodies are meaningless compared to our goals."

He hesitated. "When we met that first time at Le Pegre, I knew you wanted more of life than your heritage offered you. I could hear it in your voice. Even princess is not enough for you, and here I find you leading men in battle. Perhaps you are worthy of the blade after all."

Over the long night, the battle turned to the advantage of the Northmen who kept the Sul away from the signal fires along the cliffs. Garfann's men rallied to him, and his cordon kept Diana from rescue. At every distraction, she struggled against Garfann's hold while her mother's voice shouted: 'never surrender!'

Fures rose to tint the foggy coast blood red. A single fire down on the beach glowed, and the first of the ship's masts escaped the fog followed by scores more.

"Here they come," he said.

Diana gasped at the number of galleys and the forces on them, more than cavalry that might race to Aemgard, but a battalion with infantry to march on Bayeun. If that force landed they would overwhelm their tiny resistance, and her country would be lost.

"And I will lead them to victory," he said.

She struggled again, but his grip held.

*Patience. Some cards are yet to be played.*

A trumpet sounded a call to arms.

Along the cliffs an eighth of a mile to both sides of the cavern, bonfires blazed. Banners from each of the Northern States raised by the Le Pegre recruits flew behind the fires to highlight them for the approaching ships. Volleys of arrows from a hundred archers fired on the few Sulerian cavalry who had landed on the beach, forcing them to return to their ships. Within minutes, the fleet turned away.

"No!" Garfann shouted and turned to a soldier near him. "You. Signal the ships this is a ruse."

The messenger turned and took a step toward the cliffs but fell with an arrow in his leg.

Distracted by the stalled invasion and tranquilized by her futile escape attempts, Garfann loosened the tension on his arm, and Diana felt it. With both hands on his wrist, she pulled the knife down and pinned it to her chest. Jumping up, she slammed the top of her head into his chin. With her thumbs to the pressure point on his hand, she spun under his arm, ready to direct the point of the knife into his side.

But even with two hands, she was not strong enough to control his arm. Before he could regain his footing and with her thumbs on the pressure point, she twisted his hand into a wristlock, forcing him to drop the knife. Then she drove her knee into the back of his and he fell on his face in the sand. And with her knee on his neck, she held his arm in the wristlock. When he struggled, she twisted his wrist near breaking, and he stopped. But she would tire of holding him soon. With one hand holding the wristlock, she grabbed the blade and held it to his neck.

Freed from the melee, Dru, Rollo, and Gage ran to help her. and she sighed with relief.

"The medic is with Jeannine," Dru said.

"Help me bind him," Diana said, and Rollo and Gage bound him hand and foot.

With weapons drawn, Sulerian soldiers ran to help Garfann, but stopped at the sight of Diana's blade on his neck.

"He's mine," she said with a feral scowl.

"And who are you?" asked a Sulerian chief with the most ornate leather armor.

"I am Diana Stewart, Princess of the North. I claim War-Chief Garfann Sineura as my prisoner." She pointed to the soldier. "You are witness to this. Take a token of his to vouch for this."

"Take the bracelet," Garfann said and held out his bound hands.

Careful to avoid Garfann's grip, Gage unlatched Garfann's bracelet of silver stamped with a stylized wolf, the symbol of Makashti Sineura, and gave the bracelet to the chief.

"You've lost your command," she said. "They won't fight for you."

He laughed. "You know nothing."

*We don't have the strength to hold this many warriors captive, and I've lost enough friends.*

Diana turned to the chief. "Leave your weapons here and lead your cohort down the caverns to the beach," she said. "Honorable men will not return."

The chief gazed at the cliffs and the sea and the green plains to the trees. Turning to Garfann, he struck his fist against his chest and smiled.

"This is a fine place to die, sir."

Garfann shook his head. "Your death is unnecessary, chief. The invasion is thwarted. Do as she says."

"Gage, Rollo, escort them to the beach," Dru said. He turned to Diana with narrowed eyes. "You are enough to guard him?"

She understood his meaning not to kill her prisoner and nodded. "Yes, sir."

The chief gathered the remaining Sulerian cavalry and wounded, and led them to the cavern followed by Gage, Dru, and the sergeants.

"You plan to kill me," Garfann said.

"You're a dog that needs to die."

"I'm a hero to those men. They will only accept my head, and you can't take it."

Diana scowled. "You killed my friends."

"They didn't have to be here," he said and smirked. "Actually, I'd have preferred they not be here. I suspect they're only here because *you* brought them, and *you* bear the responsibility for their deaths."

He was right, and that made it worse. "You need to die," she said with her hand on her sword hilt but did not draw. "You would goad me into giving you the death you want but don't deserve."

He shrugged as best he could while bound as the Sulerian ships sailed into fog tinted blood red by the dawn.

"You see there on the beach," Garfann said. "They wait for me."

"Alive or dead?"

"Either." He glanced at her. "I'm a warrior, girl. Why do you delay my death?"

She glanced at him. He was a handsome man in the light, with a soldier's stocky build and a scar that curved over his shaved forehead to a topknot. *In another life, he might* . . . Her thoughts offended her, and she curled her lip.

"You used the Book of Chaos to infiltrate our lines?" she asked.

"Yes."

"The same book your mother used to kill mine."

He scoffed. "Hardly. That was the Empress's doing. The Empress fears my mother and would never let her near the book. Ah, I see now. You still blame us for your mother's death?"

"Your people killed her."

"But I didn't, and neither did Makashti."

"You celebrated her murder."

"I was young and stupid," Garfann said and shrugged as best he could. "You would take vengeance on all Suleria for the acts of assassins?"

"You are what I have to work with at the moment."

Garfann turned back to peer out to the Inland Sea. "I was told it was a good death."

"She bled to death in my arms."

"After an honorable fight," he said. "She fought well, I was told. And you feel guilty for her heroism?"

"You searched for me in the South."

"Ah, yes, there is that matter at Le Pegre years ago. Things get muddied after years and thousands of miles. You and the Empress are the only women to defy me."

"And your mother."

He scowled. "I still needed to remove your stain from my reputation. My humiliation was public."

"We were children."

He sneered. "You know nothing of the children of the East."

"And so you sought my death?"

"Concubine would have sufficed and united our countries."

He winced, his head jerked back, and his arm twitched. Foam dribbled from the corner of his mouth, and he spit on the sand. "My apologies," he said and coughed.

"Are you injured?"

"In a manner of speaking," he said, wheezing. "A gift from the Empress. Please, there's something in the pouch on my belt. Go ahead, I won't bite you."

She reached into his pouch and found powder wrapped in parchment. He opened his mouth, and she emptied it on his tongue.

After a shudder, he sighed. "They only make this in the holy city of Mokdar and only for the Empress."

"A drug?"

He nodded. "There are two sides: a velvet glove and a cudgel."

"Addict?"

"You might say. Without it, I die without honor. It's an interesting incentive for a young warrior."

"Is that what makes you rabid?" she said.

Garfann glared at her with cold eyes, then back out to the sea. "In the manic moments, I lust for death. In the sick ones, I pray for it. But there are a few moments in between where I'm at peace."

"An hour ago, you could have killed me," she said.

He glanced at her again. His were not the eyes of a madman but reminded her of Eric: a warrior needing a purpose. His were not the eccentric moves of the wild boy in her father's tent, but the deliberate moves of a soldier, who fought for another leader, another flag.

"Your death seemed wasteful," he said and turned back to gaze at the sea. "It appears now I was too sentimental."

"And now you plead for mercy?"

He laughed. "Hardly. I've been preparing for death my entire life."

Followed by Gage and Rollo, the unarmed chief returned to stand by Garfann.

"Leave with the others," Diana said.

"I'm his second and will die in his place if you choose execution."

As the sun rose above the fog, and Diana pondered Garfann's fate, Richard and Sam rode up with Company A and the Beirn Home Guard. She glanced at her father, then pursed her lips.

"Has the Council excused you from debate, Your Highness?" she asked.

"I didn't consult them. Are you injured?" he asked, pointing to a spot on her neck where Garfann's blade had cut her.

Diana shook her head.

"I received Jon's message from Le Pegre," Richard said. "Who commands here?"

"Ensign Dru Wilmette," she said.

"Find him," Richard said to Sam.

"How fares Jon?" she said.

Richard dismounted. "Jon has rallied at the Wye. He and Jacobian hold the Sul and Qu at bay."

She sighed. "I worried for him."

Dru galloped to them, dismounted, and saluted. "Reporting sir."

"Status of forces?" Richard asked.

Dru opened his mouth to speak, then glanced at Diana, but she shook her head.

"A large invasion force attempted to land, sir," Dru said. "We believe they intended to join with a light cavalry squadron here and attack Aemgarde. They ravaged Le Pegre. General Henlow and the reserves reinforced the Wye, and the survivors stopped the landing of light cavalry and infantry here."

Richard signaled to his adjutant. "Tell General Malveaux to take the army to the Wye to support General Fredricks. Company A and a battalion will remain with me." He turned back to Dru. "Well done, Ensign."

"Thank you, sir," Dru replied. "Honors should go to the men, not me."

"I'll see to that," Richard said. "Aye now, what do we do with your prisoner? Is he yours, Ensign?"

"He's mine, Your Highness," Diana said.

"His life should be forfeit for the scores lost at Le Pegre, sir," Dru said.

Richard nodded. "Thank you, Ensign. Dismissed."

"Please, let him stay, sir," she said.

With another nod, Richard led them to a fire and chairs set by the King's Guard. They sat, and Richard leaned over to rub his hands near the fire as the rising sun stole the chill from the dawn.

"You're an adult now and this is war," Richard said. "Garfann's fate is your decision. But this choice will affect the—"

"The entire North," she said.

Richard shook his head. "The North can survive any outcome. This is about you. He's a pawn in a bigger game, but how you decide will affect the rest of your life. What game do you play?"

She could not speak. Her decision could affect so many lives. "You are my king. Choose for me."

"No," Richard said. "He's your prisoner. This is your choice, and I trust you."

"I'm only recently of age and unfamiliar with—"

Richard's voice was resolute. "You are the Princess of the North and my daughter. You will choose with wisdom. Just remember who will wield power in the future."

She stared at Garfann. This was the man who hunted her for years, the person who represented all the Sulerians she blamed for her mother's murder.

She glanced at Sam. *"Revenge is selfish," he told me years ago. So what would be justice?*

*Papa had also been enraged at Mama's death and felt responsible for it. Despite that, he let the Sulerian emissaries live, including Makashti and her son, Garfann, the man who could have killed me.*

*But he didn't. We both killed a score of men tonight, but we could not kill each other.* She looked into his eyes. *In another world, another time . . . but there is too much between us.*

"Is he valuable in a bargain?" she asked.

Richard rubbed his chin. "Accepting a ransom is unseemly."

"Perhaps a favor?"

Richard turned to Dru. "In confidence, Ensign?"

"Yes, sir," Dru replied.

"I'm afraid Garfann's life has little political value to Makashti anymore," Richard said.

Garfann smiled.

"So much more a gift," she said. "And humiliation."

"You have the token of capture?" Richard asked.

The Sulerian chief nodded.

"Your death or his is unnecessary," she said. "Take the bracelet to High-Chief Makashti Sineura. Tell her we have a gift for her of her son and request she send an emissary to retrieve him.

"And tell her the emissary must escort Eavlyn Moretti, the slave Garfann calls Tina, and her family here. Those are our terms and without them there will be no exchange of gifts."

Diana glanced at Garfann, who scowled at her, but Diana saw something more in his eyes.

*That hurts. Not surrender. Not death.*

"And deliver a message to the Empress. Tell her the Book of Chaos has no power over us anymore. The North is closed to her, and her secrets are ours. Go now."

Gage escorted the chief to the beach, and Sam took Garfann's arm, stood him up, and led him to a horse.

"We'll meet again, Princess," Garfann said as Sam led his horse away.

Diana turned back to her father. She saluted as she would to her commander, and then she kneeled to acknowledge him as her king. Behind her, Dru and the soldiers followed.

"At ease," Richard said. "Well done to trade a noble Sulerian for a slave." He nodded to her and turned to Dru. "Ensign Wilmette, remain here with the healthy seniors and assign the rest to return with me to Aemgarde. I'll leave a detachment of the Home Guard here to assist you. We will relieve you all from Aemgarde."

"Aye, sir," Dru said and signaled a sergeant.

Diana stepped forward. "Your Highness, I request assignment to deploy with General Malveaux at the front."

"Denied, Corporal," Richard said. "There are bigger fights ahead, and I need you."

*Bigger fights?*

When the others left, Richard hugged Diana and gazed at her with a smile. "I must tell Jon you may have vanquished your demons."

"Garfann?"

He shook his head. "No. Something much more important."

She smiled and hugged him again, and when his adjutants brought their horses, they mounted with Diana to his right.

Instead of leaving, Richard signaled to the color guard, who rode beside Diana. Sam Rickets handed her the standard for Company A of Cherbourne: the C/A banner that led the army and announced the king; the unit of his most trusted soldiers charged with protecting him with their lives.

She accepted the standard, and one step behind Richard, rode with him at the head of the cavalry home to Aemgarde.

And for the first time, Diana felt as if the arrow was pulled from her heart, the arrow that struck when her mother died.

# Epilogue

## Of Kings and Dragons

Without the support of the invasion forces from the cliffs, the Sulerian and Quarajii armies that crossed the Wye found themselves unable to complete their mission. General Malveaux from the west, General Fredricks from the north, and General Henlow from the south caught them with their backs against the river and forced their surrender.

Diana returned to Aemgarde with Richard to festivals marking the victory. Nearby in a smaller ceremony, with less fanfare but much more liquor, the Cherbourne Militia initiated Diana into Company A. Around her neck, she wore the silver arrowhead they had given her on her first stay in Le Pegre.

With celebrations over, they settled down to business, negotiating the armistice with the defeated Sulerians and forcing their armies back across the Pelsuk into Tourik. To mark the armistice and honor the victors, the Sul sent hostages and treasure to warrant their good behavior. But no one in the North, outside the political orbit of Wikkert, trusted their assurances.

A month following the victory at the Wye, Garfann was traded for Eavlyn and her family. After all were sent home, Diana and her father escaped to vacation at their rebuilt summer cottage along the Alba.

One afternoon they relaxed after a morning ride in the foothills of the Spine and a late breakfast. A coming rain stole the light, and Maggie lit the storm lanterns which glittered off the silver-gray coin, Jones's gift, which she wore as a brooch. Browne's gift from that night, the translucent blue necklace of dolphins and mermaids, always brought a blush, so she packed it away.

As she translated the text of the map using the picture dictionary, Diana leaned back and shook her head.

"She's brilliant," Diana said.

"Who?"

"The Sulerian Empress. She began her aggression decades ago. The decline of Suleria and the Imperium was clear compared to the growing prosperity of the younger countries like ours and Venaro. The Empress unified and focused her country while the rest of us are divided and blind to what's coming. She's making the best use of her resources now, before the cold steals them from her and before we can unite against her."

Richard nodded and smiled. "You are the only person who could make that assessment." He kissed her on the forehead. "You might consider presenting that view to Wikkert."

"And sit on the antler throne in your place?"

"You are my only heir, Diana," Richard said.

"Choose a concubine and have another, Papa. The moment you expose me to the vipers in the capital, I'll be a target."

He raised an eyebrow. "You've been a target for a decade, Dee."

"Yes, but only of our enemies," she said and returned to the book.

A racket of birds interrupted and brought Diana to the window. Outside, dark clouds gathered and the air bit her nose with the sweet-sharp metallic smell of the approaching storm.

As she raised her head, a shadow like an eagle moved across the clouds. The flier dropped closer and closer, grew larger and larger, and landed not ten yards from her. Sheep grazing nearby froze, and so did she.

The dragon was terrifying and fantastic, and her jaw fell open. He was six times her length with fangs as long as her forearm. Hair covered his body, mottled blue-green except for his sky-blue belly and four legs.

She was stunned, lost in wonder, and unafraid of the beast that could swallow her whole or cut her in half with the swipe of a claw.

In the last rays of the sun, an exposed fang glinted pearlescent like the inlay on her mother's dragon-tooth box, the little box that held all her most precious possessions.

On the dragon's back was a saddle unlike the horse saddles of the North. Tied to it were a bow and arrow and fighting staff. And from that saddle jumped a beautiful woman in leather gear. Around her eyes shone tattoos that reminded Diana of a bird, and within that pattern, the Rider's eyes glowed. With a slight limp, she walked to Diana and unbuttoned her heavy leather jacket to expose a rune coin fragment like Diana's, hanging from a necklace.

Smiling, the Rider said the last thing Diana expected. "Well, you're a surprise."

Diana furrowed her brow. "Have we met?"

Arranging her fingers in the shape of V's, the Rider used them to cover her semaphores. "Perhaps now?"

"Singer! But how could . . . when did . . . how . . ."

"Call me Astria, dear. And pleased to meet you, too."

"Is this Zephyr?"

Astria smiled. "No, dear. This is Vandrare. Zephyr remains at the Source."

Diana's eyes stung. "My mother's last words were of you and Zephyr."

Astria winced but said nothing.

The dragon glanced at Diana with opalescent eyes, and honked softly, reminding Diana of her mother. With a jump and a flap of wings, he headed south to the mountains.

"He'll be back," Astria said. "I've only once seen a dragon act like that with a stranger, and that was with your mother."

"What do you mean?" Diana asked.

"When dragons are happy, their eyes sparkle."

Diana smiled. "Come inside, Father will want to see you."

As they walked to the cottage, Astria took Diana's shoulder. "We have much to talk about. Our enemies gather in the South on the east coast."

Diana put her hand on her rune coin brooch and nodded. "I fear it's part of a larger change, a change that will bring back the Chaos."

Astria nodded and tapped Diana's rune coin. "We have a mystery to solve."

# Appendix

## Special Words and Terms

**barvost** Six-legged long-haired ruminant the size and strength of an ox. Hunted for meat, but useful working animals when gelded. In males, the two middle legs are vestigial. Females hold small babies near their teats with their two small central hands.

**breshk** Vegetable, cooks down to mush like squash and releases an alcohol-like intoxicant. The high alcohol content allows it to be planted and grown all year with a growth cycle that varies with temperature. Propagates like a potato from stems or pieces of the body.

**bracer:** A cuff or arm guard to protect an archer's forearm from the bowstring.

**Chiniferra:** Holy book of the Sulerians, Turajii, and Quarajii; believed by the devout to be the literal word of God.

**cuirass**: Armor that covers the chest. Specifically, padded leather to cushion the blow of a sword and staff during practice.

**daemonberry:** A small red fruit that grows best in the winter. The flesh has the flavor of liquor and thyme because of the high concentration of alcohol, a concentration which increases as it gets colder. The berries grow in clusters on a plant with bushy green leaves.

**flitterbie:** A winged four-legged flier, about the size of the hand. They are very colorful and omnivorous with a diet of wheezits, jenalei, and daemonberry.

**grax:** A vicious four-legged pack hunting raptor, about the length of a person's arm.

**jenalei:** A small white petalled plant with a high concentration of alcohol in the sap that thrives in the cold and winter. The open leaves catch seeds that drift past and store them in a pod of neutral fluid that preserves them. It grows everywhere except on the glaciers and in the lowlands of the South and North.

**pattern:** In martial training, a pattern is an exercise comprising set moves, often with weapons.

**sabaton:** An armored foot piece or shoe covering.

**stenifer:** A tree with wide branches like a fir tree whose sap contains a high concentration of alcohol.        With red, brown, and yellow leaves year-round.

**targalan:** A four-winged omnivorous seabird often seen with gulls and pelicans or soaring with albatross.

**Wolfskin of Eldmoor:** A wolfskin that made the wearer invisible. Chaucin, the northern god of justice, took the form of a wolf and shed his skin to help the champion of the people, Thores, slay King

Sinrall. Eldmoor, or ancient Auxiere, was the land ruled the despotic Sinrall, the last King of the North.

**vambrace:** Armor to protect the forearms and wrists; padded leather for practice with weapons.

**vows:** In Martin's case, it refers to the promises of piety and chastity that a monk must make before being ordained as a priest.

**wheezit:** A winged flier with six legs and four wings the length of a little finger; serves to pollinate plants.

# The Three Moons

Three moons orbit Juro, each with various names depending on the culture.

**Lon:**
Mother Moon. The largest of Juro's three moons, with the longest orbital period. Epitomizing fertility and abundance; aids in the preservation of the world.

**Elein:**
Sister Moon. Smaller than Lon but brighter, with a slightly faster orbital period. Epitomizing community and civilization.

**Fures:**
Brother Moon, the Demon Moon, or the War Moon. Smallest of the three moons, with a red cast. Epitomizing courage and strength.

# Calendar of the Imperium

Juro's year is approximately the same as Earth's is now, although at twenty-three Earth-hours, Juro's days are shorter resulting in a Juro year of 381 days. The Sixth Imperator divided the year into 14 months of 27 days each, with the two summer months having 28 and 29 days, respectively. Though the structure of the months and days is the same throughout Juro, each region refers to them by different names depending on their local gods and customs.

In the Imperium, workdays are Lonsday morning through noon Jonday. Jonday evening is often for entertainments and celebrations, and Sunday is reserved for a day of rest, religious rituals, and sacrifice. Slaves, still common in the Imperium proper, have no such weekend of course.

| Day Name | Named for |
|---|---|
| Lonsday | Lon, mother moon |
| Furesday | Fures, brother moon |
| Winzday | Winz (fertility aspect of Junera, queen of the gods) |
| Brotday | Brotkab king of the gods |
| Elenday | Elein, sister moon |
| Jonday | Joniz (creative aspect of Junera) |
| Sunday | Helios, the sun |

# Makashti Sineura's Letter to Richard Stewart

*You are wise not to trust. But I knew nothing of the attack on your family. I am deeply sorry for your wife's passing and glad beyond measure your daughter escaped. It is to our dishonor that some among us conspired in the plot. For their betrayal I owe you a debt. Please accept this small token as you may wish to call on me in the future. And please accept my humble gift of a carpet.*

*The Empress will be disappointed that you did not kill me. And this letter is my death sentence if you choose to disclose it.*

*Choose wisely.*

# About the Author

Ray Strong is the award-winning author of *The Dragons' War*, an epic fantasy series that launched in 2025 with *Zephyr's Flight*. He began his writing journey with newspaper stories in Chicago before earning a graduate degree in engineering. That path took him around the world, where he learned from many different cultures and ways of life. Ray now lives on the West Coast with his wife and their three children, who once spent rainy afternoons acting out scenes from *Castle in the Sky*. Today, he writes full time, building rich worlds full of adventure, mythology, and magic.

### A Note *of* Thanks

Thank you for reading my book. If you enjoyed it, please take a moment to post a review at your favorite retailer. And follow me to learn about the latest news and releases about the Dragons' War series.

☐ Friend me: Facebook
☐ Follow me: Twitter/X
☐ Subscribe: Impulse Fiction
Ray Strong